MADELINE BAKER [writes?] books. She writes the [histor?]ical novels that roman[...] many bestsellers have prompted *Romantic Times* to say "Baker has the Midas touch."

JENNIFER BLAKE is the author of thirty-four successful historical romances, including four *New York Times* bestsellers. Her award-winning novels have sold over twenty million copies worldwide. The *Chicago Tribune* calls her writing "as steamy as a still July night on the bayou."

GEORGINA GENTRY, the author of twelve novels, is beloved for her passionate Western and Indian romances, which have garnered numerous awards. *Romantic Times,* which has given Gentry two Lifetime Achievement awards, has called her "one of the finest writers of the decade."

SHIRL HENKE has written over a dozen highly acclaimed romance novels. She is renowned for her sensuous writing style, and has won countless awards. *Romantic Times* wasn't exaggerating when it called Shirl Henke's novels "romance at its best!"

PATRICIA RICE has eleven romances to her credit and has won awards for both her historicals and her fantasy novels. *Romantic Times* called her last book "an extraordinary novel of searing passion and compelling intensity."

ANNOUNCING THE

TOPAZ FREQUENT READERS CLUB

COMMEMORATING TOPAZ'S
I YEAR ANNIVERSARY!

THE MORE YOU BUY, THE MORE YOU GET

Redeem coupons found here and in the back of all new Topaz titles for FREE Topaz gifts:

Send in:

◆ 2 coupons for a free TOPAZ novel (choose from the list below);

☐ THE KISSING BANDIT, Margaret Brownley

☐ BY LOVE UNVEILED, Deborah Martin

☐ TOUCH THE DAWN, Chelley Kitzmiller

☐ WILD EMBRACE, Cassie Edwards

◆ 4 coupons for an "I Love the Topaz Man" on-board sign

◆ 6 coupons for a TOPAZ compact mirror

◆ 8 coupons for a Topaz Man T-shirt

Just fill out this certificate and send with original sales receipts to:

TOPAZ FREQUENT READERS CLUB-1ST ANNIVERSARY
Penguin USA • Mass Market Promotion; Dept. H.U.G.
375 Hudson St., NY, NY 10014

Name_____

Address_____

City_____State_____Zip_____
Offer expires 5/31/1995

This certificate must accompany your request. No duplicates accepted. Void where prohibited, taxed or restricted. Allow 4-6 weeks for receipt of merchandise. Offer good only in U.S., its territories, and Canada.

THE TOPAZ MAN FAVORITES
Secrets of the Heart

Madeline Baker

Jennifer Blake

Georgina Gentry

Shirl Henke

Patricia Rice

A TOPAZ BOOK

TOPAZ
Published by the Penguin Group
Penguin Books USA Inc., 375 Hudson Street,
New York, New York 10014, U.S.A.
Penguin Books Ltd, 27 Wrights Lane,
London W8 5TZ, England
Penguin Books Australia Ltd, Ringwood,
Victoria, Australia
Penguin Books Canada Ltd, 10 Alcorn Avenue,
Toronto, Ontario, Canada M4V 3B2
Penguin Books (N.Z.) Ltd, 182–190 Wairau Road,
Auckland 10, New Zealand

Penguin Books Ltd, Registered Offices:
Harmondsworth, Middlesex, England

First published by Topaz,
an imprint of Dutton Signet,
a division of Penguin Books USA Inc.

First Printing, December, 1994
10 9 8 7 6 5 4 3 2 1

Topaz is a trademark of Dutton Signet,
a division of Penguin Books USA Inc.

Printed in the United States of America

PUBLISHER'S NOTE
These stories are works of fiction. Names, characters, places, and incidents
either are the product of the authors' imaginations or are used fictitiously,
and any resemblance to actual persons, living or dead, events, or locales is
entirely coincidental.

Contents

Gambler's Delight

---

by

Georgina Gentry

Prologue

A ragtag riverboat loaded with trashy tarts and rowdy ruffians? In a true but little known incident of the Civil War, a Yankee officer, urged on by irate citizens, decided to clean up a Mississippi River town. At gunpoint, he forced all the whores, gamblers, petty crooks, and assorted villains aboard an old paddle wheeler under orders to dump them up or down the river.

Easier said than done! No town would let the captain leave his licentious load. In vain, he chugged from one town to the next. Yet as word of his cargo spread, all the randy, rambunctious men along the river tried to climb aboard.

That much is history. Everything else, names and towns, have been changed to keep our ancestors' secrets. . . .

Chapter One

Old Captain Leroy Pettigrew peered from his upper deck at the crowd now marching down the wharf toward his boat, the *Petunia Ann*. "Buck, what in tarnation . . . ?"

Down on the dock, the big black man paused with a box on his massive shoulder and studied the mob. "Whatever they is, Capt'n," he yelled back, "looks like trouble!"

"I can see that!" The captain spat tobacco juice into the muddy Mississippi and watched the unruly group striding across the dock. Some of them carried torches and signs; some sang hymns. Bringing up the rear were Union soldiers, sunlight gleaming off their rifles and brass buttons.

"Uh oh." Captain Pettigrew abruptly recognized the town's mayor and aldermen. With a grimace he saw that the righteous, stiff-corseted members of the local Ladies' Town Betterment Society—friends of his dead wife—were bringing up the rear. There might have been a preacher or two, some curious townsfolk with time on their hands, but the most interesting people were those being herded at gunpoint toward his ragged little riverboat; tinhorn gamblers, petty crooks, card sharps, freebooters, and even Sadie, accompanied by all the girls from her bordello. A young blond beauty in a red satin dress seemed to be heading the pack.

"Oh, Buck, it's trouble!" His belly feeling as if he'd just swallowed a live catfish, Captain Leroy climbed down from the top deck of the *Petunia Ann* to face the advancing crowd. His righteous wife, Petunia Ann, had spent her whole life crusading against the scandalous thought that somehow, somewhere, someone was having a little fun—and this crowd of righteous windbags looked cut from the same cloth.

The captain joined his first mate, Buck, on the dock as the crowd pressed forward. "What in tarnation is the meaning of all this ruckus?" he shouted.

The pretty little blonde looked mad enough to bite a chunk out of an anchor. "Ask the soldiers; they're running us out of town!"

He looked around the mob. "I'm Captain Leroy Pettigrew. Who's in charge of this circus, Miss—?"

"Delight. Delight Dugan." She squared her small shoulders, trying to maintain a sense of dignity as she faced the old man. Her real name wasn't Delight, but of course, that was only one of her secrets. "I keep trying to tell the major that there's been some mistake, but—"

"No mistake." A middle-aged, portly Union officer elbowed his way through the crowd. "Captain, I'm Major Blake, assigned to the town of Nameless. At the urging of the local businessmen and the Ladies' Town Betterment Society, I'm cleaning out this riff raff!"

"Now, see here—" Delight began, but the grizzled old captain motioned for silence.

"What's this got to do with me?" the captain asked.

Delight sputtered, "That's exactly what I asked, and—"

"Young lady," said the Yankee officer, "and I use the term loosely; he wasn't addressing you!" He confronted the old man. "You've got the only boat in port

right now, and I intend to load these . . . these ladies of
the evening, pimps, gamblers, cutthroats, and general
trash on your boat—"

"Oh, no, you don't!" The old man took his hat off,
running his hand through his gray hair. "I've got cargo
to haul! With the *Petunia Ann* mortgaged from stem to
stern, I can't spare time to haul whores for the government!"

"I have never been so insulted!" Delight began,
looking into the smug and condemning faces of the respectable ladies. She hadn't been in town long enough
to know one from another, but their expressions told
her what they thought of her.

"Never mind, honey," the plump madam said, "I've
been called worse, and me and the girls have been run
out of better towns than this one."

"Sadie, that's the understatement of the year," Major
Blake huffed. "Now, Captain, because of the war, I
could commandeer your leaky old tub. Besides, the
government will pay you."

"What in tarnation am I supposed to do with them?"
Captain Pettigrew asked.

"Who knows? Who cares?" the Major snapped.
"Just dump them off in some other town up or down
the river. From now on, Nameless is a respectable,
law-abiding town!"

Cheers rose from the Ladies' Town Betterment Society. On the other hand, Delight noted, the men in the
crowd looked a lot less enthused.

Robust and full-figured Sadie waved her hand in
protest. "Half the men in this crowd still owe me last
month's bar bill."

At that remark some of the respectable gentlemen
began running fingers around their collars as if they
were choking, while stout and self-righteous wives
glared at them.

Delight got right up in the major's face. "Major, you can't do this to us! I'm not—"

"Of course I can—and I will." He signaled the soldiers, who began prodding the luckless cargo up the gangplank at gunpoint.

Just as another cheer rose from the Society matrons, a buggy galloped up on the dock, carrying two armed soldiers and a grinning, darkly handsome man. "Major, we found him," one of the soldiers shouted as they reined in. "He's drunker than a boiled owl, though."

"Ahh"—the major rubbed his hands together—"and here's the worst of them, Choc McGraw. Load him, boys!"

"Choc! Oh, Choc!" The saloon girls set off squeals of ecstasy that made Delight clench her teeth. She looked over the newcomer who, judging from the girls' rapt expressions, was obviously well-known to most of the local hussies.

He looked like a tinhorn gambler, Delight thought with disgust, tall and broad-shouldered in a fine black coat and Western hat, bright, flowered satin vest, and scarlet silk cravat.

"I can get down by myself," the rascal announced with great dignity as the soldiers reached up to help him down. He stood up, reeling a little, then promptly fell out of the buggy and onto the wharf, almost landing on a hound dog who had stopped to scratch a flea.

All the saloon sluts except Delight gasped and surrounded him. "Oh, Choc, honey, are you hurt?"

The handsome gambler stumbled to his feet, dusting himself off. "Ladies, I thank you for your concern," he drawled in a western twang. He took off his hat, made a deep bow, and would have fallen again except the soldier on each side caught him.

The major's lip curled into a sneer. "Disgusting! You've won your last pot here, McGraw—you and all your ilk!"

"Sonovagun, as I remember, Major, I still have your marker for fifty dollars from Tuesday's poker game."

The major's face turned the color of winter long-handles while the tarts snickered and the soldiers struggled to control their smiles. "Load these people onboard, men," he ordered, "we've spent enough time on this trash!"

"Wait!" Delight protested, but the soldiers were prodding everyone across the dock.

The black-clad Ladies' Town Betterment Society waved their signs and sang off-key hymns while the hound howled in harmony. Choc McGraw, looking cross-eyed drunk as the soldiers carried him aboard, was dumped unceremoniously on the weathered, un-painted deck.

"What in tarnation am I supposed to do with them?" Captain Pettigrew shouted over the singing.

"Dump them anywhere up or down the river," the major ordered, "and put in a requisition for repay-ment."

"I don't have time to nursemaid a bunch of rowdy rascals," the crusty old codger yelled back. "I got or-ders to fill, goods to deliver."

"You heard me," the major ordered, "get this load of slimy sinners out of my town!"

Buck looked toward the captain, who, after consider-ing the number of armed men on the dock, plus the for-midable Ladies' Town Betterment Society in their iron corsets, nodded reluctantly. "Let 'em board, Buck."

Delight found herself being pushed up the gangplank along with the rest, and no one listened to her angry objections. She was surrounded by tarts, trash, and all manner of rowdy rascals. Oh, what a mess she was in!

Buck cast off, and the boat drifted away from the pier. The respectable ladies on the wharf waved their signs and began to sign the "Battle Hymn of the Re-public."

"I am innocent!" Delight shouted.

A fiesty-looking black woman on her right grinned. "Ain't we all, lamb chop?"

". . . He is trampling out the vineyard where the grapes of wrath are stored. . . ."

"Tarnation!" Captain Leroy muttered over the off-key chorus, "they all remind me of my late wife."

"You were married?" Delight asked. It didn't seem likely.

He shrugged. "She was leading a temperance march, tripped over a step, and broke her neck, God rest Petunia Ann's iron-clad soul." He turned and climbed up the steps to the pilothouse while the engine coughed and choked, and he began to turn the stern-wheel in the muddy water.

How had Delight gotten into this? Money. She was doing it for the money, but she'd never dreamed . . .

With a groan, Choc McGraw pulled himself into a sitting position while the adoring whores crowded closer. "Oh, Choc, are you all right?"

"Gimme some room, girls." With reluctant sighs the garishly dressed whores backed away and drifted across the deck.

Delight marched over and glared down at him as he took out a small sack of tobacco and some little papers and tried to roll a cigarette. The tobacco spilled down his coat. Drunk and a gambler to boot—there was nothing she disliked more. "You're disgusting!"

He grinned up at her with a crooked, disarming smile. "I've been called worse, Miss . . . ?"

"Delight."

"Ahh, and I'll just bet you are!" Her face burned as his dark-eyed gaze roamed freely across her form. She was relieved when he finally turned his attention back to the cigarette he was attempting to roll, but it soon became obvious that the task was beyond his present capabilities.

"You ninny! Here, let me do that." She jerked the makin's from his unsteady hands, and expertly rolled a cigarette. He looked baffled as she stuck it between his lips.

"It seems you have more secret talents than I even suspected, Miss Delight. Not many gals can build a quirly." He felt through his pockets and brought out a match.

"Be careful with that—your breath might catch fire."

He grinned. "Why do I sense you'd love that? And I'd like to find out just how delightful you are."

"It'll cost you a double eagle to find out."

"Twenty dollars?" His dark eyes crinkled into a grin as he lit his smoke with a shaky hand. For a moment it appeared he might set fire to that shock of black hair blowing across his tanned forehead from under his hat. "The going rate is a dollar . . . or maybe a half eagle in a big town like New Orleans or St. Louis."

"I presume you're an expert on the going rate?"

He took a deep puff and winked at her. "I really wouldn't know; I don't usually have to pay for it."

"And I don't give away free samples like a medicine show." She was annoyed both with this drunken ne'er-do-well and with herself for having gotten into such a mess. Delight looked toward the dock and the crowd growing smaller by the moment as the old stern-wheeler puttered and churned up the river. Faint strains of music drifted across the water: ". . . Glory, glory, hallelujah! Glory, glory, hallelujah. . . ."

"I have never been so humiliated in my whole life!"

"You'll get used to it," Choc said. "Take me, for instance, I hadn't been back in Nameless but a day or two when I was . . . ah, invited to this party. I take it this is the first time you've been run out of a town?"

"I take it that for you, it isn't?" His attitude was the most annoying, arrogant. . . .

"Not hardly." He shrugged. "It probably also won't be the last."

She could smell the brandy as she looked down at his tall, muscular form. "You smell like a rumcake."

"I'm impossible to insult." He grinned up at her.

"So I notice. Why isn't a big, husky fellow like you in the army?"

"Which one?"

"Either one."

He pushed his hat back and smiled. "I never had much interest in fightin'—gamblin' and lovin's more my style."

"So I surmise from the women's concern. You must get around more than a tomcat."

"Sonovagun, you've got a tongue like a razor, darlin'; it's a wonder you get any customers at all. With that accent I'd say you're a Rebel."

"Don't call me 'darlin,' you cheap card sharp."

He hiccoughed. "I'm from Indian Territory so the war doesn't interest me much. I'll take poker money from either side; spends just as well. Where you from, darlin'?"

"Texas, and my name's Delight."

"Texas. That explains it. My pappy always said, 'You can always tell a Texan, but you can't tell 'em much.'"

She managed to control the urge to push him off the deck into the water. As drunk as he was, he'd probably sink like an iron horseshoe. "For ten years," she said loftily, "Texas was its own nation. Some thought it was a step down to trade for statehood."

He staggered to his feet, hanging onto the white gingerbread rail as he leaned close. "I've been all up and down the river and don't remember ever havin' the pleasure of your company, Tex. Since we'll be on this leaky old tub a while, would you take my marker for this evening?"

She looked up at him. He was taller and more handsome than she had realized. Along with the brandy, she smelled the scent of tobacco and the spicy scent of cologne. "The first thing a girl in this business learns is not to extend credit."

"My marker is good anywhere. You'll enjoy it, too, just ask any of Sadie's girls—"

"Any of whom would be willing to do it for free," Delight snapped. There was something about this half-breed, an easy, insolent charm that made her breath quicken, her pulse pound, and her teeth grind.

"I want to see if you're worth the extra money." He leaned to throw his cigarette overboard and came dangerously close to losing his balance.

"Watch out!" Without thinking, she caught his sleeve to save him, and he responded by putting his arms around her.

"Thanks, Tex."

For a moment she was caught in the circle of his muscular embrace. He was also stronger and bigger than she'd realized. His dark face was shadowed by the late afternoon sun, but his mouth looked full and sensual. For a split second she thought he was going to kiss her.

"Let's get one thing straight, you tinhorn gambler." Delight pulled out of his grasp. "You may work that oily charm on the others, but that dog won't hunt here."

"In other words not only no, but hell, no?"

"You got it. I'll bet you'd steal the butter off a sick beggar's biscuit. It'll be bad enough to be cooped up on the same boat for a few hours with a rascal like you, without extending you credit. I'd rather sleep with that hound dog, *Mister* McGraw."

"I can see we're gonna be great friends, so call me Choc. It's a nickname, short for Choctaw, my mother's tribe."

"Good-bye, *Mister* McGraw. Use your credit in someone else's bed." She turned and flounced away.

But you're more of a challenge, Tex, he thought, staring after her. He leaned nonchalantly against the post, liking the way the red satin swished when she walked, outlining her full breasts and round hips. Her bright yellow hair looked like burnished gold in the late afternoon sunlight. What was a girl like that doing working the river as a whore? What a fresh-faced beauty, and so young, too; maybe not more than eighteen or twenty. He suddenly felt old and jaded at thirty, but of course, he had more miles on him than his normal years because of the war.

"We all have our secrets, don't we, Tex, darlin'?" he whispered and watched her disappear into the interior of the down-at-the-heels riverboat. Choc looked around to make sure everyone had drifted away, then he dusted himself off, expertly rolled and lit another smoke, and leaned against the railing. How and why had he let himself get talked into this intrigue? With this motley bunch of cutthroats and whores, anyone of them might be. . . . His thoughts returned to the little blonde. How had such an innocent-looking beauty descended into this scummy, dangerous life? The war, maybe.

Choc smoked and listened to the old tub chugging through the muddy water, the shouts of deck hands, the talk and laughter of the whores and rascals in the small salon. Delight. He had never met a girl quite like her— and he had known and loved a lot of women. More to the point, she'd apparently disliked him on sight, which made her even more appealing. Choc appreciated a challenge. He felt in his pockets and came up with a couple of dimes and a handful of markers. He must stop extending credit at the poker table.

With a glum sigh he smoked and thought about how he'd let the major talk him into this. He wished he had twenty dollars; damned if he wouldn't see how skilled little Delight was. Did she hide some secrets, too? Maybe Choc would find out tonight when he talked his way into her bed.

Chapter Two

Captain Pettigrew hastily called a meeting in the faded and dusty dining room and salon. "Now, listen up, all of you!" He surveyed the motley crowd, still not quite able to believe he'd been saddled with them. Choc McGraw staggered in and leaned against a pillar. He hoped Choc didn't get too close to any of the kerosene lamps and breathe; the *Petunia Ann* would go up like a roman candle and it wouldn't be too good for Choc, either.

"Well, Captain," the fiesty blonde began, "I—"

"Tarnation, I said listen up! Now, I'm not any happier to have you on my vessel than you are to be here, but it won't be for long. Buck, how far to Simpson's Landing?" A long pause. "Buck?"

The big black man seemed oblivious to everything but the dark mature beauty who was smiling back at him. "Huh? Oh, we be there not long after dark."

"That means we gotta feed 'em supper," Captain Leroy grumbled, "such as it is. Anybody here a good cook, or do you want to eat Buck's grub?"

The pert blonde and the attractive coffee-colored wench held up their hands.

The blonde looked too young to be experienced at anything. He took a good look at the way the tight red satin strained around her supple curves. Well, there was probably one thing she was good at. Every man in the room was staring at her as if supper had already been served and she was the dessert. He gestured to the older black woman. "You there, what's your story?"

"Name's Duchess; ah works for Miss Sadie. I's a good cook, I is."

"That's right," the robust madam confirmed, "Duchess can cook . . . and do a lot of things."

Buck grinned like a possum eyeing ripe grapes. "Duchess, we ain't got much to cook, but what there is, I'll help you whip up."

"Set up some trot lines, man"—Duchess smiled, looking him over—"then if you got corn meal, bacon, and a few greens, I'll whip up vittles you ain't ate since you was in your mama's kitchen."

The two disappeared into the galley.

"Okay, reckon that's it till supper." Captain Leroy dismissed the crowd. "Right after that, I unload you all at Simpson's Landing."

Sadie sidled up, catching his arm as he turned to go. "Captain Leroy," she drawled, "it was nice of you to take us. I don't meet many old-fashioned gentlemen."

He felt himself coloring. "Didn't have much choice with them soldiers' guns."

"How come I ain't ever seen an attractive old bull like you in my place?" She purred in a slow Southern drawl that felt like warm honey running down his wiry frame.

Now he really did snort and sputter. "It ain't that I ain't never thought about it, Sadie; after all, you're a fine figure of a woman—to my mind, better lookin' than any of your girls."

"Why, you charmer, you!" She smiled and batted her eyelashes.

"I just never had any extra money," he admitted, feeling shamefaced. "I'm about to lose my boat to the bank; competition is mighty fierce with the bigger boats and the railroads and all."

She looked around the dingy dining room. "I'll bet this was once a beauty; she still has a quaint charm."

Captain Leroy felt himself warm to her. Sadie was special all right. "The *Petunia Ann* belonged originally to my late wife, God rest her soul. She wanted to do revivals and temperance crusades, but she died, and then the war began. Besides, temperance never was my style."

She leaned closer, and he smelled the scent of perfume from the cleft of her big breasts. "I'll bet you were a man of the world, a devil with the ladies in your day."

He cleared his throat modestly. "I got around some."

Sadie surveyed the room. "You know, with a lot of cleaning and polish, some new drapes, this place could almost be a nice boat."

He shook his head and sighed. "Even if I had the money, which I don't, passengers don't want to ride with me. They want a fast boat; they like racing each other down the river."

"Is she slow?"

Buck limped back into the room, white apron tied around his waist. "Is she slow? Why, last week, an island outrun us."

Captain Leroy scowled at him. "She ain't that slow."

"Not by much, she ain't!" Buck chuckled. "The *Petunia Ann* could run all day in the shade of a big tree, but we love her."

Sadie pursed her lips in thought. "Then Captain Leroy, you need to offer something the big paddle-wheelers and the trains don't have; fill a specific niche."

"No money to do nothing," the captain snorted. "I'll probably lose her anyways. It ain't your worry, Miss Sadie, but I do thank you for your kind heart. In a few hours you'll be starting fresh at Simpson's Landing."

"Yeah, I reckon." She looked almost wistful under

her rouge and rhinestones. "It was sort of comfy here. Is there a piano?"

Buck nodded. "Down at the end; under that stack of boxes. 'Fraid it's out of tune—ain't never had anything but temperance songs and 'Shall We Gather at the River?' played on it.'

"You know, we got the professor with us. Maybe he could tune it."

"I'll give it a try." A skinny man in a rusty black suit stepped forward, looking more like an undertaker than a man of musical talents. He smelled like rose hair tonic. Whether he had been drinking or wearing it was open to debate. Flexing his bony fingers, he hit a couple of notes. "Reminds me of a place I used to work down in New Orleans."

The captain shook his head. "Don't bother yourself, Professor, you'll be gone in a few hours and it ain't your problem."

"It's no bother, and some music might pass the time."

The captain shrugged as he went back up to the pilothouse atop the texas deck.

Buck limped back to the kitchen. "Umm! Something smells larruping, gal."

"Corn bread with crackling bits." She turned and smiled. "By the way, you can drop that Uncle Tom shuffle. I cook as a hobby, but I'm really Miss Sadie's bookkeeper."

He stared at her, bug-eyed. Her mammy accent was gone. "If that don't beat all! Duchess, there must be more to you than meets the eye."

She gave him a bold, appraising look. "And you, too, maybe."

"The limp's real, gal," he said. "A couple of years ago a roustabout dropped a crate on me. It would have killed me if a fella hadn't knocked me to one side."

She looked him over slowly. "The rest of you doesn't look damaged."

He grinned. "How'd you like to find out?"

"I'll think about it." She returned to her stirring.

"A bookkeeper," he marveled scratching his head in admiration. "That's something we could use; the cap'n ain't too good at the business end of it."

"You really about to lose the boat?"

Buck nodded. "We ain't doin' enough business and Cap'n Leroy don't have any money to fix her up, do repairs."

She paused and gestured toward a wooden block. "Chop up some onions for me while I roll pie crust."

"Too bad ya'll are gettin' off at Simpson's Landing," Buck said as he cleared off the chopping board. "I was just beginning to think I'd like it if you'd stay."

Duchess smiled as she stirred brown sugar into her sweet potato pie. She wondered what Sadie thought of the captain and his boat. The white madam had a small fortune in gold sewn into her corset for emergencies; getting run out of town certainly counted as one. "If I had a few more ingredients, I'd make you think you had died and gone to heaven."

He looked her over and grinned. "I'm thinkin' that already, gal."

Choc went outside after the meeting and leaned against the rail, thinking about the major. If they did all get dumped out at Simpson's Landing, Choc wasn't going to have near enough time. He grinned at the thought. If the major only knew. . . .

"Well." Delight Dugan stood at his elbow. "You seemed to have sobered up pretty quick."

"Had some of the hair of the dog that bit me," he said somberly and swayed on his feet for effect. "There's a little liquor in the old bar."

"Might have known you'd sniff it out if there was

any." She looked around. "Paint's peeling. I'll wager she was a fancy boat in her day."

"Reckon her luck's run out like a bad roll of dice." The last rays of the sunset reflected in Delight's yellow hair. He managed to control the urge to reach out and touch it, see if it was really as silky as it looked.

"Luck!" Delight snorted. Papa had lost the little German bakery in the Texas Hill country to a card sharp and then became a hopeless drunk before he died. "What some call 'luck,' others call cheating. The only thing worse than a tinhorn gambler is a drunk tinhorn gambler."

"I don't know why you're as riled as a filly with her tail caught in a cactus, darlin', but if a man had said that to me, he'd be eatin' my knuckles right now."

She laughed. "Oh, now I've insulted your honor, have I? Tell me, Mister McGraw, have you ever done an honest day's work in your life?"

"Maybe one or two." He pushed his hat back and grinned at her. Before the war, he'd been a rancher in Indian Territory; he'd sweated over branding irons, cut hay, and broken wild horses. But there was no point in telling that secret to this acid-tongued little tart.

"Are your sympathies with the South or North?"

"What's that got to do with anything?" If he was going to talk his way into her bed tonight, he had to at least get her to stop insulting him.

"Just as I thought; you've no interest in the ideals of either side."

"I plead guilty, I reckon." He was standing close enough to look down at the soft swell of her breasts in the low-cut red satin. "Indians in the Territory are fighting on both sides." He wanted to reach out and pull her up against him, see if those breasts would feel as soft as they looked. "Which side are you on, Tex?"

"The right side."

"Well then, so am I." He grinned down at her again.

"After supper maybe we'll have a little time before we get to Simpson's Landing." In the background the off-key notes of the piano drifted from the dining room. "The professor must be tuning it. Maybe we could even dance some."

"Don't you have anything better to do?" She turned and left just as he was about to put his arms around her. Choc watched her go, feeling more aroused than he had in a long while. "If you only knew, Tex, darlin', if you only knew."

The dull thud of wood hitting wood broke his reverie. Chock peered into the dusk and saw that a small boat had bumped up against the *Petunia Ann.* "Who's there?"

"Just us." A bunch of men were tying on and clambering aboard. Choc recognized some of the Union soldiers and a couple of aldermen from the mob scene at Nameless. "It was suddenly so dreary back in town," the young lieutenant explained. "What with the girls gone and the saloons and keno games closed down, it wasn't quite the same."

"Yeah," said a private, "we had forgotten how dull it is when the only piano is the one at the local tent revival."

Choc scratched his head. "I don't suppose it plays anything you can dance to."

"We was thinking," the bushy-bearded mayor said hesitantly, "we could have some fun, spend a little money, and then row back to Nameless with no one the wiser. Our wives and mothers think we're at a town beautification meeting."

One of the aldermen took a deep breath. "Do I smell sweet potato pie? Duchess must be cooking!"

"I reckon you're all welcome to stay for supper and a little entertainment for a price." Choc grinned. "Any of you gentlemen play cards?"

The young corporal nodded. "Sounds good to me."

"Later, then." Choc leaned against a post and watched the men head toward the dining room where, already, the piano was beginning to sound fiesty and hot under the professor's expert hands as he banged out "Camptown Races."

If he could play a few hands of poker, he'd have the twenty-dollar double eagle he needed. He got warm just thinking about unbuttoning that tight red satin and tangling his fingers in that long yellow hair. Her mouth looked like wet velvet, and he ran his tongue along his lips, wondering how she tasted.

Funny, he didn't remember seeing that girl in any of the river towns before; but then, there were so many towns and lots of widowed or orphaned girls with this war going on. It was hard for a woman to earn a living anyway, but prostitution—too bad. When he thought of the pert blonde, it was suddenly distasteful to him to think of men lining up outside her door, money in hand.

Well, the war was almost over. No matter who won, pretty soon he could go back to the beautiful Choctaw country and the ranch his parents had been keeping together for him. Choc watched the sun sink into the river with all its pinks, purples, and golds. The sunsets across the rolling, wooded hills in Southeastern Indian Territory were finer by far. He yearned to be back there.

Major Blake. Damn him. It was his fault Choc was aboard this tub with all these misfits. He remembered their conversation this afternoon when he'd been called to the major's quarters.

"Ah, Choc, come in." The major motioned him to a chair and poured him a whiskey. "Good to see you again."

"Yep." What was it the man wanted? Last Tuesday

Choc had taken him for a week's pay. "Glad to see you don't carry a grudge."

The portly man ran his hand through his thinning hair. "You still got all my money?"

Chic grinned and shrugged. "No. I spent it on women and whiskey; the rest I just wasted."

"Such a charming rascal." The Major chuckled. "You bring a lot of color and fun to the river, Choc; wish you'd stop drifting from town to town and stick around awhile."

Choc sipped the whiskey. It was the good stuff—now why was he wasting it on Choc? "If I stay too long in any one place, I might get lynched. Besides, there's always new suckers in every town and prettier women at each saloon."

"You amaze me," the officer remarked, clasping his hands behind his back. "This war—winning or losing it—doesn't matter one whit to you."

"Not a whit!" Choc agreed and laughed easily. "Blue or gray money spends the same, so it don't make no difference to me. But I told you one time what the South did to the Choctaws."

"I know. They loaded them up and shipped them off to Indian Territory so they could have your lands, just like they did the Cherokee, Seminole, Creek, and Chickasaws."

"That's a fact. Still and all, maybe they did us a favor. Oklahoma has been pretty good to me."

"Oklahoma?"

"It's a Choctaw word, Major; some have taken to calling it that. Roughly translated, it means, 'Land of the Red People' or 'Home of the Red Man.'

The Union officer paced the floor and frowned. "Remember I was a colonel in '63."

"I had forgotten. We played some poker when I was in that town the previous week," Choc reminded him sympathetically. "Nobody had a clue saboteurs would find out that boat was carrying guns, ammunition, and three million in federal greenbacks to pay the troops."

"Looked like green rain, all falling in little bits from the sky," the other said dourly.

"Now Major, that wasn't your fault."

"Wish Washington shared your opinion. They figured it was. Guess I wasn't as cautious as I thought I was," the officer admitted. "I do have a taste for pretty women and good whiskey, and you know what kind of trash is on the river these days and how they drift from town to town."

"Half the people in town right now were in that area that week." Choc took out his little sack of tobacco. "We'd all been run out of another town." He began to roll a cigarette. "Forget it, the war's about over anyhow."

"Not for me, it isn't!" Major Blake snapped, "I intend to build a career in the army, in Washington or New York City, where it's civilized and the weather's cooler. I've got to clear my record."

"I wish I could help you, Major," Choc said earnestly, "you're the best sport I've ever played cards with."

The major was feeling through his pockets. "Damn, I'm out of cigars."

"Here." Choc rolled him a cigarette and lit them both.

Major Blake inhaled and made a face. "Tastes like barn sweepings. This new cigarette thing is a sissy craze anyway. Those English types should have left it in the Crimean."

"It's cheaper than a good cigar, and I'm trying to quit anyway."

Major Blake leaned forward, grinning. "Broke, are you? I've talked the government into offering a reward."

Choc paused, intrigued in spite of himself. "A reward for what?"

"I thought that would interest you." Major Blake laughed. "A thousand dollars is pretty good money for your help."

"A thousand dollars is a lot of money," Choc agreed, "but I don't see where I fit in—I'm a gambler, remember?"

"Choc, you know everyone up and down the river, and you've got the devil's charm. Folks find it easy to talk to you, especially women."

"So?"

"This hasn't been the only sabotage. If I catch the spy, I'm a hero. Otherwise, after the war, I may end up assigned to a horrible place like Texas, chasing Comanches across hot, dusty plains with some vainglorious idiot like Custer." He puffed the cigarette. "Choc, with your connections along the river, it would be simple for you to nose around, see what you can find out."

"Me?" Choc touched his chest. "You can't be serious. What do I know about the army, spies, or saboteurs?"

"But don't you see?" The major rubbed his plump hands together eagerly. "You get around, know everyone. I figure the Rebel is a whore, a bartender, maybe a piano player, or even a soldier."

"I wouldn't know a spy from a New York debutante," Choc snorted. "You must be drinking as much as I do to think I could track down your mysterious Reb." He reached for his hat.

"Wait! Hear me out. There's been some more sabotage in this area, so now I figure the spy is plying her trade among some of my loose-lipped officers—maybe even right here in Nameless."

"You don't even know it's a woman," Choc pointed out. "It's a wild-goose chase."

"Not if I isolate all the ragtag river trash in one

place for a while and put someone amongst them who has enough charm to get her to talk."

"What happens to the spy?" Choc paused in the doorway.

"What do you care? Firing squad, of course."

"Tsk! Tsk! Seems like a waste of a pretty girl."

"Now how do you know she's pretty?"

Chic winked at him. "Believe me, if she's worming big secrets out of Union officers, she's downright beautiful."

"Remember, there's a thousand dollars in gold for the informant; think about that, Choc. I know money means more to you than principles or patriotism."

"Thanks a lot," Choc said sarcastically, "but I'm not much on getting someone shot, especially if your spy turns out to be a woman."

"If you don't find her, someone else will turn her in." The major leaned against the sideboard and smiled. "I've had notices posted about the reward all over the county and up and down the river this past week. Someone's going to get that gold—it might as well be you."

Choc considered. "When you put it that way, I reckon the little tart deserves what she gets. Suppose I say no?"

"I'll call in Pinkerton, and you know how relentless he is; he won't stop until he solves it."

Choc leaned against the door and considered. "If I say yes, will you give me plenty of time to investigate and keep Pinkerton on a leash?"

The major nodded. "In fact, I'd like that better because I know you'll let me take most of the credit since we're old poker buddies. Pinkerton will want publicity for himself and his detective agency."

"I don't know," Choc sighed with reluctance, "it's not really my type of thing—"

"And then there's the money," the major reminded him.

"You really know how to inspire a fella, don't you?"

"Think of charming secrets out of pretty women and getting paid to do it," Major Blake said.

Choc sighed. "I do like pretty women. Suppose I still don't think—"

"By the way," the Major said slyly, tossing his cigarette into the spittoon, "did I neglect to mention I've promised the local Ladies' Town Betterment Society that I'll clean up their town by running the trash out?"

Choc swore under his breath. "I just returned a day or two ago."

"So now you're leaving this afternoon along with all the tarts and trash. You'll need that money, Choc." Blake smiled like a man holding a royal flush.

"Since you put it that way, I'm in." Choc shrugged and tossed his cigarette into the spittoon. "What's the plan?"

"Late this afternoon the righteous ladies are having a rally and I'll be the hero of the hour, helping them clean up their town. Splash a little whiskey on yourself and be at your hotel where my men can find you."

"I don't like this," Choc grumbled. "I've got no interest in this war, except what I can make gamblin' with the soldiers; that's the only reason I came over from the Territory."

"At least you're honest about being unprincipled." The light shone on the major's balding head as he smiled. "This reward is more than you'll make off poker in a month; think about that, Choc, and the women . . ."

A sound startled Choc, and he realized he was staring into the darkness as the *Petunia Ann* splashed through the water in the darkness. "Who's there?" he called, suspecting it was yet another group of "visitors."

"Some soldiers!" a voice called back. "Word got out all the gamblers and girls is on this old tub, and we decided to tie up and have a couple of hours of fun."

"Come on aboard." Choc grinned and reached to give the young man a hand up. "Any of you boys play poker?"

"Poker? I'm just learning; can you teach me?"

Choc grinned even wider. "I might be persuaded to give lessons till we get to Simpson's Landing."

He had only a couple of hours until the boat docked. Now which of all these people on board would Major Blake figure was the spy—if any?

Chapter Three

The supper was exceptional, Choc thought as he wiped up the red-eye gravy with a hunk of crisp corn bread and watched the others in the little dining room stuffing their faces. Everyone was sending compliments back to the kitchen and Duchess was beaming. "You folks jus' wait till I get my hands on some real vittles to work with!"

Captain Pettigrew cleared his throat and shook his head. " 'Fraid they won't get a chance at another meal; we'll be approaching Simpson's Landing in about thirty minutes."

The professor flexed his bony fingers and drawled, "Just when I was just gettin' that piano in tune."

Choc watched Delight with curiosity. She hadn't eaten much, but seemed to be all over the dining room, asking nosy questions that were none of her business—but then, that was a Texan for you.

Damn! Thirty minutes didn't give him enough time to coax her into a horizontal position or come up with anything that might satisfy Major Blake, either. Oh well, maybe when they docked. . . .

The aldermen and the mayor of Nameless, hypocrites that they were, were watching Delight as she cleared their table, leering like hogs eyeing a trough full of ripe corn. The soldiers were grinning at her, too. Somehow, that annoyed Choc; or maybe what really annoyed him was how she ignored him as she took his plate, even though the other tarts were clustering around him, offering him vast expanses of plump breasts and rouged lips. Choc flirted a little, then stood up and began looking for Delight, but she had vanished.

Now what could that stubborn chit be up to? Well, he'd catch up to her on dock.

The professor returned to the piano and began to play. Immediately, the girls gathered around him, along with the aldermen and soldiers, and sang: "Oh, Susanna, oh, don't you cry for me, I come from Alabama with my banjo on my knee. . . ."

Choc sauntered over to the grizzled captain. "Looks like everyone's havin' a good time."

"Ain't they, though?" Pettigrew's gaze was fixed on the generous curves of Sadie, who seemed to be watching him, too. "I ain't had such a good time myself— and such tasty vittles—since before my late wife got righteous. Tarnation, Choc, it's near time to dock. You want to go up to the pilot house with me?"

Choc nodded, although what he really wanted to do was go to bed with Delight. Maybe out on the deck he'd run into that tasty little tart again.

They went up to the pilot house while the lively strains of "Oh, Susanna" still drifted across the vast expanse of placid water.

The old man peered into the darkness. "There's Simpson's Landing up ahead. See where all those lights are?"

Choc pushed his hat back. "Just what are all those lights?"

"Beats me! Not much of a town, really, but I never seen the dock lit up like that a'fore." He reached to pull the whistle, and it shrieked like a whore cheated out of two bits.

Choc winced. "Sonovagun. Sounds like a pig caught under a gate!"

"It do," Captain Leroy agreed. "Lots of boats have them fancy whistles that blast several notes and some even have calliopes. Petunia Ann had talked about adding one that played 'Shall We Gather at the River?' but about that time, she broke her neck, so that ended the temperance meetings."

Sadie joined them in the pilothouse just then, smiling at him. "Leroy, I didn't think I'd get a chance to say good-bye; I wanted you to know how much I've enjoyed your boat."

He grinned back at her. "I was pleased to have you and your girls aboard, Miss Sadie. If things don't work out for you in Simpson's Landing, well. . . ."

"You're a gallant gentleman," she said and beamed.

Choc had only been half listening, wondering where that stubborn little blonde was, when he took a good look at the wharf up ahead. "Looks like we got a welcoming committee."

"What?" The other two peered into the darkness.

Sure enough, there was a mob of people on the dock, carrying torches and signs, and some of them were singing hymns.

"Uh-oh," said the captain, "I think I'd better get Buck to take over the wheel and see to the docking myself."

Choc had only exchanged a few words with Buck, the professor, or any of the others. He'd been concentrating on Delight—without results. "On second thought," he muttered, "we may not be docking."

Buck was sent up to take over the big wheel even as the captain, Choc, and the others gathered on the deck. *Petunia Ann* chugged up to the wharf.

"Tarnation, what's this all about?"

". . . we have loosed the fateful lightning of His terrible swift sword. . . ." sang the crowd, waving their signs to the song's rhythms.

Even in the dim light of the torches Choc could

read: SINNERS NOT WELCOME AT SIMPSON'S LANDING and DON'T BRING YOUR TARTS TO TOWN!

As they nosed into the dock, Captain Pettigrew tried to make himself heard over the music, but then Buck blew the off-key whistle. Pandemonium ensued as horses reared and bolted. Dogs tucked their tails and ran into the night, howling. However, it did shush the singing.

Choc leaned against a post to watch, one eye on Delight. She stood next to the handsome, young lieutenant who had rowed out to the boat earlier. Somehow, it nettled him the way the lieutenant had his arm around her waist.

"Now," Captain Leroy shouted, "what is this all about?"

A plump little man with side whiskers pushed through the crowd. "As if you didn't know! We got word from Nameless on the telegraph that you'd be trying to dock with your load of trashy tarts and rowdy rascals. We're here to tell you Simpson's Landing stands foursquare against fun and frolicking!"

A roar of agreement echoed from the righteous mob on the dock.

"But I was told to bring 'em here."

A stern matron in a black dress stepped out to confront the captain while glaring at the girls on the boat. "So Nameless wants to dump their garbage in our town? Well, we won't have it, you hear? I knew your wife, Captain, a paragon of virtue, Petunia Ann Pettigrew was. Shame! Shame! Take that trash elsewhere and put them off!"

The crowd on the dock roared its approval at the lady's words, although Choc noticed some of the men on the wharf didn't look all that enthused.

Captain Leroy tried to argue, but then the irate, upright citizens began pelting him and the others onboard with vegetables. At this point, deciding that discretion was the better part of valor, he yelled up for Buck to pull back out into the river. Within moments the *Petunia Ann* was chugging away and Choc was wiping ripe tomatoes off his coat.

Duchess, however, was beaming. She set Sadie's girls to picking up the vegetables that now lay ankle deep in places on the deck. "If'fen we stay on this boat, tomorrow I'm gonna make the best stew anyone ever ate."

Choc looked at Captain Pettigrew. "Sonovagun. Now what?"

"There's Greenville aways down the river; we'll make that early tomorrow morning. I've got to begin making a profit hauling cargo, or I won't be able to make my next mortgage payment." Shoulders slumped, he headed back up to the pilot house.

Choc looked around for Delight. If they were going to be on this old tub until dawn, that would be plenty of time for what he had in mind. He grinned in anticipation. The professor winked at him and turned back toward the dining room. "I'm beginnin' to feel right at home on this old tub."

Choc didn't answer as he watched Buck helping Duchess gather up her leafy haul. Where was Delight?

He stuck his head in the salon where the men had settled down to play cards. Some were hugging up to the girls, and a group were gathered around the professor as he began to play the piano. She wasn't in there. Choc went back out on deck, looking around. As he paused by the rail, he heard a noise.

"Who's there?"

"Just some of us men from Simpson's Landing," a voice announced, and within seconds a skiff was tying up with men climbing aboard.

Choc sighed. "You gotta hell of a nerve after runnin' us off!"

"That was our women folk, and they never let us

have any fun. We decided what you got onboard is better than what we got at home, so we thought we'd enjoy the party, then float back down before sunup."

Choc shrugged. It wasn't his problem. "Come aboard then. There's dancing and a bar in the dining room, but it'll cost you."

"We expect it to." The eager bunch almost ran down the deck and disappeared inside.

Choc sauntered along the deck, peering into each small cabin window. Where was that sassy wench?

He heard a familiar voice and paused near a room. In the warm spring night the window was open. Cautiously, Choc peered through the blinds. Delight. And she was with that handsome lieutenant who had just laid a twenty-dollar gold piece on the table. "This is quite a cozy place you got here, Miss Delight."

"Oh, I just took it over and cleaned it up a little." She smiled as she took the money and put it in her reticule. "I'm glad you like it. How about a drink, Lieutenant?"

"I'd love one"—he smiled—"and call me Alfred."

She could call him dead if Choc got his hands on him. Choc was just reaching to jerk open the door when he managed to control himself. Why was he so angry? He had never minded sharing a whore before. No, he was just riled that the spiffy young officer had gotten here first, that's all. Otherwise, why should he care that the customer was now looking at the little blonde as if she were a pork chop and he was a hungry hound?

He must not create a ruckus. It would only bring attention to himself and get people asking curious questions—although Lord knows Miss Delight Dugan had been as nosy as a tax collector. Choc had planned to spend the rest of the night asleep on those soft breasts, and here he was out on the hard deck, peeking in the window like a burglar, while a man not worthy of Delight's considerable charms was presently plopped on her settee, staring up at her raptly while she poured two drinks.

The settee was pushed up against the window, so close that Choc could've grabbed the young rascal by the neck and given him a good shake. He was tempted, but just then, Delight crossed over with the drinks and set them on the table before the ardent young man.

"Lieutenant, wouldn't you like to get comfy?" She purred like a kitten full of cream. As she put the drinks down, she leaned forward so Alfred, and Choc behind him, got a good look at the soft swell in the tight, low-cut, red satin.

"I . . . I can't stay long, Miss Delight." Alfred made a little noise in his throat as if he were choking on a brass button from his shiny uniform. "Tomorrow my unit's moving, escorting artillery to Virginia."

"Now is that a fact, Alfred?" She leaned even closer. "Then we'd better not waste what time we have. Wouldn't you like to take off your jacket?"

"Why, yes, ah, I'd like to take off my coat."

And his breeches and his underwear, Choc thought dourly.

He watched Alfred stand up and turn his back as he doffed his blue jacket with noticeably trembling hands. No doubt his palms were sweaty, too. Choc gritted his teeth at the thought that any moment now, those same sweaty hands were going to be slipping down the front of Delight's dress.

Then the most amazing thing happened. As Choc watched and the young officer was still turned away to take off his coat, the pretty blonde pulled a tiny vial from between her breasts. Deftly, she poured a few drops into one drink, then slipped the vial back into her bodice. By the time the officer turned around, she was smiling at him and holding both drinks, offering

Alfred the drugged one. "Here, Alfred, let's drink to a very exciting night."

At that point Alfred's hand was shaking so much, it looked as if he might spill the drink before he could get it to his mouth. "A very exciting night!"

Delight smiled as he drained the glass, but she only sipped her drink. "Now, Alfred, why don't we try out my bed and see if it's as soft and warm as it looks." She took his hand and led him to the bed.

What Alfred had in mind lying on would be soft and warm all right, Choc thought, but it wasn't a mattress. It was all he could do to keep from jumping up and crashing through the door as Alfred sat down on the bed and stared up at her, almost drooling.

She began to unbutton his shirt. "Now, Alfred, you're about to find out why they call me Delight."

"Y-Yes, ma'am. Funny, I feel a little sleepy."

"Well, then, Alfred, why don't you just lie back on my pillows and let me undress you? We've got all night."

"Oh, Miss Delight, this . . . this is my first time."

"No! Why, you seem like a man of the world to me. I'm really looking forward to this." She had finished unbuttoning his shirt and was bending to take off his boots.

"Really?" The lieutenant sounded sleepy and his voice faint as he leaned back against the pillows. After a long moment, he began to snore.

"Lieutenant?" Delight leaned over him. "Lieutenant? Are you asleep?"

Asleep? Choc thought, as many knockout drops as the little tart had put in his drink, it was a wonder Alfred wasn't dead. What in the hell was she up to?

Even as he watched in amazement, Delight felt through the unconscious man's pockets, then went over and began to search his coat. Choc leaned even closer, baffled. He felt disappointment that she was only a thieving whore after all, about to rob a naive customer. It was common enough, but somehow, he didn't want to believe Delight would do such a thing. Yet, even as he watched, she found some money, looked at it, then put it back in the coat. If she wasn't after money, what was she looking for? Next she began to go through the man's papers, unfolding and reading them.

Choc scratched his head in puzzlement. She wasn't a thief, and this innocent-looking girl couldn't be the spy Choc had been sent to search out, so what was she doing? He watched Delight go through everything in Alfred's coat, then put it back after reading all of it. Now she turned down the lamp, threw a blanket over the snoring young officer, took a book from her reticule, curled herself up on the sofa close enough for Choc to touch, and settled down to read.

He stifled an urge to reach out and stroke her hair or touch her bare arm. Over her luscious shoulder he read the book title: *The ABC'S of Proper Ranch Management*. Must be a mistake. He strained to see as she turned to a chapter. What was such fascinating reading? "How to Geld Your Bull or Stallion." Choc winced. Why in the hell would a lady of the evening be interested in that?

It was getting chilly out here in the dark. Choc had intended to be in that comfy bed tonight, along with the warm Delight. Yet that boy now snored in her bed; she was on the settee reading as raptly as if she held a romance novel; and here was Choc out on the deck, cramped and cold under her window as the dew fell and the breeze blew in off the river.

Well, sonovagun, the boat was full of eager, pretty girls. So why was he out here looking in at the one he couldn't have? He'd go find one of the others. When he started to rise, he discovered one of his feet had gone to sleep, and he almost fell before limping away down the deck.

From the dining room the sounds of the piano and women's laughter drifted faintly. He had something else he needed to do, too, and—

His mind busy, he bumped into Sadie just starting up the steps to the pilothouse. "Oh, Choc, I . . . I was just going up to see if Leroy was lonesome; I never met someone quite like him before." She looked almost sheepish in the moonlight.

"Everyone else still about?"

"Buck is in Duchess's cabin, and people are pairing off. You alone? That's unusual for you, Choc."

"I . . . I'll pick one out in a minute, Sadie; you know I don't ever lack for female attention."

She laughed as she started up the steps. "You can say that again, sport."

"Sadie, about that little blonde."

"What blonde?"

"You know, the young, pretty one in the red satin dress. What do you know about her? How long has she worked for you?"

"For me?" In the moonlight Sadie looked baffled. "She don't work for me, handsome. Matter of fact, until she showed up in the crowd in Nameless's town square, I never saw that girl before!"

Chapter Four

He stood there blinking in surprise, letting Sadie's words sink in.

"Choc, are you all right?"

"I . . . I'm fine, Sadie. See you in the morning."

He didn't want to answer any more questions so he turned toward Delight's cabin. That sneaky, secretive Texas tart!

She was just coming out her door as he rounded the corner and caught her arm. "Where are you headed?"

She started. "What's it to you, you tinhorn? Back to look for another customer."

"Don't you have a customer already?" He glared down at her. When he took a deep breath, he smelled the slight scent of Cape Jasmine perfume from the warmth of her half-bare breasts. "If not—" He pulled her close and kissed her.

Delight meant to pull away from him, but he was strong as well as tall. She opened her mouth to protest, but his tongue probed as it slipped between her lips. It was the most electrifying sensation she had ever experienced. Without meaning to, she relaxed and let him mold her tightly against him, her breasts pressed against the fabric of his coat, his urgent manhood hard against her body. He tasted of brandy, and when she took a deep breath, she smelled the male scent of sun and tobacco and masculine cologne.

For a long moment she lost control and let him

stroke her breasts as she trembled with her own need. Was she out of her mind? She remembered her mission, took a deep breath, and pulled away from him.

"No wonder you charge so much." He was breathing heavily. "I'd pay anything right now." His tone was urgent, aroused. This man was no fool; he'd demand what he paid for.

She heard the young lieutenant inside moan softly. "I've got to get back to my customer."

Before he could stop her, she jerked out of Choc's grasp and went back inside, closed the door, and locked it.

Damn her. Choc leaned against the window and shook with sheer frustration. What was happening to him? He had always had an easy nonchalance around women, a charm that lured any girl he wanted into his bed, yet he wasn't having much luck with this one. Delight Dugan was about to make him forget everything else, even important things.

He peered through the blinds and saw Delight lie down on the bed as the young officer came to and sat up.

"Well, Alfred, did you enjoy it?"

The young man blinked, puzzlement on his features. "I . . . I guess I did. I don't remember much about it."

"Oh, I remember every detail!" Delight sighed. "You were wonderful!"

"Really?" Alfred grinned.

"Now, Alfred, let me help you with your things so you can be going." She hopped up and began to button his shirt.

"Maybe I could stay just a little longer—"

"Oh, Alfred, a girl can only take so much from a virile man like you; I need a little rest after all that."

"Oh. Okay." Alfred looked both proud and disappointed as he reached for his boots.

Within minutes Alfred was swaggering down the

deck toward the dining room where the piano and laughter echoed.

Choc frowned after him. No doubt, the young rascal was going in there to brag about what a good time he'd had in Delight's bed. Even that annoyed him somehow.

Delight started back out the door. Choc grabbed her. She shrieked in surprise, but he kissed her and cut off her cry. She pulled away and wiped her mouth with the back of her hand. "What are you doing, skulking around my door?"

"I never left."

"You're a very suspicious character, you know that?"

"You're the suspicious character, Tex." He stood blocking her path and had to fight himself to keep from taking her in his arms again. He started to ask questions about what Sadie had said, what he had just seen through her blinds, then decided against it. "If you're looking for your next customer, here I am." He reached to open her door.

She looked up at him, and he had never felt such an overpowering urge to kiss a woman before. He wanted to make a bantering, clever remark, but all he could think of was how soft and vulnerable she looked—like a little girl playing dress-up in a garish costume. Yet she was making him feel awkward and hesitant as if this were all brand-new to him.

"Why not?" She took his hand, led him into her cabin, closed the door, and held out her palm. He put the money in it, and watched her tuck it in her reticule as he sauntered over to sit down on the settee.

"Choc, wouldn't you like to get comfy, maybe take off your coat while I fix us a drink?"

"Sure." He sneaked a look as he turned his back. The tiny vial came out, and she poured a couple of drops in one drink. That ornery little chit! Just what was she looking for? Did she intend to go through the pockets of every man onboard?

He laid his coat across a chair, settled himself back on the settee, then patted the cushion next to him. "Tex, darlin', why don't you sit right here and we'll continue."

"Let's have our drinks first."

"Oh, we've got plenty of time." He winked up at her. "Say!" He sat up suddenly. "Didn't I hear a noise outside?"

Her attention was momentarily diverted. In that split second as she turned her head, Choc deftly switched drinks, then picked up the one without the sleeping potion. "Maybe I was hearing things." He held his glass up. "A toast to the fun we'll have tonight."

She leaned forward so that he got a good view of her soft breasts as she picked up her glass. "Here's to fun!"

And oh, darlin', do I mean to have some, Choc thought and drained his. "Drink up!" he urged.

She hesitated, then drained her glass. "Choc, don't you think it would be more comfortable on the bed?"

"Sure do." He let her take his hand and lead him over to the bed. He sat down while she began to unbutton his shirt. At the same time he began to unbutton her bodice.

"What are you doing?"

"Well, turnabout's fair play. Hey, why don't you get here in bed, too, and we'll kiss awhile? No use rushing."

"That's a good idea." Delight kicked off her little slippers and climbed in next to Choc, pausing to yawn as she fluffed up the pillows. "I don't know what's getting into me."

"It's been a long, hard day for everyone," he said sympathetically. "I feel pretty sleepy myself."

"Really?" She grinned up at him and yawned again.

The little wench was going to be out cold in a few minutes, and he could do anything he wanted to her. The thought made his manhood swell. He took her in his arms and began to kiss her, reaching to take the pins from her hair so he could tangle his fingers in it. He gloried in her faint gasp of pleasure.

He nuzzled her neck and Delight yawned again. "I'm just so tired," she said faintly.

"So am I," he answered, unbuttoning her bodice further with one hand while the other went to push up her skirt.

She stiffened and pulled away. "Aren't you . . . aren't you feeling sleepy?" She appeared to be having a difficult time focusing her eyes.

"Some," he said. "Why don't we both just sort of lie back on our pillows and take this nice and slow?" He began to kiss her again, his pulse pounding so hard he was certain she could hear it.

"Nice and slow," Delight murmured, and her eyelids fluttered as Choc held her close. "Nice and . . ."

She was asleep. He felt her relax, and her head fell against his broad shoulder. She was warm and soft in his arms, and there was no resistance as he pulled her small body against the length of his hard one. Her bodice lay open now. Choc looked down at the most beautiful pair of creamy breasts he had ever seen. "Oh, darlin', you are certainly worth twenty dollars, all right."

Finally, he felt as if he had the advantage over this quick-witted, secretive chit. His manhood throbbed with urgent need as he reached to push up her skirt. She smiled in her sleep and snuggled down into his arms as if she belonged there. She looked small and defenseless. Choc hesitated. He had paid for the use of her body, and this little sneak deserved to have the tables turned on her—yet it didn't seem quite right somehow. Cursing himself for a chivalrous fool, he sighed and stood up. Well, at least he'd find out what her secrets were.

He picked up the book and flipped through it. It was just a book after all, no code, nothing. What had he expected? This sweet-faced, ornery Texan couldn't be the major's spy. What a joke! He took her reticule and dug through it. Besides the twenty-dollar gold pieces he and that lieutenant had given her, she had no other money.

Whoa! What was this? He unfolded a handbill announcing the thousand-dollar reward the Union was posting for the capture of the Rebel spy. Now why did she have that? If she weren't one of Sadie's girls, who was she? Maybe she was on the run and had taken advantage of the crowd on the wharf at Nameless as a perfect opportunity to flee the area. Choc studied the handbill a long moment, utterly mystified.

Choc dug a little deeper and came up with an old letter.

Dear Miss Bertha Kleinhoffer:
I regret to inform you of your father's death. There is no estate, due to his drinking and gambling, but maybe you can continue working at your old Aunt Hilda's drygoods and apothecary shop.

It closed with apologies for the bad news and was signed with a flourish by a lawyer in Fredricksburg, Texas.

Thoughtful, Choc folded up the worn letter and returned it to Delight's things. Just who was Bertha Kleinhoffer, and how did she connect with Delight Dugan, the high-dollar whore? The sassy blonde seemed to be hiding as many secrets as Choc himself.

A sound. He whirled and looked toward the bed. He listened a moment and smiled. Delight Dugan had at least one more secret—she snored. He went over to the bed and stood looking down at her. So very young and so innocent-looking; but then, those were the kind of whores men paid best for. Gently, he rolled her onto her side and pulled a blanket up over her. Cursing himself for a fool, he slept on the settee until almost dawn.

Her stirring brought him awake and immediately, he crossed over and crawled in next to her. She rolled over and snuggled closer to his warmth, then her eyes flew open and she pulled back as if she had just touched a hot poker. "What are you doing here?"

He raised up on one elbow and looked down at her. "Now, Tex, darlin', don't you remember?"

She looked horrified. "N-not much."

"Oh, it was unforgettable," he assured her with a grin. "No wonder you charge twenty dollars."

Her face turned ashen, and she made a choking sound. "And with a gambler, a damned tinhorn gambler," she muttered, closing her eyes as if she couldn't bear the idea.

The boat whistle sounded, and they both jumped, startled.

Choc said, "Must be coming into Greenville."

She hopped up and began to button her bodice and put on her little shoes. "You lowdown sidewinder!" Gathering up her things, Delight turned and ran out.

There was no understanding women, Choc thought as he put on his boots and coat. Right now he had other things he needed to think about.

However, out on the wharf was an irate crowd, armed with shotguns and big signs, singing at the top of their lungs.

Choc looked from them to Captain Pettigrew. "Let me guess—they don't want us, either."

"You got it." He yelled to the mayor, "Will you at least let us send someone into town for supplies?"

The men on the dock conferred, nodding and rubbing their hands together greedily.

Choc took out tobacco and papers and began to roll a cigarette. "I never heard of any town council turning down a chance to make money."

Sure enough, the mayor yelled up, "Send them ashore, but keep everyone else on board that old tub!"

"Tarnation," Captain Pettigrew said, then took off his hat and scratched his gray head. "Buck, why don't you go and maybe the professor?"

Sadie said, "I'd like to go, Leroy, and maybe Duchess—she'll need some cooking supplies."

The captain nodded, looking around at those on deck. "Anyone else need anything?"

Choc shook his tobacco sack. "I could use some makin's. Here, Buck, I'll write the brand down." He searched through his pockets, shrugged, pulled out a stub of pencil, scribbled the words on a cigarette paper, and gave it to Buck along with some money. "Didn't have any other notepad. Can you read that small print?"

Buck nodded. "Yes, Mister Choc. Come on, Duchess, and anyone else goin' to town."

About half a dozen people got off. Choc yawned and headed to the dining room. Delight was serving coffee. "Pour me a cup, darlin'. I like my coffee like I like my women—hot and sweet."

"How would you like it in your lap?" she muttered, picking up the pot and advancing on him.

He jumped and backed away. "Now, Tex, darlin', I don't understand why—"

"Get out of here, you sidewinder!"

The girl mystified him. He went back up on deck and thought about love, war, and Major Blake.

In less than an hour the group returned with supplies. Within minutes the *Petunia Ann* was headed upstream again, with the scent of ham and eggs, biscuits with cream gravy, and strong coffee floating on the air. Predictably, also in less than an hour, the male citizens and Union soldiers of Greenville were also climbing aboard. Captain Pettigrew sat down at the same table with Choc and piled the fried potatoes next to his crisp bacon. "Tarnation, I'd forgotten what good cookin' is and how nice it is to have real women around."

Choc nodded. Sadie and her girls had pulled down the drapes and were cleaning windows. "They could almost turn this into a comfy haven, all right." Comfy? Hell, he was beginning to talk like her.

"Next town is Haleysburg, and if they won't take this bunch, I don't know what I'll do."

Choc eyed Delight across the dining room, but she seemed to be avoiding his gaze. It was amazing how good she looked in a frilly apron. He wondered suddenly how she'd look in blue calico about the color of her eyes? "Haven't you been making money on these men who've been coming aboard?"

The grizzled old fellow nodded. "If many more come aboard, we'll sink under their weight!"

The morning passed pleasantly, with the sternwheeler rocking with the professor's piano, the girls cleaning and polishing, and the tantalizing scent of pecan pies drifting from the kitchen. Sure enough, more men were coming aboard all the time to replace the ones who left, and the poker tables were full. Choc played cards with some of the Union officers and kept one eye on Delight, who seemed to be flirting with every man on board and asking all sorts of nosy questions, especially from the soldiers.

Now just what did that sweet Texan think she was going to do with that information? He thought about the folded handbill again. There were plenty of cutthroats and rascals on board who'd turn in anyone for a lot less than a thousand dollars. He stifled a yawn and tried to act polite and interested to an eager captain talking about a big troop movement soon to begin in the Shenandoah Valley. "I'm not really into politics or the war," Choc said.

"I suppose if you were, you'd be in uniform," the captain sneered.

He wasn't about to be goaded into a fistfight with this young hothead. Choc merely smiled and shrugged. "You're probably right."

The captain, mollified, looked at his hand and made his bet. With a smile Choc laid down his royal flush and took the pot.

As might have been expected, a stiff-necked "welcoming" party met the boat at the Haleysburg wharf early that afternoon, proclaiming loudly that they didn't want the *Petunia Ann*'s load of trashy tarts and rowdy rascals, either.

"Tarnation, what am I gonna do, Choc? I can't just keep hauling these folks up and down the river with men climbing on board, wanting whiskey and food and dancing."

"Well," Choc said, "the only thing I can suggest is to maybe take them back to Nameless."

"Are you daft? Major Blake ain't gonna let me—"

"Don't blow that damned whistle. Just sneak into the dock about dark, unload 'em, and be off before the town knows it. They ain't your problem."

"Somehow, I don't want to just dump Sadie off where folks won't be good to her. She's a remarkable woman, and I'm gettin' used to her."

Buck sighed as he wiped off their table. "It won't be the same with the professor and the girls gone, especially Duchess. Tendin' bar is a sight easier than lifting cotton bales, and the gentlemen tip well, too."

"Can't be helped," Choc said. "By the way, thanks, Buck, for runnin' my errand." He reached into his pocket for a coin, but Buck grinned and shook his head.

"I wasn't hintin' for money, Mister Choc. You'n me

goes back a long ways; I'm happy to do things for you."

"Well, thanks, Buck. I'm beginnin' to like your boat; I might just decide to stay aboard."

So now they were headed back down the river in the darkness. By Choc's calculations they might be back at Nameless by dusk tomorrow since they'd be moving faster going downstream. He grinned. That gave him tonight to enjoy Miss Delight Dugan. In the meantime the dining room served up fried chicken and apple pie, and the scent drifted to shore, or maybe it was the scent of perfume and the sound of that piano that lured men aboard all over again.

Choc intercepted Delight just as she was about to leave the dining room with that Union captain. "Sorry, but I believe the lady had previously promised me this evening."

"I don't remember any such thing!" Delight protested.

"Maybe last night you were enjoying our dalliance so much, you forgot." He caught her arm and propelled her outside with the young officer protesting weakly behind them.

"You sidewinder," she snapped, "all I've got to do is scream, and that gallant officer will come running!"

"If he does, Tex, darlin', I'll either throw him overboard or show him that folded-up reward poster in your reticule, and we'll have a little discussion about why you might be asking so many questions of everyone you meet."

She looked stricken. "How do you know about that? Did you go through my things?"

He grinned. "Now would a nice fellow like me do something like that?"

"Oh, you rascal, there's probably no telling what you'd do! I'm not a spy if that's what you're thinking.

I'm merely trying to find out who is so I can claim that reward."

"Uh-huh." He was big enough that he could propel her toward her cabin even though she was resisting. "What are you going to do with a thousand dollars in gold?"

"I want to own a ranch; it's my secret dream."

"You think you can work it by yourself?" He opened her door and pushed her in.

"I can try!" She faced him gamely.

"You are a fiesty thing, aren't you?" He didn't want to admire this secretive chit, but he did. He closed the door and leaned against it. "Just think, I could probably collect that reward myself by turning you over to Major Blake—he might be more likely to believe me than you." He saw in her eyes that she was wondering if that could be a real possibility.

"Why . . . why would he?" she asked.

"Because to be honest with you, he suspects that the Reb might be in this ragtag bunch, and he sent me to investigate."

"Honest!" she snorted. "You don't know the meaning of the word!"

"Maybe not"—he pushed his Western hat back and grinned at her—"but I think I could make a good case against you."

"What . . . what do they do to spies?"

"Firing squad," Choc replied, shrugging carelessly. "Of course, you never thought about that—just the money. For a woman they might give you a choice of hanging instead."

"If that spy is on this boat, it isn't me," Delight said. "My sympathies are with the Union."

"A Texan throwing in with Yankees? I don't think so." She might be a liar, but she sure was beautiful when she was riled, he thought.

"I'm from the Hill country; I'm German," she said.

"You surely know the German settlers sided with the North."

He considered that. Certainly he had heard of the lynching of forty men at Gainesville by pro-slavery groups and the massacre of the Union sympathizer Germans at Nueces. "Dugan is hardly a German name."

"My real name is Kleinhoffer."

"Ahh! Bertha," he said nodding, "no wonder you changed your name. What other secrets are you hiding, Tex?"

"None! Now let me out of here!" She tried to push him away from the door, but he reached out and caught her hands.

"Suppose I believe you, that you aren't the Rebel spy?"

"We could work together, split the reward." Her pretty blue eyes were so appealing he had to remind himself that he couldn't trust her.

He chewed his lip, thinking. "Do you have any clue; any good suspects?"

"No, but I aim to find out. There's lots of suspects; the professor, the captain, any of the girls or gamblers, or maybe one of those soldiers who've come on board."

"Suppose I've figured out who it is? Why should I share the money with you?"

"Oh, you cheap tinhorn—!" She struggled, but he pulled her up close where he could look down into her fragile face. The way she looked up at him with her lips partly opened set his blood to pounding.

She seemed to realize how she was affecting him. "Just who is it?" she purred and pressed closer.

"You little rascal. You'd do anything to wheedle it out of me so you could get that money."

"Oh, you don't know anything—you're bluffing, trying to get me back in bed." Delight stopped struggling and smiled up at him with those blue eyes that a man could drown in.

"I must admit, I'd considered it, but I'm not sure your charms are worth a thousand dollars."

He thought for a moment she was going to slap him, but she seemed to force herself to smile, as if she realized she wasn't getting anywhere. "Why don't I fix us both a drink?"

"Tex, you should have learned your lesson last night; I know about the knockout drops."

Her eyes widened with gradual shock. "You rattlesnake! You . . . you switched drinks on me! Oh, you unprincipled cad!"

"Unprincipled? Darlin', you're the one druggin' folks and goin' through their pockets. Suppose I tell Major Blake about that?" He pulled her closer.

Choc could feel her heart pounding against him through the tight dress, and the scent of Cape Jasmine perfume made his senses reel.

"You'd . . . you'd make me buy your silence with my body?"

"Silence? I don't think you know the meaning of the word; you chatter more than a squirrel. Kiss me and I'll think about it."

"A squirrel? Why, what an insulting—"

His lips cut off her words. For a moment she struggled against him as he pulled her even tighter into his embrace.

She wasn't going to let him pressure her into going to bed with him. She wasn't going to . . . his mouth was insistent, his lips caressing hers as one of his hands tangled in her hair. She felt his manhood throbbing against her with need.

His mouth tasted sweet and hot on hers as his fingers stroked down her back, cupped her bottom. He kissed her tenderly, expertly, until she was gasping for air. It felt good, the way he was cradling her against

him as he lifted her gently and carried her to the bed.
She saw that his hands were trembling as he began to
unbutton her bodice. She should stop him, tell him the
whole truth—but now he had the front of her dress
open and his big hands, gently cupping her breasts,
were driving her to distraction.

As he pulled her breasts up to his eager mouth, she
couldn't stop a sigh of pleasure. His warm lips caressed her nipple, and the unbelievable sensation
stilled her protests as he began pulling her dress down
her shoulders. Whatever she confessed, she told herself, he probably wouldn't believe her.

He had his hands up under her skirt, pulling her gar-
ters off, slowly rolling her silk stockings down and
kissing along her inner thighs. Oh, surely he wasn't
going to kiss her there; oh, no, not there. And then he
did, and it was the most electrifying feeling, sending
whorls of heat radiating all over her while she trembled and clung to him.

"We've got all night, little Tex," he murmured, "and
I intend to make the most of it." Then he kissed her
breasts again, and she found herself tangling her fingers in his black hair, pulling him down insistently to
kiss and caress every inch of her while she shook and
gasped, wanting still more.

She was only vaguely aware of him slipping his
pants off before he lay down next to her again.
"Darlin', you seem to like to take men's shirts off—be
my guest."

She could feel the hard male length of him against
her as she unbuttoned the top button, and it made her
hesitate.

"Go on," he urged, kissing her again in a way no
man had ever kissed her, putting his tongue deep in her
mouth, thrusting there as his hands roamed all over her
body, gently touching, stroking, and squeezing. His
fingers were warm as they caressed her skin, and she

began to unbutton his shirt again, eager now to see what he looked like.

She wasn't disappointed. He was dark, big and muscular. He took her hand and placed it on his manhood. Its heat and size made her gasp.

"Everything's better in the Indian Territory," he said and laughed. And then, suddenly sensuous, he touched her with his fingers. "You're wet, darlin' and ready for me," he whispered.

She wanted to deny it, but she didn't want him to leave, didn't want him to stop kissing and stroking her. She felt as if she were on fire and nothing could put out that blaze but this half-breed rogue. She didn't mean to—Lord knows, she'd never even imagined herself doing this—but she spread her thighs and pulled him down on her.

"My Delight," he murmured, and then he thrust into her. "Oh, honey, you feel so good!"

He was big. He seemed to be thrusting up into the very core of her. For just a moment he was more than she could take, and there was pain, but she wanted him anyway.

"Wrap your legs around me, darlin'," he commanded, his voice cracking with urgency.

She started to tell him then, but she was afraid he would pull out and end this dizzying sensation that was sweeping over her, overpowering her. Instead, she looped her legs around his strong back, and dug her nails into his lean, dark hips, urging him even deeper. "Choc, oh, Choc, don't stop, don't stop!"

His mouth felt hot as a branding iron on her lips and breasts as he thrust into her. No wonder women liked him, she thought as her excitement built—she hadn't known there could be such pleasure in this. Then she couldn't think anymore because the intensity was building and he was riding ever harder and faster, and she wanted still more and more and more. . . .

That was the last thing she remembered for a long time. Delight was only vaguely aware when Choc finally pulled out of her, snuggling her down against his chest. "Oh, Tex," he whispered, breathless. "You are something else!"

She curled up in his embrace and put her blond head on his shoulder. "The best you ever had?" she asked, needing to know.

He held her protectively. "The best ever."

They made love again and again, and finally, wrapped in his warm, muscular arms, she dropped off to sleep, lulled by the rhythmic churning of the paddles as the *Petunia Ann* headed downstream.

It was late morning when Choc awakened and glanced down at the girl still asleep in his arms. He smiled and brushed a lock of hair from her forehead. No woman had ever given him such pleasure. He realized, suddenly, that the thought of another man ever touching her again filled him with fury. She was a whore, he reminded himself bluntly—men paid to use that lovely, ripe body. Hell, he was no better—he'd bluffed her into giving in to him; Choc had no idea whether Major Blake could have been convinced the girl was the elusive spy or not.

Choc kissed her cheek, and she smiled in her sleep, snuggling even closer against him. Sonovagun, what was wrong with him that he felt so protective of this little tart?

He slipped out of bed, trying to turn his thoughts to the things he had to do today, important things. As he glanced back down at her sleeping form, he saw the scarlet stains on the sheets. What the hell?

Then the inevitable truth dawned on him. Delight Dugan or Bertha Kleinhoffer, or whoever she was, had one more incredible secret she hadn't told him. Last night his high-dollar whore had been a virgin.

Chapter Five

Delight's eyes opened as Choc dressed. Oh, my God, she had given herself to him last night. She must have been out of her mind!

He looked at her, confusion in his dark eyes. "Tex, just when I think I've got you figured, you surprise me."

"W-what do you mean?"

"Where did you get that red dress? Was it originally old Aunt Hilda's draperies?"

How did he know about dear, departed Aunt Hilda? "Don't be a ninny!" She retorted, trying to hide her embarrassment. "No woman would make a dress from old drapes—they'd be dusty and sun-streaked. It was a bolt of fabric she hadn't been able to sell."

He finished putting on his coat as she realized with growing horror that he was about to leave. "Not so fast!" Her embarrassment forgotten, she jumped up and barred the door with her body. "You promised you'd tell me what you knew, split the reward."

"I did no such thing, Tex, darlin'." He reached for his hat and winked at her. "We split the fun; that's enough."

"Oh, you rotten liar!" She was furious. "You tricked me! You don't have any more idea than I do who the spy is. I'm going to follow you right out on deck, telling everyone what a liar you are!"

"That don't make me no nevermind," he said as he

straightened his cravat and grinned, "but if I was you, Tex, darlin', I'd put my drawers on first!"

Delight glanced down and realized suddenly she was stark naked. "I hate you!" As she ran to grab a sheet, he went out the door and closed it just as she threw a glass that crashed and broke against the wood.

Delight collapsed on the bed, sobbing.

On the other side of the door, Choc listened a long moment, trying to ignore his sympathy for the Texas chit. He was a free-wheeling, high-living bachelor with no responsibilities, and he liked it that way, especially with the life he was leading right now. With a sigh he shrugged off the voice that told him to comfort her, and headed down to breakfast and a leisurely morning of cards.

Delight was so furious, she wouldn't even look at Choc the rest of the day, and he was pointedly ignoring her. Well, why shouldn't he? He had gotten what he wanted from her. Delight tried not to remember the pleasure of his embrace. No wonder women flocked after the cheap tinhorn. She had been tricked while she was trying to trick him. What a rotten rascal! And he didn't have any more of a clue than she did who the spy might be—or else, he intended to keep all that reward for himself.

Determined to ignore what had happened last night, Delight renewed her search for the spy. As the day passed and the *Petunia Ann* chugged downstream, she found herself looking over everyone on board, weighing the possibilities. The professor certainly seemed harmless enough, but in and out of a lot of bordellos and dance halls, he could pick up information easily, and he was a Southerner. But then, so was Sadie and half the people on board. All the pickpockets, the whores, and the gamblers mingled with enough soldiers to overhear military secrets. There was the captain himself, and those roustabouts and deckhands who overheard a lot on the waterfront, and Buck and Duchess. But of course blacks wouldn't help the Rebels. What about all those civilians and soldiers who had come aboard? Oh, the whole thing was probably a wild-goose chase! Suppose the major and Choc were wrong and the spy was back in town—or a thousand miles from here?

Delight sat down on the arm of a soldier's chair, put her arm around him, and kissed the dice for him for luck. In return he stuffed some greenbacks down the front of her dress. When she looked up, Choc was glaring at him. That caused her to laugh even louder, and she flirted outrageously with the men at the table. Why should Choc care? He had had his fun with her, hadn't he? Aunt Hilda had been right in her warnings; men—unscrupulous men—would say anything, do anything, to get inside a girl's drawers.

Delight was feeling more and more desperate as the afternoon lengthened. Collecting this reward had been her last hope, even if it was a long shot. When she got back to Nameless, what was she going to do for money? Well, she realized with a sigh, she was no longer a virgin. Every time that half-breed rascal looked in her direction, she got angry all over again. She would have sworn that silver-tongued devil had offered to split the reward . . . or had he? In the heat of the moment money hadn't seemed very important.

The tables were full as the sun set and the *Petunia Ann* nosed quietly into the wharf. Delight looked out the dining-room window. "I think the telegraph must have carried the word," she announced to the crowd. Choc kept right on dealing cards, but others hurried to the rail to look. Sure enough, on the dock was a large gathering of businessmen and shopkeepers, along with Major Blake, his soldiers and that one old hound dog.

Captain Pettigrew stuck his head in the doorway.

"Tarnation, I reckon we ain't gonna unload here, either."

"Who cares?" Sadie laughed. "We've about decided we don't want to get off."

The men and girls merely nodded and went on playing cards and drinking.

Out on the dock the mayor yelled, "Captain Pettigrew, are you there?"

"I'm here!" he yelled back. "I know, you don't want me to unload, but—"

"On the contrary," the mayor shouted, "we had forgotten how much business and money the girls brought in; we need the tax dollars. Can we come aboard and talk about it?"

"Well, I'll be damned!" the old man remarked.

The professor paused in his playing and shook his head. "I'm beginning to like the *Petunia Ann.*"

The girls all murmured agreement.

Delight watched as Major Blake climbed onto the deck and headed toward the dining room.

Choc yawned. "Well, Buck, if you're goin' ashore for supplies, I'm almost out of whiskey; I don't like the cheap stuff behind that bar."

"Anything you say, Mister Choc." Buck limped toward the table with his tray.

Delight stood at the next table, watching Choc with sadness. In a few minutes they'd all be scattering and he wouldn't even look at her. What had she expected? She was embarrassed to admit it, but her heart was breaking—and all he could think of was ordering a favorite brand of whiskey!

"Buck, I'll write down the brand I like; see if you can find it." Choc took out a cigarette paper and a pencil stub and scribbled a few words.

Major Blake's boots were echoing down the hall toward the dining room, but everyone else was playing cards and drinking. Carelessly, Choc tossed the scrap of paper onto Buck's tray. It missed and fluttered to the floor, landing right at Delight's feet.

"That's mine," Choc insisted, getting up from his chair. Buck rushed forward to retrieve it, but Delight bent over and picked the little paper up just as Major Blake entered the dining room.

"Captain Pettigrew," the officer said, "there's a delegation outside, wanting to talk to you and Sadie."

He came toward Choc's table. Both Choc and Buck were holding out their hands for the cigarette paper. Delight glanced down and blinked, then read it again.

Gen. Lee. Big Troop coming Shenandoah V, Choc.

For a split second she looked from the tiny note to Buck's strained expression. Then she turned to Choc. The half-breed's color had paled, and sweat gleamed on his forehead as he looked up at her. He didn't look cocky now—he looked horrified and scared.

She almost laughed out loud as the stunning realization swept over her. Choc was the spy—a double agent! The major, unknowingly, had the rascal searching for himself! Buck was carrying the messages, of course, but the evidence would only damn Choc.

"Hello, young lady," the major said with an amorous smile. "I don't remember you at Sadie's place." He began feeling through his pockets.

She had all she needed in her hand. This tiny scrap of paper could send the rascal who'd seduced her to prison or the firing squad; she could collect that reward. Both revenge and the ranch she'd always dreamed of were literally within her grasp. All Delight had to do was hand that small paper to the Union officer.

Choc and Buck knew it, too. She could tell by their tense expressions. Secrets—she knew Choc's deepest secret. Oh, she finally had that cheap gambler right where she wanted him. Revenge was going to be so sweet!

"Damn, I seem to be out of cigars," Major Blake grumbled. "Get me one, will you, honey?"

Sweat beaded on Choc's handsome face as he looked up at her. His expression revealed that he fully expected her to hand the major the evidence and collect the blood money. It was, after all, what he deserved.

In that split second she made her decision. Delight grinned and winked at the major. "Can I roll you a cigarette instead, handsome?"

The officer sat down at Choc's table, leaned back in a chair, and smiled. "If you roll it, honey, I'll bet I like it."

Very slowly, she reached into Choc's coat as he stared up at her and took his tobacco. Shaking some into the paper in her hand, she rolled a cigarette, then, smiling, she stuck it between the major's lips. Giving him her most flirtatious smile, she carefully lit it. "This is a really expensive smoke," she purred.

The major took a deep drag and nodded. "Does taste pretty good," he agreed with a smile, winking at her. "Special blend, Choc?"

Choc only sputtered. Before he could answer, she said, "I believe it's called Gambler's Delight."

The major took another drag and motioned to Buck. "Boy, bring me a whiskey; that fine brand Choc prefers."

"Beggin' your pardon, suh." Buck relaxed visibly. "I was just on my way into town to get Mister Choc some; we's out of that."

"Then be quick about it," the major snapped as he smoked. "I don't have all day!"

"Yassah," the big black man rolled his eyes and did an Uncle Tom shuffle out the door.

Choc let out his breath with a sigh, but he didn't take his gaze off Delight as he took out a handkerchief and wiped his forehead. "I-I came up empty-handed, Major, if you know what I mean."

"Damn!" grumbled the major, "I was afraid of that!" The ash on his cigarette grew longer and longer. Neither she nor Choc seemed to be able to cease staring at it. "Maybe my hunch was wrong," the officer grumbled as he finally shook the ash off. "Rebs just ambushed an artillery outfit up near Greenville, so the gal I'm looking for must be in that area."

"Sorry I wasn't much help," Choc said.

The officer took another drag and shrugged. "I just expected too much from a gambler." He turned to glare at the professor. "You there, play something— 'Camptown Races'."

The professor banged out the tune, and the laughter and chatter started again. Delight watched Choc, admitting to herself that she loved him whether he cared about her or not. Now all that mattered was getting off this boat. She turned, tears blinding her, and hurried outside.

"Wait, Delight!" He ran after her, catching up with her out on the deck.

She pulled away from him. "You don't need to worry now; the major's just sent the evidence up in smoke."

"As well as that reward that meant so much to you."

"Worse than a tinhorn gambler, a damned Rebel— why, Choc, why?"

"The Confederates have promised to declare the Indian Territory a separate nation if the South wins," Choc said. "That's important to my tribe."

"But Buck—?"

"I saved his life a couple of years ago, pushed him out of the way as a crate fell. He'd do anything for me." He put his hands on her shoulders. "How did you get into this comedy of errors?"

She was crying now. "I . . . I saw the reward poster

and drifted into the town square out of curiosity. No one would listen to me when the crowd began pushing toward the docks."

"Well, your ranch just went up in smoke. What kind of place had you dreamed of, anyway?"

She tried to pull away from him, but he was stronger than she was. "What difference does it make? I wanted lots of rolling hills, plenty of trees, clear streams. Now, I'll never get it, but that's not your problem."

He reached out and put one finger under her chin, forcing her to lift her eyes to his. "I know of a place like that, but it's not in Texas, it's in eastern Indian Territory. The war can't last much longer."

She was hiccoughing and sobbing. "I don't have any money to buy land. Don't you understand?"

"I understand one thing," he whispered, and no longer was he a jaunty, arrogant rascal. "I've always been as wild and free as an unbranded mustang, and up until now, I liked it that way. Now Delight Dugan or Bertha Kleinhoffer, or whatever the hell your name is, I'd like to see you in blue calico and a frilly apron, standing by a baby cradle."

"I don't understand," she wailed.

"God, you Texans are dense! If you think I'm going to get down on my knees, forget it. What I'm trying to say is I'd like to change your last name to McGraw."

She stopped crying, and her blue eyes widened. "Is that your real name?"

"Almost."

She waited while he hesitated. "Okay, Tex, if there're not going to be any more secrets between us, my first name is really Algernon."

"Algernon? That's worse than Bertha!"

"My pappy read a lot poetry; I had to fight half the boys in the county over it. Of course, if it doesn't suit you—"

"It suits me just fine!" She cut off his words with a

kiss and his mouth tasted as good as she remembered. He held her so tightly, she almost couldn't breathe as he lifted her off the deck and held her close. His lips were soft, yet possessive, and he smelled of sun and wind, brandy and tobacco. "Oh, Choc, I love you so!"

He kissed the tears from her cheeks. "I never thought I'd say this to a girl and mean it, but I love you, darlin', more than I ever thought it possible to love a woman."

Captain Pettigrew came out on the deck. "Oh, there you two are. The local businessmen are begging Sadie and the rest to come back, but everyone seems to want to stay aboard."

"Captain," Choc said, "you can't see the forest for the trees. Your old boat can't compete against railroads and the big packets in ordinary ways; you need to find a special niche and fill it, and you've done that. Think, man, this could be the first floating pleasure palace!"

He took Delight in his arms again. "Oh, by the way, as captain, are you allowed to perform a marriage ceremony?"

Epilogue

As you may have guessed, Choc and Delight, er, Algernon and Bertha, got hitched and went back to his ranch in eastern Indian Territory when the war ended. There they raised a passel of colts, calves, and kids, and lived a very quiet life.

In fact, the four children used to complain at the dinner table about how colorless and staid their parents were. "What did you do in the war, Papa?"

He would look down the long table to where Delight sat, clad in blue calico, demurely dishing up potatoes. "Not anything too exciting, I reckon."

"One of the girls at school's mother once baked a pie for Jeff Davis," their oldest daughter proclaimed.

"Imagine that! Now eat your peas," Delight said.

"And Lem says his Uncle Blake is in the army in Texas and gets to hold General Custer's horse whenever they go chasin' Comanches; all because of something he did in the war," the youngest son announced.

Choc grinned. "Sonovagun! I knew a Blake once; he was supposed to catch a spy, but when he didn't. . . ."

Four little faces turned toward him expectantly, but Delight gave him a warning look.

"Well"—Choc cleared his throat—"I reckon maybe it isn't the same one after all. Like I said, kids, nothing much interestin' ever happened to us in the war."

"Aw, Papa, you and Mama are so dull!"

"Ain't we, though? Now pass the fried chicken."

* * *

As for Captain Leroy Pettigrew, he married Sadie and Buck married Duchess. Sadie took the money from her corset, did repairs to the boat, even bought a fancy calliope, while Duchess took over the books and ledgers. The girls, gamblers, and the professor had all found permanent homes and jobs on the old sternwheeler, and everyone stopped worrying about the competition from the trains and the big, new boats. You see, there was no need to haul freight or cotton anymore; the *Petunia Ann* had found her destiny.

Oh, yes, many a staid businessman kissed his bland wife and kiddies good-bye with a smile as he left on a business trip aboard the *Petunia Ann Floating Pleasure Palace*. They say when you're having fun, time and speed don't mean much. With the entertainment, roulette wheel, dancing, good food, and whiskey, Captain Pettigrew was soon turning away eager male passengers. Tickets had to be bought so far in advance, Duchess raised the price to meet the demand. Buck not only ran the bar, he bought a distillery, cutting out the middle man.

The boat, repainted the color of rouge, a shade that soon was known as Petunia pink, became a legend in her own way, or maybe notorious is a better word. Everyone knew the sound of that fine calliope blasting out: ". . . buffalo gals, won't you come out tonight, come out tonight, come out tonight . . . ?" as she cruised up and down the river in all her gilt and glory, complete with mirrors over the beds and scarlet drapes.

They do say there was a series of small earthquakes right after the refurbished stern-wheeler returned to the river and her new career. Don't you believe it; locals say that was merely the righteous Petunia Ann Pettigrew whirling in her grave!

Masquerade

by

Madeline Baker

To Davis Gaines,
L.A.'s best-ever Phantom.
Thanks for the inspiration
and "The Music of the Night."

And to Annee Chartier,
who shares my passion and my obsession
not only for all things Phantom,
but for all dark, brooding heroes.

Chapter One

Los Angeles, 1993

He was a very old vampire, weary of living, weary of coming alive only in the darkness of the night.

For three hundred years he had wandered the unending road of his life alone, his existence maintained at the expense of others, until the advent of blood banks made it possible to satisfy his hunger without preying on the innocent and unsuspecting.

And yet, there were times, as now, when the need to draw warm blood from a living, breathing soul was overpowering.

He stood in the shadows outside the Ahmanson, watching groups of happy, well-dressed people exit the theater. He listened to snatches of their conversation as they discussed the play. He'd seen the show numerous times; perhaps, he thought wryly, because he could so easily sympathize with the Phantom of the Opera. Like Sir Andrew Lloyd Webber's tragic hero, he, too, was forced to live in the shadows, never to walk in the warmth of the summer sun, never able to disclose his true identity.

And so he stood on the outskirts of mortality, breathing in the fragrance of the warm-blooded creatures who passed him by. They hurried along, blissfully unaware that a monster was watching, drinking in the myriad smells of their humanity, sensing their happiness, their sorrows, their deepest fears.

He waited until the crowds had thinned, and then he began to follow one of the numerous street beggars who had been hustling the theater patrons. There were hundreds, perhaps thousands, of homeless men roaming the streets of Los Angeles. On any given night you could find a dozen or so lingering outside the Ahmanson, hoping for a handout that would buy them a bottle and a few hours of forgetfulness.

A faint grimace played over his lips as he drew near his prey.

After tonight there would be one less beggar haunting Hope Street.

Chapter Two

He was there again, standing on the corner, his long angular face bathed in the hazy glow of the streetlight.

Leanne felt his hooded gaze move over her as she left the side entrance and made her way toward the parking lot across the street. Behind her, she could hear the excitement build as Davis Gaines, who many considered to be L.A.'s best Phantom, appeared at the stage door to sign autographs and pose for pictures.

She was unlocking the car door when she felt a hand on her shoulder. Startled, she whirled around.

It was him. Up close, he was even more handsome than she had thought. His face was made up of sharp planes and angles, totally masculine, totally mesmerizing. His hair was black and straight and fell well past his shoulders. His eyes were an intense shade of blue, and as her gaze met his, she knew she had been waiting a lifetime for this moment, this man.

"I didn't mean to frighten you," he said in a deep, resonant voice. He held out a theater program. "I was hoping you'd sign this for me."

Leanne smiled. "Why would you want my autograph? I'm only in the chorus."

"But you have such a lovely voice."

She laughed softly. "You must have excellent hearing, to pick my voice out of dozens of others."

His smile was devastating. "My hearing is quite good for a man of my age."

Leanne's gaze moved over him curiously. She didn't know how old he was, of course, but he didn't look to be much more than thirty at most.

He offered her a pen, one brow raised in question.

"Who should I make it out to?" Leanne asked.

"Jason Blackthorne."

"Blackthorne." She gazed up at him intently. "Why does that name sound so familiar to me?"

"Does it?"

She nodded, then took the pen from his hand. He read the inscription over her shoulder:

"To Jason, May you always have someone to love, and someone to love you. Leanne"

He felt a catch at his heart. Someone to love ... Jolene. Leanne's resemblance to his first and only love was uncanny.

He smiled his thanks as she handed him the program, his gaze moving over her face, lingering on her mouth before moving to the pulse that beat in her throat. She was small, petite, with skin that looked as though it rarely saw the sun, hair the color of sun-kissed earth, and luminous green eyes fringed with dark lashes. She wore a Phantom sweatshirt, a pair of black tights that clung to her shapely legs like a second skin, and sneakers.

Jason clenched his hands at his sides as he fought the urge to take her into his arms, to touch those lips with his own, to sip the sweet crimson nectar from her veins.

Leanne frowned. "Is something wrong?"

"No. I was just wondering if we might go somewhere for a drink."

She should say no. There were a lot of sick people running around these days, obsessive fans, psychotics, and yet there was something in Jason Blackthorne's eyes that made her trust him implicitly.

"I know a little place not far from here," she suggested with a tentative smile.

"I'll follow you in my car," Jason said, somewhat surprised by her ready acceptance of his invitation. Didn't she read the papers? Muggings and rapes and murders were rampant in the city.

A faint smile tugged at his lips as he crossed the parking lot to his own car. Indeed, he mused as he slid behind the steering wheel, she would be far safer with one of the city's lowlifes than she was with him.

The bar was located on a narrow side street. He knew a moment's hesitation as he followed her inside, and then sighed with relief. There were no mirrors in sight.

They took a booth in the rear. She ordered a glass of red wine, as did he.

"So," Jason said, "tell me about yourself."

"What would you like to know?"

She felt his gaze move over her face, soft as candlelight. "Everything."

"I'm twenty-three," Leanne said, mesmerized by his gaze. "I'm an only child. My parents live in Burbank, but I have a small apartment not far from the theater." She smiled at him, a shy intimate smile. "Someday I hope to make it to Broadway."

"Have you a boyfriend?"

"No."

You have now.

Did he speak the words aloud, or was her mind playing tricks on her, echoing words she wished to hear?

"How long have you been with the play?"

"Two years."

"I hear it'll be closing soon. What will you do then?"

"I'm not sure."

"How long have you been acting?"

"This is my first role." Leanne smiled. "I always

wanted to be on stage, and I decided, what the heck, why not go for it? So, I tried out and they hired me." She put her elbows on the table and rested her chin on her hands. "What do you do?"

"I'm a cop." The lie rolled easily off his lips.

"You're kidding!" He didn't look like any police officer she'd ever seen. Dressed in a loose fitting white sweater, a pair of black jeans, and cowboy boots, he looked more like a movie star than a cop.

One black brow lifted slightly. "I take it you don't care for the police."

"No, no, it's just that . . ." She made a dismissive gesture with her hand. "You don't look like a cop."

"How's that?"

"No mustache," Leanne said, running a fingertip over his upper lip. "All the cops I know have a mustache."

Jason grunted softly. "And do you know a lot of cops?"

"Not really. Where do you work?"

"Hollenbeck."

"That's a rough area."

Jason shrugged. "I like it." Their drinks had arrived during their conversation, but neither had paid much attention. Now, Jason picked up his glass. "What shall we drink to?"

Leanne lifted her glass. "Long life and happiness?" she suggested.

"Happiness," he repeated softly. "I'll drink to that."

"And long life?"

His gaze was drawn to her throat, to where her pulse beat strong and steady. "Long life can be a curse," he muttered.

"A curse! What do you mean?"

He dragged his gaze from her neck. "Just what I said. I've seen too many people who've lived past their prime, people with nothing left to live for, with nothing to hope for but a quick death, an end to pain."

"I don't agree. Life is precious at any age."

"And do you think you'd like to live forever?"

"I know I would." She laughed softly. "This conversation is getting too morbid for my taste. Tell me about yourself. What do you do for recreation?"

"Nothing very exciting. Read. Watch TV. Ride my horse."

"You have a horse? Where do you keep it?"

"I have a small ranch in the hills, nothing elaborate."

"I've always loved horses. Do you think I could ride sometime?"

Jason frowned. "I sleep days, so I usually ride at night."

"How romantic," she said, her voice low and husky. "Perhaps we could go riding together sometime."

Jason swallowed hard. Was he imagining things, or was she suggesting more than she was saying? The thought of holding her close, of having his arms around her waist, of burying his face in her hair, her neck, flooded him with desire. He glanced away lest she see the sudden heat, the hunger, that he knew was burning in his eyes.

"It's getting late," he said, tossing a handful of bills on the table. "I'd better let you go home and get some sleep."

"We don't have to go," Leanne replied. "I'm a bit of a night person myself."

"Then we have more in common than a love of horses," Jason replied dryly. "Perhaps we could go to a late movie tomorrow night?"

"Sounds good."

"I'll pick you up at the stage door."

Leanne gazed into the depths of his eyes and felt the instant connection between the two of them, as if their souls had found each other after traveling through years of darkness.

She had been born for this man.

The thought entered her mind, quiet and unshakable, like the answer to a prayer.

Chapter Three

He fed early the next night, his eyes closing in something akin to ecstasy as he emptied a bag of whole blood into a glass and slowly drained the contents, enjoying the taste of it on his tongue.

Only yesterday, he had contemplated putting an end to his life. It would be so easy to terminate his existence, so easy to stand out on the terrace and watch the sun come up one last time.

So easy, but oh, so painful.

Now, as he dressed, he wondered, as he often had in the past, if he possessed the courage he would need to face such an agonizing death.

But it was a moot point. He no longer wished for death. Life was new again, exciting, and all because of Leanne. During the long hours of the day, as he slept the sleep of the undead in the basement of his house, her image had drifted across his mind. That, in itself, was strange, he thought. Never before had his rest been disturbed by images of anyone, living or dead. But even during the heat of the day, when he usually slept the deepest, he had seen her face, heard the sound of her voice, yearned for the touch of her hand.

Restless, he wandered through his house, trying to see it through her eyes. She would no doubt find it strange that there was no food in the house, that there were no mirrors to be found, not even in the bathrooms. He could easily explain the security bars on the doors and windows. After all, crime was everywhere. The old paintings, the ancient books and scrolls, would not be so easy to explain, not on a cop's salary.

He had collected quite a few masterpieces in the last three hundred years. Paintings thought lost in the wars that had ravaged France and Spain resided in the bedroom; sculptures believed to have been destroyed graced his library. He had one of Shakespeare's original plays, signed by the Bard himself. His basement was crowded with ancient scrolls, with furniture and clothing from ages past.

Perhaps he should have told her he was an antiques dealer. But it was easier to say he was a cop, that he worked the graveyard shift and slept days, that he worked weekends and holidays, and was therefore unable to attend the picnics and parties to which he was occasionally invited.

He paced the floor for an hour and then, unable to wait a moment longer to see her, he drove to the Ahmanson Theater and bought a ticket.

The play mesmerized him, as always. He'd lost count of how many times he'd seen it, had long ago stopped wondering why he found the production so fascinating.

Lost in the dark, he became one with the Opera Ghost, lusting after the fair Christine, knowing in the depths of his aching heart that she would never be his.

He heard the anguish in the Phantom's voice as the Phantom watched Christine find comfort in the arms of the handsome Vicomte de Chagny, felt the deformed man's pain as he cursed her.

But he had eyes only for Leanne. Her presence called to him until he was blind to everyone else on stage, until his pulse beat in time to hers. He felt her excitement as she sang her lines, felt her triumph as the crowd applauded.

As soon as the final curtain came down, he left the

theater, eager to see her again, to discover if she was truly as beautiful as he remembered. Surely her eyes could not be so green as those he'd seen in his dreams, her skin could not be so pale and unblemished. No lips could be so pink and well-shaped; her hair could not be so long, so thick, as he recalled.

And then she was there, walking toward him, smiling as if they had known each other for years instead of a few hours.

She was breathtaking in a pair of slinky black pants and an opaque blouse of some material that clung to her, outlining every delectable curve.

He felt his mouth water just looking at her.

"Let's go," she said, tucking her arm through his.

"My car's in the lot," he said, and for the first time since the dark curse had been bequeathed to him, he felt young and alive.

"Is this yours?" Leanne asked. She hadn't noticed what he was driving last night.

Jason nodded. "Like it?"

Her gaze swept over the sleek curves of the black Porsche. "What's not to like?" She slid into the seat when he opened the car door, her hand stroking the soft leather. "You're not a cop on the take, are you?"

Jason shrugged as he slid behind the wheel and turned the key in the ignition. "No. My grandfather left me quite well off."

"Then why do you work?"

"A man has to do something with his time."

They made small talk on the way to Hollywood. She told him about some of the funny things that had happened on stage, like the time the Phantom's boat went the wrong way, and he told her about the case he was supposedly working on.

After parking the car, they walked hand in hand toward the movie theater.

Inside, they sat in the last row. Of its own volition,

his hand took hers. The touch of her fingers entwining with his sent a shock of feeling surging through him, a jolt of such force that it almost took his breath away.

In the darkness his gaze sought hers. She had felt it, too; he could see it in the slightly surprised expression in her eyes, hear it in the sudden intake of her breath, feel it hum between them, alive, palpable.

Time and place were momentarily forgotten as he placed his hand at the back of her head and drew her toward him. Her eyelids fluttered down as his mouth closed over hers.

It was a kiss unlike any he had ever known— sweetly potent, volatile, explosive. His body's reaction to her nearness, to the scent of her perfume and the taste of her lips, was instant.

With the rise of his desire came another hunger, one that was more painful than unfulfilled passion, more deadly for the woman in his arms. Unable to help himself, he pressed a kiss to her throat, let his tongue caress the pulse beating there. Tempting, so tempting . . .

With a low groan he drew away.

"Jason, what's wrong?" Her voice was husky, drugged with desire.

"Nothing." He raked a hand through his hair. "This isn't the time, or the place."

He could see her smiling at him through the darkness, her green eyes smoky with passion.

"Any time," she murmured. "Any place."

"Leanne . . ."

"I'm shameless, I know, but I can't help myself. I feel as though I've known you all my life. Waited for you all my life."

For a moment he closed his eyes. And then he smiled at her through the darkness.

"We have time, Leanne," he whispered hoarsely. "All the time in the world."

Chapter Four

He sat on the sofa in the living room, his feet resting on a hassock, his gaze fixed on the fire in the raised hearth. The fire served no purpose save that he found it pleasing to look upon. He had no need for its warmth; he felt neither the heat nor the cold, but sitting in front of a fire on a cold night seemed a very human thing to do. And tonight, tormented by memories of his past, he had a strong desire to feel mortal again.

He had been born in a time of great superstition: when a woman with the gift to heal might be judged a witch and burned at the stake; when people believed that werewolves prowled the forests in the dead of night; when ghosts might be found wandering through castle and hovel alike.

He had never seen a ghost, and he'd never believed in werewolves, but he'd come to believe in vampires. Oh, yes, he'd never forget the night he had learned about vampires.

He'd had an argument with his wife, Jolene. He couldn't remember now what they had quarreled about, but he'd stormed out of the cottage and headed for the tavern, determined to drown his troubles in a mug of ale. He'd been working his way through his third tankard when Marguerite approached him. There had been something about the way she looked at him, the way her dark eyes had caressed him, that had chilled him to

the very marrow of his bones and yet . . . and yet it had
drawn him to her side.

Mesmerized by her beauty, by the husky tremor in
her voice, he had followed her upstairs. Never before
had he been unfaithful to Jolene, but that night it was
as if he'd had no control over his passion. And so he
had followed her up the narrow wooden stairway and
into a life of eternal darkness.

She had taken his blood and returned it to him, then
left him just before dawn, warning him that he would
need to find a place to hide himself from the sun unless
he wished to perish on the morrow.

He had not believed her—until he stepped into the
dawn of a new day. The pain of the sun on his face had
been excruciating. With a cry he had run into the
woods and taken refuge in a cave.

Trembling with pain and fear, he'd become as one
drugged, unable to move, only vaguely aware of the
ghastly changes taking place in his body as Marguerite's accursed blood wrought the hideous transformation.

He had died that day, and when he awoke that night,
he knew his old life was gone.

He had sought Marguerite the next night, begging
her to undo what she had done, but she had only
laughed softly as her hand caressed his cheek.

"There is no going back, *mon amour.*"

"There must be a way!"

"None that I know, except . . ."

He had grabbed her by the arms, his fingers biting
deep into her cool white flesh. "Except?"

"It is rumored that there is one bloodline that has the
power to transform you into a mortal again, but I have
no idea as to how it's done. I know only that the power
is not in the blood." She shrugged, as if the whole conversation were unimportant. "That's all I know."

"Whose bloodline? Where do I find it?"

"I know not. I care not. I am happy as I am, and have no wish to be mortal again."

She had pried his fingers from her arm, then patted his cheek, much as a mother might comfort a weeping child.

"Give it time, *chéri*. One day you will bless me for what I have done."

Bless her! He would have killed her had he known how. That night, he had gone home to find Jolene frantic with worry, her beautiful face ravaged by tears.

She had been disbelieving when he told her what had happened, disbelieving until the sun came up and she had seen for herself the deathlike lethargy that held him in its grip.

To her credit, she hadn't turned her back on him. Although she had been repulsed by his lust for blood, she had never stopped loving him. Blessed woman that she was, she had kept his secret until the day she died.

And that had been the hardest thing of all to bear, watching his beloved wife grow old and feeble while he stayed forever young and strong. Her soft, unblemished skin had wrinkled with the passing years, her hair, as fine as black silk, had turned white, the joy of living had gone out of her eyes, those beautiful green eyes that had ever looked on him with love.

It had been torment of the worst kind, watching her sicken and die. In desperation he had offered to save her, to make her into what he had become, but she had refused, and in the end, she had died in his arms, whispering his name.

In his youth he had been zealously religious. Always, he had believed in a just and loving God. He had been faithful in his prayers, certain they were heard. But now he was cut off from the powers of heaven, unable to offer a prayer on behalf of his wife.

That night, for the first time since Marguerite had turned him into a monster, he had contemplated putting an end to his existence. Considered it and found he lacked the courage, for far worse than the thought of dying was the knowledge that, in death, he would come face-to-face with the Almighty and have to confess his sins.

In all the years since Jolene's death, he had kept a tight rein on his emotions, never letting anyone get close to him. He had no friends, mortal or otherwise. At any rate, trusting one of the undead could be as dangerous to his existence as trusting the living, and so he had trusted no one, loved no one.

Until now.

He thought of Leanne, and her memory engulfed him with a warm, sustaining glow. She had brought light to his existence, given him a reason to live, pierced the protective wall he'd erected around his heart and forced him to accept that he had fallen in love again.

Fallen in love with a woman who looked enough like Jolene to be her sister.

A long, slow sigh escaped his lips. He could not endure the agony of watching another woman he loved grow old and die, nor could he be responsible for giving her the Dark Gift. Leanne was a creature of sunshine. He could not condemn her to a life spent in the shadows . . .

And yet he could not think of facing the future without her, not now, when he had glimpsed her goodness, felt the sweet magic that had flowed between them the moment their eyes met for the first time.

He was tired of meeting her after the theater and spending the evening in a darkened movie house or a smoke-filled bar, and since he dared not go to her house, which no doubt contained several mirrors, he brought her home.

Never before had be brought a woman into the

house. He bade her wait in the entry hall while he went inside and lit the candles. No doubt she would think it strange that he eschewed electric lights, but he much preferred candlelight to lamp light.

Returning to the entry hall, he bowed over her hand. "Welcome," he said and kissed her hand in courtly fashion.

"Do you mind if I look around?" Leanne asked.

"Please," he said. "Make my home yours."

Leanne wandered through the house, enchanted by the works of art, the sculpture. Several of the paintings were signed J. Blackthorne. The signature was bold and distinctive.

"Blackthorne," she exclaimed softly. "Of course. I saw one of his paintings in a museum." She turned to look at Jason, a question in her eyes.

"An ancestor," Jason said, "prolific but mostly un-appreciated."

Leanne studied the larger of the paintings. It portrayed a tall, dark-haired man standing alone on a sea cliff. A black cape swirled around his shoulders, buffeted by the wind. Dark gray clouds hovered above storm-tossed waves. Just looking at the painting filled her with a sense of loneliness, of emptiness.

"He was very good," she remarked.

Jason shrugged. "For his time, perhaps."

With a nod Leanne continued her tour, ever conscious that Jason was only a step or two behind her.

The rooms were sparsely furnished, and she noticed he had only a few small table lamps, none of which he turned on, obviously preferring the softer, more romantic glow of the candles that lit every room, even the bathrooms.

The living room was decorated in earth tones. A sofa faced the fireplace; there were two matching over-stuffed chairs on either side of the hearth. A book on ancient Rome sat on a carved oak table beside the couch. Heavy beige draperies covered the windows.

The master bedroom was decorated in shades of blue and white. Standing in the doorway, she had the oddest impression that the bed had never been slept in; indeed, she had the feeling that the room had rarely been used at all. Adjoining the master bedroom was a large bathroom with a sunken tub and a skylight.

In an enormous den next to the bedroom two of the walls were lined with bookshelves that reached from floor to ceiling. She paused in front of one of the bookshelves, her gaze perusing the titles. She saw Shakespeare and Homer, Louis L'Amour and Stephen King, Tom Clancy and Anne Rice's Vampire books, as well as numerous books on history and geography, medicine, art, literature, and folklore, many of which were written in foreign languages.

"Have you read all these?" she asked, amazed by the quantity and variety of books. Some of them appeared quite old, judging by their fragile covers.

"Not all," Jason replied.

Leanne smiled, thinking it would take a hundred years to read every book on the shelves.

Turning away from the bookshelf, she glanced around the room. A beautiful black marble fireplace took up most of the third wall. The fourth wall contained a large window that was covered with heavy floor-to-ceiling drapes. A big, comfortable-looking black leather chair stood in front of the hearth.

Leaving the den, she peered into the kitchen, noting that it was stark and white. Again, she was overcome with the impression that, like the bedroom, the kitchen was rarely, if ever, used. But then maybe that wasn't so strange. Jason was a bachelor, after all. Maybe he ate all his meals out.

"So," he said as they returned to the living room, "what do you think?"

"It's very nice." She made a broad gesture with her hand. "I think I like the den the best."

"Yes, it's my favorite, too."

Leanne crossed the floor to the picture window that overlooked the backyard and pulled back the heavy curtains. A full moon hovered low in the sky, bathing the grass and the outbuildings in shimmering silver.

"Is your horse here?"

"Yes."

"Could I see it?"

"If you like."

Taking her hand, he led her out the back door and down a narrow flight of steps. They followed a narrow winding path edged with ferns and willow trees until they reached a large corral.

Jason whistled softly, and a dark shape materialized out of the shadows.

"Hello, Lucifer," he murmured, scratching the big black horse between its ears. "I've brought someone to meet you."

Leanne held out her hand, and the stallion danced away, its nostrils flaring, its eyes showing white.

"I don't think he likes me," she said, disappointment evident in her voice.

"We don't get many visitors here," Jason remarked. Slipping through the rails, he walked up to the horse and stroked its neck.

Like all animals, the stallion had been wary of him in the beginning, but Jason had used his dark power to overcome the animal's instinctive fear.

Now, he vaulted lightly onto Lucifer's back and rode around the corral, guiding the stallion with the pressure of his knees.

Leanne clapped her hands in delight. "That's wonderful!" she exclaimed, charmed by the fluid grace of the horse, the sheer masculine beauty of the man. They looked as though they'd been made for each other, the devil black horse and the raven-haired man.

Jason rode effortlessly, his body in complete harmony with the stallion's. Like a dark angel, he rode bareback in the light of the moon.

After a few moments he rode toward the gate and slipped the latch. Riding up to Leanne, he held out his hand.

"Don't you need a bridle or something to control him?" she asked dubiously.

"No. He responds to my voice and the pressure of my legs."

The stallion's ears twitched as Jason lifted Leanne onto its back, and then they were riding down a sloping path that led to a trail into the hills.

Jason breathed in Leanne's scent as they rode through the quiet night, the only sound that of the horse's muffled hoofbeats and the chirping of crickets.

His thighs cradled her buttocks, his arm circled her waist, the fall of her hair brushed his cheek. He had only to lean forward to press a kiss to the side of her neck, and as he did so, he felt the longing to sink his fangs into the soft skin of her neck, to taste the warm rush of her blood over his tongue.

She leaned against him, her back pressing against his chest, her nearness sparking the embers of desire that were ever present when she was near.

"Jason?"

He grunted in response, unable to speak past the loathsome need rising swiftly within him, the need to drink of her sweetness, to possess her fully.

"Could we stop here for a while?"

He glanced around. They were in a small glade surrounded by tall trees. Wordlessly, he slid from the back of the horse, then reached up to help Leanne dismount. His hands lingered at her waist, and he drew her up against him, letting her feel the evidence of his desire, afraid she would refuse him, more afraid that she might not.

Leanne took a deep breath. It was all happening so quickly. She felt the pull of his gaze, felt herself falling helplessly in love with a man she hardly knew—a man she wanted to know better.

"Jason, tell me I'm not dreaming, that the magic between us is real and not just something I've imagined because I want it so badly."

"It's real. Never doubt that."

His eyes were dark, the blue-black before a storm. A lock of hair, as black as ink, fell across his forehead. For a moment she felt as if he were a part of the night, a dark phantom who had stepped out of one of her dreams.

Compelled by a need she never thought to question, she reached up to touch his cheek, to assure herself he was real.

"Leanne." He murmured her name in a voice filled with longing, and she had no thought to deny him.

She lifted her face, eager for his kiss, her eyelids fluttering down as his head bent toward hers.

He hesitated only a moment, battling the ancient urge to drive his fangs into her throat, to mingle her blood with his.

Instead, he kissed her gently, careful not to bruise her tender flesh. As if she were made of glass that might shatter at the slightest touch, he held her in his arms, his body basking in her warmth, in the essence of life that flowed through her.

Holding her close, he was keenly aware of the vast gulf between them. She was light and hope and innocence, children playing in the sun, lovers strolling on the beach on a hot summer day, all the things that were forever lost to him. He was the essence of darkness. It permeated his life and shrouded his soul. He groaned low in his throat, his arms tightening around her, as he sought to draw a part of her goodness into himself.

In the beginning, after he had resigned himself to Jolene's loss, to the fact that he was forever different, forever cursed, he had gloried in being a vampire. His hearing was keen, his eyesight much improved. He discovered he could cover great distances with preternatural speed. He had thought the taste of blood would disgust him, but it was a part of what he had become, and he had learned to accept it. What could not be changed must be endured.

In the beginning he had not realized how long forever was. He had not understood how truly alienated he was from the rest of mankind. With the coming of awareness, he had lost himself in learning. Later, he had discovered to his amazement that he could paint, and he had spent a century perfecting his talent, and when he grew bored with painting, he had tried his hand at writing.

It had come easily to him, and he had written scores of novels, many of which he had sold. And when writing lost its charm, he had turned into a vagabond, traveling from one end of the world to the other, but nowhere had he found a sense of home, of belonging, and so he had come back to America, a land where the bizarre was taken for granted, a place where a man who lived like a recluse was not considered odd at all.

But now Leanne was here, in his arms, and for the first time in three hundred years he felt a sense of belonging.

"Leanne," he murmured. "Can you save me, I wonder."

She drew back, a frown furrowing her brow. "Save you?"

Only then did he realize he'd spoken aloud.

"Save you from what?"

"Nothing." He gazed into her eyes, knowing the

hunger was glowing in his own. "We'd better go back."

She didn't argue, only continued to stare up at him, her expression filled with concern and another emotion he could not quite fathom. Was it fear?

And then, to his surprise, she gently stroked his cheek. "Don't be afraid, Jason," she said quietly. "You're not alone anymore."

Before he could absorb the meaning of her words, a dog came charging through the trees, saliva dripping from its massive jaws.

Instantly, Jason thrust Leanne behind him, putting himself between her and the animal's slathering jaws. A sharp command kept Lucifer from bolting down the hill.

Summoning his dark power, Jason fixed his gaze on the dog. As though it had slammed into a brick wall, the beast came to an abrupt halt. Whining softly, it eyed Jason for a moment, then turned and ran, its tail between its legs.

Leanne blew out the breath she'd been holding. Never had she seen anything like that in her life.

"We'd best go," Jason said, and before she had time to argue, before she had time to ask questions, he lifted her onto the back of the horse, then swung up effortlessly behind her and kicked the stallion into a canter.

When they reached the house, he lifted Leanne from the back of the horse, then put the stallion into the corral and latched the gate.

"Jason, that dog . . ."

"It's getting late." He drew her into his arms and kissed her. "Will you be all right getting home?"

"Fine," she murmured, all thought of the dog forgotten in the afterglow of his kiss.

"Will I see you tomorrow?"

"I'm counting on it."

Jason nodded. He yearned to read her mind, to discover what she thought of him, but for the first time in his life, he could not bring himself to steal his way into another's thoughts.

"Goodnight, Jason. Sleep well."

He kissed her once more, briefly, sweetly, and then, reluctantly, he let her go. Already, he could feel dawn coming, feel the heavy lassitude stealing over his body, draining his strength, dragging him down, down, into darkness.

His steps were heavy as he made his way to the basement. Hollywood might insist that their vampires sleep in silk-lined coffins, but then Hollywood perpetuated a lot of myths that had no basis in fact. He had no need to rest in a coffin; indeed, he found the idea macabre. Instead, he preferred to pass the daylight hours resting in a corner of the cellar, his head and shoulders covered by a patchwork quilt similar to the one he had once shared with Jolene.

Chapter Five

He saw her almost every night after that. She arrived at his house shortly after eleven and stayed until the early hours of the morning.

It was a routine that fit his with remarkable precision. He never had to worry about offering her food because of the lateness of the hour. An occasional cup of coffee, a glass of wine, were all she ever asked for.

Often, they went riding in the moonlight, sharing the quiet intimacy of the night.

Sometimes, as now, they sat on the sofa, watching television. Tonight they were watching *Love at First Bite* starring George Hamilton as the infamous Count Dracula in an affectionate spoof of vampire movies.

"He's a very romantic night creature," Leanne remarked. " 'With you, never a quickie, always a longie . . .' " She grinned impishly as she quoted a line from the movie.

Jason arched one brow as he watched George Hamilton hurrying down a New York street moments before the coming dawn, his black cape swirling behind him like the devil's breath. Romantic, indeed?

He caressed Leanne's cheek with the tip of his finger. "And would you let the count bite your neck if you had the chance?"

Leanne poked him playfully in the ribs. "Oh, I think I'd let Mr. Hamilton bite anything he liked."

"Have you ever thought of what it would be like to be a vampire?"

"Sure, who hasn't?" Leanne smiled at him, her deep green eyes dancing with laughter. "I mean, except for the blood part, the thought of living forever is very appealing, although I'm not sure I'd want to turn into a bat."

The blood. His gaze moved to the pulse in her neck. He could hear the blood moving through her veins, smell the heat of it, the warmth. The thought of drinking from her sickened him even as it excited him.

"And do you believe in vampires?" he asked, his voice low and seductive.

Leanne's gaze met his, all humor gone from her expression. "Yes, I do." She lifted one brow. "You look surprised."

"I am. Most people don't believe in monsters."

"There are all kinds of monsters."

"Indeed." He glanced at the television, his stomach muscles tightening as George Hamilton enveloped Susan Saint James in the folds of his voluminous black cape to give her the final bite that would change her into a vampire.

He felt Leanne's hand on his thigh, felt his mouth water at the thought of giving her the vampire's kiss.

"Is something wrong, Jason?"

He shook his head, and then, unable to keep from touching her, he drew her into his arms and kissed her.

His touch went through her like lightning, igniting every nerve ending, every sense of awareness. His tongue plundered her mouth, stealing her breath away, until she thought she would faint. He whispered her name, his voice urgent, almost rough, as though he were in pain.

She felt his hands slide under her sweater to settle on her bare back, felt the tremors that coursed through him as his fingertips caressed her quivering flesh. His kiss deepened, taking her to places she'd never been. His intensity frightened her even as it excited her. He seemed to know exactly what she liked, what she wanted . . . what she needed.

She gasped with pleasure as she felt his teeth nip at the lobe of her ear, then nibble the side of her neck. Desire shot through her, and with it an image of darkness that went beyond black.

"Jason!" Alarmed, she drew back.

The light in his eyes burned brighter than any candle, hotter than any sun. His breathing was erratic, his lips slightly parted. She watched him draw several deep breaths, felt the effort it cost him to release her.

"I'm sorry," he rasped. "Forgive me."

"It's all right. I'm as much to blame as you are."

"No." He couldn't keep his hands from shaking, couldn't keep his gaze from returning time and again to the pulse beating so rapidly in her throat.

Rising, he extended his hand. "Come, I'll walk you to your car."

She didn't want to go home, she wanted to stay, to spend what was left of the night in his arms, but leaving was definitely the smart thing to do.

Another moment, and she would have lost all control.

Another second, and she would have given him whatever he wanted.

Hand in hand, they walked down the stairs to the driveway.

Jason opened the car door for her, kissing her cheek before she slid behind the wheel.

She closed the door, then rolled down the window and leaned out for one last kiss.

He covered her mouth with his, drinking deeply of her innocence. "Don't come tomorrow night," he said, and before she could ask why, he turned away, taking the stairs two at a time.

From the window in the living room he watched her drive away, wondering if she had any idea of the danger she'd been in.

He sat in his favorite chair in front of the fireplace in the den, his hands clenched into tight fists as he listened to the the sound track from *The Phantom of the Opera*. The haunting words of the Phantom's plaintiff cry as he pleaded for Christine's love filled the room, echoing in Jason's heart.

The Phantom's music of the night might be a ballad of love and longing, Jason thought, but his own song was a requiem of blood and death, of darkness as deep and wide as eternity, as bottomless as the bowels of hell.

The Phantom of the Opera had lived in the darkness of life, Jason mused bitterly, but he was trapped in the everlasting darkness of his soul.

He shuddered to think how close he had come to wrapping Leanne in his embrace, to quenching his unholy thirst by stealing the essence of life from a creature who was pure and innocent.

He could not see her again. He loved her too much to put her life in danger, to risk turning her into the kind of monster he had become.

There was no hope for him, but he would not defile Leanne. She was a beautiful woman, made to walk in the sun, to find love in the arms of a mortal man and bear his children.

A hoarse cry rose in his throat, a cry that became an anguished scream of denial as he imagined her in the arms of another man, a man who could take her walking on the beach, who could make love to her in the light of day, a man who didn't live in the shadows.

A man who didn't thirst for that which made him a thief of the worst kind, stealing life itself.

* * *

For the next week he tormented himself by going to the theater, watching her perform on stage, hearing the sweet magic of her voice.

He listened to the Phantom's anguish with renewed pain. Just once, he thought, just once he'd like to see Christine turn her back on Raoul, the Vicomte de Chagny, and give the Phantom of the Opera the love he craved, the love only she could give.

When the show was over, he hovered in the deep shadows to make sure Leanne made it safely to her car. It was the worst kind of torture, seeing her from a distance, hungering for her touch, yearning to hear the sound of his name on her lips.

Each night he saw her gaze sweep the crowds waiting at the stage door, the hope in her eyes fading when she didn't see him.

And now he stood in the shadows again, a tall figure dressed all in black. Couples passed him by, never knowing he was there. Frustrated beyond reason, hating what he was because it kept him from the woman he loved, it took every ounce of his self-control to keep from destroying the innocent creatures who passed him by. He was torn with the need to lash out, to hurt others as he was hurting.

He watched a young couple pass by, and he wanted to sink his fangs into the man's throat, to turn the man into a monster so that the woman at his side would look at him with loathing instead of desire.

He fought down the growing lust for blood as he saw Leanne coming down the sidewalk. She was late tonight, and he wondered what, or who, had detained her at the theater. Jealousy rose in his throat, as bitter as bile, at the thought of her with another man—a mortal man.

His hands curled into tight fists as he watched her cross the street. More than anything, he wanted to go to her, to take her in his arms and hold her, for just a moment.

His eyes narrowed as he saw three dark shadows disengage themselves from a doorway and follow her into the parking lot.

He lost sight of her as she turned the corner, and then he heard her scream.

In an instant he was across the street, his hands closing around the throat of the thug nearest to him. The man's choked cry alerted his companions, and they whirled around to face him. One held a knife; the other a pistol.

Jason heard Leanne scream his name as the gunman fired three times in quick succession. Oblivious to the impact of the bullets, Jason lunged forward, a hand locking around the neck of each would-be assailant. Slowly, so slowly, his fingers tightened around their throats. He would have killed them, and gladly, if Leanne had not been there. The sound of her sobs penetrated the red mist that hovered in front of his eyes. With a muttered curse he let them go, and they fell in a tangled heap at his feet.

"Jason!" Leanne ran toward him, her eyes wide with fright.

"I'm all right." His gaze moved over her in a quick assessing glance. "Did they hurt you?"

"No." She stared at the bullet holes in his coat. Unable to believe her eyes, she touched each one with her fingertips, then looked up at him, her face as pale as the moon.

Hating himself because he had to deceive her, he fixed her with his hypnotic gaze, willing her to forget that the man had fired his gun, to remember only that he had come to her rescue. He left her spellbound while he went to his car, removed his coat, and replaced it with a sweater he'd left in the backseat.

Returning to her side, Jason snapped his fingers, releasing her from the power of his mind.

"Come," he said, taking the keys from her hand. "I'll drive you home."

Leanne blinked up at him, then glanced at the three men sprawled on the ground. "What about them?"

"Leave them."

"Aren't you going to arrest them?"

"No, I'm going to get you home."

"But . . ."

"Very well. Let's go back to the theater. We can call from there."

Twenty minutes later a black-and-white pulled into the parking lot. After the three suspects were handcuffed and tucked into the backseat of the patrol car, Leanne gave the officers her name and address and then told them what had happened. Jason corroborated her story.

The police officer who took Jason's statement frowned as he examined the gun. "This weapon's been fired," he remarked, opening the chamber. "Three times."

"I don't remember any gunshots," Leanne said, looking from the police officer to Jason. "Do you?"

Jason shook his head. "No."

The cop scribbled something in his notebook, thanked Leanne for her time, advised her to be more careful in the future, and bid them good night.

"Now can I take you home?" Jason asked.

"I've never been so scared," Leanne whispered, and as the knowledge of what could have happened hit her, she began to tremble violently.

"It's over," Jason said, wrapping her in his arms. "Don't think about it."

"I can't help it. I know this kind of thing happens all the time, but I never thought it would happen to me."

Keeping one arm around her shoulders, he unlocked

the car door and helped her inside, then went around to the driver's side.

Once he'd pulled out of the parking lot, he drew her up against him, holding her close while he drove.

"Where are we going?" Leanne asked as they turned onto the freeway.

"My place."

She didn't argue, merely rested her head on his shoulder and closed her eyes.

When she opened them again, they were pulling into Jason's driveway.

She was still trembling when she got out of the car. "Nerves, I guess," she murmured, then gasped as Jason swung her into his arms and carried her up the stairs and into the house.

Inside, he placed her on the sofa, poured her a glass of wine, then went into the bathroom to fill the tub with hot water.

"You'll feel better after a bath," he said, taking the glass from her hand.

With a nod she went into the bathroom and shut the door. A good hot soak was just what she needed. Undressing, she sank into the tub, willing herself to relax, to forget the terror that had engulfed her. Reaching for the soap, she washed vigorously, knowing she'd never wash away the fear or the vile memory of being touched by an unwanted hand. Thank God for Jason, she mused, and never thought to question what he'd been doing there.

Jason stood in the living room, his keen hearing easily picking up the sounds Leanne made as she undressed and then stepped into the tub. It was so easy to picture her lying there, the water surrounding her, caressing her, as he so longed to do . . .

With an oath he threw the wine glass into the fireplace, feeling a sense of satisfaction as he watched the glass shatter, falling onto the stone hearth like crystal raindrops. If only he could destroy his need with such ease.

He prowled the room, his fists shoved into the pockets of his jeans, his desire clawing at him with each step. So easy, he thought, so easy to take her, to make her his, to bind her to him forever, body and soul.

The sound of the bathroom door opening echoed in his mind like thunder.

Leanne gasped as he whirled around to face her. The heat in his eyes seemed to engulf her so that she felt suddenly hot all over, as though she were standing in front of a blazing fire.

"Feeling better?" he asked.

"Yes, thank you." She smiled at him, wondering if she had imagined that heated look.

"Would you care for more wine?"

"No. I . . ."

"What is it?"

"I'm awfully tired. Would you mind if I went to bed?"

"Of course not, but you can't sleep in those clothes."

A faint flush brightened her cheeks. "I don't have anything else."

"I'll get you something."

He went into the bedroom, his gaze lingering on the bed. He'd lived in this house for twenty years, he mused, and no one had ever used the bed. It pleased him to think of Leanne lying there, her hair spread on the pillow, her scent permeating the sheets.

Going to the dresser, he drew out a long nightgown. He'd bought it because the color was the same vibrant green as her eyes; because, for one irrational moment, he had wanted to pretend he was an ordinary man buying a gift for the special lady in his life. He had bought it and put it away. Now, he held it in his hands, the silkiness of the material reminding him of Leanne's satin-smooth skin.

"Is that for me?" She had followed him into the bed-room.

"What do you think?"

"I thought . . ." She lifted her chin and took a deep breath. "When you stopped coming to the theater, I thought you might have found someone else."

He shook his head. "There will never be anyone else, Leanne."

"Then why? Why haven't you come to see me? Did I do something wrong?"

"No." He thrust the gown into her hands, then left the room, firmly closing the door behind him. He never should have brought her here.

He stood in the living room in front of the fireplace, fighting the urge to go to her, to sweep her into his arms and satisfy the awful lust that was roaring through him, the lust to possess her, to drink and drink of her life-sustaining sweetness, and then give it back to her.

He clenched his hands into tight fists, wondering if he had the strength to continue seeing her and not pos-sess her. He knew, at the very core of his being, that their joining would be everything he dreamed of, ev-erything he yearned for.

It would be so easy to take her blood, to bind her to him for all eternity, and end the awful loneliness of his existence, but he recoiled at the very idea of condemn-ing her to the kind of life he led. To do so would be the worst kind of betrayal.

Leanne had brought joy back into his life, had drawn him out of the depths of despair and given him a rea-son to rise in the evening. To condemn her to a life in the shadows would be the worst kind of cruelty.

He should send her away now, before it became im-possible, but even as the thought crossed his mind, he knew he would not do it. Soon, he thought, soon he would send her away, but not now, when he had just found her. He hoped only that he was strong enough to keep his accursed lust at bay, that there was enough humanity left in him to let her go when the time came.

He felt his whole body tense as the bedroom door opened. Without looking, he knew she was standing there, watching him. He could feel her gaze on his back, feel her confusion.

"Jason?"

"Go to bed, Leanne." He had not meant the words to sound so harsh.

He sensed her hesitation, her hurt, and then, very quietly, she closed the door.

With a sigh he dropped into his favorite chair and buried his face in his hands, hands that trembled with the need to hold her close, to feel the warmth of her in his arms, to breathe in the scent of her hair and skin. She was so alive, so vibrant—just holding her made him feel a little alive himself.

He didn't know how long he'd been sitting there, staring into nothingness, when he heard her cry out.

Chapter Six

Bolting from the chair, Jason ran into the bedroom, ready to do battle with Satan himself if need be. But there was no one in the room except Leanne, tossing restlessly on the bed.

Her hair spread across the pillows like chocolate silk. She'd thrown the covers off, and the gown's full skirt pooled around her thighs, offering him a beguiling glimpse of shapely calves.

Another cry was torn from her throat, and he saw a tear slip down her cheek.

Before he quite realized what he was doing, Jason was at her side, gathering her into his arms.

"Hush, love," he murmured. "It's only a dream, only a bad dream."

"Jason?"

"I'm here."

She burrowed her face into his shoulder. "It was awful," she said, her voice husky with sleep. "I was dreaming about tonight, but it was worse, much worse." She drew back, her gaze seeking his. "They shot you."

He shook his head. "No."

"Yes! I saw it so clearly. It couldn't have been a dream."

"But it was," he said reassuringly. "Look." He lifted his shirt so she could see his chest. "You see? No bullet holes."

"But I saw it, I heard the gunshots . . ."

He drew her head to his chest and rocked her gently. "Go back to sleep, Leanne. Everything's fine."

"Is it?" She rested her head against his chest and closed her eyes. "You feel so cold."

Unable to help himself, he pressed a kiss to the top of her head, willing her to relax, to sleep, to forget.

"I love you, Jason," she murmured drowsily. "Please don't leave me again."

He closed his eyes, her words pouring over him like hot August sunshine. She loved him.

It was a dream come true.

It was his worst nightmare.

"Promise me," she whispered. "Promise you'll never leave me."

Ah, Leanne, my love, if you only knew what you were asking of me. If you only knew how your nearness torments and tempts me.

She pulled back a little so she could see his face, her eyes searching his. "You don't love me, do you?"

He looked away, unable to bear the sight of the pain that shimmered in the depths of her eyes. Love her, he thought, if only he didn't!

A single tear slipped down her cheek. It was his undoing.

"I do love you, Leanne." The words were wrenched from the depths of his soul. "Please, do not weep. I cannot bear the sight of your tears."

"You mean it?"

"I swear it by all that I hold dear."

"Oh, Jason!" She threw her arms around his neck and kissed him, kissed him until they were both breathless.

She was fire and honey in his arms. All his senses came alive until he was drunk with the taste of her lips, the scent of her flesh, the sound of her whispered endearments. He felt his body grow hard. The need to nourish himself with the very essence of her life burned through him, as potent, as strong, as his desire for her flesh.

He groaned deep in his throat as her body molded itself to his. Her tongue laved the lobe of his ear, his neck; her hands explored the length and breadth of his back and shoulders, then boldly traced the outline of his thigh.

"Leanne." He caught her hands in his and willed his body to relax, knowing that in another moment his desire and his lust for blood would be impossible to control.

"It's all right," she said, her eyes shining with love and trust. "I want you to make love to me."

"I can't."

"Why?"

Why, why? What possible excuse could he give her? "I don't have any ... any ..." Hell's bells, what did they call those things, anyway?

"I don't care."

He summoned a tight smile. "I do."

"I don't have any diseases, Jason," she said quietly. "I've never been with a man before."

He felt his self-control hovering on the brink of collapse. "All the more reason why we should wait."

Maybe he was right, she thought, though she couldn't help being disappointed. Her mother had always taught her that good girls didn't "do it" until they were married. Her father, a wise and solemn man blessed with the gift of foresight, had warned her that, should she let herself be defiled before marriage, her life would be at great risk. When she had asked him to explain, he had taken her in his arms and told her that he'd had a most disturbing vision of her future, a vision in which he had seen her surrounded by darkness and danger, protected only by her innocence, and then he had warned her that, should she give herself to the wrong man, she risked the chance of being forever cursed.

Thinking of that now, she was ashamed of her own weakness and doubly grateful for Jason's self-control.

"If I promise to behave, do you think you could stay with me until I fall asleep?"

With a nod he drew the covers up to her chin, then sat beside her, her hand cradled in his.

She smiled up at him and then, tucking his free hand under her cheek, she closed her eyes.

He sat with her until he felt the nearness of a new day and then, regretfully, he left the room.

In the kitchen he wrote her a note, saying he had been called to work early, and that he'd see her that night after the show. He invited her to stay the day if she liked, or to take his car if she wished to go home. He dropped the keys on top of the note, and then, his steps growing heavier by the moment, he made his way down to the basement.

He closed the door behind him, slipped the bolt into place, then wrapped himself in the quilt and closed his eyes.

Leanne woke with a smile on her face. Jason loved her. She stretched, feeling as contented as a cat. He loved her.

And she couldn't wait to see him. Bounding out of bed, she hurried out of the room. She expected to find him in the kitchen, and when he wasn't there, she checked the other bedroom. It, too, was empty.

Shrugging, she went back into the kitchen. She'd fix something to eat, shower, and then go home. It was then she saw the note.

She read it quickly and then, clutching the slip of paper in her hand, she glanced around the kitchen. She had hoped to cook breakfast for Jason. It would have been the first day they spent together, and she wanted to share the morning with him before he went to work.

With an effort she shrugged off her disappointment. If she was going to be in love with a cop, this was the kind of thing she'd have to get used to. Policemen were on call twenty-four hours a day. They missed birthday parties, and Christmas morning, and anniversaries. They worked long hours for little pay. And these days, when law officers were being maligned and criticized more than ever, a cop needed the support of his loved ones.

Crossing the floor, she opened one of the cupboards. It was empty. So was the next one, and the next. Frowning, she opened the refrigerator. Nothing.

Leanne shook her head. She could understand if he never cooked, but she'd expected him to at least have coffee in the house, a loaf of bread, salt and pepper.

Puzzled, she went into the bedroom and opened the closet. It was reassuring, somehow, to see his clothes hanging there, to see several pairs of shoes and boots in a neat row on the floor.

After getting dressed, she wandered through the house again. There were no personal items to be found; no photos, no mementos. If not for his clothes and the hundreds of books in the den, she'd wonder if this were truly his house.

With a shake of her head she picked up his keys and left the house. He could answer her questions tonight; in the meantime, she had some shopping to do.

He felt her stirring in the house above. Even though he was trapped in the daylight sleep of death, he could feel her presence as she moved from room to room, feel her confusion when she realized there was nothing in the house to eat. He should have thought of that, but then, he hadn't planned to see her again, to bring her here again.

Leanne. Leanne. Her name whispered through the

sluggishness of his mind. He yearned to go to her, but his body, held prisoner by the daylight, refused to obey.

Trapped in darkness, he willed the sun to hurry across the sky.

Leanne stood in the wings, peeking out at the audience during intermission. She felt her heart skip a beat when she found him. He was sitting in the fifth row, center section.

How handsome he was! His dark jacket complimented his hair; the pale blue shirt brought out the color of his eyes. Her gaze moved lovingly over his face, the width of his shoulders. He seemed to be in a world apart as he sat there. People milled around, waiting for the second act, laughing and talking, making their way to the front to look into the orchestra pit. She saw several girls talking to the bassoon player. He was a nice guy, funny and outgoing, and seemed to know everyone.

She took her place behind stage as the house lights dimmed and the second act began. Soon, soon she'd be with him.

Jason sat forward, lost in the Phantom's anguish as he told Christine she must make a choice between himself and Raoul.

And then Christine's voice, pure and beautiful, filled the auditorium, her words of pity melting the hatred in the Phantom's heart.

He felt the aching loneliness that engulfed the Phantom as he watched Christine leave with Raoul, and he wondered what Leanne would do if she knew the man she loved was truly a creature of darkness. Would she look at him with loathing, the love in her clear, green eyes turning to revulsion? Would she flee from his presence, disgusted by the memory of his kisses?

He had felt the lingering sense of her presence when

he left the basement earlier that night. Her scent had filled the empty rooms of his house. Her presence had been everywhere. She had placed vases of fresh flowers in the living room and kitchen, there was food in the refrigerator, food that he couldn't eat, and a bar of perfumed soap in the bathroom. She'd left a change of clothes on the bed in his bedroom, and a note that said she'd fix him a midnight snack after the show. He had found a rented video tape on top of the television.

A mirthless grin had curved his lips when he saw the title: *Dracula* starring Frank Langella. She seemed to have a fondness for vampire movies, he mused ruefully, and, though she didn't know it, for vampires, as well.

Now, sitting in the theater, listening to the applause that thundered through the auditorium as Davis Gaines received a standing ovation, Jason forced himself to admit that, just as the Phantom had let Christine go because he loved her, so he would have to let Leanne go. He could not hide his identity from her forever, and he did not trust himself to go on seeing her without hurting her, without turning her into a creature as wretched as himself.

Just one night, he thought. Let him have just one night to hold her and love her, and then he would let her go.

He lifted his gaze to the stage, focusing on her face as she stood in the background. Her eyes were bright, her lips parted in a smile that was his and his alone.

Just one night, he thought again, one night to last for eternity.

Heavyhearted, he left the theater and went to wait for her at the stage door.

Chapter Seven

Leanne ran up to him, bubbling with excitement. "Wasn't it great tonight?" she exclaimed. "Oh, I know, it's great *every* night, but sometimes it all seems so real, I forget it's just a play and find myself crying when the Phantom sends Christine away."

Jason nodded. He'd often felt that way himself.

Leanne threw her arms around Jason and kissed him. "Did you have a good day?"

"The same as always," Jason replied, and then, seeing the expectant look in her eyes, he smiled. "Thank you for the flowers and everything."

"I hope you don't mind."

"No." He took her hand in his and gave it a squeeze. "Let's go home."

Leanne hummed softly as they drove down the freeway, her hand resting on Jason's thigh, her gaze returning again and again to his profile. She loved the rugged masculine beauty of his face, the finely sculpted nose and lips, the strong square jaw, dark now with the shadow of a beard. His brows were thick and black above deep blue eyes, his cheekbones pronounced.

How had she fallen in love so quickly, so completely, with this man who was still a stranger in so many ways? She hardly knew him, and yet she felt as if she had always known him, as if her life had begun the night they met.

"Jason?"

He slid a glance in her direction. "What?"

"My folks would like to meet you."

The silence that followed her remark was absolute.

"Jason?"

"One day perhaps."

"How about next Sunday?"

"Leanne . . ."

"You don't want to, do you? Why not?"

"Surely you must have realized I'm a bit of a recluse when I'm not working."

"I know, but I'd really like them to meet you."

"I'll consider it."

"I'm sorry." She took her hand from his thigh, then looked out the window. "I didn't mean to push you, or make you think I was trying to . . ."

He muttered an oath as he pulled into the driveway and turned off the ignition. Getting out of the car, he opened the door for her, then drew her into his arms.

"I'm sorry, Leanne, I didn't mean to hurt your feelings. Please, just give me some time." *Just give me tonight.* "Come," he said, taking her hand. "I have a surprise for you."

Inside, he lit a dozen long blue tapers. "Sit down," he said, "I'll only be a moment."

With a nod Leanne sank down on the sofa. Kicking off her shoes, she stared at the candles flickering on the mantel.

A few minutes later, Jason returned. Kneeling in front of the fireplace, he lit a fire, and then he joined her on the sofa.

"Here," he said, handing her a long, slender box. "This is for you."

She opened the box with hands that trembled, and uttered a gasp of astonishment as she stared at the contents. "Oh, Jason, it's lovely."

"You like it, then?"

"Oh, yes." She ran her fingertip over the heavy gold chain, then outlined the filigreed heart-shaped locket. "But it must have cost a fortune."

"Only a small one." He lifted the chain from the box and fastened it around her neck. The heart-shaped locket settled in the cleft between her breasts. "I'm glad you like it."

"I love it. And I love you."

Her gaze met his, filled with such adoration that it made him want to shout, to sing. To weep. "Leanne, beloved . . ." He cupped her cheek in his hand and kissed her gently.

"More," she whispered, and twining her arms around his neck, she kissed him passionately, her body pressing to his, inviting him to come closer.

Her nearness, the wanting he read in her eyes, made his pulse race with desire. Too fast, he thought, they were moving too fast. If he was to have only this one night, he wanted to savor every moment.

Leanne drew back, her eyes aglow. "Tell me," she whispered. "Tell me you love me."

"I love you."

"Have you loved many women?"

"No. Only one other."

"Who?"

"A girl from my childhood. She's dead now."

"Oh, I'm sorry."

"It happened a long time ago."

He gazed into her eyes, longing to bury his hands in the wealth of her hair, to carry her to bed, and sheathe himself in the velvet heat of her all the night long—but he dared not. He would make love to her only once, just before dawn, and then he would let her go.

It took every ounce of willpower he possessed to keep from touching her. "Shall we watch your movie?"

"If you like. Have you seen it before?"

"No."

"You'll love it."

Jumping up, she slipped the tape into the VCR, then snuggled up against Jason, her head pillowed on his shoulder.

Langella made a most convincing vampire, Jason thought. Indeed, the movie hit close to home. Too close. He felt his desire for Leanne surge through him, along with a ravening thirst, as he watched Count Dracula seduce his lady love amidst a shimmering crimson backdrop while a bat hovered overhead.

A bat. He'd never changed into a bat in all his three hundred years; indeed, he didn't know if he could.

He felt his whole body tense as Dracula made a slit in his chest and offered Lucy a taste of his blood.

"I think he's the most realistic vampire I've ever seen," Leanne remarked. "I almost wish he didn't have to die in the end."

"Good always triumphs over evil, eventually," Jason remarked.

"I suppose, but he doesn't seem evil exactly," she mused. "I mean, I guess he can't help being what he is."

"No," Jason said, his voice strangely thick. "He can't."

"And he does seem to love her."

Jason gazed deeply into Leanne's eyes. "Yes, he does."

"I don't think I want to watch the end." She laughed self-consciously. "I've already seen one sad ending tonight."

"As you wish." Rising, Jason switched off the VCR. "Tell me, how does this Dracula meet his death?"

"On a ship. Doctor Van Helsing catches him on a big hook of some kind, and they hoist him into the sunlight." Leanne grimaced. "I think he ages and disintegrates, but I'm not really sure. I didn't watch that part. All I remember is seeing his black cape drifting away. It made me want to cry."

"You have a tender heart, my sweet."

"Enough about vampires and unhappy endings," Leanne murmured, reaching for him. "Make love to me, Jason."

"You're weeping," he exclaimed softly. "Why?"

"I don't know. I feel . . . I don't know, as if something awful is going to happen."

He knelt on the floor and drew her down into his arms. "Nothing is going to happen, Leanne. You're going to have a long and happy life filled with sunshine and laughter."

"I didn't know you told fortunes," she said with a watery smile.

"Only yours. You're going to marry and have children and live happily ever after."

"Am I?"

"I promise."

"And will you be the father of my children, Jason?"

"I'd like nothing better," he replied evasively, and then, to stop her from asking any more questions he couldn't answer, he kissed her.

The touch of his lips on hers, the sweet invasion of his tongue, drove all thought from Leanne's mind. She forgot her mother's admonition, forgot her father's dark warning; she could only feel. Jason's lips danced across her skin, hotter than the flames that burned in the hearth, engulfing her until she felt as though she, too, were on fire. Perhaps the heat incinerated her clothing, for she was suddenly lying naked beside him while his lips and tongue drifted over her face and neck, exploring the hollow of her throat, her navel, the valley between her breasts, the sensitive skin of her inner thighs.

With a boldness she didn't know she possessed, she stripped him of his clothing, then let her hands wander over his hard-muscled flesh. He was a study in masculine perfection, from his broad shoulders and flat belly, to his long, powerful legs. She felt him shudder with pleasure at her touch, heard a low groan that sounded oddly like pain as she rained kisses along his neck and down his chest.

And then he was rising over her, his dark eyes blazing.

"Tell me to stop if you're not sure," he said, his voice low and rough. "Tell me to stop now, before it's too late."

"Don't stop." She wrapped her arms around his neck and drew him closer. "Don't ever stop."

With a strangled cry he buried himself in her softness. She whimpered softly as he breached her maidenhead, and he cursed himself for hurting her, but it was too late now.

Too late to stop. Too late to think. He was caught up in an inferno of desire, and there was no going back.

Leanne clutched at his shoulders, exhilarated by his mastery, frightened by the torrent of emotions that flooded through her. She felt as if she were drowning, being sucked into a vortex from which there was no return. A soft, gentle blackness engulfed her, and then she felt as if she were immersed in a warm red mist.

She moaned as she felt Jason moving deep within her. Her fingernails clawed at his back, drawing blood, and then she was reaching out, reaching for something that shimmered just beyond her grasp, something beautiful.

She cried as she found it, cried with the joy of discovery, of wonder, as her body convulsed beneath his.

For a long while they lay wrapped in each other's arms. She held him tighter when she felt him start to draw away. "Don't go."

"I must be heavy."

"You are, but I like it."

He shifted to the side a little so she wasn't bearing the full burden of his weight. "Did I hurt you?"

"No."

He drew back so he could see her face. How lovely she was, her beautiful green eyes still aglow with passion, her lips pink and swollen from his kisses, her hair spread in wild disarray over the pillow. He felt a ridiculous urge to thank her.

"What are you thinking?" Leanne asked. Reaching up, she brushed a lock of hair from his brow.

"How wonderful you are."

"Did I please you?"

"Foolish girl. No one has ever pleased me more."

"I wish you'd never known anyone but me."

He saw the hurt in her eyes, the sudden flare of jealousy, and silently berated himself because the thought of her being jealous pleased him beyond words.

He stroked her cheek with the back of his hand. "After tonight, beloved, there will never be anyone else."

"Truly?"

"Truly." Jason buried his face in her shoulder, knowing he had no wish to go on existing without her.

Three hundred years he'd walked the earth, he thought, and only now, as he contemplated a future without her, did he realize the true meaning of loneliness.

Chapter Eight

He had promised himself he would make love to her only once, and then let her go. But he found it was a promise he could not keep.

Monster that he was, he could not keep from sampling her sweetness again and again, and each time he possessed her only increased his appetite for more.

Holding Leanne in his arms, he wished he could keep the sun from rising in the morning, wished her face, her beautiful green eyes filled with love, could be the last thing he saw before he slept, the first thing he saw upon rising.

He had made love to her as tenderly as ever a man loved a woman. Each moment he had spent in her arms had brought him the most exquisite pleasure he had ever known, and the most excruciating pain.

The lust to possess her wholly, as only a vampire could possess a woman, pulsed through him, and only the love he had for her made it possible to keep his accursed blood lust at bay, to touch the living warmth of her skin, to kiss and caress her, and not bury his fangs in her neck and alleviate the awful thirst that plagued him.

Still buried deep within her sweetness, he held her close, listening as her breathing returned to normal. She whispered that she loved him and then, her eyelids fluttering down, she fell asleep in his arms.

So young, he thought. So trusting.

He felt his fangs lengthen as he gazed at the pulse throbbing in the hollow of her throat.

One bite, just one. Slowly he bent over her, his tongue stroking her neck, tasting the musky heat of her skin, the salt of her perspiration.

A growl rumbled in his throat. His whole body shook as he fought the need to dip his fangs into her flesh, to swallow a single drop of her blood. A single drop. She need never know that a monster had sipped her sweetness.

Hating himself for his weakness, he bent over her, his teeth gently pricking the tender skin in the side of her neck. Her blood was as warm and sweet as he'd imagined, and he hovered over her, torn by a driving need to take more, to stop fighting what he was and seize what he wanted. She was his for the taking; she would be his for all eternity . . .

She moaned softly as he bent over her once more, and then she whispered his name.

Filled with self-loathing for what he'd almost taken from her, he drew back, surprised to find that he was weeping.

"Sleep, Leanne," he whispered brokenly. "Dream your young girl's dreams. You're safe from the monster tonight."

Leanne dreamed of darkness, a vast, overpowering darkness. And in the darkness she saw a man with hair as black as ebony and eyes as blue as a midsummer sky. He was dressed all in black. A cloak the color of death billowed out behind him as he walked toward her, as graceful as a panther stalking its prey, but it was his gaze that captured her, mesmerizing, haunting, filled with the pain and suffering of three hundred years.

She should have been afraid of him, afraid of the

power in his eyes. Instead, she reached out toward him. *Let me help you.*

He shook his head, and she saw that he was weeping, and his tears were the color of blood. *No one can help me,* he said, and the anguish in his voice was more than she could bear.

I'll do anything, she promised. *Anything you ask, only let me ease your sorrow.*

Anything? he asked.

Anything, she replied, and then he was upon her, wrapping her in the folds of his cloak. His dark eyes blazed with an unholy light as he lowered his head toward her. She closed her eyes as she felt his mouth cover hers in a searing kiss, and then she felt his teeth at her neck, a sharp pain, a sudden sense of lethargy.

A scream rose in her throat, a scream that brought her awake with a start.

Heart pounding in her breast, she sat up, reaching for Jason, only to find herself alone in the bed. She gazed wildly around the room, but he was nowhere in sight. Through a crack in the drapes, she saw that it was dawn.

She sat there for a long moment, and then, with a hand that trembled, she touched the side of her neck. Was she imagining things, or did she really feel two small puncture wounds? Slipping out of bed, she started for the bathroom, only to stop when she remembered there was no mirror in the bathroom.

There were no mirrors anywhere in the house.

She shook her head vigorously, refusing to even consider the bizarre possibility that came to mind as she climbed back into bed and drew the covers up to her chin.

She was just letting her imagination run wild.

"Just a dream." She spoke the words aloud as she closed her eyes. "Just a dream."

* * *

Leanne stared at her reflection in her bedroom mirror, but all she saw were the two small puncture wounds in her neck. For the fifth time in as many minutes, she touched her fingertips to the tiny holes. As before, heat seemed to flow from the wounds and Jason's image danced before her eyes.

She had looked at those marks in the rearview mirror time and again as she drove home. Looked at them and shuddered. Looked at them and tried to find a logical reason for their existence.

Now, still staring into the bedroom mirror, she tried to laugh at the ridiculous image of Jason bending over her, his teeth turning into fangs, biting her neck. She'd been watching too many vampire movies, she thought, had read too many books by Anne Rice and Lori Herter. She was losing her grip on reality. The marks on her neck were probably nothing more menacing than a couple of mosquito bites.

Leaving the bedroom, she went into the kitchen, grabbed a dust rag and began dusting the living room furniture. Her apartment had been sadly neglected since she met Jason Blackthorne . . .

Jason. He'd been gone when she woke up. A note told her he'd been called to court to testify in a case, but that he'd meet her that night after the show.

She'd never seen him during the day.

She thrust the thought away, plugged in the vacuum, and ran it over the living-room rug.

She put the vacuum away, then changed the sheets on her bed and bundled up her laundry. Carrying it downstairs, she stuffed it into one of the machines, then went back upstairs to fix lunch.

She'd never seen him eat.

Sitting at the table, she cradled her head in her hands. It couldn't be. For all her talk to the contrary, in her heart she didn't really believe in vampires. There had to be a logical explanation for the oddities in his life.

There had to be.

She wondered if he was still in court, and then, because she couldn't wait until after the show to see him, she grabbed her car keys and drove to his house, her laundry forgotten.

She'd left his key under a flowerpot on the front porch. A sudden unease filled her as she unlocked the massive front door. Without thinking, she dropped the heavy brass key into the pocket of her jeans, then stepped into the entry hall. She'd never before noticed how still the house was.

"Jason?"

She tossed her car keys on the small table inside the front door and walked through the house, seeing it all again as if for the first time. The rooms were all dark, the sunlight held at bay by the heavy drapes that covered all the windows. She explored every room, every closet, looking for the door that led to the room where Jason slept during the day.

She shuddered at the thought of seeing him lying in a silk-lined casket, sleeping the dreamless sleep of the undead during the hours of daylight. Unbidden, unwanted, came a rush of images as she recalled every vampire book she had ever read, every horror movie she had ever seen. All had vividly portrayed vampires as the embodiment of evil, preying on unsuspecting mortals. She felt a rush of nausea as she imagined Jason stalking some helpless woman, sinking his fangs into her neck . . .

She pressed her fingers to the marks in her own neck, shuddering as she imagined Jason biting her, drawing her blood.

With an effort she shook the image from her mind. In the den, she paused before one of the paintings signed J. Blackthorne. Jason had told her an ancestor had painted it. She ran her fingers over the distinctive signature, and then she went into the kitchen and picked up the note Jason had left her that morning.

Returning to the den, she compared the handwriting on the note to the signature on the painting. They were the same.

With growing certainty she continued her search. There was a service porch off the kitchen—and a door—a locked door. She stared at it for a long moment, and then she placed her hand against the wood and knew, without doubt, that Jason was behind the door.

Getting a chair from the kitchen, she sat down to wait.

He felt her presence in the house as soon as he awoke. He'd been aware of her nearness all day, aware of the turmoil in her mind. He knew he could use the power of his mind to put her at ease, to make her forget the questions and suspicions that troubled her. But he could not do such a thing. She deserved the truth, and he would give it to her.

He shrugged the quilt off his shoulders and stood up. His feet felt weighted with lead as he climbed the narrow stairway and unlocked the door.

She would know the truth the minute she saw his face.

Leanne's heart climbed into her throat as she watched the doorknob turn and the door swing open.

"Jason."

A faintly mocking grin touched his lips as he met her gaze. "Sorry to keep you waiting so long."

"You know I was here?"

"Of course."

She glanced past him to the darkness beyond the doorway. "What's . . . what's down there?"

"Nothing."

"Nothing?"

"You don't believe me?" He flicked on a light switch. "Perhaps you'd care to see for yourself?"

The thought of going down those stairs filled her with dread, but she had to know, had to see for herself.

Summoning every ounce of courage she possessed, she stepped past Jason and walked slowly down the stairs, wondering, as she did so, if she was making the biggest mistake of her life. What if he followed her? If he was truly a vampire, he wouldn't want anyone to know where he rested during the day.

She paused at the foot of the stairs and looked around, but there was nothing to see, only a patchwork quilt.

And a small mound of earth. She swallowed hard. Wasn't there some kind of vampire edict that made it mandatory for the undead to rest on the soil of their native homeland?

"What were you doing down there so long?" she asked when she returned to the laundry room.

"Sleeping."

There was no emotion in his voice, no inflection of any kind; it was merely a simple statement of fact.

"I thought . . ."

"You thought to find a coffin." He gave a slight shrug. "I tried sleeping in one once, but I found it . . ." He paused a moment. "Distasteful."

"How long have you been . . . been a . . . ?"

"Three hundred years."

It couldn't be true. She glanced around, thinking how bizarre it was to be having such an outlandish conversation in a laundry room. And even as she tried to tell herself she must be dreaming, she knew that everything she had feared was true. She felt it in her heart, saw the truth of it in his eyes.

For the first time, she noticed how pale he was. His skin was drawn tight over the planes of his face, and there was a burning intensity in his eyes as he stared at her throat.

Unconsciously, she lifted a hand to her neck. "How could you keep such a secret?"

"How could I tell you?"

"But . . . we made love . . ." She stared at him, the horror of what she'd done making her sick inside. She'd made love to a man who was a ghoul.

The revulsion in her eyes sliced through him, and he cursed the hand of fate that had turned him into a monster, cursed the hunger that clawed at him even now, urging him to drink from her one more time.

For a moment Jason closed his eyes. Her nearness, her goodness, reached out to him. She shouldn't be here, not now, not when the desire to feed pounded relentlessly through him. The remembered taste of her blood on his lips, warm and sweet, drew a groan from deep in his throat.

She was close, too close. Needing to put some distance between them, he went into the living room. Standing in front of the fireplace, Jason braced one arm on the mantel and stared at the ashes in the hearth. A blink of his eye brought the cold embers to life.

A sigh rose from deep within him. She knew what he was now, knew where he rested during the day, something no mortal but Jolene had ever known before. With that knowledge she held the power to destroy him . . . but it didn't matter. Losing her would destroy him as nothing else could.

She followed him into the parlor, as he'd known she would, though she stayed on the far side of the room. Foolish girl, he thought, didn't she realize the danger she was in?

Leanne rubbed her fingertips over the two small wounds in her neck. "You did this, didn't you?"

"Yes."

A look of horror filled her eyes. "Am I . . . ?"

"No!" He shoved his hands into his pants pockets, his fists clenching and unclenching as he fought to control the thirst raging through him. "I may be a fiend of the worst kind, but I would never condemn you to a life of darkness."

She touched the wounds in her neck again. "Then why?"

"Last night was to be our last night together." He met her gaze, begging for her understanding, her forgiveness. "I wanted to taste your sweetness just once."

Leanne stared up at him, the thought of never seeing him again suddenly more frightening than the realization that he was, indeed, a vampire.

"Our last night?" she repeated tremulously.

"Yes."

His gaze lingered on the pulse throbbing in her throat for a moment before returning to her face. "You'd better go now."

Wordlessly, she continued to stare at him, her eyes filled with anguish and denial.

With preternatural speed he crossed the floor until he was standing in front of her, his eyes blazing with an unholy light.

"Go home, Leanne," he said, his voice harsh and uneven as he fought to control his raging thirst. "You're not safe here."

"Jason . . ."

A low growl rose in his throat as he bared his fangs. "Go home," he said again, and his voice was filled with pain and tightly leashed fury.

With a strangled cry she turned and ran out of the room.

Out of his life.

Chapter Nine

He sat in his favorite chair in front of the fireplace in the den, staring, unseeing, at the flames. In his mind's eye, he saw the horror in Leanne's eyes when she thought he might have bequeathed her the Dark Gift and turned her into a loathsome creature such as himself. The sound of her footsteps running away, running away from what he was, echoed like a death knell in his ears.

He stared at his hands. He hadn't eaten for several days, and his skin looked like old parchment. He knew his eyes glowed with hell's own fury, knew that soon he would either have to go to ground and lose himself in sleep, or satisfy the awful craving that was eating him up inside.

An unquenchable thirst for blood.

A deep and never-ending hunger for Leanne.

Had it been only two weeks since he'd held her in his arms, tasted her sweetness, heard the sound of her laughter? Only two weeks?

It seemed a lifetime.

A lifetime, Jason mused with a bitter smile. He had walked the earth for three hundred years, and never had the hours and the minutes passed so slowly.

During the long, lonely hours of the night, as he prowled the alleys and dark streets of the city, he seemed to hear the wind taunting him with the sound of her name. Sometimes he paused outside a house, listening to the sounds of life inside: children crying, laughing. He watched people eating, talking, arguing, sleeping. And he thought of Leanne, always Leanne, of how wonderful it would be to be mortal, to share her life, to sit across the breakfast table from her in the morning, to make love to her in the light of day, to father a child.

He haunted the shadows outside the Ahmanson, torturing himself with glimpses of her face. He read the sadness in her eyes, and he was filled with bitter regret because he knew he was the cause of her sorrow. She didn't smile anymore, and the world was the poorer because of it.

One night, driven by an uncontrollable urge to hear her voice, he bought a ticket to the evening performance, sitting in the last row of the balcony so there would be no chance of her discovering he was there.

Oblivious to everything else, he sat with his gaze riveted on her face, silent tears streaming down his cheeks as he listened to her sing. Her voice, while still beautiful, lacked the enthusiasm, the *joie de vivre,* that had once set it apart from the others.

Leaving the theater that night, he had told himself she'd get over him. She was young, so young, and they had spent such a short time together. Soon she'd find someone else . . .

Now, staring into the fire's dying embers, he gripped the arms of the chair, his nails gouging the wood as he thought of her in the arms of another man.

Rising, he went into the bedroom. Sitting on the edge of the bed, he picked up the pillow she had used. Closing his eyes, he took a deep breath, his nostrils filling with her scent. In his mind, he saw her as she had been the night they made love, her beautiful body lightly sheened with perspiration, her green eyes glowing and alive. He felt again the touch of her hands as she undressed him, felt the way her fingers trembled as she caressed him, bold yet innocent. He relived every moment, every touch, embracing the pain of remembering, the shattering sense of loss now that she was gone.

Into his mind came the last soulful cry of the Phantom as he stood alone in his underground lair, bidding farewill to the only woman he would ever love.

The urge to kill, to destroy, welled within him, growing until he could think of nothing else.

Engulfed with rage, he stalked out of the bedroom, his hands clenching and unclenching at his sides. With a strangled cry he grabbed the fireplace poker, holding it so tightly it bent in his hands as though it were made of straw.

With an oath he flung it against the wall, then stormed out of the house, the lust for blood, the need to hurt someone as he was hurting, driving him beyond all reason.

He found his prey in a dark alley. The man struggled in vain, his red-rimmed eyes growing wide as he stared into the face of death. With a low growl Jason lowered his head to the man's throat. He smelled the malodorous stench of the drunk's unwashed body, felt the violent tremors that wracked the man as he realized he was about to die.

Unaccountably, an image of Leanne rose in Jason's mind, and he saw himself as she would see him, his eyes glittering with the lust for blood, his lips drawn back to expose his fangs as he prepared to drain this hapless creature of its life.

Filled with self-loathing, Jason shoved the man away and disappeared into the shadows of the night.

"Do you want to talk about it?"

Leanne glanced up, meeting Jennifer's face in the mirror. As always, Jennifer looked as if she'd just stepped out of a fashion magazine. Her makeup was perfect. Her long, honey blond hair framed her face like a golden halo. Unlike the rest of the cast, who usually arrived at the theater in jeans and a T-shirt, Jennifer always looked as if she were about to go to a Hollywood premiere. "Look like a star, be a star," she always said.

Leanne forced a smile. "Talk about what?"

"Whatever's been bothering you for the past two weeks."

"I don't know what you mean," Leanne said and burst into tears.

Jennifer sat down on the stool beside Leanne and patted her friend's shoulder.

"It has to be man trouble," she murmured with the air of one who spoke from experience.

"Oh, Jen, you don't know the half of it."

"I've got time to listen."

Leanne plucked a Kleenex from the box on the dressing table and dabbed at her eyes. If only she *could* tell someone, she thought sadly, if only she could pour it all out, all the heartache, the hurt. If only . . .

"There's nothing to tell, Jen. I met a . . . a man, and I thought . . . it doesn't matter. It's over."

"But you don't want it to be over?"

"No."

"Maybe he'll change his mind."

A rueful smile tugged at Leanne's lips. It wasn't Jason's mind that was keeping them apart. "Maybe."

"Come on," Jennifer said, gaining her feet. "Let's go get a cup of coffee."

It was unusually crowded backstage that night. Some of the cast members were giving friends and family a behind-the-scenes tour, showing them the props: the huge painted elephant that was part of the first act, the boat that ferried Christine and the Phantom across the underground lake, the numerous candelabra that lit the Phantom's lair, the enormous winding staircase, the trap door that the Phantom used during the Masquerade number. Later, they'd see Twin's Gym, where members of the cast and crew sometimes worked out between shows.

Near the stage door, Leanne saw Michael Piontek, who played the Vicomte de Chagny, signing autographs, and Dale Kristen, who had played the part of Christine Daae for over four years, a role Leanne secretly yearned to play.

When they reached the street, she couldn't help glancing at the corner where she had first seen Jason. There was no one there now, and she experienced anew the pain of their separation, the awful sense of loss that had filled her heart since the night she ran out of his house.

She blinked back the tears that threatened to fall.

"Where shall we go?" Jennifer asked.

"I'm not up to it, Jen," Leanne said. "I think I'll just go home."

"Leanne . . ."

"Please, Jen. I need to be alone."

Jennifer laid her hand on Leanne's arm. "All right, honey, but you call me if it gets too bad, promise?"

"I promise. And thanks, Jen."

"See you Tuesday."

Leanne groaned softly. Tomorrow was Monday, and the theater was dark. What would she do all day, all night, with not even a performance to help fill the lonely hours?

Shoulders sagging, she crossed the street to her car. All the magic had gone out of the play; all the joy had gone out of singing. Jason was gone from her life, and he'd taken her heart and soul with him.

Sliding behind the wheel, she drove out of the parking lot and turned down Hope Street toward the freeway.

At home she kicked off her shoes and sank down on

the sofa. For a time she stared at nothing and then, because the silence was too much for her, she switched on the TV.

It took a moment for the black-and-white images to register on her mind, and then she didn't know whether to laugh or cry, for there, clad in funereal black clothes and cape, was Bela Lugosi in his most famous role, that of Count Dracula.

The tears came then, burning her eyes, making her throat ache. She sobbed uncontrollably, wishing that she'd never gone to Jason's house that day, wishing she could have gone on loving him in blissful ignorance.

For a moment she considered going to Jason, begging him to do whatever was necessary to change her into what he was, but she knew she lacked the courage to face the enormity, the horror, of such a vile transformation. She didn't want to live forever if it meant she would never be able to see the sun again, never be able to jog along the beach on a bright summer day, never experience the joy and wonder of motherhood.

But she didn't want to live without Jason.

Tears washed down her cheeks as she watched Dracula, but it was Jason she saw walking down the long stone stairway, a candle in his hand; Jason enveloping Mina in his cloak. How many people had he killed in the last three hundred years? In the last two weeks? Or perhaps he no longer had to kill. She remembered watching *Love at First Bite* and wondered if Jason visited the local blood bank to satisfy his thirst.

A burst of hysterical laughter bubbled to her lips. She must be going insane, she thought, comparing the reality of what Jason was to Hollywood's celluloid illusions.

Jason, Jason. Why couldn't she forget him? Why didn't she hate him? But she couldn't think of him as an evil monster, not when she remembered how tenderly he had made love to her.

Sniffing back her tears, she thought of all the hours they had spent together. Never had he done anything to hurt her, never had he treated her with anything but kindness and affection.

She lifted her hand to her neck. The tiny wounds had all but disappeared. She recalled asking him why he had bitten her, remembered the sadness in his eyes when he told her that night was to have been their last. She knew now that he had planned to leave her because he was afraid for her, afraid of what he might do.

I wanted to taste your sweetness just once.

Burying her face in her hands, she sobbed, "Jason, help me. Please help me."

He paused in his headlong flight to nowhere as Leanne's soulful cry echoed in his ears. He felt her pain as if it were his own, felt her unhappiness, her anguish of spirit.

Closing his eyes, he pressed his forehead against the cool stone wall that ran along the alley.

Ah, Leanne, beloved, he thought, *if it gives you any solace, be assured that your pain is no greater than mine.*

Leanne. The need to see her burned strong and bright within him, and before he quite realized what he was doing, he found himself at her door.

He hesitated for the space of a heartbeat, and then he placed his hand on the latch. It was locked, but nothing as insignificant as a locked door could keep him from his heart's desire.

A wave of his hand and the door swung open. Quiet as a shadow, he entered the apartment and closed the door behind him.

She was in the front room. Her life force drew him as surely as a beacon.

On silent feet he followed her scent.

She was curled up in the corner of a high-backed sofa, her head pillowed on her arms, her cheeks wet with tears.

He watched her for a long moment, and then, unable to help himself, he crossed the room and knelt on the floor in front of the sofa.

"Leanne."

Her eyelids fluttered open, and his breath caught in his throat as he waited—waited to see the horror and the loathing that would be reflected in her eyes when she saw his face.

"Jason?" She reached out to him, her hand trembling. "Tell me you're really here, that I'm not dreaming."

"I'm here if you want me to be."

"I do. Oh, I do!"

Sitting up, she threw her arms around his neck and held him tight.

With a strangled sob he drew her down into his arms and buried his face in her hair. For a long while they simply sat there holding each other close.

Leanne felt the sting of tears behind her eyes. He was here, really here. It didn't matter how or why or for how long, only that he was there, holding her as if he would never let her go.

"I've missed you." She whispered the words, afraid to break the spell between them.

"No more than I've missed you."

"Truly?"

"Truly." He drew back so he could see her face. "I've felt your sadness these past two weeks. I know how unhappy you've been." He brushed her cheek with his knuckles. "I can help you, if you'll let me."

"What do you mean?"

He took a deep breath. "I can make you forget we ever met."

Her eyes grew wide and then narrowed. "You mean hypnotize me?"

He nodded. "I've done it before."

"When?"

"Do you remember the night those three men attacked you in the parking lot?"

"Of course."

"One of them had a gun. He shot me three times."

Leanne shook her head. "That's impossible."

"You saw it all. If I hadn't erased the memory from your mind, you would have started asking questions I couldn't answer." A faint smile curved his lips. "I can show you the bullet holes in my coat if you don't believe me."

She didn't want to believe him, but she knew somehow that it was true.

"Do you want me to make you forget that we ever met?"

He would do it if she asked, he thought bleakly, though destroying her memory of their time together would be like destroying a part of himself. And yet, he would do anything she asked, anything that would wipe the sadness from her eyes.

Slowly, Leanne shook her head. "No, I don't want to forget a single moment. I want . . . I want us to go on as before."

"Leanne, you don't know what you're saying."

"Yes, I do."

Jason shook his head. "No, beloved."

"You don't want me?"

"You know that's not true."

"Then why?"

"Leanne, you think you know what I am, but you don't. There's nothing romantic about being a vampire. It's a life against nature, a life against God. I could never forgive myself if I caused you harm."

"You won't. I know you won't."

"You don't know!" He pushed her away and stood up. "I never should have come here."

"Why did you?"

"Because I needed to see you one last time. Because I heard you call me and I couldn't stay away."

Rising, she wrapped her arms around his waist and pressed her cheek against his chest. "I love you, Jason. I couldn't bear it if you left me again."

"Leanne, you don't know how hard it is for me to hold you like this and not make you mine. You don't know how many nights I've wanted to take you in my arms and drain you of every drop of life."

His gaze seemed to probe the furthest reaches of her heart and soul. "How will you feel about me if one night I can't control what I am?"

His words gave her pause. He saw it in her eyes, heard it in the sudden sharp intake of her breath.

"I never should have come here," he said again. "I'm sorry."

"Don't go, please. Stay the night with me. Just one more night."

"Leanne . . ."

"Please?"

He knew he should leave her, now, before it was too late, but when he opened his mouth to tell her he couldn't stay, the words wouldn't come. Instead, he bent his head and kissed her, kissed her with all the bittersweet longing that had tormented him for the past two weeks.

And when the kiss ended, she took him by the hand and led him into her bedroom.

He saw it all in a quick glance: the dresser and nightstand made of burnished oak, the large oval mirror that reflected her image, but not his, the double bed covered with a colorful cotton throw.

Leanne stood in the middle of the room, her heart

pounding wildly in her breast as she waited for Jason to take her in his arms.

Instead, he pressed a kiss to her cheek, and when he looked at her, his eyes were filled with doubts. "Are you sure?"

She nodded, and then she reached under his shirt, letting her fingers slide up and down the length of his back. His skin was firm and cool beneath her hand.

With a suddenness that startled her, he swung her into his arms and covered her mouth with his, kissing her until she was breathless, weightless, aware of nothing in all the world but the iron-hard arms that held her. His face blocked everything else from her vision, and she stared up into his eyes, eyes that burned with a bright blue flame.

"Jason." She whispered his name, just his name, but it conveyed all the loneliness she'd felt during their separation, her anguish at the thought of never seeing him again, the deep void his absence had left in her life.

"I know," he said, his voice thick with unshed tears. "I know."

Gently, he placed her on the bed, his hands moving over her face, lightly tracing the outline of her lips, her brows, the delicate curve of her cheek.

"Leanne, beloved . . ."

He bent to kiss her again, and yet again, knowing he could never get enough of her, knowing that, if he existed for another three hundred years, he would never love like this again.

Leanne stroked his brow. It was so good to touch him again, to know that he still cared. Their separation had not been easy for him, either, she thought. There was a dark, haunted look in his eyes that had not been there before, a pain so deep it made her want to weep.

"Jason, let us go on as before."

His expression mirrored his surprise. "You can't mean that?"

"I do. I don't care that you're a . . ."

"You say you don't care," he remarked quietly, "yet you can't even say the word."

"Vampire. Vampire! I don't care what you are, only say you won't leave me, that you'll be a part of my life again."

"What kind of life can you have with me?" he asked in a voice filled with self-loathing. "How long will you be content with a man—a monster—who can never share the daylight with you, who can come to you only at night, who sometimes feeds on the living because he can't resist the urge to kill, because he can't always control his fiendish hunger, his rage?"

"I'll help you," she replied fervently. "I'll love you so completely you won't have to be angry anymore. And if you need to take someone's blood, you can take mine."

He gazed into the depths of her eyes, eyes filled with trust and hope, and for a moment he let himself believe that such a life was possible.

Knowing it was wrong, knowing that to touch her now would only bring them both pain later on, he kissed her.

Kissed her because he loved her so much, wanted her so much, needed her so desperately.

He began to undress her then, his hands moving reverently over her body as he reacquainted himself with the gentle contours of her body, the softness of her skin.

He closed his eyes, his joy so fierce it was almost agony, as she rid him of his clothes. She explored his hard-muscled body freely, letting her fingertips glide over the width of his shoulders, down his flat belly, the length of his thighs.

His response to her touch was instant, bringing a

smile to her lips and a warm glow of pleasure to her eyes. He groaned softly as he drew her up against him, the lush curves of her body filling the emptiness in his.

His mouth covered hers again in a long, hungry kiss, and he knew if he held her and kissed her for the rest of his life, it wouldn't be enough.

Trembling with the need to merge his flesh with hers, he rose over her, wondering what miracle had brought her into his life. Surely, he had done nothing to deserve her love, her trust. He was a creature of the night, a man who had been cursed, but now felt blessed beyond belief.

Her arms wrapped around him as she lifted her hips in welcome invitation, taking him deep within herself, cherishing him, loving him, until he wanted to weep with the wonder of it. She whispered that she adored him, and her words fell on his heart like sunshine, chasing the darkness from his soul, filling him with warmth and light, making him forget, for a moment, that he was more monster than man.

He held her tight as her body convulsed beneath him, felt his self-control begin to slip as he watched the pulse that throbbed in her throat. A red mist veiled his eyes, reminding him that he wasn't a man, but a monster masquerading in human form, a fiend who had no right to love this woman.

He gazed into her eyes, eyes so like Jolene's, and into his memory came an image of his wife, her beauty fading, her health deteriorating, as time and disease ravaged her face and body while he stayed forever young. He could not endure the agony of watching Leanne grow old, could not bear the thought that she would die and leave him alone.

Neither could he bear the thought of being parted from her again, and yet he knew that, if he stayed, it would be only a matter of time before he succumbed to the awful craving for her blood, a need that even now was raging through him, as hot and fierce as his desire for her flesh.

As surely as he knew he must shun the sunlight or perish, he knew that he would force the Dark Gift on Leanne rather than watch her die. And he knew, just as surely, that she would hate him for it forever.

Painful as it would be, it would be better to leave her now, before he did something they would both regret, before her love turned to loathing.

He held her close, listening to the soft sound of her breathing as she fell asleep in his arms.

He had always feared dying, feared the prospect of an eternity, writhing in the flames of hell, but he feared it no longer.

Hell was not a place awaiting his soul, he thought in despair. Hell would be waiting for him when he kissed her good-bye.

He held her until the last moment, until he could feel the sunrise trembling on the brink of the horizon, feel the promised heat of it.

She murmured sleepily as he drew the covers over her, then bent and kissed her one last time.

And still he lingered, imprinting her image on his mind that he might carry it with him through all the endless days and nights of eternity.

Tomorrow night he would leave Los Angeles. It was the only way to keep from seeing her—the only way to keep her safe.

Chapter Ten

He had left her again. There was no note this time, no written words of farewell.

With grim certainty she knew he would never come back.

With equal certainty she knew she would not let him go.

It was Monday, and there were no performances scheduled. She straightened her apartment, wrote Jennifer a short letter that would account for her absence but explained nothing. Next, she penned a letter to her parents, telling them she loved them, saying she'd met a man and they were on their way to Europe for an extended holiday.

She took a long, hot bubble bath, shaved her legs, washed her hair, and then she stood in front of the full-length mirror that hung on the back of the bathroom door, studying her face and figure, knowing that, if her plans went as intended, she'd never see her face again—wondering, in a distant part of her mind, how a woman applied lipstick and mascara without the benefit of a looking glass.

Before she could lose her courage, she ran down the stairs to the garage, got into her car, and drove toward Jason's house.

She lingered on the porch, watching the sun go down in a blaze of color, imprinting the image on her mind.

And then, resolutely, she turned her back on the myriad colors splashed across the sky. Taking a deep breath, she took the heavy brass key from her pocket and opened the front door.

The inside of the house was as still as death.

Her footsteps made no sound as she made her way to the service porch, but she was sure the thudding of her heart could be heard as far away as Catalina.

As she'd done once before, she sat down and waited for him to rise, wondering, as she did so, if there was some kind of vampire law that would prohibit them from sleeping in a bed.

She felt her heartbeat increase as the basement door swung open, and then she forgot everything else but her love for Jason, and her reason for being there.

So, he thought, he had not imagined her presence, after all.

"Leanne," he said after a lengthy silence. "Why are you here?"

"You know why." She tilted her head back, baring her throat to his gaze. "Do it, Jason, do it now."

"No!" He turned away from her, his hands knotted into fists. He recoiled as if in pain when he felt her hand caress his back.

"I love you, Jason. If you can't, or won't, try to live in my world, then I'll live in yours."

"No. No. No!" He whirled around, his eyes blazing. "How can you even consider it?"

"Because I want to be with you!" She placed her hands on his chest and gazed up at him, her eyes filled with love. "I love you. I don't want to live without you."

He drew in a deep breath and exhaled slowly, and then he took her hands in his.

"Look at me, Leanne," he said quietly. "Take a good look. Tell me what you see."

"I see the man I love, the man I've waited for my whole life."

"No. I'm not a man, and I can't pretend to be one any longer, not even for you."

He saw the protest rise in her eyes, and he silenced her with a look. "Face it, beloved. I'm a ghoul, a monster."

"No."

He lifted her hands to his mouth and kissed her palms, first one, then the other. "Go home, Leanne."

"I won't leave you, Jason. Nothing you can say will make me change my mind."

It was tempting, so tempting. He closed his eyes as he contemplated the ecstasy of bestowing the Dark Gift on her, of knowing that, as a creature of the night, she would be his forever. Never again would he be alone, his existence empty. She would bring him the sunlight he had not seen in three hundred years. He would know love and laughter, the taste of her kisses, the sound of her voice. They could travel the earth together. He could show her the wonders of the ancient world, take her to London, to Paris, to Rome. And perhaps, if he loved her enough, she'd never miss the sunlight, never regret forfeiting the opportunity to bear children . . .

He held the image close, savoring it, even though he knew he would not do it. Every day of his miserable existence, he had cursed Marguerite for what she'd done, for the mortal life she had stolen from him. He would not selfishly bequeath the same horrible fate to the woman he loved.

Slowly, he opened his eyes, drinking in the sight of her beloved face, knowing that, after this night, he would never see her again.

"I love you, Jason." She spoke the words with the simple faith of a child, as if they could make everything all right.

"And I love you," he replied fervently.

"And you'll stay with me forever?"

Tenderly, he brushed his knuckles over her cheek. "Only death will part us, beloved."

At his words Leanne shivered violently, as if someone had filled her veins with ice water. She knew then what he meant to do, knew it as surely as she knew the sun would rise in the morning.

"No!"

"Yesterday, you asked me for one last night. Now I ask the same of you."

"Jason, you can't mean to do it."

"You cannot stop me."

"I will not live without you!" She pummeled his chest with her fists. "Do you hear me, Jason Blackthorne, I will not live without you! If you kill yourself, you'll be killing me, too."

She looked up at him, her eyes awash with pain, though only a single tear trickled down her cheek.

He watched it for a moment, and then, compelled by an urge he could neither understand nor deny, he bent down and licked the tiny drop of moisture from her cheek.

For a moment he gazed into her eyes, and then he reeled back, his whole body on fire.

"Jason, what is it?"

He couldn't answer; he could only stare at her, the salty taste of that single tear incinerating his tongue, burning through every fiber of his being like a shaft of liquid sunlight.

He heard her voice sobbing his name as from a great distance, but he lacked the power to answer. He dropped to his hands and knees, his head hanging, his breath coming in ragged gasps.

"Go." He forced the word between clenched teeth.

"No, I won't leave you." She knelt beside him and placed her hand on his shoulder, only to jerk it away when the heat radiating from his flesh burned her palm. "What is it? What's happening?"

"Go!" With an effort he raised his head and met her gaze. "I'm dying."

She shook her head, her eyes filled with denial. "That's impossible."

"It's true." He groaned low in his throat as his body convulsed with agony. His blood was on fire; his skin seemed to be shrinking, melting. "Leave me." He took a deep shuddering breath. "Please, Leanne, if you love me, go from here."

She was sobbing now, her tears falling to the floor, splashing like liquid fire over his hands.

"Please, leave me," he implored her. "I don't want you to see . . ."

Using the chair for support, she stood up. If he wanted her to go, she would go, but only as far as the other room.

"I love you," she whispered brokenly. "I'll always love you."

But he was past hearing.

Chapter Eleven

Numb, she stared down at him, unable to believe he was dead. A distant part of her mind, a morbid part she hadn't even known existed, wondered why his body hadn't aged and dissolved into dust.

And then reality struck home. Jason was dead.

Slowly, she dropped to her knees beside him and cradled his head in her lap, the pain in her heart too deep for tears.

Gently, she smoothed the long dark hair from his brow. His skin felt warm and alive. Odd, she thought, when it had always felt cool before.

The hours passed unnoticed as she relived every moment she had spent with Jason, remembering how she had found herself looking for him outside the theater long before he introduced himself, remembering the instant attraction between them, the way she had known, that very first night, she could trust him.

A faint smile touched her lips as she caressed his cheek. She would have liked to walk along a sunlit beach with Jason at her side, watched the sun rise over the ocean, borne his children, grown old beside him.

She would have liked to make love to him one more time.

With a sigh she kissed him one last time, and then, very gently, she lowered his head to the floor and stood up.

Feeling empty and alone, she walked out of the house.

She hesitated on the veranda, her gaze caught by the fiery splendor of the sun as it climbed over the tops of the hills.

"I love you, Jason Blackthorne," she murmured, her fingertips absently stroking the heart-shaped locket he had given her. "I love you, and I'll never forget you." Tears welled in her eyes. "Never."

"Never is a long time."

Leanne whirled around, her hand flying to her throat. "Jason! You're alive!"

He held out his hands and flexed his fingers, looking at them as if he'd never seen them before. "So it would seem."

"But . . . but how?"

"I don't know." A wry grin tugged at his lips. "The love of a good woman, perhaps?" he mused, his finger catching a tear that hovered at the corner of her eye, "or perhaps it was the magic of a single tear shed for a monster who yearned to be a man."

They gazed at each other for a long moment, and then Leanne threw herself into his arms and hugged him tight.

"You're alive." She ran her fingertips over his face, then spread one hand over his chest, above his heart. "Alive," she murmured again. "Thank God."

He looked deep into her eyes, and then he smiled, a beautiful smile that went straight to her heart.

Lowering his head, he teased her lips with the tip of his tongue, and then he kissed her as gently as ever a man had kissed a woman, and it seemed he could taste the sunrise on her lips.

"Leanne," he murmured. "Do you think you could love this mortal man as you once loved the monster?"

"Oh, yes," she exclaimed softly, and the glow in her

eyes was warmer and brighter than the sun he had thought never to see again.

His smile grew wider. "And do you think you could make love to me now, here, in the light of day?"

Happiness bubbled up inside of her. "I think so," she replied in a voice trembling with love and joy and excitement.

"And will you spend the rest of your life with me? Bear my children? Grow old at my side?"

"Yes," she promised fervently. "Oh, yes."

Jason sighed as he wrapped his arm around Leanne's shoulders and watched the sun climb in the sky, proclaiming the birth of a new day.

It was a day of miracles, he thought, and Leanne's love was the greatest miracle of all.

She had been the sun in his sky since the first night he had seen her emerge from the theater.

Now, standing beside her, with the sunlight on his face and the warmth of her love shining in the depths of her eyes, he knew he would never dwell in darkness again.

Falling In Love

by

Shirl Henke

Chapter One

Prince Humbert Von Ruprecht-Hohenstaffen adjusted the monocle over his left eye and peered myopically at the document before him. His tightly coiled black curls bounced around his face, giving him the appearance of a young cocker spaniel. "You are certain everything is on order, Herr Cassidy?" he asked in his precisely accented English.

"Sure and it's right as rain," Shamus O'Roarke replied, his round Irish face beaming guilelessly. "I've checked every clause in the documents which Messieurs Royal and Blake drew up. The transfer is a mere formality once you sign. They've already done so." He rounded the ornate mahogany desk in the large office situated on the corner of First and Biddle and looked out the window at the enormous stone arches of Mr. James Ead's engineering masterpiece. "Just think, tomorrow all that will be yours."

"My first American investment! It is so very excited I have become. To own Eads Bridge!" The prince signed the last sheet in a very thick sheaf of legal documents and handed them back to the older man with a courtly European flourish.

"Er, there is one more wee matter to be taken care of . . ." Shamus let his words trail away delicately, as if he had all the time in the world.

"Ah, ya! Of course, the money for the first payment. I have here a check. As soon as my bank in Pomerania arranges the transfer, the rest of the two million will be paid." He handed the crisp bank draft to Shamus.

"My secretary will see that it's deposited in Messieurs Royal and Blake's account." He never even glanced at the slip of paper as he rang for "Miss Huxtable."

When Chastity O'Roarke entered the big walnut office, she made a quick curtsy and took the proffered check, along with the heavy sheaf of papers. "See to the filing of these and then summon our special courier to take the check for deposit, my good woman," Shamus instructed.

"Certainly, sir, at once, sir." Her mousy brown hair was drawn severely into a tight bun, and heavy, dark-rimmed spectacles perched on the bridge of her delicate nose. Dressed in a crisp white shirtwaist and navy serge skirt, she looked every bit a proper office girl as she scurried from the room officiously.

"And now, how about a drink to celebrate the conclusion of a most profitable business transaction?" Shamus offered, walking over to an elaborately carved cabinet standing against the walnut-paneled wall and extracting two Waterford crystal glasses and a decanter.

"Ya, ya. To becoming an American—how do you call them?" The prince cocked his head as he removed his monocle.

"Robber baron," Shamus muttered beneath his breath, then turned and said aloud, "tycoon—that's the word, sure and if it isn't!" He handed a glass to the prince. "Here's to a real American tycoon."

As the two men drank and chatted jovially in the big office, Chastity raced out the front door, flew down the stairs, and headed to the Boatman's Bank on Broadway, where they had opened a commercial account two months ago upon arriving in the city.

"Twenty-five thousand dollars! I can hardly believe it, Da!" Chastity said, her eyes glittering as she rifled through the stacks of hundred dollar bills again. "I could bathe in it. We've never made a haul like this before."

"And himself apologizin' that he could only advance us such a paltry amount with his funds in transit from Europe," Shamus said, wiping tears of mirth from his eyes.

"Messieurs Royal and Blake were sure understanding about it, but then they really did need to sell their bridge."

"Aye, and a real steal it was, too!"

Both father and daughter broke into peals of giddy laughter as the thickset man whirled his slender daughter around the big, ornate office.

Sobering, Chastity said, "We'd better clean up here and put some distance between us and St. Louis before the prince returns. I've already purchased our railroad tickets and packed our bags. Delilah's waiting for us at the station."

"Don't you be worryin' yer pretty head about the prince. I, ah, slipped a wee bit of a mickey in his brandy and escorted him to his carriage. His driver's probably pouring him into his hotel room about now. He won't wake up until tomorrow mornin'. We've got time enough to celebrate tonight."

Chastity shook her head, and her hair, now free of its wig and torturous pins, flew in a bright, fiery red curtain around her shoulders. "No chance. This is the biggest sting we've ever pulled off, Da. What if the real owners of this law office should return from their New York trip a week early? Let's just clean up the evidence, get Delilah, and get out of town."

Shamus sighed. "Always the practical one. Ye're just like yer dear sainted mither ye are, God rest her soul."

As they began to straighten up the exclusive law office, erasing every trace that they had ever "borrowed" it, they discussed their future plans.

"Where are we headed next? I was thinkin' Texas. Lots of rich cattlemen down that way, dumb as the poor brutes they buy and sell."

Chas shook her head. "I've bought tickets for Denver."

Shamus arched one shaggy gray eyebrow. "Denver, now is it? Say, there is gold in Colorado, is there not?" His green eyes began to glow with an unholy light. "Lots of rich miners . . . and mines . . ."

"Aye, there's gold, but I don't want to fleece anyone out of it. I've been thinking, Da. We've got enough for a real stake this time. We could live like rich folks, put on a fancy front for several months in Denver. I've been doing some research into the socially prominent families of the city . . ."

"And?" Shamus prompted, his curiosity piqued. There was something in his daughter's manner, uncertain, hesitant—he would almost have said shy if that adjective could ever apply to Chastity Kathleen O'Roarke, who had been a fire-haired hellion since she lay kicking in her cradle.

"I could get us an introduction—an entrance to the inner circle of the elite."

"I'm listenin'," he replied as he boxed up the last of their "props," including a brass desk plate engraved: Sean Cassidy, Attorney at Law.

"Well, you see, I read this story in a Saratoga newspaper three months ago, while we were working that resort in the Catskills." She extracted a dog-eared clipping from her reticule and smoothed it out on the desk. "Her given name is even Chastity, the same as mine.

She married this fabulously rich young heir to a timber dynasty in New England last year, then was tragically widowed only a month after her honeymoon. She went into seclusion to mourn."

"Says here she returned to Ireland to be reunited with her father. And—" He almost dropped the paper when he looked at the blurry photograph on the second side of the clipping. "Saints preserve me if she couldn't be yer twin! Just what kind of a con do ye think we can work, with ye posin' as the Widow Manchester 'n me her poor Irish father?"

"It won't be a con, Da. Rather more like a . . . well, a sort of a secret. We'll just be borrowing her identity—briefly."

He waited, watching her nervously replace the clipping in her reticule. She had been planning this for quite some time and had not said a word about it to him, which bothered Shamus. They had worked out every con, each sting, together since she had been in pigtails. "Borrowin' her identity to what end?"

"To catch me a rich husband."

Shamus looked poleaxed. If Chas had said she planned to tack a paddle wheel on her rump and churn down the Mississippi River, he could not have been more amazed. "Ye mean to really and truly marry?" he croaked, aghast.

"I'm tired of living one jump ahead of the law, Da, conning rich, greedy fools out of their money, then racing to the railroad station in the dark of night. We never stay in one town more than a few months. We're rich one day, grubbing for money the next. Oh, not that you haven't done your best for me ever since Ma died. I do dearly appreciate your taking me from Aunt Prudence's house." Just remembering her mother's puritanical sister, who heartily disapproved of Patience's scalawag husband, gave Chas a case of the shivers.

"But this is a hard life for a fine, bright girl like

yerself." He sighed. "I guess it's selfish I've been, keepin' ye to meself all these years, niver lookin' to the future when I was gone."

"Don't you start talking about being gone, Shamus Lliam O'Roarke." She rounded the desk and gave him a hard, long hug of genuine affection and concern. "I just think it's time we both retired—before some irate lawman catches up to us."

"But why this masquerade as Chastity Manchester?"

"That will be our entrance to the circles of the rich. She was from a poor background, of no particular social standing until she married Ralph Manchester. No one in Denver's wealthy circle would know her, but they've all heard of her husband's family and his wealth. She'd be welcomed after her year of mourning. And, no man would suspect her of being after his money."

"And ye'd be willin' to give up yer freedom, to tie yerself down to a man, just for security and"—he paused as if the word tasted bad—"respectability?"

"Having lots of money is freedom, Da—a freedom we've never known." Her green eyes were dark and sad.

"I've robbed ye of yer childhood, Chas. But, God is me witness, I'll see to it ye get yer husband—whoever the lucky sod may be. Lord have mercy on his soul!" he added. She smiled and gave him a mock rap to the jaw with her knuckle.

A private rail car enroute to Denver

"Ian, have you lost your bloody mind?" Lyle Dorchester, Fifth Baron of Wyndham, stared aghast at his friend, who reclined in a gilt, ornamented lounging chair calmly smoking a thin black cigar.

"No, I most certainly have not, rest assured, old chap. In fact, I'm rather looking forward to the adventure—not to mention escaping all those title-hunting mamas with their vapid little debutante daughters in tow, panting at the prospect of becoming the next Countess of Lyme. You shall be their sole prey, while I shall be free to enjoy my horses." Ian Warfield studied his distraught companion with detached amusement, his gold eyes flashing with satisfaction.

"Enjoy your horses? Humph! More likely you'll be left to muck about in the stables, cleaning up after them," Lyle retorted.

"After three months, seven cities, and God knows how many American heiresses, cleaning up after my horses will be decidedly refreshing. Not only do the stables smell more tolerable than all that damned French perfume in which these chits insist upon drenching themselves, but the horses are a damn sight more intelligent. Lord, I've had more inspiring conversations with Samson than with any American female." Ian reached down and patted the large sheep dog lying beside his chair.

"You said that very thing about all the eligible young women in London, not to mention those on the Continent," Lyle replied. "You have to marry someday, Ian."

"Ah, but not yet, Lyle, not just yet." Samson let out an ear-splitting "Wolf," chorusing his sentiments on the subject.

"For the life of me, I can't fathom why you decided to drag that rag mop with the endless tongue on tour with you."

Understanding that his master's friend was talking about him, Samson chose that moment to jump up on Lyle and give him a slurping kiss, leaving him with not only a wet face but also a fine coating of silver and white fur on his immaculately tailored coat. Ian chuckled as Lyle pushed the dog down and mopped at his face. Then he rang for his man, Brimly, to deal with the hair-covered coat.

"You take life too seriously, Lyle. The whole idea of this American tour was to have an adventure before you were leg-shackled."

Lyle sighed as Brimly entered, took one look at the mussed coat, and glared witheringly at the dog and his master. Rolling his eyes heavenward, he walked stiffly over to the plush railcar's built-in walnut cabinet, extracted a clothes brush, and began to methodically remove the offending dog hair. "Have you ever considered sewing the brute's lips shut, your lordship?" the pinch-faced older man asked.

Ian burst out laughing. "Brimly, every dog has two ends. Have you ever considered the alternative?"

"Just so, milord. That would save walking him at every water stop."

Lyle, bearing the brunt of Samson's licking, shedding, and other unseemly habits, saw less humor in the situation. "I can't comprehend why you insist on keeping that behemoth. He has no mitigating qualities, not even a decent pedigree."

"Between us, my friend, we've enough titles to stretch around the earth's equator twice over. I'm heartily sick of pedigrees."

"So you are going to chuck it all and pretend to be my stable master when we reach Denver. How long do you intend to continue this ridiculous charade?"

Ian steepled his long, elegant fingers and considered, then cocked his head and grinned up at Lyle. "At least until we reach San Francisco. I hear it's semicivilized. Denver may be filled with millionaires, but they are a crass, humorless lot. I'd rather be on the outside looking in."

"It isn't altogether a cultural wasteland. Her majesty's cousin, the Baronesss de Galoti, is performing at the Opera this season," Lyle retorted.

Ian rubbed his eyes and pinched the bridge of his nose. "I rest my case, old chap. The Sardinian Songbird serenaded me in Milan last year." He shivered in revulsion at the memory. "I've heard enough bad opera from Berlin to Boston to last me a lifetime. The only thing recommending this wilderness is its spectacular scenery and salubrious climate. I want to ride, to hunt, and to enjoy the fresh air with no interference from social obligations that will require me to listen to the screechings of a hen I may not legally shoot."

Brimly finished his task and retired, leaving his master to pace across the room and drop onto a settee facing the car's window, a respectable distance away from Ian's dog. "I know you resent being pressed to marry and produce an heir."

Ian shrugged. "I have a bastard half brother, you know. Quite a successful merchant in the Pacific sugar trade. I wish to bloody hell Kit could have inherited the blasted title."

Lyle's dark eyes grew round with consternation. "He is not only illegitimate, but part Chinese in the bargain! You know your father couldn't acknowledge him . . . even if he had so desired."

"Which he did not," Ian said bitterly. "Lord, I despise the hypocrisy of it all. So, there's nothing left for it but to seize the day while we can," he added, his mood lightening mercurially, a trait that drove his earnest younger companion to distraction.

"Dash it all, Ian, you're twenty-nine years old—and by now all of your wild oats should already be sown; I suspect a number have already sprouted."

"Lyle, you are twenty-four, not forty-four," Ian chided. "I'll settle down one of these days . . ." He took a long drink from the tall glass in his hand. "Mint juleps are definitely an American invention I have come to appreciate. Beats the bloody hell out of gin."

"Can't you ever be serious, Ian?"

"Not so long as we're in America. From here on, you are the titled nobleman who's on display. I shall merely be your groom."

"And you shall be caught out in this deception, and then there will be the devil to pay."

"Not is you can keep a secret," Ian replied, still grinning.

Denver

Utterly entranced, Lyle watched Chastity Manchester from across the crowded ballroom. The young widow had become the toast of Denver's glittering social scene. Wealthy, mysterious, and divinely beautiful, she also possessed charm sufficient to grace the most so-phisticated French salon. He was smitten. Unfortu-nately, so were half of the wealthiest mining magnates in Colorado.

Of course none of them had a title, even if one or two could claim to be as handsome as he, after their own rough American fashion. Perhaps he could im-press her with a visit to Everett's place in the moun-tains. There was only one way to find out. He must invite her and see if she would make room on her busy agenda for him. He began to wend his way across the floor toward her with two glasses of champagne. "For you, dear lady," he said, handing her one of the crystal goblets with a flourish.

"Why thank you, Baron," Chas replied with a blind-ing smile.

"I am so delighted you chose Denver for your return to society," Lyle said.

"It was so difficult, you know," Chas replied with a dramatic downward flutter of her lashes. "Poor Ralph had taken me simply everywhere up and down the eastern seaboard. The memories were too, too painful.

So I decided upon going West and Denver is the only real city between St. Louis and San Francisco."

"Exactly the reason we chose it," Lyle said.

"We? I thought you were traveling alone?"

"Er, I am. That is, I have an entourage of servants and occasionally one tends to think of them as friends."

"How very un-English of you, but delightful nonetheless." Chas raised her glass to meet his. Of all her suitors the earnest young baron was certainly the sweetest. He was also one of the nicest looking with his curly chestnut hair and wide blue eyes. If only she could feel some spark, some . . . ah well, he was rich and even-tempered. The rest was all romantically impractical dribble she could ill afford.

Lyle returned her smile and clinked his glass against hers, then raised it in a toast. "To the most beautiful woman in Denver—no, in Colorado—no, in all of your western United States."

Chas laughed. "Are all Englishmen such flatterers, or just those with titles, Baron?"

"Please, you must call me Lyle—and yes, some Englishmen are flatterers, but not I. I speak only truth."

"Well, Lyle, then you must call me Chastity, and I shall reserve my opinion about whether or not to trust your ardent declarations. After all, we've only met twice."

"You wound me—there have been three occasions. But, I would like to have the opportunity to become better acquainted. I have a friend—well, actually he's a friend of my father's, and he owns a country estate a few hours' ride from the city. It's a hunting lodge, and the scenery is quite spectacular. Although he is off in South America at present, my family has a standing invitation to use the house. Would you and your father care to be my guests there next week?" Before she could reply, he rushed on, saying, "I do realize it's frightfully sudden with your busy social schedule, but it would be ever so much fun."

Chas smiled at his eagerness. He was hers if she wanted him. Perhaps it was time to make a decision. Their cash reserves were running low. Keeping up the pretense of being a wealthy widow in a city given to as much opulence as Denver had quickly depleted the bulk of their savings. "Why, Lyle, I do believe a few days in the mountains sounds perfectly delightful."

"We'll have a whole stable full of superb horse-flesh—I've brought along my best English thorough-breds. You do ride, don't you, Chastity?"

Chas had never ridden anything more spirited than a plow horse back in Wichita, but all ladies of quality rode. "Of course. I shall look forward to it. Do let me check with Papa to make certain he's free next week."

With a smile Chas excused herself from the adoring baron and scanned the ballroom with keen eyes—just in time to observe Shamus O'Roarke sliding their host's diamond-studded watch into his coat pocket! *I swear, leave that man alone for a moment, and he can stir up more grief than a yellow jacket in an outhouse!* She glided across the floor and seized her father's hand in a steel grip.

Shamus winced, then muttered low beneath his breath, "For a wee thing, you've always possessed un-common strength, me darlin'."

"Don't you darlin' me. Give me that watch. What do you think you're doing? We're supposed to be rich, re-spectable people, not common pickpockets," she grit-ted out as she dragged him into an alcove surrounded by huge potted ferns.

"There is nothin' common about me skills at liftin' gold and diamonds. Besides, I need to keep me fingers in practice," he said with a huff, straightening his suit jacket.

"You won't be lightening any more pockets or working any more cons after I marry, Da. That's what this is all about—going straight."

Shamus shuddered at the horrible prospect. Then, seeing the glittering green light in Chas's eyes, he dug into his pocket and slipped her the watch. "Ye goin' to slide it back onto its fob? That's a real tricky maneuver, Chas."

"No. That only works when I can jostle a man in a crowd. I'll have to return it to Mr. Wharton's room. Perhaps he'll just think he forgot to put it on before the soiree. Why don't you engage him in conversation while I slip upstairs and figure out which is the master suite. Oh," she caught herself before dashing off, "Lyle—the Baron of Wyndham—has invited us to spend next week in the mountains. I think he's the one, Da."

As her fiery curls disappeared into the crush of people, Shamus forgot all about Waldo Wharton, the bombastic silver king whose watch he had just pinched. Instead he turned his attention to his daughter's young suitor. *Well, I'll just take yer measure a bit before Chas goes and fixes her heart on ye.*

Chas opened the last door at the end of what had seemed like a mile-long hall and was finally rewarded by the sight of an immense room filled with dark masculine furniture and game trophies on every wall. Waldo Wharton was an avid hunter. Now, if she could only locate his jewelry case. She made a swift inspection of the big dressing table, then moved on to the armoire. The shallow top drawer was filled with diamond stickpins, two other watches even gaudier than the one her father had filched, and an assortment of tasteless men's jewelry worth a king's ransom. She tossed the watch on top of the pile and closed the drawer, but just as she turned, voices echoed from down the hall.

"And I sez to that theater manager, 'Jist exactly who

is this here feller, Shakespeare? I never heard of him.' 'N he sez ta me, 'Why, Mr. Wharton, he's the world's greatest play writer!' Well, I don't mind tellin' you, Gus, I paid fer every brick in that god damned building so I sez, 'What's he ever done fer Denver? Take his picture down and put up one of me!' "

Both Gus and Waldo broke into raucous laughter as Chas frantically searched for an exit. How on earth could she explain being in her host's bedchamber? All her plans would be ruined! But maybe they were not headed for this room.

"I really want to see that twelve-point buck you got hanging over your bed, Waldo. Must be a beauty," Gus said, his voice quite close now.

Chas's eyes fastened on the immense rack in despair. She raced to the big casement window, the only one ajar in the large room. Hiking up her watered silk skirts and petticoats, she thanked her lucky stars that hoops and bustles were out of fashion and swung one leg over the sill, hooking her high-heeled slipper onto the trellis beside the sash. She vanished in a blur of apricot silk just as the bedroom door opened and Gus and Waldo entered the room.

Clinging to the splintery wood with white-knuckled fingers, Chas prayed they would not take long to admire the trophy. One quick glance at the brick patio below was enough to cause her to squeeze her eyes tightly shut and cling to the trellis like a leech. All she could do was wait.

Ian strolled across the gardens behind Wharton's gargoyle of a house. *What a bloody monstrosity,* he thought. The garish mansion combined all the worst excesses of Denver's nouveau riche tastes in architecture, which mutilated the Queen City's skyline with Italianate towers and cupolas, mansard roofs and crenellated walls, crowed by cast iron trim on everything. Mrs. Wharton did, however, have exquisite taste in English roses, a small touch of home. Ian smelled the heavenly scent, perfuming the night air as he listened to the sounds of music and laughter drifting from the press inside. He had never felt so free in his life. Here he was in a comfortable open shirt and old trousers while poor Lyle was inside all starched up in his formal wear.

All Ian had done for the past weeks was work the horses, ride and sleep ... well not just sleep. There was that perfectly luscious little Polly O'Mally from the Golden Slipper Saloon, who had shared his humble bed on quite a few occasions since he had arrived in Denver. As soon as Lyle was done socializing for the evening, he would drive his friend back to their lodgings, then send word to Polly. Perhaps she had a friend for Lyle. The lad was all together too caught up with some American heiress who had taken his fancy.

His ruminations were cut short by a sudden sharp, cracking noise directly overhead. Startled, Ian looked up just in time to be enveloped in a swirl of apricot silk as the wearer of the skirts crashed down on him, knocking them both to the ground with a sickening thud. She was eerily silent.

The female had not let out so much as a squeak as she fell. Ian couldn't speak either. All the air had been squeezed from his lungs when she landed atop him. Praying his body was intact, Ian took a deep breath when the intruder scrambled off him. He rolled into a sitting position, coughing loudly as she yanked frantically at her skirts.

"Get off me, you oaf," she whispered, shoving a great mass of bright red hair out of her face.

Ian looked into the most striking pair of emerald eyes he had ever seen. "Get off you? You came plummeting out of the bloody sky and damn near broke my neck and that's all you can say? You landed on me, m'dear." Lord, she was a fetching piece, with clear ivory skin and delicate features, although, at the moment, her eyes were blazing and her mouth set in a petulant moue.

Chas glanced up at the broken trellis, which dangled from the wall precariously. Thank God Wharton and his friend had quit the room just before it gave way. It had taken every ounce of her willpower not to shriek like a banshee when she fell. This servant had probably saved her from breaking her neck.

She freed her skirts from beneath him and smiled, preparing to make an apology, but once her eyes met his, she froze. He was the most gorgeous male she had ever seen, with heavy-lidded gold eyes and dark blond, wavy hair that curled softly around his shoulders. His face was darkly tanned as if he were an outdoorsman, yet there was an elegant refinement about him. The thick, arched eyebrows, that long blade of a nose and those finely sculpted lips all bespoke generations of breeding. And the voice, low and husky, was most definitely English. "Who . . . who are you?" she finally blurted out, then blushed.

Ian watched the positively delicious way her tongue rimmed that pouty little mouth before she spoke. His eyes swept from that enticement downward to the swell of her breasts, and thence to the sweet curve of one silk-clad calf, which lay entangled between his thighs. In her haste to pull her skirt from beneath him, she had rucked it up, baring her leg all the way to the knee. "I rather think I'm entitled to ask you that question, considering that it was you who mounted me, as it were."

Chas's normally agile mind shut down like a faro game on Sunday morning. "I, er, I'm Chas . . . Chastity O . . . I mean, Chastity Manchester. The Widow Manchester, a guest of the Whartons," she said, scrambling away and covering her legs as she attempted to stand.

"And you are?" She covered her gaffe by taking on her haughtiest air, and looking disdainfully at his frayed shirt and ordinary twill breeches—although there was nothing ordinary at all about the way he filled out the simple clothes. A thick whorl of gold hair peeped out from the top of the open collar, and his shirt strained against the breadth of his shoulders. His long legs and hard thighs were shockingly revealed by the tight breeches, which molded to every muscle as he rose, graceful as a sleek mountain cat, and began dusting himself off.

"I'm Ian. Ian Warfield, the Baron of Wyndham's head stableman and groom," he said with an insolent grin that obviously flustered her. So much for the chit's attempts to look down her nose at him. She began to fuss with her gown, an enticing creation of sheer silk that clung to her breasts and waist like a lover's caress. "Beautiful but soiled," he said, causing her to jerk up her head, sending the last remaining pins flying from her hair.

"W-What did you say?" Damn! This man rattled her. Of course a near brush with death might just as well have something to do with her case of nerves.

"Your dress, lovely as it once was, is, alas, quite soiled—ruined I suspect." He extended one long arm and seized a piece of the skirt, which had ripped loose from the waistline in her fall.

Chas slapped his hand away. "Don't touch me."

He tisked and shook his head reprovingly. "Is that any way to act? I just saved your life, or at least your legs. You would've broken them, falling from that height." He ignored her shocked gasp and looked up at the open window and teetering trellis. "What the devil were you doing up there? Are you per chance a circus aerialist practicing before you perform for Wharton's guests?" He knew bloody well she was nothing of the sort.

"That, sir, is none of your business," she replied in a frosty voice, attempting to slip past him toward the rear of the house. Perhaps she could get one of the maids to send Shamus with her cloak and make good their escape. *I'll wring Da's neck for this!* Then his words froze her.

"If you aren't an employee or a guest, then perhaps I have apprehended a thief slipping from Wharton's private quarters." He watched her stop in midstride and turn to face him, gathering her tattered dress around her as regally as a queen.

"No! I mean, of course I'm not a thief—nor am I a circus performer. You see . . ." she licked her lips as she forced her brain to function, improvising as she went along. "It's all too horribly humiliating to explain." She forced the tears, a trick she had mastered as a girl.

He watched her performance with a grin twitching at the corners of his mobile lips. "Do try."

"I . . . I was accosted in the upstairs hallway by one of Mr. Wharton's friends. He, sir, is no more a gentleman than are you! He forced me into that room and made most improper advances." She shivered and sobbed, hugging herself forlornly.

Ian was unmoved. "So you climbed out the window and tried to make good your escape from this bounder by pretending to be just another gargoyle on this atrocious mansion?"

Even without the sarcasm, the whole thing did not sound very probable, but what else could she say? "If you had one shred of decency, you would assist me to the servant's entrance and have the maid send for my father. We *are* guests of the Wharton's."

"And you are also a superb little actress, m'dear. Too bad I'm not a gentleman, else I'd be forced to fall for your fanciful tale."

Chas had had enough of this arrogant lout. "You . . .

you horse butler, you," she gritted out furiously, just as a familiar voice caused her to whirl around in utter dismay.

"Chastity! My dear lady, what has happened to you?" Lyle rushed onto the patio from the library doors.

"It would seem the lady has suffered a slight accident, your lordship."

"I'm quite unharmed, really, Lyle, but I would prefer if we didn't discuss this in front of servants," she said, swishing past Ian and taking the baron's arm. "In fact, I'd prefer not to discuss the incident at all. Please, could you escort me to the rear entrance and summon Papa?"

With a distressed shrug at Ian, Lyle did as he was bidden. "I have the most splendid news, Chastity. Your father has cleared his calendar for us. The two of you will be joining me at Hornsby's estate for the week."

Ian watched them disappear around the corner, a frown creasing his brow.

Chapter Two

Chastity's eyes widened in amazement as the carriage rounded the bend and the Hornsby estate came into view. Set against the magnificent backdrop of jagged, rust-colored mountains, the country chalet looked like a gingerbread house from a fairy tale book, with steeply gabled roofs and blue shutters cut elaborately in geometric designs.

"It's enchanting! How can your friend bear to leave such a lovely home?" she asked Lyle.

The young nobleman was delighted with her reaction. "Well, actually this is only one of his homes. He's quite the gadabout, an eccentric millionaire industrialist, retired now. Turned scientist. He studies fish."

"Fish, ye say?" Shamus echoed incredulously. "All I've ever known to do is catch 'em and eat 'em."

Delilah let out a trilling meow of agreement, and everyone laughed as Chas stroked her beloved cat.

"Cats are such agreeable pets—so quiet and well mannered. And they don't knock one down or slobber on one either," Lyle said, reaching over to scratch one dainty white feline ear. The cat allowed the liberty, but fixed him with baleful green eyes, letting him know who was in charge.

"You sound as if you're describing that awful beast loping beside your groom," Chas replied, looking out the carriage window where Ian rode, herding a string of the baron's thoroughbreds, assisted by a large, shaggy, gray and white dog. The beast had so much hair covering his face, she wondered how he could see where he was going.

Lyle laughed. "I just realized. His name is Samson."

Chas joined in the laughter. "And he'll more than meet his match if he ever tangles with Delilah here!"

"Ye say Mr. Hornsby studies fish?" Shamus was intrigued by the idiosyncrasies of the English nobility, especially since it appeared one was about to marry into the family.

"Ichthyology, it's called. He travels all over the world, collecting rare varieties. Some of them are quite literally priceless, I understand," Lyle replied. "Right now he's off in South America after something called piranha. The little blighters are supposed to be able to pick a cow's bones clean in minutes."

"I once knew a gambler on the Miss—"

Shamus's words were cut short when the pointy heel of his daughter's dainty slipper surreptitiously came down on his instep. Hard. "Do tell us more about the chalet, Lyle," Chas said sweetly after flashing a warning glance in her father's direction.

"It's quite a place, modeled on the Rothchild's Swiss summer house outside Geneva. There is a billiard room, the formal dining room which seats thirty comfortably, three parlors, and quite a library. Then, of course, there are the grounds."

As they pulled closer, the magnificent formal gardens, complete with topiary mazes, brilliantly colored flower beds, and beautiful blue-green pools came into view.

"It *is* a fairy-tale setting," Chas said in awe.

"I shall be pleased to give you a tour of the grounds tomorrow," Lyle replied as the carriage pulled to a halt in front of the chalet's wide wooden doors.

Ian swung down from his horse with the negligent ease of a man born to ride. He walked over to the carriage with Samson following at his heels and took the stepping stool from the coachman. Setting it in place, he opened the door with a flourish. "Welcome to Hornsby's Haven, your lordship," he said to Lyle with a puckish wink. Samson chorused with a hearty woof.

Lyle eyed the beast warily. "Do send him off before the lady gets out. Her cat might not find him any better mannered than Brimly or I do."

With a chuckle Ian turned to the big sheep dog and gave him a command. The shaggy behemoth took off, trotting behind the stablemen who had come up to take the horses away. The baron stepped down, but just as he turned to assist Chas from the conveyance, Brimly, who had been sent ahead to prepare for his master's arrival, bustled officiously down the front stairs. He was irate over the performance of the Hornsby servants.

As Lyle was thus occupied, Ian turned to Chas, poised at the carriage door, and offered her his hand, saying, "Let's see this marvel of feline manners."

"Delilah doesn't take to strangers," Chas replied, protectively handing the big white ball of fluff to her father so she could alight. As soon as he clasped her hand, it seemed as if electric sparks raced up her arms. Her eyes met his, startled and wide. She jerked her hand away quickly and alighted, holding onto the side of the carriage door. The cat, sensitive to her mistress's case of nerves, let out a low hiss as Shamus handed her out.

"It would seem you and Delilah have a great deal in common," Ian replied with a grin. "Do you have claws beneath those dainty silk gloves? I already know you spit like a she cat," he murmured softly.

"You are insolent. I cannot imagine why Lyle doesn't fire you." She held the cat between them like a shield as Shamus climbed down, watching the exchange with confusion.

"The two of ye have met before?"

"You might say your daughter dropped in on me rather unexpectedly the other evening," Ian replied as Chas's face crimsoned.

"Come, Father, let's see the chalet. I'm certain Mr. Warfield has matters to attend to in the stables. That is where you reside, isn't it?" she asked in dulcet dismissal as she swished up the steps to where Lyle and Brimly were arguing.

"The colleen has a sharp tongue on her," Shamus said to Ian with a chuckle.

"Rather more like Delilah's fangs or I miss my guess," Ian muttered beneath his breath as he turned toward the stables. After the guests had retired for the night, he would slip into the library and avail himself of some of Hornsby's excellent cognac. He had a feeling by the time this week was over, he would more than deserve the treat.

"Da, have you seen Delilah? I'm afraid she's hiding somewhere, or else she's slipped from our suite out into this big house."

Shamus was ready for bed, clad in a nightshirt and cap. He scratched his thinning gray hair and quickly shambled back into his bedroom to look for the pesky cat. "Sneaky beastie, she's not here. Ye know she loves to explore every time we come to a new place. She'll return soon enough once she's seen the lay of the place."

"You go to sleep. I'll find her," Chas replied, giving the old man a kiss on his cheek.

"Ye wouldn't want to be runnin' into the baron after hours all alone in the house, now would ye?" Shamus asked with a sly grin.

Chas drew herself up. "Certainly not. I'm supposed to be a respectable widow lady, not a common swindler out to bait a trap."

Shamus's beetle brows drew together indignantly.

"And niver was there a thing *common* about the way we pulled off a con." Then seeing her crestfallen look, he patted her shoulder awkwardly. "Ah, colleen, ye know I want what'll make ye happy . . . but are ye sure it's this Sassenach baron ye want?"

In truth she was not. Lyle was sweet and pleasant, but she felt nothing beyond a sense of mild embarrassment whenever he pestered her with ardent compliments on her beauty. *There's no . . . no . . . electricity.* Now why did that idea leap into her mind—along with a wickedly gleaming pair of gold eyes? "I'm going to find Delilah," she replied evasively and slipped away, heading for the door to the hallway.

Downstairs, Ian strolled in blissful solitude. He and Lyle had played a few relaxing games of billiards before his young companion turned in. Then the earl had gone to the library and poured himself that promised cognac, thinking over their predicament. Damned if he did not feel responsible for the younger and infinitely more naive baron. Lyle had a schoolboy crush on the beauteous Widow Manchester and would probably succumb to her charms.

Marriage was a dismal enough prospect at the ripe old age of thirty or such, a duty one must eventually perform to provide heirs for one's family title. But Lyle was only twenty-four, a mere babe in the woods compared to Ian's far more worldly twenty-nine. He would bet the window was almost as old as his friend, and far more experienced. She would certainly lead him a merry dance. Damned if he trusted the chit. She was not what she seemed. That bizarre incident at the Wharton's last week had yet to be explained.

"I'm being overprotective. Lyle will just have to take his bloody lumps like any other man," he muttered, hoping the infatuation would wear off when his friend's grandmama sent another letter, reminding him of Emily Veryan, the daughter of a neighboring baronet with whom he had grown up, and the family's preferred match for him.

Ian wandered through the big, empty house, imbibing a bit freely of the cognac, induced by a combination of guilt and boredom. Watching old Everett's fish might soothe his nerves, he decided, heading out the side door into the Japanese garden where exotic gold fish swam in a large pool. Their bodies, brilliantly spotted in red, blue, black, white, and yellow, flashed in the shallow water, illuminated by a silvery moon. He drew near the small bridge that arched above the pond when sudden sounds of splashing broke the still night air.

"What the devil?" Ian looked onto the bridge where Chastity Manchester's damnable cat was teetering precariously as she stretched one forepaw into the water, attempting to snag one of Hornsby's expensive Shubunkin. The fish, used to being fed from the bridge, at first clustered in a brilliant multicolored array around the disruption in the water, but soon darted away from the sharp, hooking claws of the cat when they sensed the danger. The cat's purchase on the edge of the bridge was loosening in direct proportion to her frustration. She hung further over the water, finally tumbling in, tail over nose, with a startled yowl and a loud plop!

Ian swore as he raced toward the shallow pool to rescue Everett's exotic fish from the crafty thief. Delilah's head quickly emerged from the water as she paddled with as much dignity as she could muster in her wet, bedraggled state. The stupid fish darted around her, and she paused to swipe at them, her sharp white fangs snapping hungrily in concert with the extended and lethal-looking claws.

"Get out of there, you bloody little thief," Ian yelled, kneeling on the bridge and reaching down to pluck the marauding cat from the water. She hissed and sank her teeth into his fingers. He jerked back his hand and swore, then grabbed her by the scruff of her neck, lifting her from the water, a thrashing whirl of claws and teeth.

"You vicious bastard! Trying to drown a helpless little cat!" Chas launched herself at Ian's back, her fists pounding against his shoulders. "Let Delilah go this instant."

"She was eating the bloody fish—not to mention my hand!" he yelled, trying to ward off her blows with one arm while trying to rescue his other one, which felt as if it were being fed into a buzz saw plied by several particularly industrious lumberjacks. "Tell her to let go of me!" He shook his arm, trying desperately to fling the cat away.

Delilah was wrapped securely around his arm now and was hanging on for dear life as her prisoner waved his wounded arm in ever widening arcs above the water. Already soaked and furious, she was having no more baths tonight, thank you, even if it meant forgoing a fish dinner. Delilah listened as the two humans shrieked at each other, letting out an ear-piercing yowl of her own when her tail dipped into the water.

"Let her go, you brute!" Chas lunged forward across his back, grabbing for the howling cat.

"Get the bloody hell off me or we'll both—oh shit!" Ian felt his grip on the bridge plank slip when Chas's weight shifted to his shoulders. In a whirl of arms and legs they tumbled headfirst into the shallow water. The fish fled to the perimeter of the pool in an expanding circle of flashing color as Ian hit bottom with a solid thud.

Chas landed on top of him, knocking the air from his lungs, which quickly sucked in a sufficient amount of the pond to significantly lower the water level. Mercifully, the impact forced Delilah to relinquish her death grip on his mangled arm. She paddled away after the bright ring of Shubunkin.

Chas rolled off Ian's back and landed in the shallow water on all fours. Flinging a sopping wad of hair out of her eyes, she glared at the coughing, gasping man who was struggling to his knees. "If you've drowned my cat, you'll pay for it. You—"

"If your cat's damaged any of those fish *you* will pay for them," he gasped out. "They're Everett Hornsby's specimens. And as for your darling Delilah, she's a bloody sight drier than we are!"

Ian gestured to the edge of the pond, where the white cat sat, furiously licking her soggy tail. He finally managed to stand up on the slippery bottom and started to trudge toward the bank. His first mistake was looking from the cat to her mistress.

Bloody hell, the chit was practically naked! Her robe had come unfastened and hung open, revealing the swell of her breasts and other delights all too clearly through the translucent white silk of her nightrail. One rosy, hardened nipple winked impudently at him as she rose like Venus from the waves.

Chas struggled to her feet, but her brocade robe and the voluminous nightrail beneath it tangled around her legs. Before she could reconsider, her hands reached out and grabbed Ian's arm as she started to slip.

He jerked away with an oath of pain, for it was the arm the cat had just lacerated with teeth and claws. She held on and was flung against the solid wall of his chest. A heavy mass of sodden red hair flew into his face as he continued to curse. Her body was molded against his and suddenly the heady scent of lilacs filled his nostrils. He could feel himself growing hard as her breasts seemed to melt into him and the delicate bones of her hips rubbed intimately against his lower belly.

"Let me go," she said in a greatly subdued whisper, starting to tremble—and not all of it because of the cool night air on her wet skin.

"What, no more shrieks and curses, Puss?" He tight-

ened his good arm around her, ignoring the pain in the
one Delilah had shredded. All the blood had suddenly
rushed to another part of his body. "It's a good thing
the bedrooms are on the far side of the house, else
we'd have awakened quite an audience by now—the
baron, your father, and even old Brimly. I wonder who
would be the most shocked, hmm, Puss?"

"Don't call me Puss." Chas pushed ineffectually at
his chest, trying to put some space between their heart-
beats, which seemed to be thudding in a swift, matched
cadence. She felt the strangest heat beginning to pool
low in her belly, and her breasts tingled.

"Ah, but you are quite a puss—spitting one minute,
purring the next. You're an enigma, Chastity," he whispered, lifting a wet curl away from her face, drawn to
those lush, soft pink lips and that darting, clever little
tongue. "You even wield your tongue like a puss." He
lowered his mouth to hers just as she opened it to gasp
in outrage.

Chas had been kissed often in the course of the cha-
rades she played to separate foolish men from their
money, but she had never had a real suitor—until the
baron. *Lyle!* What was she doing, clinging to this common stable hand, allowing him to take liberties with
her person—liberties that the very proper baron would
never consider? She felt the persuasive heat of Ian's
lips and tongue as he plied his considerable skills.
Forcing her treacherous body under control, she bit
down on his tongue. He withdrew with a startled oath.

"Beware. Cats bite as well as scratch," she said,
shoving him away. Seizing her waterlogged robe and
gown in both hands, she slogged to shore near Delilah,
scooped up the instigator of the debacle, and walked
toward the house with as much dignity as she could
muster.

"Sweet dreams, Puss," he called after her, half
amused by her soggy retreat, half infuriated by her

sudden rejection. "An enigma indeed," he muttered to himself as he waded from the water in search of more alcohol, this time for medicinal purposes.

As he saddled the horses the next morning, Ian was decidedly out of sorts. His right hand and arm were crisscrossed with angry red scratches and punctures, and his head was splitting from overindulgence in Hornsby's cognac. "Lyle would have to decide on a bloody scenic ride this of all mornings." He finished cinching the sidesaddle on a spirited mare and led the horse out to where the other mounts waited in the vindictively bright sunshine.

Samson, his tail thumping, woofed loudly as Lyle approached them. Ian winced and castigated the dog with a sharp command.

"I say, old chap, you do look a bit green. Hornsby's cognac, eh?" Lyle asked with a chuckle. At Ian's noncommittal grunt he patted the neck of his horse and continued, "You're not the only one feeling not quite the thing. Chastity almost begged off our morning ride. Something about not sleeping well last night, but I convinced her that some fresh mountain air would do her a world of good. She'll sleep better tonight after a day's exercise."

"She had plenty of exercise last night," Ian muttered beneath his breath as Lyle rushed forward to escort a resplendent Chas to the corral. Her riding habit of apple green poplin perfectly accentuated her soft curves and long legs. He remembered how every inch of her had looked—and felt—in the water last night. He gave her a leering nod and felt inordinately pleased when she blushed and looked away. Odd, she did seem a bit pale as she eyed the horses nervously.

"Not feeling up to the ride, Mrs. Manchester?" he dared.

"Certainly I am." She ignored the horrid cat mo-

lester and smiled brilliantly at Lyle, who was so eager
to show off his English racers. *If only I knew how to
ride.* Every lady of breeding was an accomplished
horsewoman. Chas had to ride, even if it killed her . . .
which it well might. Remembering Shamus's admonition—"Wrap your leg around the pommel and hang
on for dear life until it's over"—she approached the
horses. The damn things looked tall as sycamores and
as skittish as Delilah at a dog show.

"Aren't they magnificent? I just knew you would
like Jersey Lady. She's spirited and intelligent," Lyle
said as he scratched the mare's forehead.

"I can see that," Chas replied uneasily, tugging the
heavy weight of her riding habit train. *Damn fool
thing. If I could just wrap both legs around the horse,
I'd feel better.* But ladies never rode astride. She
reached up and patted the horse nervously, trying at the
same time to pretend Ian wasn't having such a disquieting effect on her. He leaned indolently against the
fence post with one booted foot crossed over the other,
looking altogether splendid in a white shirt open at the
throat and a pair of tan breeches that looked painted
over his sinewy legs.

The mare tossed her head and nickered as Ian's big
dog trotted up to them. Chas drew away from the horse
and glared at the intruder. "Must that onerous creature
go everywhere with us?"

"Samson is quite good with the horses." Although
she had asked Lyle, Ian had answered.

She turned to Ian and said dulcetly, "I was not refer-
ring to the dog."

Lyle looked from Chas to Ian and back, baffled by
his cheeky grin and her sarcastic retort. "I say, perhaps
we'd best mount up and be off."

"Allow me, m'lady," Ian said, uncurling his lithe
form from the post and cupping his hands to give her
a leg up onto the tall thoroughbred.

The minute her foot touched his hands, there it was, that damned electric jolt again! "I am not a lady. I'm American," she said waspishly, trying to ignore the way his big hands felt, boosting her so effortlessly.

"Not a lady? Ah, Puss, how fortunate for me," he whispered so low only she could hear.

He's toying with me, the cad. Her anger quickly evaporated, however, for keeping the leggy mare under any semblance of control seemed nigh impossible. So did staying on top of her. Chas's leg was hooked so tightly around the pommel she knew she would limp for a week—if she didn't break her neck first and end it all.

They started out at a slow trot which nonetheless felt like her teeth were being loosened. Fortunately, Lyle was enjoying playing host so much he talked nonstop, only pausing in his panegyric on the beauties of Colorado long enough for her to nod or smile in assent before continuing.

As he trailed along at a discreet distance, Ian watched the way Chas sat, or rather, bounced on the mare. She was not only a terrible rider, she was a terrified one, and her fear was transferring itself to the high-spirited animal. Another enigma. Why would a wealthy society lady be an untutored rider? And if so, why would she attempt to hide the fact? There was a great deal the chit was concealing, and his foolish young companion was oblivious to it all. That crafty old Irishman was a mystery, too. He was glib, but hardly possessed the polish to have married off his daughter in rarefied eastern society.

She's nothing but bloody trouble. I hope Lyle will forget her when we move on to San Francisco in a few weeks. He watched Samson race across the open meadow through bushy clumps of blue and white columbine, dashing back and forth in pursuit of butterflies and any creature that took his eye. Ian heard Lyle chattering to Chastity, but ignored their silly conversation in favor of enjoying the day and the view of her delectable little rump bouncing up and down on the sidesaddle. Before he knew it, he was mentally stripping her of the riding habit's heavy folds. The task required little imagination after seeing her in Everett's fish pond the preceding night.

Chas could feel the groom's mocking gaze burn into her backside, distracting her from Lyle's charming company. That accursed dog was not helping either, racing around like a berserk thing, leaping up in the air as he chased insects. Luckily, he disappeared over the rise between several large boulders, and she was able to once again concentrate on controlling the mare. Just as she was beginning to relax and even laugh at several of Lyle's comments, they rounded a curve in the trail. A furiously barking Samson drove a frightened prairie hen directly toward them. The frantic flapping of the bird's wings, combined with the blur of the gray and white mountain of fur chasing it, caused all three horses to prance and sidestep nervously. Chas was so startled she inadvertently yanked on the reins, hurting the mare's sensitive mouth and causing her to rear, squealing angrily. Terrified now, Chas dropped her reins and grabbed frantically for the horse's mane, but her leg was slipping off the pommel and she began to slide from the bucking mare.

"Kick free of your stirrup," Lyle yelled, fearful she would be dragged, as he fought to bring his horse under control and ride to her rescue. Before he could wheel his mount around, Ian had grabbed the mare's reins and had the horse somewhat under control, but not in time to save Chas from a very undignified head-over-heels fall. She landed with a plop in the thick red dirt, her left foot still caught in the stirrup, causing her skirt to flip back and expose a long expanse of leg.

As she thrashed, trying desperately to sit up, Ian

commanded Samson to sit and stay, then yelled at her, "Stop that bloody flopping about. You're frightening Lady and she might just step on you."

Before Chas could give him a blistering retort, Lyle was at her side, his face pale and his eyes wide with fright. "Good Lord, are you harmed?" Careful to avoid looking at her delightfully exposed limb, he extricated her foot from the stirrup and helped her sit upright and cover herself decently.

Blushing furiously, Chas coughed, then winced at the pain in her tender posterior. She glared at the dog who was responsible for her ignominious fall, then at his owner. "If that woolly mastodon every comes near me again, I will shoot him with my derringer!"

"Samson often scares up rabbits when we ride, and the horses aren't disturbed by them, but the noise of the bird's wings and the motion at eye level spooked them. I'm so frightfully sorry, Chastity. Please accept my deepest apologies," Lyle said. By this time Ian had secured the horses and approached, towering over them.

His eyes were dancing with mirth as he held up his scratched right hand, seeming to say, turnabout is fair play. "If you had a better seat, Lady wouldn't have thrown you."

Chas hissed, "My seat is just fine, thank you." But when Lyle helped her stand up, she could not resist rubbing the aching muscles.

When Lyle walked over to gather the horses, Ian leaned close to whisper, "I apologize. Your seat *is* quite fine, a very good seat indeed. But one in need of work." His eyes swept over her body in amused inspection.

"Laugh at me will you . . . you . . . you English horse butler! You forget your place!" She turned and stomped off, still rubbing her backside, dreading the prospect of remounting that damned horse. "Lyle, do you think we might walk for a bit—just to cool down the horses?"

The sound of Ian's rich chuckle echoed in her ears.

"I think the baron is taking a real shine to ye, Chas," Shamus said the next day as they drank their morning coffee in their suite before joining Lyle for breakfast. "What if he asks me for yer hand in marriage?" His thick brows creased together into one long, woolly slash.

She looked at him impatiently. "Isn't that the whole object of our masquerade, Da? You'll approve, of course."

"There is one wee matter, colleen, that ye've not considered." His normally florid face mottled an even deeper red. "Ye're impersonatin' a widow lady . . . and, Chas, I know ye've niver . . . that is . . ."

"At twenty-three I'm not only a spinster, but a virgin as well. I know," she sighed. Never having wanted the encumbrance of a husband when she was growing up, Chas had not given much thought to men except as marks to be bilked of their money. But maturity and increasingly closer brushes with the law had forced her to reevaluate their situation. "I'll manage to take care of it some which way," she replied evasively, turning to enter her dressing room.

Why did a pair of mocking gold eyes and a dazzling smile flash into her mind?

When Chas returned to the parlor of their suite, dressed elegantly in a morning gown of bright yellow muslin, Delilah was grooming herself at the window ledge. She hugged the feline, who butted her head affectionately and gave Chas's cheek several rasping licks with her scratchy pink tongue.

"Be a good girl and don't try to eat any more fish! Stay in our rooms here."

The cat regarded her mistress with inscrutable jade

eyes until Chas left the suite with Shamus. Then she turned her attention to the window. The spreading branches of the oak tree beckoned. What was a self-respecting cat to do? She leaped.

After finishing a delightful late-morning breakfast, Chas and Lyle left Shamus in the library and strolled out onto the patio behind the house, looking out at the Japanese gardens and the fish ponds. Suddenly a blur of white sped across the lawn, closely trailed by another, much larger blur of gray.

"Delilah! That wretched monster will tear her limb from limb! And I'll tear Ian Warfield's heart from his chest, bloody and beating!" Chas picked up her skirt and dashed over the lawn just as the cat sped up a large elm. Samson circled the tree barking furiously.

"Get away, you miserable rag mop disguised as a dog!" She shoved at the dog's shaggy shoulder with all the effect of a gnat trying to roll a boulder. "How dare you attack my cat?"

"How dare your cat try and eat Hornsby's fish? Again." Ian strode up to her from the opposite direction just as Lyle and Shamus ran up behind her.

"Get that . . . that flea-bitten fur bag out of my sight," she gritted at Ian, then looked up to the top branches of the elm where the cat huddled, puffed to twice her normal size. "Oh, Delilah, darling. Don't be afraid. We'll get you down." She turned frantically to Lyle. "She's not an outdoor cat. She's never even climbed a tree before in her life."

Lyle began to remove his jacket. "Never fear, Chastity. I'll retrieve her. As a lad I climbed more than my share of trees," he said with a reassuring smile.

"Lyle, no! It was Warfield's dog that caused this debacle. He is your servant, and I think he should fetch Delilah down," she said, turning with a saccharine smile to Ian.

"It's quite all right. I really am a stout climber," Lyle protested.

But Ian made a mock bow to the seething beauty. She looked delectable as a daffodil in that yellow frock. "I'll handle this, your lordship. She's quite right. It is my dog, and you can't abide Samson much better than Mrs. Manchester here." He gave the big sheep dog a stern command, and the canine trotted obediently in the direction from which he had come as his master began to climb the brittle limbs of the Chinese elm tree.

"Damn stupid feline, you would have to choose the flimsiest tree on a bloody thirty-thousand acre estate," he muttered as he pulled himself up near the top. Several branches made ominous groaning sounds as his boots bore down on them. When he reached Delilah, she gave a threatening hiss and backed farther out on her slender perch. He reached out his unpunctured hand and she swiped at it, claws flexed.

"So, it's to be like that, is it?" he growled.

"I say, do be careful, Ian," Lyle called up worriedly.

"Yes, you might drop Delilah," Chas chimed in sweetly.

"I have it," Lyle said, snapping his fingers. "What we need is the gardener's orchard ladder. I shall be back with it in a trice. Hold on and don't move, Ian!" With that he raced across the lawn and vanished behind the barn, hallooing for any yardmen who might be wandering about.

Ignoring the two blithering idiots below, Ian began to yank off his shirt, ripping away the buttons in his haste. The limb that bore most of his weight was sounding none too promising. A slow crackling noise emanated ominously from beneath his feet. He wound the shirt around his unmarred arm, using a bit of it to cover his hand and still allow enough flexibility to seize the stupid, spitting creature who glared at him.

"How in bloody hell did I get myself into this? I should've let Lyle break his fool neck." He crawled out and slowly extended his protected arm toward Delilah. She growled low, narrowing her eyes to jade slits, then backed off again. He pursued her, and the crackling beneath him became more pronounced.

Just before the limb snapped, he lunged for the cat, seizing her by the back of her neck. Then the whole world seemed to tilt as he tumbled downward, clutching at passing branches to break his fall, succeeding far better at nearly dislocating a shoulder. He lost the contest with Delilah about halfway to the ground when the cat leaped free of his grasp and easily clawed a hold on the tree trunk. Amidst Chas's shrieks and the rustling of elm leaves, the grassy earth rushed up to greet him.

Ian opened his eyes and had begun to experimentally wriggle his toes, testing to see if he was intact, when Chas's voice roused him. "Oh, Delilah, you could've been killed!" She stepped over him and reached up on tiptoe for the fractious feline, affording him a nice view of her slender ankles beneath the hem of her skirt.

The cat gave a murph and began to jump down from the limb directly above him, which had miraculously remained unscathed despite the pounding his body must have given it. But instead of leaping into Chastity's outstretched arms, the perverse creature sprang past her and landed squarely on his body—the lower part of his body, a very sensitive part of his body.

"Stupid beast, this is not a fish!" Ian rolled over with a snarled oath, clutching himself as Delilah jumped gracefully away and sat down a few yards distant, where she began to groom herself without a care in the world.

Chas turned from the cat and knelt beside the man lying on the ground. From the strength of the colorful oaths spewing forth, she ascertained he was not in imminent danger of expiring on her. He again rolled over onto his backside and threw one forearm across his face, shielding his gaze from her. Ian Warfield was half naked and all male.

Against her will her eyes traveled across the sleek powerful muscles of his arms, up to that glorious bare chest she had only had a peek at before. She'd thought it tantalizing when all she could see was a tuft or two of dark gold hair. Now the entire cunning pattern of the springy mat was visible. She followed the thick pelt as it narrowed in a vee that ran down his hard belly to where the waistband of his pants should have been—had it not been ripped open in his fall. His fly buttons were half missing as well! Chas couldn't stop her trespass as she watched the rise and fall of that flat abdomen with its navel lightly surrounded by a wisp of golden hair, which continued downward, finally vanishing, alas, beneath the cover of his breeches.

Never in her twenty-three years had she wanted to touch anything as much as she did at that moment. He was injured, wasn't he? Surely she had to offer assistance. Scooting nearer, Chas placed her soft palms on his hard chest, feeling the heavy pectoral muscles jump and flex.

He flung his arm away from his face and glared up at her, his heart hammering from the near brush with death, not to mention castration by this female's feline. Every inch of his body was scratched or bruised or both, but he did not feel any of it from the instant Chastity Manchester touched him.

The delectable tip of pink tongue rimmed her lips before she breathlessly asked, "Are ... are you all right?"

"Bloody lovely. I always enjoy a brisk drop of thirty feet or so before luncheon. It so perks up one's appetite, don't you think?" He struggled to sit and succeeded only in raising up onto his elbows.

One errant curl of dark blond hair drooped across his forehead. "You look like a fallen angel," she whispered.

In spite of himself, Ian grinned. "I do believe *fallen* is the appropriate word." He stared into her wide green eyes, lost in their fathomless depths. Why had he never noticed how thick her lashes were? Or how pert her tiny upturned nose was? Or how sweetly her pointy chin curved up from her slender throat?

"I am stark raving mad," he said hoarsely as he reached up and placed one hand at her nape, pulling her into his embrace. She came willingly.

Chapter Three

All that night Chas tossed and turned in her bed, restless and miserable. Finally, she gave up and rose, slipping on the one remaining robe she had brought with her from Denver. As she belted the soft satin, she remembered how she had come to ruin the other one, wrestling with that wretched stable man in the fish pond.

"All of this is your fault," she said, glaring at Delilah, who sat draped decadently across the cushions of a maroon velvet sofa, the heads of George Washington, Thomas Jefferson, and Benjamin Franklin staring disapprovingly down on her from the elaborately carved back of the John Belter piece. The feline gave both the carved heads and the human one a smug blink of her green eyes, then stretched and yawned as if to say, "Well, now that my sleep's been disturbed ..." She stood and bowed up her back, front paws extended in a languorous movement of fluid grace. Her whole body rippled as she stretch-walked across the cushions of the sofa and jumped onto the floor, then began to twine around Chas's legs.

Chas picked her up and walked over to the window, gazing out across the immaculately manicured lawns toward the dark cluster of wooden buildings in the distance—the servant's quarters. Ian Warfield no doubt slept near the horse paddock. Being the head groom, he probably had private, if spartan, quarters. She scratched the cat's ears, then ran her fingers through the long, silky fur of its back.

"He's the reason I can't sleep, damn his eyes. I've never felt this way before, Delilah. All breathless and quivery whenever he's around. And when he touches me . . . that kiss this morning . . ." Words failed her as the heated splendor of it washed over her again. Just thinking about Ian made her ache.

"I desire him," she whispered aloud, her voice hoarse from the shock of the sudden revelation. "How perfectly preposterous. I've never been interested in any of the men I've ever met except for finding ways to fleece them. Now when I decide to honestly marry one and find the sweetest, noblest, *richest* eligible bachelor, how do I react to him? As if he were a charming younger brother. And I actually get heart palpitations over an arrogant, impoverished stable hand! I must be going insane, Delilah."

The cat licked her hand and nuzzled her. Whether it was in consolation or agreement, or both, she was not certain.

Could she marry Lyle while his groom held her in such shocking thrall? And there was the matter her da had broached the other day. Her virginity was, most ironically, a real impediment. How could she explain it to the baron?

"If only the real Chastity Manchester had been wed to some gouty old fart, I could convince Lyle the marriage had never been consummated, and he'd probably be delighted." But one of the silver kings the baron hobnobbed with in Denver had known the unfortunate young man. No, that would never work.

Then an idea flashed into her mind, an idea so outrageous, she squeezed Delilah without realizing it. The big Persian let out a startled squeak of dismay and wriggled free. Leaping to the floor, she took several angry swipes at her back, then looked accusatorially up at Chas. But Chastity Kathleen O'Roarke was oblivious as she stared raptly out the window, toward the stables. A calculating smile began to curve her lips.

"I wonder if Da brought his medicine chest along with him? Oh, please! You're always consistent, Shamus you old rascal, don't surprise me this one time." She could scarcely wait until morning to search his room while he was downstairs.

Her opportunity came even sooner than she expected when the old con man rose earlier than was his usual wont to meet Lyle for breakfast. She knew he was concerned about his daughter marrying a Sassenach and was no doubt intent on asking the baron all sorts of embarrassing questions. There was no hope of preventing it, and Lyle seemed to bear the old Irishman's scrutiny with amazing good humor.

As soon as the door to the suite closed, she rolled out of her bed, where she had feigned sleep, and headed for the dressing closet in her father's room. "He always travels with that snake oil chest," she murmured, surveying the pile of boxes and trunks that contained Shamus's stock and trade. From the slums of Dublin to the Five Points of New York, he had worked every type of con known and even invented a few new ones along the way.

One of his most famed "methods of extraction," a term he employed for the separation of money from marks, was the sale of exotic and very expensive patent medicines. An old Gypsy woman had concocted the aphrodisiac for him. Chas could still remember how her enormous black eyes glittered hypnotically as she explained the potency of just a single drop swallowed by the intended victim.

Chas had never seen it work, of course, but Shamus swore it was one of the few legitimate elixirs in his collection. If it would make Ian receptive to her seduction, she would be delighted. He would have to be the one who attacked her in a fit of lust in order that she might blackmail him into silence about the event afterward. If at the same time the drug rendered his memory a wee bit fuzzy, all the better. She refused to consider that she was unable to view losing her virginity to Ian as distasteful.

Chas dug through the trunks, looking for one small leather chest with an antique silver latch on it. Finally she located it, buried beneath the false-bottomed magician's box, which Elmo the Sorcerer had given them when they lived with the traveling carnival. Fumbling with the clasp, she finally opened it and then began reading the labels on the vials.

"Ah, here it is! Spanish Potion of Eternal Love." The cautions on the bottle were enough to give Chas pause, but not for long. The idea of that vile, overbearing devil slobbering at her feet and begging her to share his bed definitely held a strong appeal. She would get her revenge on the maddening Englishman and solve the dilemma of her virginity at the same time. What better way to get over an infatuation than to quench the mystery of lust?

"Now, Delilah," she said as she closed the medicine chest and slipped the small vial into her pocket, "we have some careful planning to do."

Appealing to Shamus O'Roarke's larceny was the easy part. There was nothing he loved move than to cheat at cards, and the old rogue had never lost his talent for sleight of hand when it came to picking a pocket or palming an ace. She arranged for Lyle and her father to play a friendly game of poker that evening after dinner. Then while Brimly was serving them cognac in the library, she pleaded a headache and excused herself, urging them to have a good time.

"I'd be ever so happy if you'd stay and be my lucky

charm," Lyle pleaded. "I have a feeling I'm going to need all the luck I can muster against your father."

And I'm going to need it for your groom. "Just don't let him deal seven card stud," she said with a wink at Shamus, who made a face at her. It was his favorite game—and he always managed to deal himself flushes.

By the time she reached her room, her knees were weak and her breath was short. "Great, at this rate, I'll never even make it to the stables." Chas squared her shoulders and looked at herself in the cheval glass mirror. Her hair was too fussy, all done up in elaborate ringlets with jeweled combs holding it high on top of her head. And her dress, elegant and sophisticated navy blue crepe, was too formal—and difficult to remove. What if he ripped it off of her?

Her heart skipped a beat, and her mouth went dry. She should have been terrified, but she wasn't. The thought of Ian's hands cupping her breasts, his lips pressing fierce kisses on her throat, his tongue teasing and tasting her mouth as he had yesterday beneath the elm tree drew a warm, restless surge of hunger from her. "I can do this. I will do this," she whispered aloud as she began to pull the combs from her hair.

Ian was feeling anything but amorous as he sat soaking in a big wooden tub of hot water, which Brimly had had two footmen carry over from the main house's kitchen. "If there's an inch of my body that her infernal cat hasn't bitten or clawed, it's bloody black and blue from that little fall out of the tree yesterday." He winced as he flexed his right shoulder. Probably dislocated the damned thing in his attempt to grab hold of that branch to break his fall.

"If there were any justice I should've landed on *her* this time! Or at the least, squashed that hellish feline into a Persian carpet!"

And then what had he done, idiot to the last, but pull Chastity Manchester down and kiss her until they were both nearly intoxicated. Thank heaven Samson had come bounding after Delilah and interrupted them before it went any further. Lord, Lyle and his fool gaggle of gardeners would have stumbled upon them in a position compromising enough to make a romantic like his young friend demand he do the gentlemanly thing and marry the chit!

"Lyle may be honorable, but I haven't a decent bone in my bloody body—and somehow I strongly suspect neither has Chastity Manchester."

He leaned back in the tub and closed his eyes, recalling the way she had reacted to the kiss, with such fire, yet with befuddlement and surprise. She combined the most peculiar traits—sensuality and sophistication with a stubborn sort of virginal innocence. Absurd! She was a widow, and in the year and a half since her husband's passing, a woman of her beauty and adventurous nature must surely have taken lovers.

She was as attracted to him as she was infuriated by him, this in spite of seeming to set her cap for Lyle. What game did the mysterious widow play? Whatever it was, her desire for him was genuine, not the artificial posturing of a vapid heiress enamored of his title or wealth. Was her whole western trip a lark, much as it was for two bored, rich noblemen such as he and Lyle? A disquieting thought, but then she was a disquieting female.

A sudden creak on the hinges of the door to his room caused Ian's eyes to snap open—only to behold the subject of his ruminations. Chas stood poised in the doorway, holding a bottle of Hornsby's best Bordeaux in one hand, clutching the lapels of her sheer silk wrapper with the other. Long, flame-colored curls fell in splendor past her shoulders, contrasting with the virginal whiteness of the silk robe.

God, how it clung to every sweet curve of her body. And how well he remembered the feel of that body.

"What the bloody hell are you doing here? Viewing the remains?"

His voice was accusatory and his eyes full of anger. Chas wet her lips, depleting the supply of moisture in her mouth, and tried to frame a seductive answer. She held the bottle aloft. "I sneaked into Mr. Hornsby's wince cellar and pinched this. Is '66 a good year for Margaux?" She had chosen the heaviest red she could find in order to cover any taste of the aphrodisiac. When she had opened the vial, it looked like ink and smelled like turpentine.

"And you just had to have someone special to share it with you. Why not the baron?"

"Lyle is engaged in a very competitive game of stud with my father." She moved slowly into the room, watching him watch her from his recumbent position in the tub.

"And you thought you would engage in another variety of stud with me?" His eyes were heavy lidded, his expression mocking.

Chas felt the heat of the blush crawling up her throat, she who never betrayed a flicker of emotion even while working the biggest sting. "I've come to make peace between us." Why, when she really intended to seduce a man, was it so much more difficult than when she only pretended to do it? Chas sat down on a rough pine chair beside an equally crude small table and set the bottle down, letting the white silk robe slide artfully open, revealing a long, sleek stretch of leg from ankle to midthigh.

"You should've been named Delilah, not your bloody cat," he said in a hoarse voice.

A small, almost feline smile spread across her lips. So, she was having an effect on the arrogant devil. "I dare you to come out of that tub and have a drink with me. I promise I won't scratch you where she did."

He surveyed the sheer, almost translucent, white

silk, barely concealing her breasts. Long, fiery curls spread across her shoulders, partially curtaining her face as those cat green eyes studied him. "Suddenly, I understand how Hornsby's fish must have felt," he said softly. Shrugging his shoulders, he added wryly, "If you would like a drink, before *your* fishing expedition, there are a couple of glasses in that cupboard on the wall."

She looked to where he pointed with one lean, elegant finger. A small wooden cabinet was nailed against the rough planks. He still made no move to rise from the water. Good. Let him play a waiting game. She could pour the wine and slip the drug into his glass all the more easily. *I'll bet you won't be so cool and arrogant in a few minutes!*

"Your obedient servant, sir," she answered, gliding up from the chair to open the cabinet and take out two chipped tumblers. "I took the liberty of opening the wine before I brought it down. I rather imagined you might not have an opener."

His mouth quirked in a leering grin. "Please, m'dear, no lies. We both know that my 'opener' is the reason you're here."

"If you persist in being so crude, I might decide to leave." She used her haughtiest voice, unreasonably angry at his assumptions about her morals.

She poured two sizable draughts of wine into the glasses, using her body as a shield when she palmed the tiny vial and slipped a drop into his drink. Then she considered what a rude bastard he was being and plopped in another drop for good measure.

"How the hell did you keep from freezing to death in that gauzy thing?" he asked. It was a chilly, rainy night.

"I wore a heavy cloak. It's hanging on the peg by the stable door."

"How resourceful. You did make a dramatic entrance."

She turned and held out a glass to him, willing her hand to be steady. "Come and get it."

Bloody hell, he was hard as a poker, and his heart was pounding like one of his racers after doing a dozen laps around the track! "At your service, madam." He stood up in the water, then reached for the towel lying beside the tub and began to rub his thick hair dry.

Chas watched the water droplets run through the dark gold pelt on his chest. Muscles flexed and rippled as he scrubbed his head dry, hiding those mocking, searing golden eyes so she could feast on his naked flesh unobserved. God, what a splendid specimen he was! Lean and sinuous and tanned to the waist. Then her eyes followed the course of the water glistening on his skin, lower, down beyond where she had seen that thin band of gold hair vanish into his breeches yesterday. His staff looked huge to her virginal eyes. A frission of fear washed over her. Perhaps she'd been a bit hasty about that second drop from the vial.

Ian put down the towel and looked at her wide green eyes. "I trust I meet with your approval." It was not a question. Tossing the towel across one broad shoulder, he took a step toward her. "I fear in spite of your precautions with the cloak, you're going to get very damp in a moment."

She thrust the glass into his hand as he reached for her, not because she wanted him to imbibe the aphrodisiac—anyone not blind could see it was quite unnecessary! She simply wanted to stall for time, to gather her scattered wits—and her nerve. "Let's drink first."

He took the glass, but set it impatiently on the table without taking a swallow. "First another of those kisses, I think." He pulled her against him and felt the soft warmth of her body through the sheer silk wrapper. His wet flesh quickly soaked through the flimsy stuff as they melded together. His fingers splayed against her back, pressing her tightly to him. He tangled his other hand in her hair, inhaling the lilac sweetness of her while he buried his face in the fiery curls. Her neck arched back, baring her throat to his hot, seeking mouth, while at the same time pressing her flat stomach against the hardness of his erection. He groaned and kissed her throat, trailing wet, fierce nips and licks of his teeth and tongue upward to graze her delicate jawline with his lips. Then he rained light, brushing kisses over the hollows of her cheeks, her temples, nose and brow, pulling her thick lashes between his lips as he kissed her eyelids.

Finally, as he felt her clinging to him, panting softly, he centered his mouth on hers and she opened for him. His tongue plunged inside to taste her. She was every bit as unique and delicious as he remembered. He felt her clever little tongue spear against his in a delicate duel. They danced, twining and darting, then he sucked against it, drawing it deeper into his mouth until she moaned helplessly.

Chas thought yesterday's kiss incredible. But it had been a mere prologue for this. The whole earth seemed to tilt on its axis as his mouth took hers, sucking, brushing, pressing, probing until she was mindless, lost in the passion of the moment. Then he withdrew, shaky and breathless. Chas could feel the sudden chill of night air and looked down at herself. The whole front of her wrapper was soaked, imprinted with the form of his body where it had pressed so tightly against hers. Her nipples protruded in sharp points against the translucent silk, which clung like second skin to her breasts, belly, and thighs.

"We'd better slow down, else we'll never make it to my bed," he said ruefully. " 'Tis a small, rude pallet, but infinitely preferable to the rough floorboards here.

I shouldn't want any splinters in that delectable derriere." His palm cupped one small buttock and squeezed gently to emphasize his point. In truth, he feared he was going to spill his seed like a green schoolboy if he did not regain control of himself. This impossible American had a more potent effect on him than any woman he had ever desired.

Chas turned, dazed, to where the two glasses sat side by side on the table. *My God, which was which?* Before she could decide, the matter was taken from her hands when Ian picked them both up and handed her one, then tipped his against hers, in a surprisingly elegant gesture for a stable man.

"To peace between us," he said, waiting for her to drink.

Bemused, she took a sip. It tasted all right. Surely his must be the drugged one. He upended the glass, draining it, then looked at her with a dare in his eyes. She followed suit.

"We've made peace. Let's make love." He set both glasses down and swept her into his arms. Carrying her over to his small pallet, he lay her down on the sheets.

Soft, surprisingly good linen caressed her back as he began to unfasten the satin frogs holding the robe together. With deft skill he peeled the wet, clinging silk from her body, kissing her bared, cool skin as he did so. The room began to get warmer and warmer, her skin more and more sensitive. When he threw the robe against a chair and lowered his head to her breast, she thought she would expire from the sweet ache.

Ian drew one hard, rosy pebble into his mouth and bit gently on the tip. When she arched up with a startled gasp, he rimmed the pale pink edges with his tongue, then sucked greedily, using his hands to shove the soft milky globe higher into his mouth.

A sharp rapping on the outside door to the stable interrupted them. With a muttered oath Ian straightened up, giving her mouth a quick kiss. "I'll be right back. Remember where we were." He rolled up and took his breeches from a peg on the wall, jerking them on awkwardly and buttoning the fly with great difficulty.

"Whatever you want, it had better be important."

Chas heard his strident voice from where she lay on the pallet. A low exchange of conversation ensued between Ian and one of the stable hands, but she had no interest in it. The room began to whirl around her in a dizzying surge, and her whole body, already sensitive and tingling as it always was when she was in Ian's company, now caught fire. She burned. Her breasts seemed swollen and tender, her belly tense and quivery. But the hungry discomfiture centered lower, in that most secret, mysterious place where no man had ever trespassed. She was dying for Ian's touch.

Her fevered brain finally registered with horror what had happened. "I drank the damned aphrodisiac! Oh, sweet saints, what will I do?" What if he did not return—and very soon? Panic alternated with blind lust as she lay quivering on the bed.

Minutes seemed like hours before Ian returned, cursing the stupid stable hand who had let one of the horses eat his bedding and develop colic. After giving the thoroughbred a colic remedy, he gave instructions to the boy and rushed back to Chastity. The moment he walked through the door to his quarters, she rolled up on all fours on the bed, her expression as feral as a tigress.

"What the devil—" His words broke off when she leaped from the bed and launched herself across the small room, flying into his arms. Her hands seized fistfuls of his shaggy hair, pulling his head down to hers for a fierce kiss. Her hips arched against his, and she wrapped her legs around his waist, scaling him in a frenzy.

Ian strode back to the bed as Chas tore his breeches,

ill buttoned in the first place, and began to tug at the gaping wasitband, while at the same time continuing her assault on his lips.

"Mmm . . . easy, easy, Cha . . ." His protest was muffled by her mouth as it closed over his again in the midst of raining frantic kisses all across his face. He started to kneel on the pallet, but her frenzied writhing unbalanced him, and he fell sideways, landing on his back with Chas straddling him. Her hands resumed tearing at his breeches, but the very proximity of her position atop him impeded her success. She groaned in frustration.

"Allow me, my scratching little she-cat. Remember your promise about not emulating Delilah," he said, lifting her off him and attempting to pull down his pants, but she was after him again before he had them to his knees.

"Bloody hell, Chastity!" *Chastity!* What an idiotic name for this greedy little puss. Then he felt her hands on him, stroking him, and all thoughts fled. He pulled her down on him and kissed her savagely while kicking his breeches the rest of the way off. She kissed him back like a demented thing, her long nails digging into his shoulders.

Ian molded her to him and rolled up on top, pinning her wriggling little body beneath his larger one. His staff ached to plunge into her, and she was certainly ready for him. He seized her busy hands by their delicate wrists and pinioned them above her head, then moved the tip of his phallus between her eagerly spread thighs, rubbing the silky wet heat of her petals. In spite of her bucking, he finally made contact with the center of her softness and arched forward to plunge deeply inside her.

Just as he completed the stroke and her wet sheath enveloped him, he looked into her eyes. The shock jolted his mind almost as much as the physical bliss of feeling her surround him jolted his body. "V-virgin. You're a bloody virgin!" he accused in amazement, releasing her wrists. In spite of the sundering of her maidenhead—or perhaps even because of it—she arched up against him frantically, rolling her hips with such eager abandon he could do nothing but follow the primal rhythm of mating.

Chas clutched at Ian's powerful biceps and ran her fingers up over his shoulders, then dug her nails into his back, clawing him to draw him closer, deeper. His strokes grew swift and hard, pounding against her inflamed flesh, making her senses sing even as her body cried for more, more. It felt so glorious she could not bear it, but could not bear for it to stop either.

Ian lowered his mouth to hers and took it in a searing kiss, plunging his tongue between her parted lips, emulating the thrusting dance of their bodies. How quickly it would end. No. He could not bear for it to be over so soon. Seizing her hips with one big hand, he stilled her swift bucking and slowed their pace, taking her in long, deliberate strokes—shivering, delicious strokes. She was so small, so tight, so wet, so hot. He tried not to think of anything but holding on, not for his own pleasure but for her ultimate release. This woman needed him as no other ever had, and he knew he could not disappoint her.

Chas felt the heat build to a roaring inferno, the sensation radiating from the core of her body outward to every inch of skin, every pore. The crisp hair of his chest abraded her aching breasts, caressing them every time he slid in and out. His hard, long legs twined with her slender soft ones, the rough texture a compliment to her own smoothness. His beard scraped her cheeks as his lips firmly brushed hers between fierce penetrating kisses. And for all the intensity of her pleasure, she hungered for something beyond it. What lay beyond infinity?

Chastity Kathleen O'Roarke found out. The subtle rippling contractions began slowly. Her nails dug into his back as her head thrashed from side to side on the pallet. "Please, harder, faster, more," she pleaded, her own voice so hoarse she could not recognize it. The contractions grew from that low, languid tremor into keen, penetrating spasms that ended with a starburst of such fiery bliss she literally came up off the bed, raising his larger body with her.

Ian felt her release begin, and it drove him instinctively to move according to her pleas, giving her more of what she needed, thrusting hard and swift as the sweat beaded on his face and his phallus swelled and spilled its seed in great waves of ecstasy.

His shuddering climax appeased her compulsive hunger in such a rush of satiation that it left her utterly limp and spent. "Sweet, so sweet," she murmured dreamily against the salty sweat of his throat.

Ian collapsed on top of her, never having given so much of himself to a woman in his mortal life. In fact, the act had been so fiercely intense he had feared for his mortal life in one or two flashes of cognizance during the coupling. Dazed, he rolled off her and gathered his scattered wits. The first thing he saw were the smears of blood between her thighs and on his staff.

"You were a bloody virgin." *Stupid thing to say.*

"Bloody does seem to be an appropriate word," Chas said as she rolled up, shakily trying to hide her nakedness from him with a corner of the sheet.

He felt himself color. "You attacked me like a tigress in heat," he said defensively as his eyes narrowed on her. She still looked a bit disoriented, and her pupils had been strangely dilated. "Did you take some sort of drug?" Then he remembered the way she had foisted the wine on him and he had refused the glass at first. "You intended for me to have it—one of those oriental aphrodisiacs." He thew back his head and roared with laughter.

Chas looked around her for a weapon, anything to bash the insensitive oaf's brains in—what little of them he possessed! The first thing that came to hand was a pillow shoved in the corner of the pallet. She smashed it at his head, sending feathers flying all over the room, then rolled from the bed and, seizing one of the tumblers from the table, hurled it through the down-filled air.

Ian ducked and it broke against the wall. He jumped up, but she had the second glass in hand, and it connected wickedly with his midsection, then bounced onto the pallet. "Will you calm down before we're both cut to bloody ribbons with broken glass?" he said, spitting feathers from his mouth as he spoke.

As he advanced on her, Chas seized the wine bottle by its neck and brandished it like a cudgel in front of her. "Stay away from me, Warfield."

She looked so ridiculously fierce, a slender naked woman with riotous red hair tumbling across her bare shoulders, emerald eyes blazing as she waved her pathetic weapon at him. He stopped a few feet in front of he and crossed his arms over his chest, looking down at her defiant little face.

"What the bloody hell's going on? You set out to drug and seduce me. You wanted me to take your virginity. Why? You're a widow—or are you?" A sudden light of comprehension washed over him. "Who are you, Chastity? Chastity! I'd bet my last pound sterling that's not your name."

"It most certainly is!" she replied, tightening her grip on the bottle. *Think fast, Chas.* But it was difficult since hers were the addled wits, not his. Nothing in this plan was going right. He was supposed to be only a means to help her marry his employer. The sexual interlude was supposed to mean nothing. Chas never

imagined it would be so fiercely sweet and wonderful.
And somehow she knew it was not the drug that had
made it so, but Ian himself. He was her drug. Now the
thought of marrying poor bumbling Lyle seemed even
more unappealing.

"Well, I'm waiting, Puss?" He felt the most irresistible urge to take her in his arms and hold her protectively. She looked so small and vulnerable, clutching
that ridiculous bottle.

"Well . . . my . . . my husband, saints rest his soul,"
she interjected piously, "he couldn't . . . that is he
never . . . well, you know. And I didn't want the man
I married to find out and think less of poor Ralph."

"Balderdash! I've heard he was a young, vigorous
man." His eyes narrowed. "You're pretty good at spinning tales, Puss. Just like the whopper you fed me at
Wharton's soiree. But I didn't believe you then and I
don't now."

She backed away a step. "That's your prerogative,
Mr. Warfield."

With a lightning-quick move he yanked the wine
bottle from her hand and threw it onto the pallet.
"What are you after? Lyle?" His eyes narrowed when
he saw a confused, guilty look flash across her face.
"You want a title, Puss? Is that it?" He shook her
shoulders roughly. "Any man will do—so long as he's
a baron? How would you like an earl?"

Chas snapped out of her bemused confusion when
his hands seized her, but his words cut to the quick. "I
might like an earl, yes," she spat defiantly, twisting
away from him and rushing to retrieve her robe from
where it had been tossed in the corner. It was still
damp as she struggled into it.

"You won't get so much as the baron when I tell him
how you came after me."

She pulled the silk wrapper protectively around herself, biting her lips not to plead with him. "You

wouldn't dare. Lyle would fire you. It would be your word against mine—a stable man's against a lady's."

"Some lady! Did you doubt your own charms so much you thought I'd need some extra inducement to betray the baron?" he asked nastily.

"Obviously you needed no help to betray Lyle." She turned from his harsh, condemning expression and walked past the tub, its water now cold as the passion they had shared.

Angrily, Ian stepped around the other side of it and grabbed her arm. "Not so fast, Puss."

"I told you not to call me that!" she said furiously, shoving at him with all her might. The back of his knees caught against the edge of the tub and he tumbled into it with a loud splash.

Chas fled into the rainy night, leaving behind the sounds of his angry curses and her good brown velvet cloak hanging on the peg outside his door.

Chapter Four

Chas had no sooner curled up on her bed when she fell into a deep, dreamless sleep. At dawn she awakened in the cool silence as faint, rosy fingers of light pulled away the shadows pooling in her sumptuous bedroom. Delilah lay snuggled against her side. Chas sat up, at first dazed and disoriented. The cat opened her eyes and blinked crossly at being so rudely disturbed. As the girl's eyes swept the room, she saw her white silk wrapper lying at the foot of her bed, wrinkled and smeared with faint traces of blood. Her blood!

She picked up the fluffy white cat and hugged her forlornly as the preceding night's debacle flooded back into her memory. Her plans had seemed so logical and practical on the train to Denver. Now, however, everything was turned upside down. Marrying a rich man who was kind and indulgent would mean security for her future and even more important—it would provide a safe life for her da. Shamus was getting older and his hands were not so quick, nor were his legs nimble enough to jump on passing trains fleeing the law. Sooner or later he'd be caught and face prison.

"I have to think of him, not myself. As if being married to someone like Lyle would be so awful," she whispered to Delilah. But Lyle's sweet, earnest face with its pale eyes and soft brown hair did not make her heart thrum with forbidden excitement. Only Ian's mocking smile and heavy-lidded gold eyes sent the sparks flying. Damn him. She did not—could not—want an impoverished menial! Who would take care of Shamus? On Ian's meager wages as a groom, he'd barely be able to provide for a wife.

"As if he'd ever ask me to marry him after last night." Her voice broke as she pushed the cat aside and slipped from the bed, only to feel the soreness between her legs. He had hurt her, but oh, what divine, unimaginable pleasure had come along with the pain. Pleasure a woman should experience on her wedding night—not when she threw herself like some demented creature in heat onto a man she stalked just to seduce and use. He had every reason to hate her.

Chas could still see the contempt in his eyes and hear the sarcasm in his voice when he discovered her deception and the stupid mistake with the drug. "He'll never forgive me." Desolately, she balled up the white silk wrapper and threw it in the waste basket, then walked over to the bellpull and summoned a maid. She needed a hot soak and time to think.

Her courage restored, Chas came downstairs several hours later, dressed smartly in her best chocolate brown crepe traveling suit. She headed toward the dining room, but before she reached it, Ian materialized from the servant's door at the opposite side of the hall and leaned indolently against the wall, blocking her path. In his hands he held her velvet cloak.

Smiling insolently, he held it out. "This is yours, I believe."

She snatched at it, but he held it just out of her reach. "Give it to me."

He eyed her suit. "You're dressed to travel. Turning tail and running out, Puss?" Why did she have to look so damnably delectable?

She struggled to remain calm. "It's time we returned to Denver. My father has business matters to attend."

He took a step closer. When she seized the cloak, he

reached out and lifted her chin, forcing her to look up into his eyes. "Are you all right?" *Idiot. She looks bloody beautiful!* "I was afraid I might've hurt you last night. After all, you did get rather ... carried away."

She blushed scarlet, wanting to vanish into the pattern of the Aubusson carpet beneath her feet. "Me?" she squealed indignantly. "You were the rutting stable man, pounding me with that great—oh!" She gasped in shock and her hands flew to her mouth as she looked around the deserted hall, horrified someone had overheard her most indecorous remark.

"If I recall—and, mind, I was the only one in full control of his faculties—you leaped upon me like Delilah upon a tit-mouse."

"You are no gentleman, Mr. Warfield." She would not let him see the tears of humiliation that burned her eyelids.

"That all depends on the definition of the term, Puss," he replied enigmatically.

Chas clutched the cloak like a shield before her, then turned and fled back up the stairs.

"Won't you reconsider, Chastity? I had hoped to take you for a shoot, and the Davidsons, who own the adjacent country place, were so hoping to meet you." Even as they climbed aboard the carriage, Lyle continued importuning Chastity. She set Delilah's travel cage on the seat beside her, its occupant bristling with outrage at being forced to endure the indignity of confinement.

"One thing ye'll learn about Chastity, me boyo. Once her mind is set on a course, the Lord 'n all his hosts'll not be swayin' her from it," Shamus said with a grin. He patted the agreeable young Sassenach on the back in consolation. Last night he'd won nearly a thousand from the baron and not so much as a blink of complaint out of him! "We'll see ye back in the city next week."

Lyle nodded. "Don't forget to mark your calendar for the opera. I have the use of Everett's private loge seats. I know you'll enjoy it," he said to Chas.

She forced a bright smile, trying not to look toward the corral where she knew Ian was putting one of their thoroughbreds through a workout. "I shall look forward to seeing you next week."

As the carriage pulled away, Lyle stood staring disconsolately after it. Ian waited until it vanished around the bend, then strolled up, casually observing the woebegone look on his young friend's face. "You look as if you were seventeen and had just been sent down from Sandhurst."

"That was you, not me," Lyle said distractedly.

Ian shrugged. "Yes, but I didn't give a damn and you would have." He studied the baron's face. "Lyle, er, you aren't getting serious about the widow, are you?"

"Why ever not? She's a wealthy heiress, good bloodlines and all that. Even if she isn't British nobility, I'm quite certain my family will approve."

Ian rocked back on his heels. "Will approve? You sound as if you're going to marry the chit."

Lyle's chin shot out pugnaciously. "I might—that is, if the lady would have me. I . . . I haven't asked for her hand yet."

"Bloody hell. You *are* serious! But you've only known her for a couple of weeks. And don't be so certain about how your mother would take to having an American daughter-in-law. She's had you in matched harness with Emily Veryan since you were in leading strings."

"Well, I am no longer in leading strings," the baron replied indignantly. "I think I shall press my suit.

Chastity is so high-spirited, so wildly free . . . so, so American."

Remembering Chas last night, leaping on him like a pouncing puma, Ian's face colored. "Yes, she's high-spirited right enough." He paused a beat. "I think she's just after your title."

"Stuff! Her father would much rather she marry an American than a British peer. He told me so."

Ian snorted in disgust. "There are some things about the two of them that worry me, Lyle."

Lyle turned his attention to Ian, noting the uncharacteristic nervousness in his normally unflappable friend. "What things?"

She was a married virgin! But I took care of that little inconvenience for you! He cursed silently. "She does seem to fabricate some rather strange tales—such as the one the night we met her at Wharton's. And her father is a bit peculiar, don't you think? Seems more like some circus peddler than a banker."

"Shamus is a rogue, but a likable one. He cheats at cards, but so does the Duke of Cumberland and no one holds the eccentricity against him." Lyle's eyes narrowed on Ian, and a surprised look flashed across his face. "Say, my womanizing friend, the incorrigible rake who's always sworn to hold no *tendresse* for any female, you haven't gone and fallen in love with Chastity?"

"Don't be ridiculous. Of course not. And I don't think you have either. You're too young to be married."

"As your mama, the dowager countess, persists in reminding you, you're too old to be single," Lyle remonstrated smugly.

While the two friends argued, Chas and Shamus rode farther away from the chalet. In spite of the beautiful summer day, she looked crestfallen. Her father studied her with troubled eyes. "Ye don't seem very happy even though the baron's coming right along. Nice young fellow, even with him bein' Sassenach."

Chas fiddled with the clasp on her reticule. "Lyle is a sweet young man . . ."

"But?" he prompted. When she did not answer, he answered for her. "Ye don't love him."

"I never began this project with the intention of falling in love—just finding a rich husband."

"Aw, Chassie, colleen, it's no good. Don't ye see? I know ye're doin' this as much fer me as fer yerself." When she started to protest, he put up his hand to forestall her. "Don't be denyin' it. 'Tis as plain as the nose on me face. If ye really wanted to go through with yer plan, ye'd have told the baron the truth about yer past—and if he was the right man fer ye, he'd not have given a fig for it. Instead, ye pack up and fly off, skittish as Delilah when that hound of Ian Warfield's was chasin' her."

At the mention of Ian's name, her cheeks flooded with color, but before she could frame a reply, a shot rang out, and three riders with their faces hidden by red bandannas rode in front of the carriage, blocking its passage.

"Thet first shot wuz only a warnin'," one said to the driver, who had been eyeing the rifle lying alongside him on the seat.

While two of the men covered the driver and took his gun away, the third rode up to the side of the carriage. Bushy eyebrows hid his narrowed, colorless eyes as he studied Shamus and Chas. "Yew must be the one—thet rich as sin eastern society lady—Miz Manchester."

Chas studied the outlaw with dread. "Who are you and what do you want? I have some jewelry in my trunk, and my father has some money with him," she added quickly. The man's cold eyes and scarred face

looked ominous above the concealment of the ban-
danna.

"We ain't interested in a few puny trinkets er small
change. Yew got lots more back in Denver. We been
studyin' up on yew ever sinc't yew got to town. Figger
yer paw here, he'd be real glad to fetch us a ransom—
whut with yew bein' his only daughter 'n all," the second bandit chimed in as he held his gun on the driver.

Shamus's face paled. "Ransom? But, but . . . I don't
have . . ."

"What my father means is, his money's all back in
Ireland. It would take months—"

"Cut the malarkey, lady. We ain't no fools. Yew kin
git money sent from banks back east. All yew gotta do
is sign yer John Henry," Beetle Brows said with an
ugly laugh.

As he talked, the third man yanked the driver from
his seat, then climbed up onto the carriage. "I'm ready,
Zeb."

"I tole yew not ta use our names, yew ijit!" the
leader said furiously. "Git down, ole man," he commanded Shamus. "I reckon yer driver here can walk
back to thet fancy huntin' lodge in a couple o' hours.
Meanwhile, yew kin take the extry horse 'n ride fer
Denver. If ya wanna see yer gal here agin, don't tell
nobody nothin'. Jist bring a hunert thousand in cash ta
the ole Jig Saw Mine. It's about ten miles east—up thet
trail." He waved to a narrow road dissecting the main
one.

"An don't try nothin' funny. Them mine shafts is
like honeycombs. Yew come with the law 'n' yew'll
never find us—or yer purty li'l redhead here," the second man added as Zeb yanked Shamus from the carriage.

"No! Ye can't do this!" Shamus protested. "I . . . I'll
go with ye. Let me daughter bring the ransom. She has
me power of attorney," he added desperately, but it was

no use. In a flurry of dust the carriage vanished up the cutoff trail, leaving Shamus and the driver with one horse between them.

"What do you want to do, sir?" the driver asked.

"It'll damn certain do me no good to ride to Denver. I'll be needin' the horse, boyo," Shamus said as he swung up on it and rode hard back to Hornsby's chalet, praying Lyle Dorchester was as fond of Chas as he seemed to be—and as rich!

"A ransom? Three armed ruffians!" Lyle paled as Shamus's tale unfolded. By the time the old man had explained that Chas was not the Manchester heiress, and the only cash he could raise was a paltry few thousand left in a Denver hotel safe, the baron sank onto the steps in front of the chalet in shock.

"You mean those men will harm Chastity if you don't come up with one hundred thousand by tomorrow?"

"I know it's a lot of money, yer lordship, but Chas is me only child . . . and I was hopin'—"

"The money's no problem. I can raise it easily," Lyle said, brushing aside Shamus's pleas. "If one hair on Chastity's head is touched, I'll kill those blighters!" Then he turned to Shamus with a startled expression on his face and asked, "I say, old fellow, her name really *is* Chastity, isn't it?"

With Shamus's assurance, the baron headed to the corral to have their fastest racer saddled for the ride to Denver.

Ian had observed the tail end of the exchange between Lyle and that crafty old Irishman. When his friend approached the stable, he intercepted him. "What the devil is Shamus doing back here and whose horse was he riding?"

"Chastity's been kidnapped by three outlaws.

They're holding her for ransom. I'm going to Denver to get the money!"

Ian felt as if he'd been kicked in the gut. "Hold on—explain a bit more." The thought of his Chas being pawed by any of the crude-looking men he'd encountered in his travels west made his blood run cold. "Who are these men? Where have they taken her?"

As Lyle's disjointed story poured out, an ugly suspicion began to form in Ian's mind. "So, let me get this straight—you're pulling a hundred thousand out of *your* account for this ransom? The fabled Manchester millions don't exist?"

"Oh, they exist right enough—back in Ireland or wherever it is the real widow and her father are currently living."

A harsh, cynical expression flashed in Ian's eyes. "This could all be nothing but another deception."

"Are you saying you'd be willing to risk Chastity's life on that?" Lyle asked incredulously.

Ian sighed and ran his fingers through his hair, cursing. "No. You ride to Denver for the money, but I'm going to those mine shafts. If she had that wretched cat with her, Samson can find her."

"I don't know," Lyle said uneasily.

"They might harm her even if we do pay them. Kidnappers are rarely a trustworthy lot." *Neither is a deceitful woman trying to trap a rich fool into marriage.*

Within two hours Ian had located the mine shafts with the help of Woo Chen, Hornsby's Chinese cook, who had been employed by the Jig Saw Mine when it was operational. Ian was armed to the teeth with one of Hornsby's Winchesters and a Colt Peacemaker, as well as a detailed map drawn by the little Chinaman, of the intersecting shafts deep inside the mine. Now if only Samson could quietly sniff out Chastity and her cat.

"I wager ten to five I find her playing cards with her *kidnappers,* waiting to collect a fortune," he said cynically to the sheep dog, but the doleful look in Samson's eyes reflected a deep gut instinct he felt as well. What if she were really in danger? According to Chen's map, there was an outside ventilation tunnel leading to the lower levels; it should be hidden somewhere in the clumps of chokecherry bushes up ahead. He headed in that direction with Samson trotting quietly behind.

Inside the mine Chas stared at her captor as he sat devouring his lunch of smoked trout. Delilah meowed plaintively from her cage. All three of the lummoxes who had kidnapped her appeared to be brothers, possessing the same kinky reddish hair, coarse features, and dim wits.

It was distressing that once they had gotten clear of Shamus and the driver, they had removed their bandannas. Chas had a terrifying intuition that they did not plan to release her, even in the unlikely event her da could raise the ransom. Zeb was the eldest and a fraction smarter than his younger siblings. He stood guard at the top of the shaft, on lookout for any trespassers such as lawmen, leaving one brother to guard her and the other wandering about, God knew where, in the labyrinth of tunnels.

"I could sure use a bite of food," she said in a soft voice, hoping to elicit some sympathy—and draw him nearer. She was untied, apparently considered too weak and stupid to attempt escape. The rock clutched in one hand, concealed in her skirts, would prove otherwise if she could only get close enough to use it. Finding a way out of the tunnels was quite another matter, but Chas would deal with that when the time came. The dumb brute apparently had no pity, for he only grunted and continued eating. "Or just a sip of water from your canteen. Please." Delilah let out a thin wail at the same time, which probably accounted for his acquiescence.

"Durn fool females is always whinin'," he groused, picking up his canteen and shambling across the shaft to where she sat, daintily perched on a crate. When he shoved the canteen at her, she drew back with a small pouty moue that had charmed dozens of marks.

"Could you . . . would you please wipe the edge, I'm terribly delicate you understand, but . . ." She fluttered her lashes.

He grunted again and wiped the neck of the canteen across his greasy sleeve, then shoved it into her hands. "Here. Thet's good enough."

Chas let the heavy metal slip through her fingers and bounce onto the floor. When he cursed and stooped over to pick it up, she raised the rock and knocked him squarely on the back of his skull. He pitched headfirst into her lap, out cold. She rolled him off her and quickly searched him for weapons. Pulling a rusty Colt .45 from his belt, she stuck it in her pocket, then took the kerosene lantern from the wall in one hand, secured Delilah's carrier in the other, and set out.

"We're free, but we're sure not in the clear," she murmured low to the cat as she tried to retrace the myriad twists and turns they had made after getting off the rope bucket that had lowered them from the surface. Zeb waited at the top. No chance of escape in that direction. "There must be other ways out. Mines always have more than one entrance . . . or at least I think they do . . . I hope they do."

Once she moved away from the main shaft, the lantern gave off only a dim flicker and she had to grope her way along. The possibility of wandering blindly in the tunnels until they both starved to death was a grim thought Chas refused to consider. Then she heard a noise, somewhere below her. Heavy breathing. It was probably that awful third brother. He might be guarding a second exit. She set down Delilah's carrier and the lantern, and crouched at the edge of a steep drop off, obviously an open shaft that intersected hers.

The noise of breathing drew closer. Chas leaned out, clutching the old .45, wishing desperately for her small Zig Zag derringer, a weapon she was a good deal more proficient at handling. Without warning, the dirt and stones at the lip of the tunnel's floor began to give way and a big chunk broke loose under her weight. Chas hurtled downward with a small avalanche of rocks and landed squarely on top of a sturdy male body, knocking them both to the floor. Delilah's cage was caught in the same fall and bounced down, landing upside down at Chas's feet. The cat blinked indignantly, but remained silent.

Ian shook his head, trying to clear away the stars that danced in whirling circles behind his eyes. All the air had been driven from his lungs. The last time he'd felt this way was when— "You!" he choked out incredulously.

"Ian, what are you doing here?" The mystery of the panting she had heard was quickly solved as Samson planted a sloppy kiss across her face, then moved over to elicit a sharp hiss from Delilah when his nose pressed too closely to the bars of her carrier. He withdrew with a yelp and a bloodied muzzle.

By this time Ian had regained his wind and struggled to one knee, looking down at her, sprawled with bare legs on the ground. "Do you make a habit of dropping in unexpectedly? Or do you save that treat especially for me?" He reached down and hauled her to her feet.

"Quiet!" she hissed. "I coshed one of them over the head to escape, but Zeb is at the entrance, and the third one is around her somewhere."

"Oh, he's around somewhere real close, leetle lady," a raspy voice said with an ugly chuckle. "Drop yer guns."

Samson began to growl low in his throat, but Ian restrained him with one hand while tossing his Peacemaker and Winchester away. One look at the .10-gauge shotgun aimed at them convinced him they had no chance. "Easy boy." He turned the dog with a simple hand command, then yelled, "Go, Samson." The dog vanished into the darkness of the tunnel he had just traversed.

The outlaw turned the shotgun for an instant, then decided it was more prudent to keep the big Englishman covered than to waste a shot on the fleeing mutt. "Jist move thet way, both of yew."

"My cat. Let me get her. She might be hurt," Chas said, scooping up the carrier and clutching it to her.

They were returned to where she had escaped. A very irate outlaw sat rubbing his head in the dim light cast by the stub of a candle.

"Go git thet lantern. It's by the south entrance of the upper shaft where she left it," their captor commanded his brother.

"Aw, Lev, I got me a fierce pain in my haid—"

"Yew let a puny female git the better of yew, Nev. Serves yew right! Besides, gittin' hit in yer haid wouldn't hurt yew none noways." He glared at his brother until Nev shambled off to retrieve the missing lantern.

In minutes Zeb had been summoned from his post above, and the trio held a debate over what to do about the newest development.

"I say we do 'em both now 'n' pound leather outa heer," Nev averred, with a sidelong glare at Chas, as he rubbed his head.

"Naw. I think he's alone," Lev replied, avarice gleaming in his pale eyes.

"I ain't planned on this fer weeks ta let a fancy pants limey and a spoiled rich gal git the better o' me. We stay 'n' wait. Her pa'll brang the cash once't he sees this feller ain't comin' out with her." Zeb turned to the two captives, now seated on the rocky floor beside De-lilah's carrier.

"Whut about the dawg?" Nev asked.

"Whut about it? It run off. If'n it comes back, shoot it," Zeb said impatiently. "Now, tie them two up good. I don't figure on playin' any more hide 'n' seek in them mine shafts. We worked 'em enough years ta be quit o' 'em fer good."

The two younger brothers trussed up Ian and Chas under Zeb's watchful eye. Then all three outlaws went to separate entrances where they could watch all possible approaches to the mine just in case of a trap.

After they left, Ian and Chas huddled in the flickering light of Lev's stubby candle.

"They plan to kill us when this is over, don't they?" Chas held her voice steady.

"I imagine," Ian replied distractedly, searching the bare mine shaft for some implement with which to escape.

"Ian, why did you come after me?"

"Not now, Chastity. That is your name, isn't it?" He added dryly, "Not that it suits you at all."

"It's Chastity Kathleen O'Roarke, and it certainly did suit me until last night," she replied huffily.

He snorted in derision. "You were the one who came equipped with the aphrodisiac, not me, Puss."

"Don't call me—oh, why not? Call me anything you want. I've been a fool. All I wanted was some security for Da and me."

"And a titled Englishman could provide that. What was Lyle supposed to do—whisk you across the Atlantic one step ahead of the law?"

"How do you know we'er wanted by the law?"

"Shamus was rather in a panic when he returned. He confessed the whole bloody masquerade. I surmised the rest," Ian replied, remembering somewhat guiltily that he had believed her in on the kidnapping. He saw a piece of shale lying a few feet away, rolled over to it, and began to saw awkwardly on the cord binding his hands. It would take hours, but he persisted.

Chas surprised herself by blurting out, "I never wanted a title!"

"But you *did* want a rich husband." He raised one golden eyebrow sardonically as he continued to work on the ropes.

"I did." She lowered her lashes, then swallowed and said softly, "Do you want to know a secret, Ian?"

He stopped his struggle for a moment and looked at her. Even in torn clothes with her hair tangled around her face and dirt smudging her nose, she was the most desirable woman he'd ever seen. "What secret, Puss?"

His voice was low and husky, like rich warm molasses. Chas felt the heat steal into her cheeks. She wet her lips with the tip of her tongue and studied the way his broad shoulders flexed as he worked against his bonds. Well, if they were going to die here, she might as well tell him. Courage failed her as she stared at his beautiful golden countenance. *A fallen angel.* He would mock her.

"Well, Puss? I'm waiting." *I'll have a least one kiss before we're done,* he thought. "Did you know you have the most delectable little mouth?" he whispered.

Her head snapped up and she stared at him. He was still sawing ineffectually at his bonds as he watched her. "Mouth! That's it," she said suddenly.

Ian looked at her as if her mind had snapped. "Stay calm, Puss."

"Puss—Delilah—it's her mouth. Oh, never mind, just let me try something." Chas rolled over to where the remains of Nev's lunch lay on the floor. She grabbed the last chunk of greasy fish and then rolled back to Ian. "Turn around and let me rub this on those ropes. Delilah will eat anything fish flavored."

He cocked one eyebrow in disbelief, then shrugged.

At the rate he was progressing, anything was worth a try. He scooted back to back with her and let her grease up the ropes. Then he rolled over to Delilah's carrier and stuck his hands against the opening.

"Watch out—she may—"

"Ouch!" A string of curses followed.

"Bite," Chas finished her warning.

Gritting his teeth, Ian again shoved the ropes against the carrier, trying to hold his hand as far away as he could from the cat's sharp incisors. "She's worse than a bloody vampire. I'll probably get both wrists slashed and bleed to death."

Delilah, starved and having smelled the fish from her confinement all this time, quickly chewed away until Ian was able to rip the frayed hemp apart. "Good girl, Delilah," he crooned as he tackled the ropes on his feet, then knelt and began to work on Chas's bonds. As he pulled her to her feet, she stumbled against him.

"My legs are sort of numb," she apologized.

His arm held her tightly, and he smelled the oddly endearing combination of lilacs and smoked trout. "What was that secret you were about to divulge, hmm, Puss?"

Her heart slammed in her chest as she looked up into his eyes. "I . . . I don't care that you're not rich, Ian . . . After last night I realized I couldn't go through with my plan. Lyle is ever so sweet, but I can't marry him. I don't love him . . ."

He lifted her chin with one fishy finger and grinned down at her flushed, lovely face. "We'll take this up later, Puss, after we're out of here."

Chas threw her arms around his neck before he could release her. "Just in case we don't get out of here." She reached up and kissed him hard on the lips, then whispered, "I love you, Ian, and I wouldn't mind living in a stable with you—as long as we could take my Da along with us." She looked at him hopefully.

Ian cursed as he lowered his mouth to hers, unable to stop himself.

Delilah, having tasted just enough of the trout to whet her appetite, grew restive and began to trill a protest as her sharp claws fastened on the wooden bars of her carrier. Her humans were ignoring her! She shook the carrier door, which had been damaged in her earlier tumble, and succeeded in snapping open the latch. Silently, she slithered out and darted over to where the last fragments of fish were scattered and began to devour them.

Ian forced himself to pull Chastity gently away, holding her at arm's length. "Those barbarian brothers may be back any second. We have to get out of here." Just then a shot echoed from above, followed by several more. "Quick, I know a back way into this hole." He clutched her hand and reached for the candle.

"Delilah!" Chas saw a fluffy white plume vanish around the corner and darted after it. "No girl, come here." She turned frantically to Ian. "We can't leave her! She helped free us."

Muttering curses, he took after the two females as the firing from above stopped.

"It probably warn't nothin' but a mule deer, yew jackass," Zeb's angry voice yelled out. "Save yer lead. No good if'n yew shot thet rich old galoot afore he gits the money anyways."

Ian rounded a turn in the tunnel and heard Chas's gasp just ahead. Before he could stop himself, he collided with her. They stood frozen, facing Lev, who grinned nastily. He was holding Delilah with one huge hamlike hand by the scruff of her neck, choking her. "Jist slow down 'n raise yer hands real easy 'er I'll snap it's scrawny back." His other hand held a gun leveled at Chas and Ian.

Just as Lev took a step forward, Delilah wriggled one hind foot loose and raked his arm with her claws.

The outlaw cursed and raised her up, preparing to fling her hard against the stone wall, but before he could do so, a blurry streak of gray pounced at him from behind, knocking him to the ground with a loud whump. Delilah jumped away in midfall with a loud hissing screech and danced sideways, bowing up at the dog, who paid her no attention now that he was engaged in a wrestling match with Lev. Samson growled fiercely as he bit into Lev's right arm, instantly disarming the outlaw and splintering bone.

"Good boy, Samson!" Ian quickly moved to retrieve the gun from where it had landed across the tunnel, but before he could do so, the other two outlaws materialized from behind him.

"Whut the hell's goin' on?" Nev said as he saw their prisoners free and some immense woolly, bearlike creature with fangs devouring his brother.

"Shoot, yew ijit!" Zeb commanded Nev.

Ian threw himself against Zeb just as the outlaw leader cocked his pistol. The earl knocked the gun aside, and the two men fell to the floor. Meanwhile, Nev was still gaping, trying to decide if he should aim at the leaping Ian or at the whirling ball composed of his brother and the mountain of fur.

Chas gave him no time to make the decision. She seized a piece of rotted timber lying against the wall and whacked him squarely across his face, knocking him to the ground where he landed on the seat of his pants, then toppled backward, out cold.

Ian rained a series of short, powerful punches to Zeb's nose and jaw, quickly bludgeoning him unconscious.

Samson was by now sitting on top of the squirming Lev, who lay whimpering curses while his captor seemed to beam for approval from his master.

Delilah ignored the whole unsightly fracas and began to groom herself with swift, furious licks to her snowy coat. That crude oaf had dared to muss her with his dirty paws!

"Ian, thank God!" Chas threw down her cudgel and ran over to him as he climbed off Zeb after retrieving the outlaw's gun and sticking it in his belt.

Ian gathered her up in his arms and kissed her lustily. "You're a handy female to have around in a crisis, Puss." He looked over at the preening cat. "Both of you."

"Oh, Ian, we've done it! We're free." Then she noticed the heated look in his eyes, and her cheeks flamed as she recalled her earlier declaration of love. "You said we'd talk after the danger was over. Well . . ." she prompted hopefully.

"I seem to recall something about your not wanting a title or a rich husband—only a humble groom—if he'll agree to be saddled with your rascally father in the bargain." His eyes were dancing as he pulled her up for another long, breathless kiss. "Will you marry me, Puss? Even if it means living in a stable?"

Her green eyes sparkled like emeralds. "Even if it means living in a mine shaft—anywhere! I just want to be with you, Ian."

His expression changed from one of delight to devilish amusement. "Puss, there is one thing I should tell you. I don't think you and Shamus will have to live in a mine shaft or a stable—"

"Colleen, Ian are ye all right?" Shamus's voice echoed down the tunnel before he came into view. Then he rounded the turn, and his eyes nearly popped from his head. "Well, saints preserve us, what have we here?" His bushy brows raised, he whistled low, taking in two unconscious outlaws, and the third flattened beneath Samson. Then he saw Ian holding Chas in his arms.

"Everything's under control, Shamus."

"And it's that glad I am, yer lordship. When the

baron explained about ye after ye went ridin' off, I got ta worryin' ye'd only get in more trouble. Real upset he was, yer young friend, thinkin' about havin' to explain yer demise ta the dowager countess 'n' all."

Chas stared at her father as he rambled on, until finally the words began to sink in. "Your lordship? Dowager countess? Have you gone daft, Da?"

Then she turned to Ian and really looked at him, her beautifully handsome, arrogant, sophisticated, witty, educated *stable man*. The truth dawned on her. "You! You were playing games all along, weren't you? Masquerading as a common menial while all the time you were laughing at us rude colonials, weren't you?" She jabbed a finger into his chest as she advanced and he retreated.

"Now, Puss. I was trying to tell you when your father—"

"And all this time I was so worried about Da, what would become of him with my marrying a poor working man—and a Sassenach at that!" She poked him again, her eyes shooting green fire.

"I love you, Puss, and I think you shall make a splendid countess."

"Oh, you do, do you? And why should I marry a man who'd keep a secret of his identity from the woman he says he loves?" She took another step forward, poking him again.

Ian took another step backward, fighting down the laughter at her spitting fury. "You kept a few secrets as well, as I seem to recall, Puss." He reached out for the furious woman just as the back of his knees connected with a cross timber wedged between the floor and the wall. They went down in a tumbling heap. Chas landed on top of him, pressed tightly to his chest, which rumbled with laughter now.

"I've certainly fallen for you enough times, Chas. How can you doubt my love?"

She looked into that beautiful fallen angel's face, and her anger was spent. An answering chuckle, rich and joyous, bubbled up inside her. "Oh, my darling, I could spend the rest of my life on top of you!"

Ian chuckled, "Ah, Puss, you haven't the foggiest what you just said—but you soon will."

As their lips met and the world receded, Shamus calmly covered the two reviving outlaws with his guns. Samson herded the third kidnapper over to where the old man patiently waited. Then the dog eyed Delilah, cocking his head speculatively.

"Don't even think it, boyo," Shamus said to Samson. "The females always come out on top, don't ye know?"

Keeping the Fire Hot

by

Patricia Rice

Colorado, 1882

Dawson Smith smiled down at the flirtatious piece of fluff and lace on his arm. Gloria Jean had the smile of an angel. Her perfumed scent reminded him of the magnolias back home. She was as slim and curvaceous as the women of his midnight dreams. He didn't know if she could cook or keep house, and he really didn't care. He just wanted a sweet-smelling woman in silks and satins in his bed, and he wanted her now.

But he couldn't have her. Gloria Jean was an innocent meant for some man to marry, and Dawson Smith had no intention of being that man. He chuckled at some comment made in her lilting voice. Amusement crinkled the corners of his dark eyes and curved the lines of his narrow lips. Gloria fluttered her lashes and hid behind her fan, certain he was smitten. Dawson knew what she was thinking and didn't discourage her.

"You will be at the cakewalk Saturday, won't you, Mr. Smith?" she asked coyly, casting a shy glance at his marvelous cleft jaw.

"Wouldn't miss it for the world, Miss Gloria. Will you have an entry?" Lost in the teasing flutter of her baby blue eyes, Dawson wasn't paying much attention to where he was going. He was busy imagining the lovely white skin beneath all that feminine frippery and deciding which of the girls at the saloon he would use to work off his lather.

Lost in his imagination, he nearly tripped and fell over a small urchin sitting cross-legged on the boardwalk, whittling at a piece of wood.

The urchin's bedraggled and filthy felt hat fell into the dusty street. The small figure leaned over and fished the hat from the dirt, slapping it back atop a tumbled nest of cinnamon-brown curls. Without rancor, the child drawled, "Watch it, Dawson. The drool is goin' to stain your fancy coat," then went back to whittling.

Dawson grabbed the hat, beat it against a porch post to knock off the dust, then pulled it down over the youth's head. "Jamie, you need a bath. Why don't you go jump in the river?"

The youth snorted and glanced from beneath the hat brim at the vision in lavender silk clinging to the arm of the elegantly dressed saloon keeper. Dawson was nearly as grand as his lady in a gold silk waistcoat that contrasted nicely with a tailored buff coat and tight trousers. He was the best-dressed man in all of Altona, Colorado. Although, since most of the rest were miners, that wasn't saying much.

"We'll go skinny-dipping together sometime," the youth promised with a sneer.

Dawson laughed. "We'll do that. Why don't you get yourself over to Davidson's? He's got a load of inventory in and could probably use a hand."

The youth didn't even lift his hat in farewell as he climbed from the boardwalk and ambled down the dirt street toward the mercantile. Gloria Jean just shook her head and fluttered her fan.

"I swear, Mr. Smith, I don't know what this town's coming to. A child like that ought to be in school, learning to mind his manners. What kind of parents let their children lie about the streets all day? And in such clothes! Perhaps we ought to take up a collection."

Dawson was already heading in the opposite direction from the urchin. "Jamie is past teaching. And if you took up a collection, Mulligan would only drink it up. Why don't you tell me more about that cakewalk I mean to win on Saturday?"

After Dawson left the glorious Gloria at her home some time later, he wended his way back toward his gambling saloon, whistling to himself. Maybe he ought to buy Lulu a lavender confection like the one Gloria had worn, and then he could have the pleasure of removing it, one frothy layer at a time.

At the image of the flame-haired saloon girl discarding the ladylike costume, he grinned. She'd rebel at the laces and lift her skirt, and the only layer he'd find beneath would be the dark bush between her legs. That was why Gloria was a lady and Lulu was a whore.

Dawson refused to reminisce on what he'd once had and thrown away. Home was a million miles away, and the lovely Southern belles that inhabited it were as forbidden as Gloria Jean. When life had handed him lemons, he'd made spiked lemonade out of it. He wasn't going to complain.

Seeing Jamie lifting a bag of grain bigger than he was, Dawson set out across the street to give the kid a hand. Now *there* was one who had a right to complain. His mother dead, himself cursed with a drunken lout for a father and bullies for brothers, Jamie stoically worked his way through every odd job in town in return for meals and whatever anyone wanted to give him. Dawson couldn't conceive of complaining about his own lot when faced with Jamie's. At least Dawson had grown up in the loving comfort of family and home. It had been his own damned fault that he'd lost it.

He lifted the grain bag from Jamie's shoulders and

proceeded, whistling, into the mercantile. The kid grabbed a couple of bolts of cloth and raced after him.

The shopkeeper said nothing as the wealthiest man in town dumped a sack of grain at his feet like any common laborer. After all, Dawson Smith wasn't any more than a saloon keeper, despite his fancy ways. Jamie added the cloth to the table with the others, then ambled back out for the next load. Dawson tipped his hat and grinned at the frowning mercantile owner, then followed the youth out.

"Watch out for Larkin," Jamie whispered as Dawson bent to pick up the last sack of grain.

As if looking for a better grip, Dawson put the sack down while Jamie hoisted more cloth in his arms. "Larkin? Big dude in green shirt?"

"Yeah. Heard him bragging about his dice. He'll take you for a roll if you let him." Lifting the bolts, Jamie ambled back up the stairs as if not a word had been exchanged.

Dawson followed, carrying the grain. Jamie would never admit he couldn't carry the grain himself, nor would he thank Dawson outright for helping, but he always repaid a favor in kind. Thinking of the money the big man named Larkin had been winning at the tables on the previous night, Dawson thought the favor had been more than repaid. He flipped Jamie a coin as he sauntered from the mercantile and headed back toward the saloon.

Jamie hastily stashed the coin in her vest pocket, grimacing as her fingers brushed her sensitive breasts. They were bound so tightly she could barely breathe, and the binding itched, but she was accustomed to the discomfort. It was better than the alternative.

The coin in her pocket was more than Old Man Davidson would probably pay, she thought as she finished her assigned task. He usually gave her the tail ends of cheap muslin from old bolts as payment, but she knew she could take the scraps over to the dress-maker's and get a few coins in return. That would be enough to buy some potatoes and beans to put on the table tonight. Dawson's coin would buy a little extra.

As long as she kept food on the table, her father wouldn't complain about the space Jamie took up in the hovel she called home. He hadn't been in a state to do much complaining for a long time, but she still lived in dread of being thrown from the only home she had ever known. She could scarcely remember her mother, or those times when her father had threatened to throw them both out for being useless, but the threats lingered somewhere in her subconscious, and were the driving force of her existence.

She wasn't a man. She couldn't work the mines. Instead of growing to be big and strapping like her father and brothers, she was even scrawnier than her mother. She wished wistfully that she knew things—feminine things like embroidery and sewing that might bring in an extra coin, but her mother had died before she could teach her. Not that there had ever been much in the way of needles and thread in the Mulligan household. Any way you looked at it, Jamie Mulligan was pretty much a waste.

But as long as she could bring home food and cook a meal, no one complained about her. After selling the muslin—and surprisingly, a nice piece of gingham—to the dressmaker, Jamie bought the potatoes and dried beans, and a scoop of coffee. Maybe she could sober her father up enough in the morning so he could go into the mines without staggering.

She didn't think of her life as a particularly harsh one. It was the only one she knew. She had a roof over her head, and had made a nice pallet for herself in the kitchen. Her father and brothers slept in the front room, when they were home. The only clothes she'd ever known were the hand-me-downs from her brothers, but they suited her purpose. By now, everyone in Altona who might ever have known she was a girl had forgotten or had moved away. She was just another one of the Mulligan boys to all who saw her.

Except Dawson. Dawson was a puzzle, and that's a fact. Finding herself whistling the tune the saloon keeper had been whistling earlier, Jamie slipped into the kitchen and put on a pot of water to boil. The old pot-bellied stove had overheated one too many times and would probably burst apart at the seams one of these days, but Jamie was careful with the wood. The door hinge was loose anyway, so she couldn't build up too much of a fire without sparks leaping out.

Her thoughts drifted back to Dawson. She had a distinct memory of the day Dawson Smith had come to town. She'd been only thirteen. Her mother had been dead for over three years. She'd been wearing Frank's dungarees and an old flannel shirt ten sizes too big for her when she'd walked into the doctor's office out of curiosity and seen Dawson sitting behind the desk. He couldn't have been more than twenty-three or -four, and he'd been wearing a slick mustache to make himself look older.

She'd introduced herself, and he'd said "Jamaica Mulligan," and slapped a thin file folder onto the desk. It had been the first time since her mother died that she had been called Jamaica. She'd never been called it since.

Peeling the potatoes, Jamie dropped them into the boiling water. Dr. Dawson Smith had learned the hard way that a mining town like Altona had no patience with educated folk, and certainly no money for doctors. He'd also learned to call her Jamie and treat her like a boy as everyone else did. He'd had enough sense to figure that out all by himself. A town filled with drunken miners and cowboys on a Saturday night wasn't the kind of place for a thirteen-year-old girl with no protection.

Now, after seven years, Dawson had apparently forgotten her sex as well as everyone else had, just as he'd forgotten his chosen profession. A place like this did that to a person. Strangers came to town and either learned to shed their Eastern ways and become part of the hard-working, hard-drinking crowd, or died trying. Dawson, at least, had found a way to maintain his civilized demeanor even while running one of the biggest, rowdiest, most expensive gambling establishments this side of the Rockies.

Now that money was starting to flow out of the mines with some degree of regularity, the town was becoming a little more civilized. In the years since Dawson had arrived, it had grown from a boom town of wooden shacks to a small city with substantial buildings and plate-glass windows. The merchants arriving now had wives and daughters who wore silks and satins instead of the rough cottons and wools of the first arrivals. None of them remembered the wife of an engineer who arrived just in time to bury her husband after a mine explosion. Nor did they remember Red Mulligan when he had been the burly foreman of that same mine. They only saw the drunk staggering down the street, gossiped about the son who had robbed the train a while back, clucked their tongues, and forgot about him. And his family.

The engineer's widow had been Jamie's mother. There wasn't much a delicate woman could do out here but marry, and she'd chosen Mulligan—for what reason, Jamie could not guess. He'd already had three strong boys by his first wife and needed a mother for them. But why he had picked a woman who was half his size and not strong enough for his kind of life was also beyond Jamie's comprehension. She supposed she ought to be grateful that they'd found each other or she would never have existed, but it made her wonder about the oddities of human nature.

She tested the hunk of bacon in the beans simmering on the back burner, threw in a handful of salt, and called it a meal. Dad and Frank would be home from the mine soon. She filled her plate, ate the contents hastily, and slipped out the door just as the whistle blew. Her father and brother could eat what she left on the stove. She didn't need to hang around to see if they consumed more food than liquor tonight.

The only time Jamie ever found herself wishing for new clothes was when she passed the open door to Dawson's saloon and saw all the fancy men and ladies at the tables with heaps of greenbacks lying in front of them. It wasn't the ladies' clothes she coveted. She hadn't grown up on the streets of Altona and learned nothing. The women at those tables weren't "ladies." They didn't earn their way at the gambling tables, but in the rooms upstairs. Jamie wasn't entirely certain what went on in those rooms, but she had a fairly reasonable imagination and had grown up in a household of men. She didn't want to know any more than that.

No, it was the men's clothing that drew her eye. If she could just disguise herself as a gentleman instead of an urchin, she could sit at those tables and make more money in one night than she did now in a month.

She slipped down the alley beside the saloon. She had found a top hat out here once, but Frank had found her hiding place and amused himself one night throwing cards into it. The cards hadn't hurt it much, but once he'd emptied his stomach into it after drinking an entire bottle of rotgut, the hat had never been the same. That had been the extent of the gentlemanly attire she had acquired. But she kept a sharp eye out every time she came through here.

Whistling softly, Jamie slipped through the back door into the storage room. If Dad and Frank knew she had easy access to the saloon's liquor supplies, she'd never hear the end of it, but they never questioned her whereabouts. She was fairly certain they had forgotten her gender, too, and her age. She was little better than five feet tall and people kept expecting her to grow taller, so they still thought her a young boy. In fact, she was twenty now, going on twenty-one, and she wasn't likely to grow any more. She didn't intend to keep anyone informed of that, however.

Cookie the bartender came back and saw her sitting on one of the crates. He threw her a towel and jerked his head toward the back room. "Get the glasses washed up. There ain't many dishes. Lulu quit again."

Lulu was the whore who'd been here longest. She did all the cooking for the others and they were supposed to pay her at the end of the week. She regularly quit when the money wasn't forthcoming or when someone insulted her cooking. Since it wasn't the end of the week, Jamie wondered who had insulted her now.

It didn't matter. Dawson would come down and whisper sweet words in Lulu's ear and she would be all smiles again before evening's end. Jamie climbed up on a crate to retrieve the dishpan, then filled it with hot water from the kettle steaming on the stove. She added some cold water and filled the pan with dirty glasses. She wondered idly what it was that Dawson said to the ladies that made them smile and flutter their lashes around him.

She wondered a lot of things. She had a naturally curious mind, a teacher had once told her back when she was still attending school. She wondered why Dawson didn't marry someone like Gloria Jean and live in a fancy house like the banker. He was rich enough and good looking to boot. He even smelled good, which was a blessing around here. He sure enough liked women, so that couldn't be the reason.

She was drying the stack of glasses and pondering these curiosities of human nature when the object of her speculations walked in. Dawson often came back here to check on supplies or just to see what she was up to, so his presence didn't surprise her any. She threw him an earring she had found on the floor. He caught it in one hand and absently slipped it into his pocket.

"I don't suppose you can cook, Jamie, my friend?" he inquired, wandering about in the chaos that was Lulu's version of a pantry. He found a sack of peanuts and carried it back into the kitchen, offering Jamie a helping.

"Nothing fancy," she agreed. "But if you have a cookbook, I could figure it out. What happened, Rosa bounce one of Lulu's biscuits again?"

He cracked a peanut shell and popped the contents in his mouth before answering. Jamie had long ago decided that Dawson Smith was the most handsome man she'd ever seen. He'd gotten rid of the silly mustache, but now he had long sideburns that framed his already angular face and emphasized the squareness of his jaw. His hair was thick and dark and curly, and he forgot to get it cut as often as he should. It was brushing the back of his stiff collar now, and Jamie wondered if she ought to ask if he wanted her to trim it like she did her father's.

He was her best friend, her only friend. She'd gladly do it for free, but his concentration was elsewhere tonight, and she didn't intrude.

"A cookbook. That's an idea. Reckon Davidson would have anything like that over at the mercantile?"

Jamie smiled and propped herself cross-legged on top of an upended crate. Dawson wasn't really thinking about cookbooks, she could tell. She knew things about people they didn't think she knew. There were advantages and disadvantages to being ignored by everyone. She thought she could pretty well have her father and Frank hung if she wanted to divulge some of her secrets and she had once told Dawson as much. Most of them weren't as dramatic as that, however. One of the other secrets she knew of was that Dawson was a physician with a fine mind, who couldn't be satisfied with pouring liquor and playing the gaming tables. He could do both those things while his thoughts were on a peculiar medical symptom he'd heard someone discuss. She'd seen him do it more than once.

"You aren't worried about Rosa's appetite, are you? Nobody can eat Lulu's biscuits. It doesn't have anything to do with Rosa carrying a baby."

Dawson's gaze finally focused and fell on the urchin perched insolently on the crate. If it weren't for the lively crop of curls beneath her hat, he could easily mistake her for one of Dickens's chimney sweeps. He licked his finger and ran it down her grimy cheek, leaving a pale white streak.

"You need a bath. Go upstairs and tell Lulu to fix one for you. She's not good for anything else tonight."

Jamie shrugged. As much as she liked the baths she occasionally sneaked, they weren't a good idea. People looked at her oddly when she was clean, she had noticed. They started counting backward and wondering how long she could be a fourteen-year-old boy. It was better not to attract too much attention.

"You and Lulu have a fight?" she asked helpfully, distracting him.

"Lulu and I fight all the time, and it's none of your business. How did you know about Rosa's baby?" He might have ignored her earlier questions, but he'd heard them. Given an inch, Jamie Mulligan would take a mile of questions. She had a mind like a steel trap and Dawson preferred to step around it when he could. She knew entirely too much about everybody, and she was too good at putting pieces of a puzzle together.

There were one or two secrets that he would like to continue to keep.

Jamie gave him a scornful look that made Dawson want to laugh. She had slanted green eyes that she kept half-closed most of the time, but they crinkled up and flashed now. He'd already insulted Lulu and Rosa this evening. He might as well round out the numbers with this junior version here.

"I've got eyes and ears and a brain between them," she answered scornfully. "Is Lulu going to talk Rosa into not having the baby?"

This time, it was Dawson's turn to scowl. "She'd damned well better not. Is that what you heard? I'm going to strangle that woman, just see if I don't. You stay right here and I'll bring you her corpse. We'll bury it together."

Jamie grinned as Dawson shoved a box out of his way and headed for the door. "Give me a game after?"

"Name your poison," he called over his shoulder.

"Twenty-one. Penny a point," she called to his departing back.

"Damn, but you'll own the whole building," he muttered before disappearing into the nether regions where she couldn't follow.

Cookie came back to collect the tray of clean glasses and bring her a tray of dirty ones. He gave her casual sprawl a look of irritation. "You ain't bein' paid to lollygag, boy. Don't know what the boss keeps you on for."

"My good looks and sweet tongue." Jamie hopped down from the crate and stuck out the aforementioned appendage.

Cookie grunted and slammed back out to the front.

Instead of dumping the glasses in the water and washing, Jamie wandered to the pantry and assessed the contents. She liked working here. No one asked her to lift fifty-pound sacks of grain. No one cared if she were male, female, or somewhere in between. As long as she did her work, she went unquestioned. And it gave her someplace to go when Dad and Frank were drinking.

Finding the flour, lard, and soda, she threw the appropriate combination into a bowl and began to knead it.

By the time Dawson made it back downstairs to the kitchen, the room smelled of freshly baked biscuits and coffee. He remembered he hadn't eaten any supper, and his mouth watered. Jamie was casually ignoring him, bent over the dishpan in an affected position of industriousness. He knew she hated washing dishes and avoided it every chance she got. His gaze roamed the chaotic room that was Lulu's kitchen.

He grinned as he found the fresh baked biscuits, still steaming hot, on a pan near the stove. Ignoring Jamie as she was ignoring him, he sauntered over to the pan, picked up a biscuit, and threw it back and forth to cool it off. The little brat had even sliced some salted ham and left it on a platter. He pulled the biscuit apart, drinking in the scent. They were fluffier and fatter than the ones his mother used to bake. Slapping on some ham, he bit into the sandwich with gusto. His eyes swept the room in search of the coffee.

The pot sat in the middle of a table she had cleared—right beside the deck of cards. She was going to hold him to his promise.

He had two women down, and a man with loaded dice at the tables. He really needed to tend to business. But he couldn't resist the offer. He was perfectly aware that the little brat counted cards. She could ace just about any man out there when luck was running her way, and she damned well knew it. But he'd let her have her fun. The biscuits were worth every cent he'd lose.

Making up a stack of miniature sandwiches and

pouring himself some coffee, Dawson straddled a chair
and cut the deck. He didn't even have to call. She was
drying off her hands and settling on a stool before he
could say a word.

"I'm not going to let you rob me blind tonight," he
warned.

"You don't ever *let* me do anything." she said con-
temptuously. "I walk all over you because I'm good."

Dawson laughed. He genuinely liked this arrogant
little brat. Ever since the day she'd walked into the old
doc's office and informed him her name was Jamie and
not Jamaica and he'd better remember it, he'd followed
her career. It hadn't taken him long to realize why she
wore the boy's disguise. Any unprotected woman in
this town was free game to the miners and cowboys
who rolled into town on a Saturday night.

After running into her menfolk a few times, Dawson
was even more aware of her reasons for hiding. One
brother had disappeared into the night after a man who
had won his paycheck turned up dead. There wasn't
any proof that a Mulligan had done it, but the suspicion was heavy. Another brother had been caught rob-
bing a train with a gang of outlaws and been sent to
jail. The father and the remaining brother were no-
account drunks who occasionally managed to make it
down into the mines and earn enough pay to keep them
liquored up the rest of the time. With family like that,
she was better off pretending to be a boy. He worried
about her, though. By now she was surely old enough
for the drunks in that family to see her as a woman.
And unfortunately, he didn't think a blood relationship
would stop them from wanting to sample her charms.

Dawson threw down his cards and watched her clean
off the table again. Damn, it was a good thing they
were only betting pennies. She'd started out with two
and now had twenty-five. "How old are you now,
Jamie?" he inquired casually.

She gave him a suspicious glare and shuffled the cards. "Old enough to know better. Where's Lulu's body?"

Since Lulu was busy sharing her luscious self with a man she didn't mean to charge, it took Dawson a moment to remember their earlier conversation. He chuckled as he remembered the sight of that very live body and the corpse he'd threatened to haul down. "Lulu's body is otherwise occupied right now. I'll kill her some other time. I talked to Rosa instead. She's got enough saved to get to San Francisco. I gave her the name of a place she can go. She can arrive as a wealthy widow and make herself respectable if she wants."

Jamie didn't offer any comment. Had she been a respectable lady like Gloria Jean, Dawson would never have talked about such things as pregnant prostitutes to her. But because he often forgot what she was, she had learned a great deal more about life than most ladies would ever know. She had a very real understanding of why the women upstairs did what they did, even if she wasn't entirely certain what it was that they did. More than once when Jamie had been worried about losing the roof over her head, she'd wondered if one day she wouldn't find herself doing the same thing.

Dawson polished off the last of the biscuits after noting that Jamie had had her fair share. "You applying for the position of cook?"

"Lulu would skin me alive," Jamie answered evasively.

"You're probably right, but I can insist that she needs a little help. I could eat these biscuits all day."

"That's about all you'd eat. I don't know much else. I don't suppose Lulu would be willing to teach me." The words were more statement than question; Lulu didn't exactly have the patience for teaching.

"I'll find a cookbook," Dawson promised, rising from the table as he folded another losing hand. "I'm going to catch you cheating one of these days, and I'm going to make you cook for free."

Jamie didn't have any objections to that. As Dawson left to relieve Larkin of his loaded dice, she glanced around at the well-stocked kitchen and larder. She could make a bed up over there in that corner beside the stove. She'd straighten this mess out and practically have a room to herself when she was done. And all the food she could eat. Of course, in a place like this, she'd still have to disguise herself as a boy, but one couldn't have everything.

She'd have to let Dawson catch her cheating next time. She didn't cheat often—just when she was particularly desperate—but she knew how to do it, all right. Dawson would know why she did it. That ought to bother her; she had some pride. But with Dawson, it didn't seem to matter so much. He'd find some way to talk around Lulu if he knew that cooking here was what she really wanted. Cheating would be the signal that she was ready to move into his kitchen.

They'd always understood each other that way. Gathering up her pennies, Jamie slipped out back the way she had come.

It was odd how two such disparate people could become friends, but somehow, she thought of Dawson as just that. Maybe it was because they were both oddities in this town. Dawson walked a fine line between respectability and dissipation. He dressed like the bankers and merchants, talked like them—heck he had more money than most of them. At the same time, he ran a notorious establishment in a town that valued upright and honorable living. He was a gambler and a saloon keeper and he rented rooms to women of loose morals. That tipped him toward her side of town. Except that she really wasn't a part of the immorality of her father's friends any more than Dawson was. It was only poverty and family that kept her where she was, and there wasn't much she could do about her family.

Of course, it also helped that Dawson was the only person in town who occasionally remembered that she wasn't a boy. She didn't particularly enjoy being a boy, but she had never had much opportunity to be anything else. She occasionally wondered how she would compare if she got cleaned up and decked out like Gloria Jean, but she didn't concern herself much with impossibilities.

She wouldn't be female if she hadn't considered marriage as an escape from her present plight, but she might just as well imagine traveling to San Francisco and seeing the ocean. She didn't have occasion to meet any respectable men, if such creatures existed out here. And she had more sense than to think she would be better off if she married a miner or cowboy who would smack her around whenever he felt like it, go whoring whenever he had the urge and return to her bed smelling of cheap liquor. She'd seen the wrong side of marriage too often to want to be a part of that.

She knew she was smart and that one day she would figure a way out of this predicament. The opportunity just hadn't appeared yet. Becoming Dawson's cook just might be the chance she'd been waiting for.

She slipped into the dark kitchen of her home and grimaced at the sight of the dirty pan left sitting on the warm stove. The heat had cooked the remains of the beans into adobe plaster. An empty whisky bottle lay in pieces on the rough wooden floor, and the dregs had seeped into the planks where they would stink forevermore. She'd end up begging Dawson for that job if she wasn't careful.

The room reeked of tobacco smoke and body odors. Come Saturday, maybe she could raid her hidden cash for enough coins to persuade her father and Frank to go down to the bathhouse. They were rank beyond be-

lief right now. She threw open the room's one window
and attempted to air out the cabin.

She was too weary to do more than that. She had to
sleep while they slept and be up and out of here before
they awoke. From the looks of it, the whisky was
gone; she knew from experience that they'd be like en-
raged grizzly bears until they found more booze. The
last time the liquor had run out, she'd been belted
across the room just for looking at them crooked. If
she had to get by on six hours' sleep in order to save
her teeth from being knocked down her throat, she'd
do it. She liked her teeth too much to lose them.

Jamie contemplated accepting Dawson's offer of a
bath as she carted the last crate into the mercantile.
She could feel the perspiration streaking down her
forehead, and the noon sun was about to fry her brains.
Mentally, she lowered herself into perfumed suds and
lathered her hair in cool water. Physically, she accepted
the grudging scraps Davidson offered as payment and
headed for the street.

Occasionally, she wondered what it would be like to
be a whore. They had all the perfumed baths they
liked. She'd heard they had satin sheets. They would
eat well when Lulu bothered cooking. They had money
to spend on anything they liked. And they could save
enough money for train trips to San Francisco; a place
Jamie really wanted to see.

But then she'd watch the filthy miners and weaselly
shopkeepers climb the stairs after Lulu and Rosa and
the others, and her stomach would turn over. Instinct
told her that any occupation involving men was one to
be avoided.

So she decided to treat herself another way. Instead
of stopping at the dressmaker's to turn her material
into cash and get stuck running errands, she wandered
out of town to the creek cascading down the mountain

into a hidden pool. A few of the cowboys knew about the place, but they wouldn't be near town today. The townspeople never roamed much farther than the last building on the street unless they were in a stagecoach or carriage, so they didn't know the stream existed. She'd lose an opportunity to make a little cash, but it was worth it.

The water was heavenly. She had a sliver of soap from the last bar she'd bought, and she used it lavishly on her hair. She hated it when her head itched. She didn't care if her face was dirty, but she liked clean hair. And she didn't like to smell.

The water was just deep enough to come to her shoulders, so she couldn't drown. She didn't know how to float or swim, but she bobbed up and down in the water and scrubbed until the soap was gone, then soaked in the coolness. How nice it would be if she could stay here forever. The water washed against her skin like the finest satin, and she closed her eyes and let it lap around her, trying to imagine what it would be like to wear silk. She thought it must be a lot like wearing water.

But the sun was already moving down behind the mountain. She had to get back and convert Davidson's scrapes to cash and buy food for supper. She shivered when she climbed out and a light breeze flicked over her wet skin. She was pale and beginning to prune. She grabbed a piece of the muslin and rubbed herself down. She'd wash the scrap and sell it another time. The others would be sufficient to buy potatoes.

She hated donning the filthy clothes, but she hadn't been organized enough to bring clean ones with her. Her only thought had been to escape to the stream and lose her troubles for a little while. Now she was going to have to put her thinking cap on and figure out how she was going to get through town with shining cheeks and wet hair. Even fourteen-year-old boys tended to show traces of a beard.

A muffled explosion rocked the mountain as she was pulling on her trousers. Jamie looked up in surprise, searching the sky for thunderclouds. And then came the dreaded sound of a tolling bell and siren. The mine.

There were accidents in the mine all the time, but it had been years since there had been an explosion or a collapse. Fear clutched at her insides as Jamie grabbed up the rest of her clothes and ran down the mountainside, dodging rocks and spindly aspen like a leaping jackrabbit. Her father and Frank had gone in to work today, still half-drunk from their payday binge. They might be drunks, but they were all the family she had left.

Just then, another horrible thought occurred to her. Without them, she would be homeless in every sense of the word. The house they lived in belonged to the mine. If anything happened to her father and Frank, she would be without family and without a home.

People were already running up the road toward the mine. Horses and carriages mixed with women and children on foot. In some way or another, everyone had an interest in that mine. Jamie flew down the hillside to join them.

She smacked right into Dawson's arms as she slid off the bank into the road. He grunted, grabbed her arms to steady her, and looked down to see what he had caught.

His eyes widened, and he hastily jerked off his coat and shoved her arms into it. Taken by surprise, Jamie looked down at herself. She was carrying her oversized shirt and hat and wearing only her combinations and trousers. Like everything else, the thin cotton was larger than she was. Men went around like that all the time. But she hadn't taken the time to bind her breasts.

She jerked his coat around her and pulled on her hat over her wet hair.

"Get back to the saloon. Have the girls begin making bandages out of those old sheets I've been saving. Clear the tables and chairs out of the way and see if you can gather some blankets for pallets. And get that damned shirt on." Dawson shoved her in the direction of town, against the steady stream heading up the hill.

Still shaken, Jamie ran to do as instructed. People tended to forget Dawson was a physician as much as they forgot she was a girl. They never looked further than what they could see. But she knew what he was telling her: for the first time since Dawson had arrived in Altona, they were going to need a hospital, and the saloon was going to be it.

Jamie jerked off Dawson's coat as she dashed into the empty saloon and was still fastening her oversized shirt when she yelled up the stairs at Lulu. At this time of day, most of the women were still in bed, sleeping off the previous night's exertions. But at her frantic call they straggled down the stairs or leaned over the railing in various stages of undress. Jamie had never seen so much fancy undergear in all her life, but she didn't stop to consider it.

"Don't goggle, little boy," one of them called as Jamie waited anxiously for Lulu to make an appearance. There wasn't much point in talking to the others until then. She'd just have to repeat the message a dozen times.

Lulu finally appeared, fully dressed in scarlet silk with a slit from her ankles to her thigh. The feathery boa around her neck looked like it would tickle, but Jamie didn't have time to admire the fashion show. "Dawson said we've got to make bandages out of those old sheets. He said to get as many blankets together as you can. I'll start shoving these tables out of

the way. There's like to be a lot of injured coming in
soon."

Lulu frowned, sauntered down the steps, and removed Jamie's hat. She dropped it on the floor, then
crossed to the front door. "Mine blew, did it? There's
like to be a lot of dead, if you ask me." She gazed out
at the empty street, then turned back to Jamie and narrowed her eyes. "You're not a boy, are you? And that
damned wily Dawson knows it. Get out of here, kid.
We'll handle this."

Furious at being dismissed as a child, Jamie grabbed
up her hat and stalked out the back way. Once out of
sight, she headed for the kitchen. She could hear Lulu
giving orders and chairs being shifted across the floor.
Maybe she wasn't needed in there, but she could be of
some use in here. She had to do something or go crazy
waiting for news from the mine.

As she got the fire stoked and set pots of water and
coffee on to boil, she remembered her unbound breasts.
Combined with her clean face and wet hair straggling
to her shoulders, she didn't have much of a disguise.
She prayed the women would keep their mouths shut,
but any hopes she might have harbored about coming
to cook here had come to an end. Lulu would never allow another female on her turf.

Hiding in the storage room, Jamie bound herself and
rubbed some soot on her face. Her hair would bounce
back into tight curls once it dried. There wasn't much
she could do about it until that happened. She'd just
have to look like a long-haired boy and keep to the
kitchen.

She heard the voices yelling first, then the stamping
of feet as the first of the injured were carried into
town. Dawson's voice was loudest, directing the men
into the saloon, then shouting orders at the women.
The idea of using prostitutes as nurses didn't seem to
strike anyone as amusing. When the first one appeared

in the doorway looking for hot water, Jamie had a bucket ready for her.

As the afternoon wore into evening, the frantic rescue efforts continued. Jamie didn't have a glimpse of Dawson. Lulu came back and carried out the coffee as if it were her own. Jamie made biscuits enough for an army, and sliced up every piece of meat and cheese in the place. Somehow, it all disappeared. Her arms were beginning to ache from pumping water, but the demand never slowed.

When Cookie wandered back and discovered the urchin sweating over the stove, he raised his eyebrows and pumped the next bucket.

"Have they got a list of the dead yet?" Jamie asked fearfully, removing another pot of coffee.

"No list. Ain't seen any Mulligans either." Cookie poured the water into the kettle and started out with the coffee. He gave Jamie's ear a sympathetic tweak. "I'll let you know iffen I do."

That was the best she could hope for.

Things slowed down a bit after full dark. The saloon was filled with the sound of women weeping and men moaning. Occasionally she could detect Dawson's low voice giving instructions. She didn't know why she could pick his out among so many, other than because it was somehow reassuring. Lulu had just carried out another pot of coffee, but she wasn't being very communicative. She just sent Jamie an enigmatic look and helped herself to the pot.

When the demand for hot water finally died away, Jamie curled up in a corner, so thoroughly exhausted she didn't think she could move a muscle. She couldn't bear the thought of returning home. If the place was empty, she would know the worst. This way, she could hold on to hope a little while longer.

She must have dozed off. The clatter of an empty

coffee pot against the iron stove jarred her awake. She jumped up, wearily wiping her eyes.

Dawson was there, leaning with exhaustion against the stove, attempting to pour coffee from dregs. He was stripped of all his finery and down to shirt-sleeves—bloody shirt-sleeves, Jamie noted. Without a word, she filled a clean pot, added wood to the fire, and set the water to boiling.

Dawson leaned against the sink and watched her move with the grace of a shadow from stove to sink to pantry. There wasn't any lamp back here but the one over the sink. When she stood beside it, he could try to trace the outline of the breasts he had seen so clearly earlier today, but she'd apparently bound herself again. He didn't need to ask how old she was. He'd found the old files and looked it up.

"Jamie." His voice came out as little more than a weary whisper, surprising him.

She drifted back to the stove and added grounds to the coffee pot. She didn't look at him, but he could tell she was listening. Her whole body was tense beneath the loose shirt and trousers.

"They've brought in a list of the missing."

He didn't have to say more. She knew what that meant. The roof of the mine had caved in. Those trapped behind or beneath it were either dead already or would be soon. She knew with a sudden and sharp clarity whose names would be on the list. He wouldn't have mentioned it otherwise. He wouldn't have come back here at all.

"They were drunk. They probably didn't feel a thing." She said quietly, trying to relieve him of the burden of finding a way to break the news gently.

There wasn't much Dawson could say to that. They both knew that her father and brother might still be alive and suffocating in the methane gas from the explosion. Or they could be lying under timbers, dying slowly from blood loss or internal injuries. They also knew the likelihood of anyone digging through the debris in time to save them or any of the others was next to nil. It was better to think of them as already dead.

"I'll help in any way I can," he offered.

Jamie nodded. "If you don't mind, I'll sleep here tonight. There's space over by the pantry. Somebody might need something during the night."

Dawson preferred to send her home. Horrible as her life might be, she was still a young girl, and he wagered she knew little of the life the women in this place lived. He'd rather she didn't learn more. But he also knew Jamie well enough to know she would never have made the offer if the alternative hadn't been worse.

Dawson nodded his head. "I appreciate that. There aren't any blankets left. Can you make yourself comfortable?"

She gave him a fleeting grin. "Flour sacks make great pillows."

If he were the kind of man who cried, he'd cry now at the sight of the bravery behind that quivering smile. There were full-grown women out there right now who weren't accepting the news of their losses with half the fortitude of this one, and most of them had comfortable homes and families to fall back on. Dawson chucked her under the chin and walked out. He was too exhausted to consider any other alternative for her right now. Another woman he might have hugged and kissed and comforted. Jamie Mulligan would rightly have socked him in the gut for trying.

Jamie crawled out of her hiding place at the first crack of dawn. She could hear people stirring in the other room, but she wagered there was time to run home before anyone came looking for her.

Her hair had dried into a tangled frazzle. She jerked

her hat over it, tightened the binding under her shirt, and slipped out the back door.

The dawn promised a day as bright and warm as the previous one. She guessed nature didn't take mining explosions into account. The clouds didn't weep for the dead and injured. Thunder didn't roar and rage at the injustice of it all. Life went on as it always did.

As if to emphasize the point, a bird began to sing from the rooftop, and a rooster crowed.

Scowling, Jamie slipped down back alleys and roads to her home. It looked more miserable than ever in the morning light. It was the place where her mother had made cookies and told Christmas stories. She had learned to walk on those floors; she had polished that window more times than she could count; she had even persuaded a morning glory vine to sprout and bloom along the step. It was her home—but it didn't belong to her anymore.

Inside, the empty rooms echoed hollow as if they knew the life had gone out of them. The dirty pot of burnt beans still sat soaking where she'd left it yesterday morning. The kitchen floor still reeked of the liquor she hadn't had time to scrub out. In the front room, her father and brother's dirty clothes still lay scrambled in the disorderly pile where they had left them two nights before. They would lie and rot now. Jamie didn't mean to wash them again.

She might be sentimental about her home, but she couldn't afford to be sentimental about her family. With organized efficiency, she searched every inch of space in the front room for anything that might be of value to her. Old clothes were worthless, but she fished through pockets for pennies and knives that might bring a coin. She found the last of Frank's paycheck under a board by his bed. She wrapped up her mother's Bible in a stack of quilts. Her mother's clothes had been sold or used for rags long ago.

She would have to find a place to store the few pots and dishes that represented her kitchen. In the meantime, she would carry these few things back to Dawson's. Maybe Lulu wouldn't throw her out as long as the saloon remained a hospital.

Back at the saloon, Jamie stashed her quilts in the corner she had claimed for her own and went about making breakfast. Everyone was probably tired of biscuits, but she knew nothing about making bread. She could fry an egg if anyone wanted one, but she didn't see much point in frying one up ahead of time. Men drank coffee any time, so she got that started. She wished she knew how to do more.

Lulu came storming down a few hours later, slamming the door and yelling at Jamie to get out. By then, Jamie had already made more pots of coffee than she could count and she was running low on lard for the biscuits. She looked up at Lulu with surprise, inspected the last tray of biscuits in the oven, and shut the oven door.

"You getting tired of biscuits too?" she asked with a hint of irony.

"I'm damned tired of biscuits and I'm damned tired of His Royal Asshole telling me what to do! Now get the hell out and let me cook a real meal." She slammed an iron skillet on the stove and headed for the pantry.

"I'd be more than glad to help if you'd just tell me what to do," Jamie offered.

Lulu carried out the last of the lard and glared at her. "Unless you're willin' to work under the covers like the rest of us, you'd better get your skinny ass out of here. If I hear one more word about your glorious biscuits, I'm going to slit someone's throat." Ominously, she moved toward the tray of knives.

Jamie left. She hoped her possessions would be safe. She couldn't imagine even Lulu in a rage bothering with a few old quilts.

When she returned to the house to see if she could figure out how to salvage her kitchen supplies, she found the place already occupied by a couple of men who had "Company" written all over their faces.

Jamie tried to slip in and grab a skillet and pot before they could see her, but her hand slipped and the noise of metal against metal brought one of the men to the kitchen. He grabbed her wrist and wrenched the pot away.

"A man dies and thieves are already scavenging the remains. Get out of here, brat, before I call the sheriff." He shoved her toward the door.

Jamie fell from the force of the blow and was scrambling to her knees when the second man entered. He bent to help her up, but she shook him off with fury, backing away from both of them.

"It's Mulligan's youngest," the second man offered. "He probably ain't got nowhere else to go."

The first man frowned and stared at her as if she were emitting a bad odor. "They're talking about starting an orphanage for those that don't have any family. We could take him down to the church."

Jamie panicked and began to back toward the door. The idea of an orphanage was ludicrous. It would have been ludicrous back when she was ten and her mother died; it was even more so now. But she had no intention of explaining that to these men.

"I just want my things," she demanded. "They're my things. I need them. I've got a job."

That was a blatant lie on all counts, but these men seemed relieved not to have to do anything else. They hunted around for a sack or a box and began helping her gather her kitchen tools. They made no apology whatsoever for taking away her home.

Her back stiff, she carried out the big box full of pitifully worn-out household goods. She had no idea where she was going; she just knew she wasn't going to stay around and become an object of pity. Lord, she thought with a sigh, her father wouldn't even have a funeral, buried as he was down in the mine. They were just going to open up his house, heave everything out—including his daughter—and rent it to some other unlucky fool. Life wasn't fair.

She'd screamed and raged at the injustices of life when she had been younger, but tears and anger hadn't changed a blamed thing. She was a quick learner. When she had realized tears didn't work, she'd found something else that would. Playing the part of urchin had protected her. Working for pennies had kept her from starving. She would simply have to find something new to put a roof over her head, and crying wasn't going to do that.

She knew what she wanted to do, but she'd need Dawson's cooperation. She disliked asking anybody for help, but if she had to it would be easier to ask him than anyone else.

Carting the box to the back of the saloon, Jamie hid it among the old crates and boxes of liquor stored there. Then, dusting herself off slightly, tucking her shirt in neatly, and straightening her hat, she went around to the front door and entered just like a regular customer.

Dawson didn't even look up. He was bent over a man lying on a pallet on the floor, removing a bandage. Jamie waited awhile for him to look up, but when one of the other patients asked for water, she went to fetch it. Soon, she found herself going from pallet to pallet, supplying the needs of the injured or the women who waited beside them.

It would be a more depressing sight if she didn't keep telling herself that these were the lucky ones, the ones who had gotten out alive. These women still had their fathers and husbands and brothers. These men would live to see another dawn. She had no need to cry over their pain and suffering. She merely eased it where she could with sips of water, a cool cloth, or a few words of comfort.

Dawson finally noticed her and dragged her back to the empty kitchen. He held her collar and shook his head as he looked her up and down. Then he pushed her toward the stove.

"Fix yourself something to eat. You look like something the cat dragged in."

That hurt. She had just bathed yesterday, and she had taken the time to dust herself off as best as she could. She was hideously conscious that her overalls had only one strap and hung on her like a gunny sack tied around the middle with rope, but he'd seen her in these a thousand times. She scrubbed self-consciously at her face with the back of her hand and tried not to glare at him. After all, she couldn't get him riled when she'd come to ask him a favor.

"I need your help," she blurted out, with none of the finesse she'd planned on using.

He stiffened briefly, then crossed the room to fill a plate with the mess simmering on the stove. He shoved it at her and pointed at a chair. "Eat. You can talk to me while you're eating."

She sighed and took the place indicated. Even to her empty stomach, the congealed mess looked unappealing, but she nibbled at it anyway. She had been taught not to talk when chewing, and she glared at Dawson as she tried to chew the piece of rubber in her mouth. So much for being polite.

Finally, she swallowed and reached for the water he'd poured for her. The coins in her pocket made her braver as she sipped.

"I need a loan."

Dawson raised his eyebrows and sat down across from her. "What for?"

She had been afraid he would ask that. He had every

right to know what the money would be used for, but if she told him, he wasn't likely to loan it. "I need some clothes," she finally said. "I'll pay you back, I swear."

"How do you mean to do that?" His look contained oceans of suspicion and an equal amount of weariness. He'd more than likely been up most of the night.

Jamie squirmed. She even considered eating some more. But he was going to know sooner or later. He was too smart not to. She set her chin bravely and met his eyes. "I want to be a gambler. I want some decent gentleman's clothes so I can sit at the tables."

Dawson gave a long whistle and eyed her with a certain amount of respect. "You're a rare one, you know that? I can't think of another woman in this world who would come up with a solution like that."

Jamie knew better than to feel eagerness, but she sensed it creeping up on her anyway. Holding in her excitement, she kept a wary eye on him. "Will you give me the loan then? I can pay you back a little bit every night out of my winnings."

He lifted the hat off her head and dropped it to the floor. He got out his handkerchief and wiped at the soot she had rubbed into her cheek. Unable to peer any further beneath her disguise, Dawson tilted his head and examined her carefully. Then he shook it slowly, sending Jamie's hopes plummeting to the ground.

"You make a pretty boy, but you'd make a damned awful man. How many five-foot men with smooth cheeks have you seen running around?"

Not many. Jamie slumped in her seat and stared at her plate with distaste. She supposed she could live in alleys for the summer. If she stole food from backyard gardens, she could save everything she earned and maybe rent a place cheap come winter. The idea of living without a roof over her head made her whimper in-

side. She'd always known she was poor, but she'd
never been homeless.

Dawson came around the table and pulled her up by
her shirt sleeves. He gathered the loose material in his
hands until he had it taut enough to see something of
her actual shape beneath the cloth. He eyed her criti-
cally. "It's a wonder you haven't maimed yourself
wrapping yourself that tight. How in hell do you
breathe?"

Mortified, she jerked away and slapped at his hands.
"I manage. I'm sorry I took up your time. I've got
work to do."

He caught her loose overall strap and kept her from
escaping. "Even if you could cook more than biscuits,
Lulu would feed you to the snakes if I put you back
here where I can't keep an eye on you."

Jamie gave his restraining hand a glare of disdain
but didn't say anything. She just looked at him, waiting for him to make up his mind and let her go.

He gave her another once-over and shook his head.
"You're no bigger than a termite, but maybe that will
work to your advantage. I'm going to loan you the
money."

She stared at him, hope widening her eyes, displaying the full glory of sooty lashes and emerald glitter.

Dawson shook his head again. "I'm going to kick
myself for this—I most assuredly am. There's one con-
dition to the loan." She waited without speaking.
"You're going to buy ladies' clothes."

Her newborn hope died. She gave him a pained look
but kept her dignity. "I'll not be one of your whores,
Mr. Smith."

He winced. He hadn't been "Mr. Smith" in years.
Not even "Dr. Smith." "Do you really think I'm as bad
as that? I thought I had at least one friend who saw
past my reputation."

Puzzled, Jamie searched his face. He seemed genuinely hurt by what had been a perfectly natural assumption. But Dawson never let his feelings show for long. Abruptly, he was whistling and looking her up and down. Carefully, she inquired, "Then what, precisely, did you have in mind?"

He grinned. "A lady gambler. I want you to be my new dealer at the blackjack table." Seeing her disbelief, he hurried to add, "You'll work for me. I'll not have you counting cards against the house. I'd have to throw you out. I'll pay you a regular wage, and you'll be where I can keep an eye on you. Cookie might have to chuck a few men out at first until they get used to the idea, but we'll make them understand you're not one of the girls."

A lady gambler. She could dress like a real lady. She could be a woman. It was an impossible dream. She looked down at herself, trying to imagine what she would look like in silk and lace, and found it impossible. She looked back up and saw Dawson's smug expression. It was more than impossible to imagine. It was impossible any way she looked at it.

He couldn't watch her twenty-four hours a day. She wouldn't want him to. It was going to take everything she possessed to pretend she was a lady for eight hours at the table. For that long she might endure his looking at her as just another one of his employees. More than that would rip at her insides. She knew it instinctively. She didn't want to know what it would feel like to have him ignore her as a woman. Worse, she didn't want to know what it would feel like to have him look at her as he looked at Gloria Jean and his other women. She shook her head in dismay at the thought and gathered her courage.

"I won't want anyone to know who I am. Give me some fancy name to use like Rosa or Lulu."

Dawson looked at her with curiosity but nodded agreement. Jamie could tell his mind was already working at the problem, finding new angles, solving them faster than she could think of them. She wasn't in the least surprised when he answered.

"That's an excellent idea. I'll let them think you came from out of town. I've got a driver going into Denver for supplies. I'll have him stop at the first stage station on the road and you can hop off there. I'll be out with your new clothes first chance I get. You can arrive on the stage as if you're brand new to town, tell everybody I sent for you. What name do you want us to use? You've got time to think about it."

She heard what he was saying, but only one part stuck in her mind. Pursing her lips, she looked at him suspiciously. "You're going to buy my new clothes? How're you going to do that?"

Dawson grinned and looked her over carefully. "You think I never bought ladies' clothes before? You just wait and see. Besides, you can't be doing it. That will ruin your disguise if people see you."

Grudgingly, she had to agree but she had been looking forward to choosing her own clothes for a change. She'd never been able to go to a store and pick out so much as a piece of underwear. He might as well own the blamed things if he was going to pick them out.

With a decided lack of grace, she consented. "I want some of those fancy things like Gloria Jean wears," she informed him. "I want to look like a real lady."

Amusement danced in his eyes as he took her measure. "Gloria Jean is twice as big as you. I'll get you something suitable."

"I don't want any kid clothes!" she answered, alarmed. "I might be small, but I'm twenty years old, Dawson Smith. I want to dress like a lady." She stifled her anger, afraid she would lose her one chance if she annoyed him. But she couldn't resist adding, "Could I have a gown with green and pink stripes? I saw one like that over at the store once."

He shrugged and nodded. "I can only get you one like that if I can find one like it," he warned. "But I'll do my best."

She sighed and nodded. "When's your driver leaving?"

"First thing tomorrow." Dawson started to leave, then noticing that she stood there aimlessly, he turned. "You got a place to stay?"

She stiffened her backbone, pulled on her hat, and nodded energetically. " 'Course. I'll be here first thing tomorrow then."

In two steps, he had her by the back of the collar again. Jamie kicked backward, but he didn't release her. "Mrs. Leavenworth owns a boardinghouse. I've got a room there I keep for my personal guests. Go over there and tell her I'm expecting company in a day or two and that I want you to stay there until they arrive. She won't believe you, but she'll send someone around to ask me before she throws you out."

Jamie jerked away. "I don't take charity. I'll find my own place."

"If you're going to be a lady, you've got to stay where ladies stay. That's what Mrs. Leavenworth is for."

She gave him a furious look from under lifted eyebrows. "Ladies? Is that why you keep a room there? To keep *ladies* there?"

"If I had time, I'd wash your mouth out with soap. Now get over there, give Mrs. Leavenworth my message, clean up, and get yourself back over here to help me. I've got to get these people out of the saloon soon so I can open back up."

If she'd had a gun, she would have shot him when he walked off. No, she wouldn't. She wouldn't shoot a man in the back. Maybe she'd strangle him in his sleep. That wasn't any better. She couldn't think of any way of killing him where he couldn't kill her first.

She'd think of one sometime. If she was going to work for the bastard, she would have to wind up killing him. She was beginning to feel some sympathy for Lulu.

Jamie groused all the way to the boardinghouse and back, but she couldn't suppress her excitement entirely. She didn't know what she would look like in new clothes, but she was hoping she'd look better than Gloria Jean. Finally, she had a chance to be *somebody,* instead of a filthy little urchin everybody ignored. She was practically dancing with the excitement of it.

Somehow, she managed to get through that day. She was used to not seeing her father and brother from one day to the next, so she didn't exactly miss them. She didn't like staying at Mrs. Leavenworth's, but it was a place to sleep. She hauled her quilts and Bible over, deciding it might be a shade better than sleeping near Lulu's kitchen. The old lady scowled and clucked and insisted on checking the covers for fleas, but she'd already had word from Dawson. Jamie suspected Dawson's arrangement with the landlady might be cut short if she stayed here for long, but that was his problem.

She asked for a tub and hauled buckets of water up to the room. The old lady seemed to approve of that notion and even sent up some warm water. After locking the door, Jamie peeled off all her filthy clothes, scrubbed herself good with a bar of soap she found in the basin, then started on her clothes. She wasn't about to start her new life wearing filthy clothes over clean skin.

She hung her wet garments on hooks near the empty fireplace and went to bed naked. She couldn't remember ever sleeping on clean sheets. She stretched luxuriously on the feather mattress and decided staying at Mrs. Leavenworth's boardinghouse might even be worth listening to the old hen cluck. She could almost die happy right here and now, except she wanted to know how it would feel to wear ladies' clothes before she went.

She was too excited to sleep soundly. This side of town was quieter than where she was used to sleeping. The quiet kept her awake. Jamie heard the birds chirping before dawn, and even though it was still dark, she leapt out of bed.

Her clothes were still wet and clammy, but she wasn't overly concerned. They would dry eventually. And soon, she could don new ones.

That thought brought her to a standstill. She'd only commissioned Dawson to buy her one outfit. She would have to keep that outfit clean all week until she could have it laundered on Monday when there wasn't any gaming. She would have to wear her boy's clothes when she wasn't working.

It was a depressing thought, but Jamie saw the sense in it. She actually began to find advantages as she made her way over to the saloon and the wagon waiting out front. She hadn't dared ask Mrs. Leavenworth for something to eat before she set out at this hour, and her stomach was growling, but she was used to that. She slipped beneath the canvas in the pre-dawn darkness. No one would even know she was gone.

Except maybe Dawson. He came out and leaned into the interior calling, "Jamie? Are you there yet?"

"Told you I would be." She popped from her hiding place and sat on an empty crate.

"I brought you some food. I don't know how soon I'll get out there, and the stage station isn't known for its repasts." He handed over a sack that weighed enough to be a week's rations.

"Add it to what I owe you," she said gruffly.

"You'll earn it. Now get down back there and out of the way. I'll see you in a day or two."

She felt odd when Dawson brushed his knuckle under her chin, but Jamie attributed it to her empty stomach. He walked away without looking back, and she felt odd about that too. There seemed to be this big gaping hole where her middle used to be.

She climbed behind the boxes and pulled out a loaf of bread. She'd eat something first, and then she'd feel better.

The wagon lurched off as she hungrily broke her fast. She couldn't keep Dawson Smith out of her mind, though. He must have been working too hard at taking care of those miners. There'd been a sadness to his eyes this morning that she hadn't seen before. But Dawson Smith had it all—she couldn't think of a thing that he could be sad about. Maybe one of his patients had died.

Once her hunger was satisfied, she settled down for the ride. The day was hot enough that she didn't mind the dampness of her clothes. She didn't look much like a boy today, but there was no one to see her. She didn't know what she was going to do when she reached the stage station, but that wouldn't be until nightfall. Maybe it would be dark enough to disguise her more feminine attributes.

She wasn't fond of the idea of having to continue to wear boy's clothes even after she got her new ones, but it looked to be unavoidable. Aside from the fact that she had to keep the gown clean, she really couldn't afford to wander around town parading herself as a lady. Everyone would know she worked at the saloon, and without a father or brother for protection, she would be even more vulnerable than she had been before. Unless she wanted to hide at the boardinghouse for the rest of her life, she'd have to hang on to her disguise—at least until she made enough money to go to San Francisco.

She reckoned that wouldn't take too long. She knew how to save every penny she made, and if she could operate as Dawson's blackjack dealer at night and as her usual self during the day, she could save money quickly. By this time next year she aimed to have a dozen fancy gowns and be living where she could see the ocean.

Those dreams took her past noon, but the boredom of the ride gave way to serious doubts as the day wore on. She slept through a few of those hours, but by the time they stopped at the stage station Jamie was wondering if she wouldn't do better to go on into Denver and disappear.

She found she couldn't bring herself to do it. It wasn't that she'd miss Altona—the Colorado town meant nothing to her. She could turn her back on it in a minute. Dawson Smith was another matter entirely.

As she leapt from the back of the wagon with her food sack, Jamie decided she must be out of her everlovin' mind. Dawson Smith didn't care about her. She'd be just one more employee to bring him riches.

But she couldn't forget that look in his eyes this morning when he'd seen her off. She couldn't erase his casual touches. No one had ever bothered touching her before. No one had ever bothered trying to help her. Hell, no one had even taken the time to be kind. Except Dawson.

So she would go through with this farce and see what happened. What would it hurt? If it didn't work out, she'd come up with some other idea.

Dawson arrived by noon the next day. Jamie suspected he had ridden all night after working all evening in the saloon. She took one look at him and sent him off to sleep in the bed she'd been renting at the station. He handed her his satchel and willingly collapsed into the cubicle behind the drawn curtain.

By the time he woke, Jamie had figured out most of the various ribbons, buttons, and hooks on the froth of clothing and underwear he had brought. It had taken her quite a while to guess at the proper use for the

"dress improver" that looked like half a petticoat with
steel ribbing, but its purpose had dawned on her once
she had the skirt in place and realized that the rear
sagged. She hadn't been able to adjust the corset laces
to make the bodice fit properly, though. As a result,
she was having some difficulty fastening the gown. It
still gaped open at the top.

But the gown had broad pink stripes up and down
the skirt, interspersed with fine lines of green and me-
dium stripes of ivory. Jamie had no idea what the material was, but it was so smooth and soft and shiny, she
didn't much care whether it was satin or silk. The bodice was a soft green trimmed in tiny pink rosebuds, and
the ivory lace at the throat would cover her modestly,
if she could only get the hooks fastened. She would
have given a year's wages for a mirror, but she could
only fidget and admire the thin slippers and silk stockings on her toes while waiting for Dawson to wake.

The impatient rustle of stiff fabric eventually
brought Dawson completely to his senses. Through the
cubicle curtains he caught a glimpse of the fancy dress
he'd had the seamstress hastily make up. There hadn't
been time to create something at the height of fashion,
but a kid Jamie's size didn't need all those extra
lengths of fabric and ruffles draped all over her. He
pushed aside the curtains to sneak a peek.

He almost fell out of the bunk. He closed his eyes
and opened them again to make certain he was awake.
The vision didn't change any, and he didn't have
enough imagination to conjure up the sight he was
seeing—not even in his dreams.

Dawson tried to concentrate on the absurdities. Her
tangled mop of cinnamon curls wasn't exactly the elegant upswept coiffure he'd seen in Lulu's fashion
plates. But, Lord, those eyes. Those long-lashed eyes
had always been ridiculous for a boy, but she had kept
them concealed most of the time behind that old hat

brim. Now they were wide and excited and sparkling like rare emeralds, and they were very definitely feminine—so feminine that he was forced to ignore the tumble of curls.

He looked away from the scrubbed pink and ivory of her smooth cheeks and down to the bodice clasped inexpertly in delicate fingers. He didn't know why she hadn't fastened the bodice, but he could almost find the careless urchin in her half-dressed stance—if he squinted his eyes and ignored the obvious.

He gave up pretending when he saw it was futile. The urchin had breasts that would make Lulu green with envy, breasts that she could scarcely conceal given the state of her bodice, breasts that would give a man something to dream about for a lifetime. Not large, loose breasts, but round, full, young breasts that had probably never been touched.

Dawson groaned, rolled on his back, and covered his eyes. He was going to regret this. He could feel it in every aching part of his body. He liked women altogether too well. He liked the way they smelled, the way they rustled when they walked, their gentle voices and soft skin, the way they looked in silks and satins. He liked the way they looked in nothing at all. And he was suddenly thinking of how very lovely Jamie Mulligan would look in his bed.

That wasn't the worst of it. He faced that fact with his eyes wide open. He'd had to face it every day of his life for these last seven years. Virgins and ladies and all self-respecting women with marriage on their minds were out of his reach. He could flirt with them, escort them about, be in their company and enjoy what he could see and smell, but he couldn't touch. He could only touch the women whose favors he had to pay for. Jamie fell in neither category, but it would be very easy to seduce her into the latter one.

He didn't think he was that kind of cad, but he knew

every ounce of this self-control was about to be tested. Steeling himself, he threw his legs over the side of the bunk and stood up.

Jamie drew back in surprise, nearly losing her hold on the gown. Dawson thanked his foresight in providing her with a chemise to go under the corset or he would be looking straight down her front. Obviously, he'd overestimated his ability to judge a woman's size. No wonder she couldn't get the gown fastened.

He forced himself to inspect her coolly, nodding his head in approval and gesturing for her to turn around. "Let me help you with that," he said, without mentioning the intimate garment by name.

Jamie obediently swung around and Dawson grasped the corset laces and tugged. He had considerable experience in women's undergarments, both taking them off and putting them on ladies of pleasure, but he found himself singularly fumble-fingered right now. Jamie was more nervous than a frog in a frying pan, and she wriggled and jumped at every tug of the lace. He couldn't help but look to see how he was doing, and the more he looked, the more he wanted to look.

Muttering curses under his breath, he tied the laces off as best he could, then jerked the bodice up where it belonged. He could tell as she fastened the front hooks that the seamstress had made it too small. No amount of corseting was going to help. He had meant to provide his new dealer with something modest and respectable, but there would be no disguising her considerable assets behind the tightness of the silk.

Jamie choked and protested as Dawson fastened the hook at the waist. "I'm going to suffocate in this!" she complained, whirling around and inspecting her finery. "Are you certain ladies go around like this all day? How in hell do they eat?"

That was the Jamie he knew. Stepping back to admire his handiwork, Dawson smiled. "Mind the language, Miss Mulligan. Dresses don't make the lady. If you want to keep those miners in line, you've got to impress them with your respectability." He shrugged wryly. "And it's my fault if the gown is too tight. I underestimated your size. You kept yourself very well-hidden."

Since he was looking at her breasts, Jamie had a good notion what he was talking about, and she blushed crimson. "Looks like I'd do better to keep myself hidden," she answered curtly. "Go on out and I'll change. The stage doesn't come through until morning."

She was quite properly right, but temptation wasn't easy to resist. They were out here in the middle of nowhere with only the stationmaster as chaperone, and he was no doubt in the stable mucking out stalls. Jamie was glaring at him through suspicious eyes, but Dawson knew her well enough to know what would happen if he touched her. She was a kindred soul if he'd ever met one. They'd been drawn to each other from the start, although at the time there hadn't been this sexual discovery between them. His discovery, not hers—not yet.

Sighing, he took her advice and walked out. He was much too aware of how vulnerable she was right now. He could wait a while, give her time to recover her usual aplomb. When she was ready to fight back, then he would think about her as a woman.

Such noble denial was going to be a damned sight more difficult than he had anticipated, Dawson discovered a short time later when Jamie reappeared wearing her urchin's clothes. The overalls and overlarge shirt might as well be invisible for all he could tell. He knew every curve hidden beneath them, and he found it difficult not to touch her to confirm what was there and what wasn't. The way she wouldn't look at him, he suspected she felt something similar.

"Are you going to be all right here another night?" he asked, staring off at the setting sun. "Or do you want me to stay and keep you company?"

She sat on the front stoop and wrapped her arms around her bent knees. "I'll be fine. You're the one who hasn't had enough sleep."

She didn't go into detail. She didn't need to. She was worried about him making that long ride in the dark, and about what would happen if he stayed here with her. Dawson found her concern rather touching.

"I want to be there to greet you when you arrive in all your finery. Do you think you'll be able to fasten those hooks now that the undergarments are properly adjusted?" He didn't look to see if she blushed at his casual reference.

"I can do it," she replied stiffly.

Dawson couldn't resist. He turned and lifted her chin up so he could see her eyes. "I wager you can do anything you put your mind to, Miss Mulligan. I'll be on my way, then. Ol' Paint can get me home in the dark even if I fall asleep."

" 'Ol' Paint,' " she snorted. "There's nothing old about that animal of yours, and it certainly isn't a paint. Why do you call it that?"

"Why do you call yourself Jamie when your name is Jamaica? I understand Jamaica is a beautiful tropical isle. It suits you." He held her chin, pressed a kiss to her forehead, and walked off whistling.

Jamie contemplated murder again, but strangulation was her weapon of choice this time. She wanted to wrap her hands firmly around his neck. She just didn't think she'd get around to choking him if she did.

Jamie returned to Altona just before sundown the next evening. She stepped off the stage in all her finery, wearing lace gloves and a feather in her hat and smiling demurely when men stopped to whip off their own hats and stare. Dawson was there to meet her, as promised, and she took his arm just as she had seen Gloria Jean and his other ladies do.

She was surprised at how much she had learned just from watching him with the other ladies in town. When he bent toward her with that knowing smile of his and a small quip, she spread her fan and hid her answering smile behind it. When he introduced her to men she had known all her life, she fluttered the fan, and said her "how-do-you-do's" in a soft voice that made them lean closer. They never knew what hit them.

It was a powerful feeling, and she could really get carried away on it. She swept triumphantly into the saloon on Dawson's arm and watched chins drop all over the room. She hadn't had an opportunity to see herself yet, but she must make an acceptable female or they wouldn't be looking at her that way. Of course, the way Dawson had looked at her the day before had given her all the confidence she needed in that direction. He was a connoisseur of women, and even he'd had a time looking at her.

She figured it must be her figure that made the difference. The rest of her hadn't changed, except that now she was cleaner, and her hair was swept into a soft twist. The gown was too tight and probably too revealing, so that attracted as much attention as anything. She wasn't going to become vain or anything over all this ruckus; new women around here were always made much of. She just liked knowing she could be accepted as a woman like the others.

Jamie worked the tables that night under Dawson's careful scrutiny. The men were so eager for a chance to meet the lovely young woman Dawson introduced as Jamaica that there was soon a waiting line. They behaved themselves for the most part. Jamie minded what Dawson had told her and played the part of very proper lady, and the men responded accordingly. It wasn't until later, when some of them got a little drunk, that they began to make unwarranted overtures.

At the first questionable remark, Jamie raised her hand in the air and snapped her fingers. Cookie immediately appeared at her side, and she pointed out the culprit. He was unceremoniously removed from the saloon. That quieted the remainder of her admirers for awhile.

When Cookie was otherwise occupied, a drunken cowboy tried to get a little more personal, reaching for her chest. Dawson silently appeared behind him and grabbed the man by the collar. When the cowboy protested, Dawson jerked the man around and slammed his fist into his captive's stomach. The crowd grew suddenly quiet, but before the man could get to his feet, Cookie appeared. Dawson and his bartender carried the cowboy into the street and heaved him.

It was late and Jamie was getting tired of the tension, but she continued smiling and playing until Dawson came back and put a hand on her shoulder. She gave him a questioning look, and he gestured with his head.

"You've done enough for tonight. Let's get you out of here."

She rose quietly, her heart pounding. She didn't know why it was suddenly galloping like a runaway horse. She just let Dawson slip his hand around her waist and lead her away. With a small gasp, she realized having his arm around her waist wasn't at all the same as resting her hand in the crook of his elbow. She felt like a nervous fool as he took her out the front door.

"Where are we going?" she whispered once they were outside.

"I'm going to escort you to the boardinghouse. I

don't want to give any of those jackasses ideas by letting you go alone."

She didn't want to be giving Dawson ideas, either, but it seemed rather vain to assume that he might have any. She held her tongue on that subject. Dawson praised her performance, and Jamie let the first real compliments she had ever received wrap warmly around her. The night's tension slowly evaporated as they traversed the dark streets together, the only sounds their own quiet conversation as they walked.

He stopped at the front door of the boarding house. Smiling faintly, he kissed her hand, and left her to go to her room alone—except for the butterflies accompanying her in her stomach.

"We're going to have to get you a new dress," Dawson said grimly as Cookie hauled off his blackjack dealer's latest would-be lover.

Jamie was in the kitchen, sipping coffee, when he made this announcement, and she looked at him with surprise. Then she glanced down at her gown. It was the same one she'd worn for six weeks. It hadn't changed any, and she'd been very careful with it, sponging it clean each night. She looked back at him questioningly.

"Don't stand there looking so damned innocent. I'm going to commission a dress that covers you to your ears. I can't take much more of this." Dawson paced restlessly around the kitchen, shoving chairs and crates out of the way. The outward appearance of the room hadn't changed much in the last six weeks, but mysterious changes had been occurring behind the scenes. He'd looked in the pantry several times this past week and had found edible food in it instead of a hodge-podge of empty tins and unlabeled bottles. He didn't have to look far to find the culprit.

At his words, Jamie grew teary-eyed, but she hugged

her precious gown and threw back his words with her own growls. "I'm not paying for any more dresses, Dawson Lee Smith! I like this one." She ruined the performance by finishing in a whisper, "I'm doing a good job, aren't I?"

She might as well have stabbed him through the heart. If he had learned anything at all these past weeks, it was that Jamie Mulligan could be tough as nails when she had to be, but soft as a creampuff if he so much as offered a harsh word. He'd yelled at her once, and she'd yelled back, left the saloon like an outraged alley cat, and started weeping the minute she'd hit the street. He'd been careful not to repeat that performance.

But he was damned tired of seeing filthy miners pawing her, slimy gamblers eyeing her, and the rest of the riffraff around here treating her as if she were their own. It seemed every man in town assumed the right to handle her but himself. Knowing full well the source of his frustration, Dawson groaned inwardly, tipped her chin, and wiped her tears with his handkerchief.

"I'll let you choose the gown," he murmured. "You shouldn't have to pay for one that doesn't fit right. Just please, for my sake, pick one with a high neck."

He was so close, Jamie couldn't even manage a nod. All she could do was stare up into his eyes until he released her. It wasn't butterflies in her stomach anymore, it was a herd of elephants stampeding around, threatening to crush her to death every time she got this close to Dawson Smith. She stepped away hastily when he let her go.

"I'll walk you home now. I think we've both had enough for one night." He offered his arm and Jamie took it, fully aware the elephants would return as soon as she touched him. She didn't know what was wrong with her, but she knew Dawson was the cause.

They slipped out the back entrance, away from the

noise and garish lights of the front. Jamie liked these moments when they could walk in peace, discussing the evening's events. She could always make Dawson laugh, even when he was looking his saddest. But when he scolded her and offered to pay her more money if she wouldn't roam the streets running errands in her boy's clothes, she managed to refuse him. It was a matter of pride. She wasn't going to live off him, and when he finally found the woman he wanted, she was going to have a fortune to carry away with her when she left. The amount she had saved already seemed like a fortune.

They were too tired to have much to say this night. Dawson kept his hand protectively at her back, but they both knew she was as sure-footed on these rough boards during the night as she was during the day. The rowdy noise from the saloon must have disguised the footsteps coming up behind them.

"Here he is, Jack! I've got him." The gun butt came swinging down toward Dawson's head before he could completely dodge it.

It glanced off his temple and slammed into his shoulder, and he staggered sideways, groaning. Jamie let out a full-blooded shriek that should have woken the dead, but the second man already had his arm wrapped around her waist, jerking her from her feet.

Jamie continued shrieking as he wrestled with her, trying to cover her mouth while holding her flailing arms and legs. Dawson almost laughed, but he was too furious. He came up out of his wounded crouch with both fists swinging. One connected soundly with the jawbone of the man who had struck him, but the other missed its target as his victim stepped sideways and returned the punch. As he bent double with the pain, Dawson cursed himself for not having seen it coming.

"Bill, help me with this she-wolf! You're the one who wants her. Come and get her." The man holding

Jamie wrapped his arm around her throat and jerked her chin upward. She responded by bringing her head back so fast that it smashed his nose. He yelped, and she kicked backward, hitting his shins with her high heels.

The man called Bill seemed intent on finishing off Dawson first, but at his partner's howl of pain, he stood up and moved toward Jamie. He couldn't see her smile of triumph as he approached, but he heard her war cry when he reached for her and she released a swift kick. Held off her feet as she was, she was just the right height to strike him where it hurt most. Bill crumpled with a howl of agony.

On the ground behind him, Dawson jerked his derringer from his boot. Slamming his shoulders against the back of Bill's legs as he bent in pain, he toppled his attacker and aimed the derringer at his accomplice.

"I'd drop Miss Jamaica now, if I were you. She's not big enough to shield all of you, and I learned to shoot at my mama's knee."

Dawson heard Jamie's gown tear as the fool at his feet lunged and caught her skirt at the same time that the other man let her down. She gave a cry of half-distress, half-fury and turned to kick the man who had torn her precious gown. As her shoe connected with Bill's face, Dawson decided he was going to have to see to it that the sheriff licensed her feet as lethal weapons. The jerk should have got off his knees before he grabbed for her.

Jamie's screams must have finally penetrated the noise in the saloon. A herd of men came stumbling out the front door, hands on their revolvers, and even the sheriff wandered over from his office to see what was going on. Dawson shoved his knee in the back of the man on the ground and let his customers chase after the one fleeing down the street.

"I'm going to put a bullet through your head if you

ever try this stunt again," he warned his captive. The man struggled, but the derringer shoved to his temple held him still long enough for the sheriff to grab his arms.

Dawson jumped to his feet as soon as the sheriff had a handle on Bill. His gaze instantly swung in search of Jamie, but Cookie and Lulu were leading her back into the saloon. Heart pounding in his ears, he watched her until she was safely out of sight, then set about cleaning up the evening's fiasco. He had to get this thinking straight before he went after her.

Dawson stared at the door to the room he kept above the saloon. Lulu had told him where to find Jamie, but he was half afraid he'd open the door and find her gone. The other half was afraid that he would find her waiting. Squeezing his eyes shut, he quickly knocked, then threw open the door.

When he opened them again, she was there, perched on the edge of the bed, staring at something she held in her hands. She scarcely looked up when he entered. The lace on her bodice was ripped, revealing more of the shadows between her breasts than was good for his well-being. He could see her white petticoat through the tear between the silk skirt and the bodice. The gown could possibly be repaired, but he doubted if Jamie knew how to do it. She wasn't even attempting to piece it back together.

Her curls had grown longer and drooped in ringlets around her neck now. He had to will his hand to his side to keep from touching one. "Are you all right?"

She shrugged and slid whatever was in her hands beneath her skirt as she glanced up at him. "I'm fine. I'd better go."

Dawson straightened his shoulders stiffly beneath his coat and winced. She looked at him curiously but didn't offer to help him off with his coat or see to his injury. "Physician, heal thyself," seemed to be her attitude. He acknowledged the appropriateness of the platitude. His physical injuries weren't precisely what he had in mind for healing, though.

He eased the coat off. "I don't think it would be a good idea for you to go back out there tonight. The sheriff has Bill locked up, but he's got three brothers still roaming the street, and they're probably all as drunk and surly as Bill. You're better off staying here tonight."

"I don't think so." She stood up, palming the object she kept hidden.

When she crossed the room to his dresser, Dawson followed her. He didn't bother to see what she was returning to the Bible he kept there. He'd had about all he could stand for one night. He'd had about all he could stand for these last six weeks. He caught her shoulders and swung her around.

Jamie gasped a little when Dawson's mouth finally came down on hers. She'd dreamed about what it would be like, but dreams couldn't match the reality. It wasn't just the kiss. His lips were warm and hard and demanding and joy rose in her soul at their touch, but it was all the other little things that made her want to weep with happiness and need and terror. His fingers on her shoulders were long, fine-boned, and so very gentle that they were more caress than possessive hold. In waistcoat and shirt-sleeves, he was more blatantly male than she'd ever known him, and her hands tentatively came up to rest against his chest. She could smell the faint scents of sweat and cigar smoke and whisky; being this close to him made her head swoon. His fingers were pressing more intimately into her now, pulling her closer as his mouth demanding things she found herself all too willing to give. She gave a small, lost cry and pulled her mouth away.

Dawson didn't let her go but pressed her head into

his shoulder. She stood there shivering in all her ruined finery, letting him hold her. She couldn't imagine being anywhere else in this world right now, but then, she wasn't thinking any further than the arms holding her tight.

"I'm sorry, Jamie. I didn't mean for things to happen this way. I meant to take care of you. I meant to do the honorable thing for once in my life, but I can't remember why right now."

His hand stroked her hair, and she leaned into him, not wanting to see his face. She knew she'd see pain there, and she didn't want to cause him pain.

"It's all right, Dawson. You don't have to be honorable around me. I'm not much of a lady," she admitted.

Above her head, he chuckled. "You're better than a lady. I don't think there's another like you in the whole wide world. When I came out here, I thought all ladies smelled sweet and wore silks and never argued. It took me a little while to realize all women who smell sweet aren't ladies. I went through a spell when I decided ladies didn't exist except in my imagination, but now I know better." He lifted her chin up and kissed her nose. "If virtue makes a lady, you're a lady, little one. But I've decided I like ladies who can kick like a mule and scream like a rooster better than those weak kinds who sit on verandas and sip lemonade."

Her smiled wavered slightly as she tried to push away. "You're a nice man, Dawson, even if you are a little strange. I'd better go now."

He released her but made no move to escort her out. He stood with his hands in his pockets, his dark hair falling across his brow, and watched her through shadowed eyes. "I don't want you to go, Jamie," he replied, almost angrily, as if she had forced the words from him. "If I were a free man, I'd do whatever it took to make you stay."

Realizing what he'd said, he turned on his heel and

walked toward the door, his head bowed. "I'll call Cookie to walk you home."

Jamie stayed where she was, staring at him. "I think you'd better explain, Dawson. I'm not a kid anymore. You can't say things like that and expect me to just leave."

Yes, he could. He rested his forehead against the door, battling with his better self. He ought to tell her to get out and stay out, but he knew he'd hurt her if he did that. He couldn't bear to hurt her. But he'd hurt her worse if she stayed.

Cursing, he swung around and glared at her. "You're not a kid, but you're an innocent. You deserve a chance at a good home, a husband and family. I can't give you that. It was a mistake for me to think you could stay here. I'll have Cookie post guards at the boardinghouse."

Jamie crossed her arms and sat down on the bed. "I never pegged you for the marrying kind anyway, Dawson. If you had been, you could have married one of those rich ladies you're always out with."

Dawson looked at her with bewilderment and amusement. Jamie was good at provoking that kind of confusion. "I wouldn't marry any of them if they were gift-wrapped and handed to me. They're no different from the wife I already have."

She looked as if she'd been socked in the stomach, as she had every right to do. Dawson ran his hands through his hair and tried to ease the awkwardness. "You're the kind of woman I'd have now, if I had a choice. I want someone who would stand beside me even when I'm making a damned fool of myself. I want someone strong enough to keep on going even when the odds are against them. You're the only woman I've ever met like that, Jamie. I just met you ten years too late."

She gave him a considering look, then crossed her

legs under her and made herself comfortable. "Are you really saying you'd marry me if you weren't already married? That's quite a line, Dawson."

He shrugged and leaned his shoulders against the door. "I've never used it before, if it is. For the first time in my life, I'm even considering what it would take to get a divorce." He paused, then continued in a quiet voice. "Would you marry a divorced man, Jamie?"

She wrapped a curl around her finger. "The way I look at it, a piece of paper isn't going to keep a man if he wants to roam. You've proved that already. Is that your wife in the picture?" She nodded in the direction of the Bible on his dresser.

He scowled. "You shouldn't be going through my things."

"That's the only reading material you've got in here, Dawson. What did you expect me to do while I waited?"

He crossed the room and shook the Bible until the picture tumbled out from its hiding place. He glanced at it and handed it to her. "That's my wife. I had it taken a month after we'd been married."

Jamie ran her finger over the lovely curves of the woman's face. "She's pretty." She held the picture closer to the light and frowned. Then she glanced back to Dawson. "Is your name really Smith?"

He blinked, then grabbed the picture away. He turned it over. There wasn't any indication of a name anywhere on it. Irritated, he threw it back on the dresser. "What does it matter?"

Jamie shrugged in an unladylike manner and nibbled on the curl wrapped around her finger. "Just thought it would be nice to know the name I might have had."

"You're nuts." He crossed the room to keep from sitting beside her. "The name is Mallory, Dawson Mallory."

Jamie shut her eyes and swayed slightly where she sat. He looked at her with concern but didn't dare reach out to grab her. He knew where that would lead. He wished she would get off the damned bed.

"I don't suppose your wife's name is Laura, is it?"

He shook his head in disbelief. "You know my wife?"

"Nope." Her eyes flew open and she stared at him. The green of her eyes wasn't glittering. "You know I told you once that I could probably have my father hanged if I wanted?"

"That was just talk. You were mad. I didn't take notice."

She snorted inelegantly. "You should have. I've got one brother in jail for armed robbery and another with a warrant over his head. You didn't really think they turned bad all on their own, did you?"

"It never made any difference to me. I was just concerned about how you kept those big louts under control, but you wouldn't let me close enough to do anything about it."

"You'd better take a seat, Mallory." She pointed at his desk chair. "You're not going to like what I have to tell you." He narrowed his eyes but obligingly straddled the chair, pulling it directly in front of her.

As if suddenly struck by a new thought, she tilted her head. "Why did you leave your wife?"

"I had a run-in with a lynch crowd, cut the man down. They took objection to my interfering and I had to shoot a couple of them. I'd been wanting out for some time. Mississippi isn't what it used to be. I couldn't stand to see what was happening there. I asked Laura to come with me. She refused." He jerked off his tie and threw it on his coat. "I didn't exactly leave her. She just refused to accompany me. I've been sending her money every month, so she can't say I've deserted her. That's one of the reasons I started this saloon. I couldn't send her the chickens and jam I got as payment for my physician's services. I thought maybe if she thought I was well off, she'd come join me."

"Laura." Jamie looked sadly at her fingers. "Did you love her very much?"

"Come on, Jamie, let's get on with this. If you've got something to say, then say it. I married Laura while I was still in school, when I still thought ladies smelled sweet and didn't differentiate much among them. I would have been content if things had gone as planned. I can't say that I loved her. I didn't even know what the word meant."

She stiffened her shoulders and met his eye. "She's dead."

He didn't flinch. "She can't be. The money I send her has to go somewhere. My sister would have told . . ." He looked momentarily sick and watched Jamie closer. "She lives with my sister in the house we inherited from our parents. My sister writes. Laura seldom did."

"You'd better send someone to get the Bible from my room," she said softly.

Dawson shoved the chair back so abruptly that it fell over. He called to one of his men downstairs, gave him curt orders, then slammed the door shut and righted the chair, sitting back down again. "Give it to me now, Jamie."

"You're not going to like it," she warned, watching him carefully.

"I'm not liking what I'm suffering right now. If you don't tell me, I'm going to truss you up and throw you on the stage with me and we're going back to Mississippi to get the whole story."

"You'll not find her there. She's buried under a rock by that old cave down the mountain." When his eyes looked a little wild, she hurried to add, "She died of snakebite."

"I'm going to strangle you, Jamie," he said slowly, enunciating each word clearly. "Now give it to me straight."

She gave him an angry look. "I'm trying. It's not as if I'm used to telling these kind of things. My father tried stage-robbing a few years back. He thought it would be easier to get his pay direct from the cash box, I guess, but he never caught the stage with the mine payroll. I didn't know what he was doing until he came back one time all liquored up and blabbed the whole story to my brother. When he passed out, I snuck in and searched his clothes, but all I found was a letter and a locket. I hid them in my mother's Bible."

Dawson waited without speaking. Jamie sighed and tried again. "When he stopped the stage and found there wasn't any payroll, he made the passengers cough up their cash. There were only two, a man and a woman. The man protested and my father said he knocked him over the head. Neither of the passengers had much money, but . . ." She tried not to look at Dawson. "He thought he could make some use of the woman. He sent the stage on and carried her up to the cave, but she got bit when he lowered her from his horse."

Dawson buried his head in his folded arms. "My God, she actually came to me. How long ago?" Then realizing how he'd allowed his hopes and despair to overcome common sense, he looked up and scowled. "How do you know it was Laura?"

"Three, four years ago, and her name was on the letter. So was yours. And the locket is the same as the one in that picture of yours. I didn't see her, but the letter tells it all. I used to keep wondering who poor Lee Mallory might be. I never put it all together until I saw that picture tonight. She didn't call you Dawson."

He shook his head, disbelief still apparent in his expression. "She never liked the name. She always called me Lee. What did the letter say?"

Jamie sighed and knit her fingers together. "Maybe you ought to wait and read it yourself. I always wondered what happened to the man who was with her. You'd think he'd have yelled his head off and sent out a search party once he got back to town."

Dawson's face changed to stone. "The man who was with her?"

She gave him a disgruntled look. "I told you, there was a man with her. My father knocked him out. My father was worried he'd be recognized and laid low for some while after."

Dawson frowned but a knock at the door signaled the return of his messenger. He got up, opened the door enough to take the book from the man's hand, then shut it firmly again. He stared at the worn black Bible as if it were a snake, then riffled through it until he found the letter. He looked up, waiting for Jamie to explain the missing locket.

"There's a pocket in the front. It's in that."

When he pulled the chain out of the small pocket on the inside front cover, an expression of resignation crossed his face. "It was my mother's. I gave it to Laura the day we married." He snapped it open. "She used to keep my picture and a lock of my hair in here." He rubbed his thumb over the empty place where the picture should be. "I guess she didn't want to remember what I looked like."

He slipped the locket in his vest pocket and opened up the letter.

From across the room, Jamie said, "She carried that in her purse. My father was rather upset that it wasn't folding money."

The sad expression returned briefly as Dawson glanced down at the familiar handwriting on the yellowing page. His look turned wry as he began to read.

When he looked up again, there was a trace of bitterness twisting his mouth.

"The only thing that brought her out here was a divorce. The man with her was an old friend from back in Mississippi. No wonder he didn't hang around to see what happened to Laura. He figured I'd hang him if I found out what happened."

"Her taste in men sure didn't improve over the years." Jamie unfolded her legs and started toward the door. "I'll have Cookie see me back to the boarding-house."

Dawson swung around and slammed his shoulder to the door before she could reach for the knob. Jamie couldn't read his expression so easily this time, and she lowered her eyes. His black waistcoat fell open to reveal the wrinkled creases of his shirt, creases she had made when he'd held her. Staring at the broad expanse of his chest didn't help any. She didn't know where else to look.

"I don't have a wife," he said flatly, speaking to the top of her head.

"I'll go with you, show you where the cave is, if you want. I know where to get some flowers to put on the grave." She'd never felt so nervous in all her life; she wasn't the nervous type. She'd have died of it if she had been. But she didn't know what was going through Dawson's head right now, and she didn't want to admit to what was going through her own.

"I know where the cave is. I suppose I better write my sister and tell the scheming witch what happened to Laura. She probably thinks Laura just decided to take off without bothering over the divorce."

He didn't move one way or the other, and Jamie didn't either. "It probably takes a lot of money to keep up the house back there," she whispered. "There's not a lot of ways women can make money."

Dawson grunted and finally reached out to touch her

curls. "You're probably right. But she should have told me instead of keeping me thinking I was still married."

Jamie shrugged. "She didn't know any different."

"You're not going to let me throw a tantrum, are you? I can't kill a dead man for killing my wife. I can't strangle my sister for taking my money. I could go after my ex-friend and beat him into a pulp for not going back to look for Laura, but he's not worth the effort. What am I supposed to do now, Jamie?"

She finally lifted her eyes to meet his. She saw sadness there, and loneliness, and a tenderness that made her heart ache. "Go ask Gloria Jean to marry you, I guess. Her daddy's got a big, fine house. You won't even have to build your own."

His lips tilted slightly at one corner. "Gloria Jean would drive me to drink after more than two hours straight in her company. I told you, I've learned better than that."

The look he gave her burned a path straight through her center, and Jamie had to look away. "You can tell your sister to move out here if she wants a house, then sell the one in Mississippi. That way you can keep your money and she can look after you."

Dawson leaned both shoulders against the door and crossed his arms complacently over his chest. "I can look after myself, thank you. If I go back to being a physician, I'll have all the chickens and jam I can eat. My sister can sell the damned house and do the same. I want a woman in my bed as well as my kitchen. I don't think my sister will suit."

Jamie backed away slightly but kept her gaze fixed on his face. "You told me I was too innocent. You'd have to get Lulu if you wanted a woman in bed as well as your kitchen."

He gave her a horrified look. "Lulu? Do you hate me that much?"

"I don't hate you. Don't look at me like that,

Dawson. You know damned well I'd do anything for you. Don't go rubbing it in."

His look now was of self-satisfaction. "Then you'll marry me."

"Marry you?" It was Jamie's turn to look horrified. "I just told you my father was a stage-robber and my brothers worse, and you want me to marry you? That's a lot of bull-malarkey, Dawson Lee Mallory. What a fine family tree that would make. How many murderers, thieves, and cheats do you have on your side?"

Dawson's eyebrows flew to his hairline, and he moved so quickly from the door that Jamie wasn't prepared. He swept her off the floor, threw her down on the bed, and sprawled next to her, pinning her with one strong arm before she could jump up again. He kissed her mouth before she could open it to protest, then traced a path of kisses along her jaw after she went too limp to fight. She stirred restlessly beneath him, needing something she couldn't put a name to, but he didn't enlighten her immediately.

"Didn't your mama keep a family record in her Bible?" he whispered against her ear when he reached it.

By this time, she was trying to squirm away. His hand drifted to her barely covered breast and teased lightly along the curve. Jamie stiffened but couldn't move. It felt too good. She'd never known his touch could feel so good. A flame ignited in her lower abdomen. As if he knew, Dawson laid a torch to the kindling by moving his thumb gently across the silk over her nipple.

She struggled to remember his question and managed a whimpering, "Yes."

"And didn't it name your daddy?" he asked softly, watching her face now as his fingers played their dangerous game.

She couldn't frown like she wanted. Her eyes were too wide with the wonder of the sensations he was creating inside her. But when she didn't answer, he stopped expectantly, waiting for her reply.

"It just gave the day I was born, right after the date she married her first husband and the day he died." She couldn't follow the line of his thoughts, couldn't follow any thoughts at all. She wanted him to touch her like that again.

Dawson shook his head and nibbled on her lips again. "Damn fool women. They haven't got a lick of sense. She didn't even put the date in when she married Mulligan?" When Jamie shook her head, he turned his attention to where his hand was pushing aside the torn lace of her gown. He parted it to reveal the firm, full curve of her breast, then unhooked the top fastening of her corset so he could slide his hand inside and untie her chemise.

Jamie gasped, then sighed and closed her eyes as he rubbed his finger over her nakedness. She wasn't even going to fight him. Dawson shook his head in mock dismay and pressed a kiss to the lovely valley the torn gown revealed. Then he covered her again and looked down at her face.

"Remember the day you first saw me, when I pulled out your file from the old doc's office?"

Jamie nodded, keeping her eyes closed.

"I read that file. Your mother went to see the old doc when she first came to town. When she arrived here she was already pregnant. She got here to find her husband was dead, and she was carrying his child. She had no money, no place to stay, and she did what any sensible woman would do to protect her unborn child. She married the first decent man who asked. She just didn't know Mulligan well enough to know he wasn't what he seemed. Your name may be Mulligan because you were born after they were married, but your father was named Gregory Latimer. You're not any blood relation to those scoundrels you grew up calling father and brothers."

Jamie's eyes popped open. "I'm not a Mulligan?"

"Honey, do you think you ever looked like a Mulligan?"

She shook her head slowly, her eyes still wide with wonder. "I never got big," she murmured.

He gave a laugh. "And they never got pretty. Did anyone ever tell you that you've got the biggest, prettiest green eyes this world has ever seen?"

Jamie shook her head again. This time, her gaze was completely focused on the marvelous man leaning over her. He wasn't touching her breast anymore. He was caressing the line of her jaw, but the look in his eyes was enough to keep the fire inside her alive and growing. He looked as if he wanted to devour her. He looked as if he wanted to love her. He took her breath away.

"I'll tell you every day of our lives if you'll consent to marry me, Jamaica Latimer. Tell me yes, and I may find the strength to let you get away long enough for me to find a preacher."

Jamaica Latimer. She savored the sound. It was almost as good as her new gown. Not as good as Jamaica Mallory. She couldn't believe he meant it. "You could marry anybody," she whispered.

"I don't want to marry just anybody." Dawson's hand teasingly returned to the torn lace. "I want to marry a five-foot warrior who will fight me every inch of the way when I'm wrong and stand behind me every mile when I'm right. I want to marry a lady who knows how to make those ignorant louts out there behave. I want a woman who squirms under me when I touch her." His hand cupped her breast, and she arched upward, offering herself. Daringly, he took a sip of the nectar offered, and almost forgot where he was. Forcing himself away, he looked down at her with a distinct glitter in his eye. "I want a woman willing to carry my baby, and if you don't say yes pretty soon, you could be doing that without benefit of my name."

Jamie blushed and tried half-heartedly to pull away. "You don't love me, Dawson Lee. You're only supposed to marry people you love."

"Damnation, woman," he growled near her ear. "What do you think I've been trying to tell you half the night? It's not as if you're giving me much encouragement. I love you, Pint-size. Now will you marry me?"

Jamie gave him a considering look, then drew an assessing gaze down the length of the powerful body half covering her before returning to his face. "I think I can manage to keep loving a man too big for his britches, if he can keep those britches on except when he's with me."

He rubbed his "britches" knowingly against her hip. "I can manage that real well, I expect. Can you manage cooking something besides biscuits?"

"Just keep the fire hot, Dr. Mallory," she murmured, wrapping her arms around his neck and pulling him down to her.

The wedding was held in the saloon at noon the next day, and no one was surprised at the two main participants. There was some consternation, however, when the groom called his bride "Jamie" and the bride referred to her newly wedded husband as "Dr. Mallory," but identities were ephemeral things and the case of champagne that appeared after the ceremony was not. All concerned indulged the newlyweds and called them by their new names while helping them drink their wine.

It wasn't until nine months later when the first child was born and called Jamie Mulligan Mallory that peo-

ple went around with stunned looks and wondered if
the youngest Mulligan boy could really . . . ?

They looked at the beautiful young mother garbed in
satins and lace, remembered the urchin in dirt and rags,
glanced at the ecstatically handsome father, and shook
their heads. It couldn't be.

Besieged
Heart

———◆———

by

Jennifer Blake

Chapter One

"Will you surrender?" asked the wizard.

Princess Mara, leaning against the castle battlement with the spring wind almost whipping the linen coif from her golden-brown hair, considered the question with care. Without turning to face the man who stood a discreet distance behind her, she said, "Is that your counsel? If so, I never thought to hear it from you."

"I only ask your will, Your Highness; I don't seek to sway it." In a swirl of heavy robes, the wizard, her chief adviser, moved a step closer before continuing. "Yet consider well. The delegation approaching is the second to be sent by Baron Ewloe. If you refuse this demand to lay down your arms, and the castle falls, he will hang the garrison to a man. He has a taste for blood."

"Yes, I am aware." Mara's gaze was fixed on the scene below. In the slanting rays of the sun, their plight was painfully clear: the beleaguered castle walls, the injured defenders, the dust and the stench, and the skeletal faces of children too near starving to cry. Their defenses were pitifully meager, while beyond the keep lay the mighty force ranged against them, with its siege engines, supply wagons, and endless tents topped by snapping battle flags.

"The baron will turn his men loose on the women," the wizard continued with indisputable logic. "You yourself will be forced to wed him as he demanded when he first appeared at the gates. In the privacy of your chamber he will exact his revenge for your defiance."

Mara shivered with dread. She said, "You think I was wrong to oppose him? I could not meekly accept his suit, allowing him to lay claim to my lands and gain legitimacy for his pretensions to my brother's throne. Moreover, I despise him."

"My predecessor suggested that you chose a champion," the wizard said with biting softness. "You refused."

"Indeed I did." She lifted her chin. "A man strong enough to challenge the baron and defeat him in ritual combat might also take what he pleased as his reward. What was to prevent this champion from then claiming me as his prize?"

"Honor. I would not have trespassed."

"You?" Her silvery gray eyes widened with surprise as she turned to stare at the man standing a strict six paces away.

The wizard was powerfully built. The black robe that rested on his broad shoulders was embroidered with mystic symbols of gold and silver and only emphasized his great height. There was little else to be discerned about him. The cowl of his robe was pulled forward to shield his face from view.

Princess Mara had never seen her adviser's features, for he always kept his distance, allowing no one to come close. It was a calculated practice of the office, one designed to maintain the wizard's mystery.

When she was younger, and he only an apprentice, she had tried from sheer perversity to bridge the space separating them. The wizard had retreated each time, maintaining his strict span of steps. Later, when out of sheer loneliness she'd sought his company, he'd still kept his distance. His guardedness disturbed her at times.

The wizard inclined his head and said, "It would have been my privilege to kill the baron for you."

"You have no training in the use of weapons," she said.

"You are mistaken, Your Highness." He let the correction stand without embellishment.

A frown drew her dark, winged brows together. "You would pretend to be a knight?"

"I dreamed of it, worked toward it, once. Now I live only to serve you."

Were the words sincere, or merely an empty platitude tripping off his tongue because he thought it was expected? She could not tell. She said, "Your services are too valuable to be risked. In any case, it's far too late for such measures."

"Perhaps not," he said in swift contradiction. "The baron is as vainglorious as he is cruel. He might think it great sport to kill your champion before your eyes. That weakness could bring about his defeat."

The baron was a man of vast experience on the tilting ground, one who took pleasure in mutilating his foes. He had never been bested. With some irony, Mara said, "I fear the results would be the same, only you would be dead."

The wizard's cowl tilted in consideration. "Your concern is a boon beyond price."

"Not at all. It's only that I have more need of you in the audience hall than on the jousting field." The words were steady despite the odd sensation the quiet timbre of his voice stirred in her heart. Looking past him at the somber scene below, she added, "I already have much to answer for when my brother returns from the king's wars. I would not like to be forced to explain how I came to lose both of my advisers."

The man before her had held his position little more than a month. It had been inherited from his father, the old wizard, who had died from the ailments of advanced age combined with the deprivations of the siege.

Of course it was common knowledge the old man had not been this one's true father. The new wizard had been a baseborn child without a name, a foundling taken in at a tender age and schooled in Latin, history, and numbers, as well as the arts of magic and healing. He had also been taught the king's laws and, of course, the diplomacy of the court.

That he was something less than diplomatic with her now was due to the dire nature of their discussion; he was usually more punctilious in his address. He had long ago perfected his manner toward her, for he had been her unofficial adviser since she was eleven and he a lordly fifteen.

If this wizard was sometimes more forceful in presenting his views than the old one had been, the princess was not inclined to complain, for he was also more able in war. Without his suggestions for defense, counterattack, and midnight sallies for provisions, it would have been necessary to surrender the castle weeks ago. Regardless, the decision which lay before her was hers to make, just as the consequences would be hers to bear.

After a moment, the man watching her said, "You realize we can hold out only another week, two at most?"

"I am not blind."

"Then you are resigned to your fate."

"Dear God, no!" The words burst from her lips before she could catch them back. She swung sharply from him once more and gripped the stone of the battlement wall so that its roughness bit into her hands. Fighting to regain her self-control, she took a deep breath, then released it with a sigh. She said more quietly, "No, but what other choice is there for me?"

"You could vanish, thereby cheating the baron of his purpose."

A wan smile touched her lips, then was gone. "You mock me. There is no escape."

"But there is," he answered. "I have the power to arrange it. You will be so well-concealed that the baron could take the castle apart stone by stone and never find you."

"Run away? A coward's choice, surely?" She closed her eyes briefly. "I fear it may be my duty to wed the baron. Perhaps if I am contrite and submissive to his will, if I am properly humble, he may be lenient with my people."

A low laugh came from inside the cowl. "Submissive? You? You would spit in his eye if he tried to humble you. He would have to beat you to near insensibility to achieve it—and he will."

"You think you know me so well? I am capable of many things, given the right reasons." She refused to look at him, afraid he might see her abiding horror of her future.

"I know you much better than you realize," he said roughly. "Come away now, before the delegation arrives with its demands—before it is too late."

She shook her head, her linen coif twisting in the wind. "I must not desert those who depend on me."

"You cannot stay."

The words held a much harder edge than any she had ever heard from him. She turned to him with cool disdain in her gray eyes. "Who are you to tell me what I must do?"

"The man who will save you, my princess," he said in a clipped voice. "With your will, if possible—against it if necessary."

She drew a sharp breath of disbelief. Neither the wizard nor his father had ever offered her anything except the greatest deference. Rigid with fury, her lips parted to castigate the man in front of her.

The words were never spoken. The wizard lifted his hands, the full sleeves of his robe spreading wide. From the robe's folds swirled a soft, lavender-gray fog. The scent of it was sweet and beguiling. The fog thickened, rising around her in a whirling cloud to enter her nose, her mouth, the very pores of her skin.

She could see nothing but the wizard's eyes within the protection of his cowl. They were rich black, deep as night, shining with a tender threat. He stepped toward her, coming closer. His nearness was overpowering. Then she felt his hard and powerful arms as they closed around her.

Or perhaps she imagined the last, for an instant later she was falling, spinning, out of control. She felt as if she were being thrust beyond the setting sun, into the pitiless void where stars die unnoticed and time is but a shimmering silver light, traveling back and forth, but never standing still.

The dazzling brightness of sunlight across Mara's eyelids woke her. She absorbed the heat like a benediction. She felt so cold and heavy, as if she had lain in the same position for countless ages, certainly far too long for comfort. Yet moving seemed more of an effort than she was capable of making.

Memories flashed through her mind. She sat up abruptly, only to cry out at the sudden, pounding ache that knifed through her head. She sat perfectly still, her eyes squeezed shut, until the pain receded, fading with the gradual slowing of her heartbeat.

Birds, she could hear birds. The air was clean and fresh and pleasantly warm. Beneath her was a bed of dried leaves that felt thick and resilient. A breeze made a quiet, rustling melody in the trees overhead.

Mara opened her eyes by slow degrees. She was in

a wood of tall oak and pine. Sunbeams slanted through the branches like light through cathedral windows. She had never, to her knowledge, seen the place before.

Just beside her was the sturdy trunk of a tree. Moving gingerly, she shifted herself so that she could lean against its rough bark. There were pine needles caught in her hair and clinging to her mantle. She plucked one from her sleeve and sat turning it in her fingers, staring at it as if it were some rare prize. It felt real, but was far larger and more brightly green than any she had ever known.

A quiet sound, like a careful footfall, caught her attention. She looked up, then sat quite still.

There was a man standing not six feet away. Tall and wide of shoulder, he was wearing garments of a strange, tightly woven material that clung to his frame, defining the strong musculature of his chest, his narrow waist, and slim hips. His hair had the rich, brown-black sheen of a falcon's wing, while his eyes, looking at her from beneath straight brows, were dark and assessing. The broad expanse of his forehead indicated intelligence; the fine molding of his mouth hinted at a generous spirit; but the square jut of his chin was a clear sign of an uncompromising temperament. In one hand he carried a contraption of polished steel and wood that appeared to be a weapon. Alert, poised for action, he had a knight's air of confidence and quiet power.

A princess did not allow a man, even one such as this, to tower over her. Mara pulled herself to her feet while holding on to the tree behind her for support. Summoning her pride, she wrapped it around herself like armor. "Who are you?" she asked. "What is this place?"

Appreciation flashed in the man's midnight-black eyes, then was gone. "The name's Rayne, honey,

Rayne Winslow," he drawled. "And just who might you be?"

"I am Princess Mara of Carreg Cennen, sister to Prince Stephen, sixth of his name, who holds—"

"Right," the man drawled. "And I'm the king of England. Are you an actress, maybe, or did you just escape from a looney bin in your bathrobe?"

This stranger was watching her as if he found her vastly entertaining. Uneasiness pricked her. With great dignity, she said, "I have no idea how I came to be here. If you will tell me where we are, perhaps my position will be clearer."

"You're in the good ol' U. S. of A., sweetheart."

"I am unfamiliar with the locale. Is it east or west?"

"East or west of what?"

She frowned, her gray eyes darkening. "Of the castle, naturally."

"No castles anywhere around here that I know of," he said blithely before continuing. "You know, you sure do talk funny."

"My speech," she said with some hauteur, "is not half so comical as your own, and is infinitely more coherent. If you cannot answer a simple question, perhaps you can be of service otherwise. I command you to escort me out of this wood and to the nearest respectable house. Then you may summon some person of authority."

His humor faded. "Command," he said softly, "and be damned."

Anger and fear battled inside her. She had never met a man who treated her with less respect; in fact, had never met one who gazed at her so directly. If he had no regard for her position, no consideration for her birthright, then there was no telling what he might do to her.

At the same time, his insolence rasped on her nerves. She was used to homage and obedience, and her instinct was to exact them. She said, "I could have you taken up by the guard and thrown into a cell."

"Fine. Do it." He waited a second, then added with a wry grin, "Or have you mislaid your varlets and other men-at-arms? Not to mention your dungeon."

It had been a mistake to issue a threat she was not positive she could carry out—that knowledge did nothing to soothe her temper. "Are you peasant or freedman, archer or foot soldier?" she demanded. "Are you even loyal to my brother?"

"I don't know your brother from Adam." The man's face tightened as he spoke. He had, perhaps, taken note of the low standing which she considered he might occupy.

"Then where does your fealty lie?" she said.

"Here," he answered in unyielding tones, "with myself."

She blinked, momentarily disconcerted. "I see. Then perhaps you will serve as my escort if I tell you there will be a suitable reward for the task."

Fury flared in the dark depths of his eyes, followed by a look of utter contempt. "No."

She bit back a retort, knowing it was wiser to reason with this mysterious man. "Then what will it take to persuade you?"

"Ask me," he said. "Politely."

She took his point, and was even able to respect it. It was her habit to express her wishes in the form of a request; she was not autocratic by nature, nor was she uncaring of the feelings of those who served her. Still, pandering to this ruffian was something else again. If she had been less off-balance, less out of her element, it might have been easier. Or perhaps not. He disturbed her in some elemental manner she did not entirely comprehend.

"I believe I can find my own way, after all," she said, her shoulders straightening with pride.

"Great." He nodded and turned on his heel. With long, easy strides, he began to walk away.

She could not believe he would leave her so readily. It was puzzling. If he had any pretension to gentility, he should have felt honored to be of assistance to her. If he was of some middle rank, he should have come to her aid as an obligation, or to curry favor with her brother. If he was only a peasant, then fear of reprisal should have moved him to instant obedience.

It was possible he was none of those things, but only a rude forest outlaw. But if that were so, he should, at the very least, have taken her in his charge for the wealth to be gained from her ransom. He might also have kidnapped her for more personal use—tales of the ravishment of women unwise enough to wander alone into the forest were not unknown.

It was possible, of course, that she did not stir him to such a deed. The thought was unsettling. She directed a frown at the man's broad, retreating back.

It was then that Mara heard the deep, drumming sound high above her. It grew louder, a muffled rumble that turned rapidly to a booming roar. It was approaching, becoming a mind-shattering thunder that reverberated against the sky and seemed to shake the very heavens. Then something dark and dangerous streaked above the treetops with a deafening, deep-throated scream.

Her cry of terror was almost lost in the noise. Her every limb shaking, she squeezed her eyes closed and dropped to her knees with her hands over her ears.

In an instant, the man called Rayne was beside her. He closed his hands over her arms to lift her to her feet. Drawing her close, he murmured, "Hey, it's all right; you don't have to be scared. It's a plane, that's all, just a plane."

It was difficult to say which was more shocking, his words or the familiar way he had put his hands on her.

She should withdraw from him, and would, immediately, as soon as she was steady enough on her feet. In the meantime, there was comfort in his hold, and a deep security she had not known since she was a child.

She stiffened. Dearest heaven. What was she thinking?

She pushed away from him, though she had to hold his hard forearms an instant for balance. Removing her hands, she clenched them together in front of her. "What—what was it you called that . . . that thing?"

"An airplane. You know, the machine men use to fly?"

"To fly." Her voice was blank as her mind refused to absorb so fantastic a thought.

"Sure, like a bird. After all, Princess, honey, this is the twentieth century."

The twentieth century . . .

The idea was too incredible, too far beyond what was even remotely conceivable. She shook her head as she murmured, "No, no. Impossible."

"Cross my heart. Look, maybe I had better get you someplace where you can lie down. You don't look so good."

She could imagine. She felt chilled to the center of her being. Her lips were so stiff she could barely speak, and her hands trembled if she did not keep them clenched.

Twentieth century.

Seven hundred years. Seven hundred years into the future.

You could vanish . . .

No—it could not be. Could it?

What had the wizard done? What had he dared do to her?

The man from the future, this Rayne, was taking her elbow, urging her to come with him. She snatched her arm from his grasp. "Don't touch me!"

The man lifted his hands, backing away. "Fine. If that's what you want, honey, you've got it. But I'm leaving. You can come with me, or you can stay here. It's all the same with me."

He did not linger to hear her answer. Swinging around once more, he strode into the woods.

In a few seconds, he would disappear into the forest, leaving her alone in this strangely beautiful place that had suddenly become so alien. She let him take a half-dozen steps before she called out. "Wait!"

He paused, but did not look back.

"I'm coming." She picked up her skirts and began to walk after him.

She thought he would return to guide her, or at least remain where he was until she reached him. He did neither. Moving off again, he glided swiftly through the trees as if this woodland were his home and he had never known any other.

She could not catch up with him. Rotted tree trunks and snaking vines tripped her. Briers caught at her mantle and snagged in her linen coif, tearing it free of her hair. She abandoned it, hurrying after him.

But her footsteps could not match the length or speed of those of the man ahead. She had to break into a run just to keep him in sight. A stitch formed under her rib, and she longed to halt a moment to ease it, but to do so would mean losing sight of her rescuer or calling out to him to stop. Self-respect would permit neither.

The sight of a low building through the trees was a godsend. She thought they must be approaching the cottages of a village. Perhaps there would be a manor, or even some nobleman's seat where she might take shelter until she could decide what she must do.

She had been too optimistic. The building was no more than a woodsman's cottage made of logs. It stood alone in a clearing in the deep forest, with no other habitation of any kind in sight.

Disappointment flooded through Mara, bringing trepidation in its wake. She stopped for a moment. However, the strange man called Rayne was outdistancing her. She followed again with dragging footsteps.

It was only as she came closer to the cottage that she noticed how oddly it was constructed. Quite commodious in its dimensions, it had a roof of colored metal almost like armor, and a chimney of handsome red brick from which rose a trail of smoke. The logs were cut and fitted to such perfection that it seemed impossible human hands could be responsible. There was real glass in every window, and a finely fitted and molded door.

The interior was very like a typical cottage in that a main open space apparently served several functions, but there the resemblance ended. Surfaces had the polish of marble or the sheen of fine silver. Walls were covered with an amazingly smooth paper on which were painted intricate, brilliantly colored designs. Underfoot was a continuous rug which had the feel of wool sheared from the softest of lambs. Light appeared at the flick of a finger. There were no drafts, no dirt, no odors—only cleanliness and bright space.

Mara stood dazed while she watched Rayne prepare a hot drink, marveling at the graceful metal arc from which water miraculously flowed. He placed it on a table, then indicated that she must be seated. As she moved forward, he glanced at her face and his gaze narrowed.

"You've hurt yourself," he said. "Let me see."

Her face was stinging where a dangling brier vine had raked it. As she reached up to touch it, she felt a raised welt and a trace of what might be blood. Then the stranger was in front of her, taking her face in his large, firm hands and turning it toward the light.

His gaze met hers, black clashing with gray, and seemed to probe for something. She felt it like an invasion. Her heart jolted, then began a heavy beat, while her breath made a soft sound as she drew it between her parted lips.

His lashes flickered, then lowered like protective shields. He fastened his gaze on her scratch. "A minor wound," he said in low tones. "Come closer to the sink, and I will tend it."

He released her, turning away toward a double basin of silver metal that was set into a long, trestle-like board, and enclosed across the front with small doors. She followed him, but a frown pleated her smooth brow. There had been something in his voice just then, some inflection, some change in the tone or choice of his words, that was disturbingly familiar.

Impossible. This man was too brusque, too presumptuous, too lacking in veneration to be anyone she had ever known. That he had so casually placed his hands on her person was clear proof he was unaware of her identity. It was only her need for reassurance in this peculiar situation that had given rise to such a wild surmise.

Yet, this Rayne's touch was not unwelcome as he used a warm cloth to clean her face, then applied a soothing salve from a tube. She knew she should object, should turn away from him, but she did not. Instead, she stood quite still while her stomach muscles contracted, and she fought the surprising heat that rose inside her.

She felt a vague regret that he was not a forest outlaw. If he had been, he might have presumed to caress her with his hard, warm hands. . . .

Madness. Whatever the wizard had done to her had affected her mind. She must take care, for she had never in her life been so without protection, had never been so alone with a man.

As the man called Rayne finished his task, she used the only defense she had at present, one that had always served her well. "Thank you," she said in regal dismissal.

Turning from him, she moved with dignity to seat herself and take up the hot drink that had been served for her.

She took a sip, then grimaced, looking up at him with an expression of inquiry.

"Coffee," Rayne answered as he brought his own cup and took a seat across from her. "Don't tell me you've never tasted it before."

She swallowed and shook her head. At least the brew was warming, and would, perhaps, help calm the unsettled feeling inside her.

"I don't think I caught just what part of the world you came from," he went on. "Or how you came to be flaked out back there in the woods. And that title of yours—would you like to run it by me one more time?"

She hesitated over his unfamiliar phrases, but their meaning seemed clear enough. It wasn't necessary, of course, to give him the information. She said, "It hardly matters."

"Because you don't intend to stick around? Fair enough. You can use the phone over there, if you need to arrange transport."

She glanced at the instrument he indicated, but could not begin to guess its purpose. To disguise the fact, she said, "Transport?"

"Car, plane, train, bike. What cloud did you fall off of, Princess?"

He was having fun at her expense; she could see the flash of it in his eyes. "I believe," she said evenly, "that I can find my way without . . . transport."

"Walk? You've got to be kidding—it's all of twenty miles to the nearest town."

"A town?" she said with sudden hope. "Is it near Carreg Cennen?"

"Actually, it isn't near much of anything. It's in Louisiana." As she merely stared at him, he added, "Louisiana? America? The New World? You know— explorers, Columbus, independence, and all that?"

She closed her eyes as weariness overcame her. She had never heard of any of the places and things he mentioned with such blithe assurance.

"Come on, somebody must have brought you out here and left you," he said. "Somebody, somewhere, must be wondering where you are."

"I don't—that is, there is no one, not at the moment."

"Or not at all? What are you hiding, honey?"

"Nothing!"

His gaze was narrow, and far too knowing. Then he smiled, his eyes flashing with what might have been humor—or was it a threat? "Nobody wants you, and you don't have a clue about where you want to go. I guess that means it's just you and me, Princess."

Chapter Two

The princess, Rayne saw, did not trust him. It hurt. He knew it was unreasonable to feel this way, because she did not know him. But the fact that she did not—that she could not recognize him in this guise he had assumed—was even more painful.

He had always known that she did not see beyond his wizard's robes, of course. He was her counsellor, her confidant, someone always there when needed. She depended on him, consulted him in all things, discussed her thoughts, feelings, and instincts with him.

Yet she never saw him for who and what he was or how he felt—she never saw him as a man. It was supposed to be that way; still, it had troubled him from the first and grown increasingly intolerable with each passing year. The constant contact with the princess forced upon him by the siege had made the circumstances almost more than he could bear.

All the same, he felt naked before her without his robe. He had been only fifteen when he had donned it and walked at his father's heels into her presence; it had been years since he had stood before her without that concealment. So many years of bending his mind to her problems, of ignoring his own needs, of hiding his silent, useless adoration.

She had been little more than an imperious child when he first saw her, yet even then it had made his heart ache to look at her. He had wanted to fall on his knees and offer her every last ounce of his strength, every benefit of his hard-won skills—even his very life.

His father had known it; that was why the old wizard, on his deathbed, charged his apprentice with keeping the princess from harm. And Rayne thought he had kept faith with his father, if not with Princess Mara. He had prevented her from falling into the hands of the baron.

She was, instead, in his hands.

To reveal himself now, to show her precisely how much she was dependent upon him, was tempting beyond belief. He longed to know what she would say, how she would look at him, what she would think.

It was a risk he could not take.

He was so very much her wizard—her subject—that he was afraid she would never be able to see beyond the title. If she could not, then the relationship between them might be irreparably damaged—and he could not bear to lose the unique position of trust that he held.

No, she must discover his dedication and his strength for herself. She must acknowledge him as a man who could aid and protect her with his body as well as his mind. He wanted—needed—the grace of being accepted as her champion.

He had tried to tell her, had tried to make her see that it was the only way to save her. She would not listen. Now she must. He had to force her to realize that submission to the will of the baron—to any who didn't cherish her as she deserved—would make for a miserable existence. He would force her to it. He had to, before it was too late.

However, there was more than that to this interval out of time. The princess needed a respite from the siege, from its terrors and responsibilities. Her features were drawn with sleeplessness and fatigue, and there were dark circles under her eyes. She had lost more weight than she could spare, giving her a look of fine-boned fragility. And yet, to his eyes, she had grown only more beautiful.

Afraid his feelings would show on his face, he resumed his pretense of being a twentieth-century man. Parting his dry lips, he said, "Are you hungry? I can rustle up a sandwich and some soup."

She glanced at him and away again even as she swallowed and moistened her lips. "I—yes, food would be welcome. But what I should like above all things is a bath. This place . . . everything is so very clean. Even you . . ." She trailed to a stop, then asked in an almost humble tone, "Would such a thing be possible?"

He should have known, Rayne thought with a mental wince. She was so fastidious, and water had been precious during the siege, too precious for frivolous things such as bathing. He jumped to his feet. "By all means. Come along, and I'll show you."

He would have liked to stay to see her amazement over the hot water that gushed from the spout at a touch, the scented soaps, and thick toweling. Instead, he gave her instructions and a robe of soft cotton, then left to busy himself in the kitchen. Heating canned vegetable soup and slicing ham, he tried not to think of Princess Mara taking off her clothing in the bathroom beyond the thin walls.

Rayne had no particular difficulty with the fiendishly efficient appliances; he was able to project himself into this future world in such a way that he had a working knowledge of its inventions. Simple food was not beyond him, then, but it had been a long time since he had prepared a meal for himself. A wizard, like a princess, was used to being served.

Trimming fat from a ham slice, he almost took the end of his finger off—and might have had he not snatched the finger away. He cursed softly as he

checked the damage. Regardless, it gave him the germ
of an idea. It might be beneficial for Mara to have
a reminder that menial skills and labors had their
value—as did menial rank.

When she returned from her bath, he marveled at her
beauty. Never had he seen Mara fresh from her ablu-
tions, with her hair lying damp and curling across her
shoulders and down her back. It made him want to sink
his hands into the shining mass, to lift it and feel the
heavy tresses drape around his fingers.

The warm bath had relaxed her, he thought, for some
of the strain had left her features and her eyes appeared
calmer. Her skin was flushed a delicate rose. Moisture
lay like soft spring dew in the hollow at the base of her
throat, an invitation to kisses. He stood for a long moment, held in thrall by half-formed impulses, before he
swept a hand toward the table where her food waited.

He watched her as she ate: the way the light from
the window touched a honey-gold strand of hair lying
on her breast, the fan shape of the shadows cast by her
lashes, the tender curves of her mouth. As her wizard,
he had never been able to stare at her. The lowered
eyes, the bowed head, were too ingrained, both as a
sign of veneration and as protection for feelings he
could not acknowledge, much less display. To be able
to look at her as he pleased was exhilarating.

So absorbed was he in his own entertainment that he
missed the moment when she lowered her fork and
propped her head on her hand. The first thing he noticed was that the shadows of her lashes had become
thicker, darker, as her eyelids fluttered closed. An instant later, she swayed, asleep in her chair.

He leapt to his feet, catching her in his arms as she
slid from her chair. She had been more exhausted than
he knew. Or perhaps it was only the too-abrupt release
of the long, intolerable tension of the siege.

Swinging her high against his chest, he took a step, then stopped.

He had touched her before—in the woods, and again as he cleaned the scratch on her face. Back there on the castle battlement, before he'd sent her to the future, he'd clasped her arms so as to encompass her in his mind. Each of those small encroachments had been gratifying.

But this was different. He was holding her, semiconscious, in his arms. She was literally in his possession.

She was so delicate, so slight a weight. She rested perfectly in the cradle of his arms, her cheek against his heart. His chest lifted with a deep breath of wonder. At the same time, the warmth of her body flowing into his own ignited desires so long and sternly suppressed that he shuddered now in an effort to contain them.

He stared ahead and down the hallway leading to the bedroom. A ferocious frown drew his brows together as he wavered between honor and instinct.

The urge was too strong, while life, the future, and the exact extent of his powers were too uncertain. Or perhaps his resolve was weaker than he knew.

Moving abruptly, he strode down the hall and shouldered into the largest bedroom, the one with the great bed of a size fit for a king. Placing the princess gently upon the surface, he took off his boots and lay down beside her. He turned to his side, reaching to draw her into the curve of his body, fitting her slender hips against his pelvis, her legs along his own, her back against his chest. His arm fell naturally across her waist. His hand brushed her breast, and slowly, carefully, he cupped it.

He could feel her heartbeat against his wrist, could register the even rise and fall of her breathing against his rib cage. The scent of her hair was in his nostrils, and her slender curves burned their shape into his very being.

Such sweet torture. He wondered how long he could endure it. But even as the thought crossed his mind, he knew that the greater pain would be when it came to an end.

He could allow her only a single, short night of rest, no longer. There were limits to his abilities. He could stop time and hold events suspended only so long. One complete revolution of the earth, twenty-four hours; that was the total span during which he could keep the baron endlessly marching toward the castle at Carreg Cennen.

There were other restrictions, too, most of them concerned with life and human emotion.

He could not conjure up something from what wasn't there, therefore could not supply food for the hungry mouths at Carreg Cennen.

He could delay birth or death for a short span of time, but not forever.

He was powerless to create life or end it by magic alone, so could not cause the death of the baron with its application, no matter how much he might enjoy that ability.

He could not prevent hate, greed, rapacious desire, or other base faults, therefore could not stop war.

He could not make anyone fall in love—or out of it. Including himself.

Once, in a moment of despair, he had asked his father for some spell or potion to make himself irresistible to the princess.

"Think carefully on this wish," the old man had answered in gentle chiding. "Would you be happy with a heart won by such a trick? No, you would not, for what may be gained by such means can be lost in the same way. It becomes a mere commodity to be bought or sold, rather than life's rarest gift. Seek not, then, to compel love. It must be freely given, or it has no value."

His father had been a wise man, but he had never been forced to stand by while the woman he loved contemplated giving herself to a bloodthirsty madman. If love could not be compelled, Rayne thought, then perhaps respect—laced with a little awe—would be enough. He would have to try. There was no other way.

Shifting his weight, he leaned over Mara, supporting himself on one elbow. His gaze roved over her face, skimming the high cheekbones, the gracefully arched brows, the straight nose and tapered chin. The curves of her lips had the tender texture and soft color of rose petals.

Temptation stirred, stretched, broke its time-worn bonds. He dipped his head and brushed his lips across the shell-like arc of her ear, tasted the smooth flesh of her cheek, settled gently on her mouth.

She stirred, sighing as she eased closer against him.

Panic surged through his veins. He drew back and remained perfectly still while his heart hammered against the wall of his chest.

She did not wake. Rayne closed his eyes and softly released his breath. With exquisite care, he lowered his body to the coverlet and rested his head on the pillow, the same one on which she lay.

A lock of golden-brown hair fell across his lips. Not for the world would he have brushed it away.

A cracking explosion brought Mara upright out of bed. She stood in the middle of the strange room, disoriented and trying desperately to shake off the remnants of a sleep deep as death.

As the echoes of the mysterious sound died away, she saw that it was early morning, for a glimmer of light shone around the edges of the window curtains. She was alone, which was just as well. The robe she had been given with its odd front closure, had fallen open to the waist. Folding it closer over her chest, she paused.

Somewhere in her slumber had been a fleeting dream with a promise of joy. She could not quite recall it, but she felt its loss just the same.

The chemise, tunic, and mantle she had worn the evening before had been cleaned and left lying across the foot of the low bed. She would like to dress; she would feel much less vulnerable when she had donned proper attire. However, she had noticed no maidservants, in fact, no servants of any kind.

Her head came up as another explosion sounded, then another. This was not a plane, or whatever it was that the man, Rayne, had called the roaring thing in the sky. The noise sounded sharper, more immediate. She thought it came from just beyond the walls of the house. Her curiosity stirred as the prospect of immediate danger passed. She would like to investigate—surely she could manage to dress herself without assistance.

A short time later, she emerged from the sleeping chamber neatly clothed, with her hair captured by a gold fillet she'd found wrapped in her mantle. The rooms of the house were empty and still. There was no sign of Rayne. His absence could have some connection with the violent discharges that still shattered the early quiet at close intervals.

Sunrise was just streaking the heavens in shades of lilac and gold when she stepped outside. She gave it no more than a glance before descending the low steps and following a stone path which led around the house in the direction of the noise.

Rayne was standing in a clearing with the weapon he had carried the evening before raised to his shoulder. It appeared not unlike a catapult, or perhaps one of the small cannonades with handles which the baron had used during the siege. As she approached, Rayne fired it off again in rapid succession.

Instantly, a paper target in the shape of a man, located many yards away, was perforated at the chest in an overlapping pattern of holes. Mara gasped in amazement.

That low sound brought Rayne's head around. " 'Morning, Princess," he said, lowering his weapon. "Did you have a good night?"

"Indeed." It was not a subject she cared to discuss, since she could not remember falling asleep or how she came to be in the bed where she woke.

"You'll be wanting to make your breakfast, I expect," he went on. "You'll find everything you need in the kitchen."

"Make my—I'm not sure I understand." There were so many wonders inside the house that she could not begin to conceive of dealing with them.

"You know . . . cook food for yourself. Eggs, toast, whatever else you want. You do cook?"

Stung by his dry tone, she said, "I was given some instruction in the principles of ordering a household, including the preparation of foodstuffs, but you must understand that a princess does not concern herself with the actual work. Others attend to that."

"Yeah? What do you do when no one is around? Sit and starve?" His amusement was obvious.

"There are always servants."

"Well, there aren't any here," he said easily. "If you want to eat, you'll have to whip up something."

"I can't do that."

His humor faded. "Then I'm afraid you'll have to go hungry. I fed you last night because you were tired and a guest. You look sufficiently rested this morning, and it seems you may be staying a while. I expect you to see after yourself."

"Don't be foolish." The instant the words were spoken, she wished them back, knowing they sounded prideful.

"Oh, yes, you're royalty," he said with sardonic emphasis. "I suppose that means it's beneath you."

"No—no, but you apparently know much more about such things." It was, for her, a concession to even attempt such an explanation.

"Not me. Cooking is a woman's area of expertise."

"But not mine," she said distinctly. "I know diplomacy, court etiquette, the art of conversation, and how to embroider tapestry. I can provision a garrison, arrange the storage of grain and cattle paid in tribute—even repel a siege. But I do not know cookery."

"You'll learn," he said, his tone uncompromising.

She lifted her brows in disbelief. "Because you say it must be so?"

"Exactly."

"You are deluded," came her prompt reply. "I do nothing I have no wish to do. Nor will I stay here where I am ordered about like a skivvy."

As she moved to leave him, he stepped to block her way. There was a steady light in his dark eyes and a firm set to his mouth. "You will stay," he said with grim certainty. "You have no choice."

"My good man," she said with a laugh of sheer surprise, "I am not your prisoner."

"No?" Reaching out, he took her wrist, holding it lightly in his supple fingers. "Escape me, then."

She met his gaze so close above her. It was as hard as granite and totally implacable. She had an odd feeling that he could look into her mind, could read her sudden knowledge of how little defense she had against him. Her breath caught in her chest while her heart shuddered in a response not entirely due to anger or fear.

It was intolerable.

She set her feet and jerked her wrist, trying to free it from his grasp. His fingers tightened mercilessly.

The pain was abrupt and excruciating. She felt the bones of her wrist grind together. Her knees grew week, and she heard a roaring in her ears. She cried out with a thin sound embarrassing in its helplessness.

She was freed instantly. Rayne swung away from her, then paused, his shoulders set and his hands clenched into white-knuckled fists. He stood in perfect stillness, and when he finally spoke his voice was harsh with something that might have been regret, but could as easily have been carefully repressed violence.

"I didn't mean to hurt you, but you—you try my patience, and I don't have the time for it."

"You?" she said in indignation as she cradled her wrist. "It is I who have no time. While I stand here listening to you prattle of food, my people may be dying. And I am not there. I am not . . . there."

Her voice trailed away; she was too full of emotion to continue. She turned from him in a swirl of fabric and walked swiftly to the house before he could see her anguish. For a moment, she feared he meant to follow, but when she reached the cabin door, she was alone.

When she'd calmed herself, she realized her folly. Perhaps this Rayne was right in what he had said: she might have no real choice except to remain here with him. What else was she to do when she knew nothing about this new world with its odd landscape, its peculiar construction materials and fabrics, its frightening weapons and means of locomotion? But if she must stay, wasn't it rash to antagonize the man?

She had to admit that the situation could have been handled more diplomatically. Yet he had touched her on the raw with his smiles at her expense, his penetrating glances, and superior strength. He made her doubt

who and what she was, made her question how she
should behave toward him.

Added to that, he seemed to think he held her captive. He had even put his hands on her in anger. What
more might he do?

No. She could not stay. Once she was well away, she
could surely find some means in this land of wonders
to return to her rightful time and place.

For the moment, however, she could do nothing except remain in the house. Not that it would serve as
much of a refuge; this Rayne had followed behind her
after all, watching over her like a sheep dog guarding
its charge.

Rayne broke his morning fast with the juice of
golden apples, also with smoked pork strips and eggs
in fresh butter. The food was cooked upon a rectangle
of white porcelain which grew hot without flame. He
toasted perfectly even slices of bread by dropping them
into twin slits made in the top of a shining silver urn.
Swift, economical of motion, he moved between the
peculiar cooking devices with easy competence. Amazing.

So absorbed was she in watching him work that
Mara almost forgot to be hungry, until he slid a laden
trencher of porcelain onto the table and sat down before it. There was only one such trencher, and it held
everything that had been prepared.

She was to have none of the delicious-smelling fare.
He had told her how it would be, and it appeared that
he meant what he said. Her stomach protested—her
very soul cried out for the sustenance—but she remained silent.

She thought of rising and making something to eat
for herself, but she did not know how the magic of
producing heat was performed. To ask Rayne to show
her would be to capitulate to his decree, something that

she refused to consider. She had become accustomed to thin rations, after all.

He was enjoying his food; that much was obvious. He ate his meat in large bites, and crushed the toasted bread between white, even teeth. Yet he was not sloppy about it. He used one of the peculiar Italian utensils known as a *forchetta,* rather than a knife, and he wiped his fingers and mouth with the kind of beautifully dyed linen usually reserved for summer tunics.

The elegance of his belongings and his manners did not make her think better of him. He was overbearing and lacking in a proper respect. She despised him.

He also made her uneasy. Never had she been so aware of a man, of his inherent strength and the force of his personality. There was something elemental about him, as if all pretense of conventional behavior had been pared away to reveal dangerous natural instincts. In the face of these things, defiance was not just a vital urge, but a necessity. She could not, would not, allow him to dominate her. It went against her upbringing. It was contrary to her nature. Most of all, it offended her pride.

He made no effort to speak to her while he ate. It was possible he had nothing to say, but it seemed more likely that his silence was meant as a rebuke. He was trying to intimidate her. She did not mind—she would just ignore him. She had decisions to make and plans to perfect.

Rising to her feet after a few minutes, Mara left the main room and moved down the hallway to the sleeping chamber. She half-expected that Rayne would call her back, perhaps command her to watch him finish his meal. He did not. With a sigh of relief, she stepped inside and closed the door behind her.

She moved swiftly to the window and flung the curtains aside. The glass in the frame was like none she had ever seen, as was the wire mesh behind it. Still, the mechanisms to hold them both in place seemed simple enough to manipulate.

With the window opening clear, she stood a moment, listening. No sound came from the main room. She raised her skirts and put her leg over the window sill.

Once out of the house, she kept to the edge of the woods, circling so as to remain unseen from the front windows. There was a track she had noticed which led from the house and into the woods. If she followed it, surely it would connect with a main road which might take her to a village or a manor, or perhaps even the keep of some nobleman. It seemed worth the attempt, as she and Rayne could not, surely, be the only two people in this land.

Once she reached the track, she set a fast pace, for there was no way of knowing how long it might be before Rayne discovered her absence. She did not doubt that he would come after her; his determination seemed of that nature. He meant to best her; he seemed to think it his privilege and his duty.

One moment the forest was close around the track, the next she came out into the open. Before her lay a hard, black surface that stretched for a quarter of a mile or more before disappearing over the rise of a hill. It was, she thought, a road rather like the wide, stone-paved thoroughfares left behind in Britain by the Romans, and yet it was more level and far smoother. She stood frowning at it as she tried to envision what kind of men and tools had been used to construct such a wonder.

Then, from some distance down the road, she heard a low, rushing hum. It grew louder with its fast approach, becoming a high-pitched roar. Mara felt a faint vibration under her feet. From over the rise, there came a great metallic vehicle shining silver in the sun.

It was not a plane, but something else that rolled on

fat black wheels along the ribbon of hard surface. No, there were two vehicles. One was larger and more bulky than the other, and emitted an even louder roar. The bigger of the two was giving chase to the smaller, bearing down on the other vehicle as if it meant to crush it.

Mara leaped away from the hard surface and whirled to dash back into the forest's concealing shade. From the protection of a large tree trunk, she stared warily at the black ribbon while her heart thudded against her rib cage.

Abruptly, she was caught by one arm, then flung around so that the bark of the tree scraped her back. A hard body pressed against her, flattening her against the trunk from head to heels. She caught a sharp, gasping breath, then held it trapped in her lungs.

"I should have let them get you," Rayne said against her ear as the great metal vehicles thundered past them.

She exhaled in a rush of what might have been relief or shock—or both. Her voice constricted, she said, "Why didn't you?"

"Because," Rayne answered in low tones as he eased closer still, "I discovered that I want you more."

Chapter Three

Mara drew a swift breath. The words Rayne had spoken were no idle jest or jeering banter. She could feel the truth of them as he pressed his pelvis against her.

No man had ever wanted her for herself. At least, none had dared show it.

The baron had certainly harbored no personal desire for her. To him, she was only a route to power. Marrying her would be a political ploy, and bedding her an act no more important to him than pressing his seal into the soft wax at the foot of the marriage contract.

If other knights and nobles of her court had felt passionate regard for her, they kept it to themselves. There was little benefit to be gained by lusting after a princess. She was not free to bestow her heart, and usually too well-guarded for stolen kisses or secret trysts.

Until now.

She was here with Rayne, alone. She wondered what he might dare—and whether she had the courage to discover it.

Where had that impulse come from? She could not tell, not while she was trapped by his hard hands and her blood surged in her veins with such a violent, uneven rhythm. No one had ever affected her in quite this way.

"You forget yourself, sir," she said in husky reproof, waiting for his response with mingled terror and expectation.

He laughed. "You mean I'm forgetting who you are? It's hardly likely."

"I mean," she said, "that you forget your place. And mine."

He shifted a little to let her feel his arousal more fully. "I have no place here, nor do you. We are only a man and a woman with nothing between us except a few rags of clothing and good intentions."

"One of us has good intentions. The other—"

"Yes?" he said softly as she paused.

The dappled sunlight falling through the tree limbs overhead gleamed in his hair and danced in his eyes. It made him seem like some woodland creature, fierce and a little fey . . . and familiar. Doubt stirred inside her, but she pushed it aside. He was only an outlaw, after all.

"One of us," she said deliberately, "has the intentions and instincts of an animal."

His face lost all expression. "Why, Princess," he said with a sardonic edge to his voice, "you should have told me before. I would have been happy to oblige your animal urges."

This was going too far. She said quickly, "I didn't mean—"

"Oh, I think you did, sweetheart. And so do I."

Holding her gaze, he slowly lowered his head and touched his lips to hers.

Warm . . . his mouth was warm as the fine spring morning, and just as beguiling. Without haste or undue pressure, he teased her lips into exquisite sensitivity, testing the delicate molding and tucked, moist corners. Her lashes fluttered down as a tremor leaped along her nerves, spreading to the deepest reaches of her body. Her limbs, which had become so taut, were suddenly pliant and accepting.

His lips parted infinitesimally then, and she felt the soft tip of his tongue engage hers in subtle play.

Blindly, she followed his lead, enticed by the sweetness, the fine-nubbed abrasiveness, of the tender invasion. There burgeoned inside her a peculiar, aching excitement. Lifting her hands with a soft murmur, she smoothed his shoulders and the strong column of his neck, then closed her fingers mindlessly on the thick silk of his hair.

He froze, then withdrew. So strong was her sense of loss that she kept her eyes closed for long seconds while she sought to banish all sign of it.

She had wanted him to go on holding her, had not cared what else he might do. He must never know this. She could not hand him that fearful weapon. But how was she to conceal it?

"I suppose that was a kiss," she said, assuming a tone of cool irony. "Thank you for the demonstration; it appeared competent. If I should feel the need to have it repeated, I will summon you for the task."

Rage darkened his face. She watched it grow, and was desolated, but it could not be helped.

"My kisses are not given on command," he said, each word slicing like a knife.

"No?" The reply was soft, but there was barbed certainty behind it. She even smiled.

"I am my own man. You are my guest—and, yes, my prisoner. If I desire to kiss you, I shall. Otherwise, you will have nothing of me."

The words wounded her self-respect. They were meant to, she knew, but knowing didn't erase her need to repudiate his assertions. "You have no right to hold me captive, and I will not submit to it. As for any other indignities, you venture them at your own risk."

"Who will prevent me from doing as I please with you?" he demanded. "Who will keep and defend you? Where is your champion?"

His voice. Beneath the anger was maddening reason. It was a sound she knew. More than that, he had slipped into a cadence and accent very like her own, or like that of someone she knew well.

Could it be? Was it possible? If it was, could she ever forgive him?

In icy disdain, she answered, "I am no weakling. I can and will defend myself."

An expression of cool determination invaded his features. He reached to take her arm in a firm grip. "Then guard yourself well."

She was jerked forward, off-balance. At the same time, he bent from the waist to catch her at her midriff and lift her over his wide shoulder. Surprise and the sudden pressure across her abdomen stole her breath. Before she could move or protest, a hard arm clamped around her knees. Rayne settled her with a quick shift, then began to talk with long, swift steps back down the track toward the cottage.

Bouncing upside down, Mara felt the nose-tingling pressure of blood rushing to her head. It combined with her fury and indignation to pound in a blood-red haze before her eyes. She wanted to scream, wanted to kick and beat at the man who held her—she would have liked to order him taken and whipped, then flung into some dungeon.

The certain knowledge that none of it would help her kept her still. She grasped desperately at the folds of his shirt to steady herself and found handfuls of taut flesh. She felt him flinch as her nails bit into him, but she did not care.

"Put ... me ... down," she said through clenched teeth.

He made a deep noise somewhere between a grunt and a laugh, and leaned with a swooping movement to duck under a tree limb before plunging from the track into woods.

When she'd recovered her breath from the dizzying

swing, she tried again. "Put me down or I'm going to be sick all over you."

It seemed he intended to ignore that possibility. Then suddenly he came to a halt and she was catapulted backward. Arms like iron bands caught her in mid-flight, locking across her back and under her knees. With a jarring swiftness she was hefted against the firm musculature of his chest.

"Better?" he asked with jeering politeness.

It was better, yes, but also far worse. She was more comfortable, but she could see the satisfaction in his face, feel how powerless she was against his superior strength. She wanted to kill him, yet she also felt a reluctant admiration; if she were honest, a secret anticipation; and curiosity that would not be denied.

"Why? Why are you doing this?" The words, meant to be imperious, came out as a strangled plea.

He glanced down at her, then away again before he began to walk once more. The words taut, he said, "Surely you can guess."

"I prefer to know."

"Ransom, maybe. The pay off should be considerable for a princess."

"I suspected that at first, but now I somehow doubt payment is your aim."

Watching him, she saw no sign of strain on his features. Neither was there the slightest faltering in his step or weakening of his arms around her. His strength really was exceptional.

"You don't seem to know your way around," he offered almost at random. "You need somebody to take care of you."

"I suppose you have nothing better to occupy your time?"

"Let's say I expect the reward to be worth the effort."

"Reward? And what might that be?"

"It depends. The matter is open for negotiation."

There was, she thought, a certain grim evasion in his voice. With great daring, she asked, "Another kiss, you mean, or perhaps more than that?"

He came to a halt, and stared down at her. A fleeting hunger crossed his face, then was gone. "Whatever pleases you," he said evenly, "including your own sweet self."

The temerity of the man was beyond belief. "Not very likely!" she retorted.

"We'll see."

His tone carried a palpable threat. Turning her head, Mara saw the cottage was before them. He had taken a shortcut through the woods.

Inside, everything was just as they had left it: the scraps of his breakfast in the dish, the dish and the eating utensils still on the table. The pan where he had cooked the pork and eggs had cooled, leaving the grease congealed in the bottom.

"Home, sweet home," he said as he stood her on her feet, holding her arm to steady her. She drew herself up, turning away in the direction of her sleeping chamber.

"Hold on." He tightened his grasp. "I think it would be a good idea if you cleaned the kitchen, then made yourself something to eat."

Clean? Cook? They were back to that? It was a far cry from what she had half-expected. She stared at him with disbelief before she spoke. "I am no scullery maid."

"We've already established your status, Princess," he answered with irony. "I'm talking practical measures here. There's only one pan, and you need to clean it before you can use it. I'm not going to do it for you."

"I don't require your service, just as I don't require your food."

"Don't be ridiculous," he said sharply. "You're nothing but skin and bones. You need to eat."

His description of her form was most irritating. She said, "My appearance is no concern of yours."

"It is if I have to look at you," he corrected her as he put his fists on his hips. "Will you do as I say, or are you going to make me force you?"

Her head was high and her gray eyes clear as she faced him. "You may be larger and stronger than me, but there are no means you can use to compel me against my will."

"No?" he inquired with soft emphasis.

"No." She lifted her chin as she answered, but her voice was not as commanding as she would have liked.

"You're dead wrong," he said, taking a step closer. "You are in my hands, as surely as if I had captured you like one of your old-fashioned knights. Do you have any idea what that means?"

She retreated a step, her voice uneven as she said, "Nothing at all, for I refuse—"

"Refuse, by all means—for what good it will do you." He advanced another long stride so she was forced to back away from him. "You have no defense against me."

"I will resist with all my power."

"Do that. It will make a fine excuse to strip you naked and beat you."

"You wouldn't!" Her eyes widened as she searched his implacable features. She stumbled backward another step.

"Wouldn't I?" he said, his words matching his steady footsteps as he moved after her. "That is only the beginning of what I might do. I could make you walk unclothed before me. I could allow you no privacy while you bathe or attend to nature's needs. I could make you lie nude beside me in my bed. I could use you as I please, when I please. What," he finished leaning toward her as she came up against the edge of the table, "is there to stop me?"

"Decency," she said in desperation as she put out her hand to ward him off. "Honor."

His smile was feral. "I am not noble, certainly have no royal blood. What have decency and honor to do with me?"

She had been wrong, He could not possibly be her wizard, as she had come to suspect. "Honor" had been a by-word with her wizard—"honor" and "caring." If this Rayne had sounded like him for a brief moment, it was due to nothing more than his mocking imitation of her own speech.

She swallowed hard in dismay. Suddenly light-headed, she closed her eyes. She felt so very dizzy. Hunger, that was the reason—certainly it wasn't disappointment or grief.

No, it was just that she had eaten so little these past weeks. Even the night before, she had been too exhausted to do more than taste what had been prepared for her. It was stupid, really, to defy her captor over something so necessary as food. She should have chosen her ground more wisely.

Captor.

What a bitter taste the word left on her tongue.

She wanted to fight him tooth and nail, but it would do no good. She could not defeat his hard strength if he chose to use it; she had few illusions on that score. In which case, it would be best if she did not compromise her dignity by giving him reason to lay hands on her.

She must surrender to his demands; there was no other way. She would, no doubt, survive the damage to her pride, but could she endure the humiliation to the soul?

She moistened her lips, said, "If I agree—"

"No conditions," he said. "They will not be met—they never are."

She looked away from him, struggling to find the words to appease him. At the same time, a great desolation rose inside her, and she felt the acid sting of tears behind her eyes. There had been such promise in the thought that this Rayne might be her wizard. Now it was gone.

The glaze of hardness faded from his face. He eased away from her, though without giving her room to escape. "Yes," he said quietly, "bowing to pressure is sometimes the wiser course. Retreating leaves you free to fight another day."

It was a gesture of unexpected consideration and understanding. She turned her head, searching his strong features.

His lashes came down over his eyes, shuttering them. "The pan first," he said, and there was no compromise in his voice.

She hardly knew where to begin. But as she carefully called to mind Rayne's earlier movements about the kitchen, she soon figured out how to raise the lever above the double basin to make the water flow, and also where to find the colored scouring sand.

Rayne, who had seated himself at the table prompted her from time to time. As she began to cook, he provided detailed instructions on where the food was kept in the white metal box that was somehow cold inside, and how to release the pork and eggs from their indestructible packaging. He also told her what to do to produce heat from the white ceramic rectangle set into the long work area.

A flush of irritation rose to her cheekbones now and then at the faintly superior tone of his voice. She also suspected he was laughing at her behind his hand. It seemed unfair—she couldn't help it if she had no skill at these tasks. People weren't born knowing such things. Besides, she had always been too busy. So much of her life had been taken up by her duties.

Duty, always duty. It was a word that had been hammered into her from childhood. There had never been time for nonproductive chores, for play or friendship or, later, the pleasures of flirtation; she was lacking in skill in all these things, especially the last. She had formed the usual unsuitable attachments of young girls, but there had been no time to dwell on such minor infatuations. They had all passed. Except for one.

She had long been intrigued by her wizard. His presence near her gave her secret pleasure; the vibration of his voice alone sometimes affected her with a low, sweet thrill. She relied on his view of the world, sought his counsel when she was troubled, summoned him for the comfort of speaking her mind and knowing that no one else would ever hear what had passed between them. He was hers and she knew it, depended on it, could not bear for it to be any other way.

Now and then, she was possessed by an insane need to rip away the cowl and robe that concealed him and force him to face her, to allow her to see him as he truly was. She never quite dared. It was not that she feared what he might look like. Rather, she was terrified that if she exposed him, he would leave her. The concealment he wore was for their mutual protection; it placed a physical barrier between them so that they might come close in spirit. If it was not there, then everything would be changed. Still, she had often thought—even dreamed—of what he might be, how he might appear.

Yes, she had wondered. Now she had to be absolutely sure.

Taking up an egg to crack it into a bowl, she looked across at Rayne with a searching and pensive gaze. "Who are you really?" she asked. "What is your rank?"

Rayne was silent for the space of a long breath. There was a delicate purpose in her tone that made his stomach muscles contract, as though absorbing a blow. His voice sardonic, he repeated, " 'Rank?' All right, I'll bite. I have none, and no use for it."

"Everyone has it whether they need it or not," she said with a frown. "It's a matter of birth."

"A man is what he makes of himself here, no matter how he was born."

The look she gave him was doubtful, but she didn't argue. "Where are your people?"

"I have none."

"You were an orphan," she said thoughtfully. "A foundling, perhaps?"

He could not refuse to answer. "My parents were a couple of crazy kids who had no business making a baby. I was put up for adoption."

She gave him a narrow look before she busied herself, removing the bacon from her pan and pouring eggs into the hot fat to scramble them. Finally, she spoke without looking at him. "In the place where I live, there was once a fine and powerful knight who loved a beautiful nun. He lay with her one day in the woods, and a child was conceived. When the knight learned of the nun's disgrace, he renounced his title and estates to his uncle, then went on crusade as penance for his misdeed."

"A dumb thing to do," Rayne said in compressed tones. "Your knight should have stayed to protect the lady."

"It was a moral question," Mara said with a quick shake of her head. "He felt he had no right to happiness, for he had trespassed against his own code as well as the laws of God—but never mind. While in the land of the Saracens, the knight died. The nun, hearing of it, was distraught. She wandered away from the convent into the hills when her time came upon her. She gave birth to her child in a cave, and there she also died."

Rayne knew he should at least try to deflect her. "Do all your stories have sad endings?"

"This one is not a total tragedy," she answered with calm perseverance. "The child, a boy, was found by a wise old man, a wizard who took him as his son and taught him all he knew, then set him free in a library of books from the ancients to learn what else he might."

"Touching," Rayne said. Taking his courage in his hands, he added, "So what became of him?"

"He grew into a fine man, a wizard of great wisdom also. He offered, once, to kill his great-uncle for me."

"A bit unnatural of him." Rayne watched as she carefully transferred her cooked eggs to a plate.

"Not at all," she answered, barely glancing at him as she picked up her plate and brought it to the table. "His great-uncle, Baron Ewloe, is a man of cruelty and vaunting ambition. He gained his title from his nephew, who died in the crusade—the young wizard's father, you see—whom some say the baron encouraged to go and fight the Saracens. It wasn't enough. The baron also wanted my brother's throne. He besieged the castle while Prince Stephen was away, seeking to use me to obtain his prize."

"And did your wizard kill the evil baron for you?" Rayne said tightly.

She poured juice in a glass, then carried it toward him. "I could not allow that, for his counsel is irreplaceable. He should not have expected it."

The words carried a soft note that touched Rayne's heart like the stroking of gentle fingertips. Never in this life, surely, would his princess have allowed him to hear it if she had guessed his identity. Never.

Mara sat down opposite him and picked up her fork. Turning it in her hand for a doubtful moment, she

reached with it to poke at her egg, then proceeded to
cut off a bite and pick it up to transfer it to her mouth.
She was quick, he had to give her that; she'd caught
the knack of the unfamiliar implement at once.

It was good to see her tuck into the food, regardless
of the measures he had been forced to take to arrange
it. His fault, that; he should have chosen a better ploy
to demonstrate his so-called power. He wondered if she
would ever forgive him.

As casually as he was able, he said, "Too bad you
didn't have a few rifles there at your castle. They
would have made short work of any siege."

"You mean the weapon I saw you using earlier? Tell
me, will its projectile pierce armor?"

"Like paper—the kind of armor you're talking
about."

"Formidable. It also seemed effective at some distance."

"A trained soldier could stand on the highest tower
of your castle and pick off the attackers—even this
baron himself. He would never know what hit him."

Her eyes were dark as she gazed somewhere beyond
his shoulder. Abruptly she focused on his face. "Have
you ever met a man in a contest of honor with such a
weapon?"

Rayne's heart thudded in his chest as he began to
suspect the direction of her thoughts. Trying for a careless air, he said, "That method of settling fights died
out long ago—at least in theory. The problem is, rifles
and most other modern weapons are too lethal. Honor
becomes a moot point when both guys are likely to get
killed."

"I see," she said with a sigh. "As you say, it is too
bad."

As she turned her attention to her meal again, she
noticed that she had failed to supply herself with

bread. Rising, she moved to retrieve the loaf that lay on the cabinet in its wrapper.

As he watched her, Rayne realized that though she did not recognize him, she had gained an appreciation for his strength. It was possible she thought he might have a chance on the field of honor—then again, it could well be that she simply did not care whether a chance-met woodsman lived or died.

She had truly valued her wizard, at least enough to keep him from danger by denying him the right to face the baron. He had that consolation.

Or was that it? Could it be possible that she knew who he was, but that he had forfeited the right to her regard? Perhaps she was no longer concerned for her wizard since she had met him face to face. Possibly she was even anxious to send him out onto the field. If he defeated the baron, she would be reinstated in her proper place. If he lost, he would receive what he deserved for daring to abduct her and show disregard for her person.

He must test her somehow. He had to know.

As she returned with her bread, he swung around in his chair and stretched out his long legs so they blocked her path. "I believe I'll have a cup of coffee to keep you company while you eat," he said with lazy suggestion.

"As you please," she said, lifting her skirts in one hand as though she intended to step over him.

"I meant for you to bring it," he said as he shifted to prevent her passage.

"Did you?" she said pleasantly. "I can't imagine why."

"I thought we had settled this discussion."

"You were wrong. We settled that I would fend for myself in the matter of my own food preparation. Nothing was said about acting the servant for you."

"We settled that I am able to command you," he corrected her, then allowed his voice to soften. "Still, you might, if you wished, do it to please me."

Her gaze was defiant as she met his clear look. "And why should I feel any desire to do that?"

He smiled and deliberately tilted his head. "You know why."

He saw her eyes narrow slightly, and felt a tingle of alarm along his spine. Then her lips curved in a slow smile. Reaching over him to put her bread on her plate, she swung away and moved to where the coffee pot sat on its warmer.

Rayne watched her find a mug and fill it, leaving the brew black and unsweetened, as he had taken it earlier. Gaze lowered, she turned and walked toward him with it, moving with slow care so as not to spill a drop.

He should have known. He might have, if he had not been so gratified that she would comply with his wishes, so puffed up with conceit that she had noted and remembered his preference for black coffee. He didn't notice the grim set of her mouth, didn't see the tremor in her fingers—until she reached across him toward the table, until the cup was poised over his lap.

The cup tilted. Hot brown liquid poured out, streaming, steaming as it cascaded downward.

Rayne cursed as he flung away from it, his chair overturning behind him. Mara danced away from him and the falling chair, but slipped in the coffee splashing across the floor. The cup flew out of her hand as she fell. He grabbed for her, but became entangled in her skirts. Taking her with him, he twisted with her as he landed on his side, absorbing the brunt of the crashing fall.

He lay for a winded instant, then heaved over, dragging her under him, placing her on her back with her wrists captured in his hard fingers. Drenched in coffee, breathing hard, he settled a portion of his weight upon her.

His right thigh burned from hip to ankle, though his body against her soft, warm wetness was growing hotter still. Mara, protected by her layers of skirts, appeared to have taken no injury.

She recovered first. She braced, then arched her back in a frantic effort to throw him off. Shifting, he used his weight to hold her immobile. She heaved this way and that, struggling while he pressed her down until his body felt welded to her every curve and hollow, and he could feel her panting breaths in the very center of his being. He shifted a fraction, and the heated hardness of his arousal nudged against the softness between her thighs. Her writhing under him pressed her more firmly against it.

Abruptly, she ceased struggling to lie perfectly still. "Let me go!" she demanded in tight rage. "Did you think that I would obey you, all meek and mild, for the sake of a single kiss?"

"I never said it was for a kiss." His voice was less than even as he sought to control the urges that boiled in his blood and mounted, distilled to their essence, to his head.

"What, then? There is nothing else between us that comes close to affection."

That wasn't true, but if she did not know it, then his holding her helpless was only exacting revenge for her defiance. That made him no better than the baron.

He breathed hard and deep, trying to think, to decide how to bring some good from this situation he had created. It was impossible while his every instinct screamed for him to take the woman in his arms. He wanted her now—this moment—before it was too late.

Soon, soon, he must reverse this precarious spell and take them both back to Carreg Cennen. If he did not, they would be trapped here in this future time where everything was strange and new, and where there was nothing between this woman and himself except anger and fear and the kind of desire that, if satisfied, must inevitably turn to hate.

Rayne snapped his eyes shut and gave his head a hard shake to dislodge his raging inclinations. Releasing Mara, he pushed away from her and climbed to one knee. Reaching to take her hands, he then drew her up beside him.

She came, but there was a frown between her eyes. Curling her fingers around his, she clung to him when he would have let her go. In a strained voice, she said, "What is it? What is wrong?"

"If you value your virtue," he said with contained force, "you will take yourself well away from me."

Her lips parted on a soft sound that might have been surprise or distress. Wide-eyed, she searched his face, until her gaze caught and held his own.

Her pupils were dark and reflective, the surrounding gray irises silver-edged and shimmering with some inner light. Her face was flushed, but her features were composed—if she despised him now, she hid it well.

She was everything that was good and fine, bright and beautiful and unobtainable. She was proud, but then she had nothing for which to be humble. She was autocratic, though never unfair. If she was arrogant, it was for self-protection, and because there were those who would deny her worth, being without value themselves.

She was his princess and his only love, and if he could not save her as he'd planned, he could still serve her. If she would permit it.

"Forgive me," he said, lowering his eyes, inclining his head as he had been so strictly taught by his father. "I meant . . . no harm."

She drew a short, sudden breath. For long seconds, there was not another sound. The sunshine falling through the window caught the spilled coffee with a bronze gleam, and threw its reflection upon their faces in dazzling lozenges of light.

Then she reached to touch his cheek, trailing her fingers down it, along the turn of his jaw, and over his lips to their center as if memorizing the lines. "It is possible," she said quietly, "that I will obey you in that . . . if you will kiss me a second time."

He did not breathe, could not even blink. "If I should dare," he said in a constricted whisper, "I may not be able to stop."

She hesitated. He saw the glimmer of tears along her lashes, and the slight upward tilt of her chin as she made her decision. Her voice so soft it could barely be heard, she whispered, "Then . . . don't."

She knew him. She must, for how else could his princess come so near to offering herself to him? She would never extend that grace to a stranger, one who had done nothing except thwart her and attempt to dominate her. She was intelligent beyond most; she knew what he was doing, knew why and accepted it. He had won.

They would go from here soon, and he would fight for her. He would fight because he must—because surrender or defeat was unthinkable. Then she would return to her rightful place, and so would he. These next few hours would be all they could ever have as mere man and woman.

But could he take advantage of the power he had used to bring Mara to this point? It would not be right or honorable. Moreover, she might not be inclined to forgive that betrayal so easily when they regained their proper stations.

Yet, how could he refuse? To injure her pride by spurning her invitation would be just as unforgivable.

He wondered with grim honesty if this last was merely an excuse to obey the clamor of his blood. Was he searching for a reason to reach out and take hold of

a secret dream before it slipped away, before the cease-
less passage of time left him with only regret?

No. The answer was there before him. Had she seen
it, too? Did she know it was the only course? Did she
recognize that as long as they could each pretend she
didn't know who he was, then this moment could be
taken, whole and clear, from their past and their present? It would be theirs, without apologies or consequences, something to set in amber and keep against
the long, cold years that lay ahead.

And if all else failed, he thought in despair, it was
within his power to ensure that she did not remember
this short time to come, would never recall that he had
loved her.

Yes, it would be better that way.

Being a wizard was good for that much, if nothing
else.

Chapter Four

Mara had known he would not fail her. He never had.

As Rayne reached out to take her into the strong circle of his arms, she moved to meet him, pressing close against the hard strength of him, then closer still. She wanted him, needed him, could not bear in that moment to be denied the comfort and solace of him.

He was her wizard, her support, the other half of her heart and mind. She had known it well for long years, but had lacked the courage to acknowledge it.

She knew it now, just as she knew him beyond doubting. No one else could bend his head to her with such a precise degree of consideration and deference that yet lacked even the shadow of humility. No one else had ever sought so diligently to protect her—even when it was from himself. If he had revealed to her the hard edge of his nature, it was for a purpose. If she was surprised, the fault was her own, for she had known there was steel inside him, but had never ventured to test the tempered strength of it.

In his wisdom and power, Rayne had taken her prisoner to show her how intolerable being at the command of the baron would be to her, how much she would hate being mere chattel won in war. He had thought to make her see that submitting under force to the will of another person would be an endless humiliation fit to shrivel the spirit and bring death to joy and pride. He had succeeded.

But he had also erred, for he had shown her how it would be to surrender to his will. He had—whether he intended it or not—shown her the face of love.

"Come," he said, and lifted her in his arms. She turned her face into his neck, brushing her lips against the pulse which throbbed there, as he carried her along the hall and into his sleeping chamber. She was placed on the great, low bed with its silken-smooth sheets of celestial blue.

Or was she?

As he settled beside her, he pressed his lips to her eyelids, first one and then the other, to close them. Suddenly, she was in a bluebell wood with the fresh scent of May around her and the warm sun on her skin. She was blissfully naked, and the cool stems of bluebells tickled and caressed and cushioned her. His hands were as delicate as the grass, brushing over her, leaving the shivering, beaded skin of gooseflesh in their wake.

A soft breeze stirred her hair, lifting a strand so it made a satin curtain over her breast. He leaned closer to find the taut rose nipple through the tresses, laving it with his tongue, taking it delicately between his teeth, then gently, gently into his mouth. All the while, his hands stroked her thighs, the slender turn of her waist, and smoothed in questing circles over the flat, white surface of her abdomen.

Languor, rich and sweet, rose inside her. She lifted her hand to clasp his shoulder and found the skin firm and sun-warmed, with the muscles underneath as unyielding as those of a statue of bronze. She pressed her palms to him, as if she could feel more fully that way, and followed the ridges and planes of his body. Diligently memorizing, she skimmed over his chest, sensing his heart beating under his ribs and the strong lift of his breathing. She brushed over the inflexible, heated surface of his belly, then trailed her fingertips to where the firm length of his maleness sprang. Turgid, expectant, it stirred under her fingers, fitted into her hand.

He was naked also. She might have been embarrassed had it not seemed so natural, and so wondrous. Where had their clothes gone, and how? Oh, but what did it matter? She drew a long, slow breath of infinite pleasure.

"Magic," she whispered, and felt him stiffen as if he were surprised she could sense it. Abruptly, there was only a room and a bed with turned-back sheets, and too many confining pieces of fabric covering their bodies once more. Disappointment touched her and she made a soft sound of loss.

Then the vision flooded back with even greater intensity. She could smell bluebells and eglantine roses mixed with woodbine, honeysuckle, and warm, warm clover. The sunlight gilded their skins, flooding them with its heat.

"Disregard whatever you don't care for and it will fade from your sight," he said in quiet explanation. "Embrace what gives you pleasure, and it will be yours."

Laughing in exuberance, she rolled against him, twining her legs with his while she flicked her tongue over the hollow at the base of his throat. Never had she felt so free or so alive. Here, no duty awaited her; there was no position to maintain, no dignity to preserve. For this brief interval, she could be truly herself. There was glory in it, and also an undercurrent of pain for the knowledge that it could not last. She felt a deep need to share the wonder of it, as Rayne had shared with her the warm beauty of his fantasy.

"Shall I embrace you then?" she said, and still smiling faintly, lifted her lips for his kiss.

He gave it, molding his mouth to hers, and sliding his tongue around hers in sinuous play. She took the silken strokes, letting them fuel her languid delight, and returned them with half-shy, half-bold explorations of her own. The swell of his chest against her was her reward—that and the delicate touch of his hand between her thighs. He eased a finger into her, gently teasing, stretching, while his palm closed over the center of her being in firm possession.

A ripple moved over her, like the billowing of a curtain in a soft wind. Abruptly, she felt voluptuous, abandoned—the purest sensual glory flowed molten in her veins. In the same instant, she recognized the lap of warm water around her, sensed the drift of rose petals like a thousand tiny kisses upon every inch of her exposed skin.

Slick . . . her body was slick with warm, rose-scented oil. She was immersed in a shallow pool lined with marble and filled with aqua-blue tinted water from which drifted pale white wraiths of steam. Overhead arched a great corbelled roof set with thick panes of glass against which rain spattered in a drowsy cadence. Rayne, his skin burnished to bronze magnificence by oil and water, trailed a line of kisses from her lips to the point of her chin and down the smooth white line of her throat. He brushed his face against the gentle curves of her breasts and tasted their crests with his tongue. Marking the path with the heat of his mouth, he continued lower. He licked across the wetness of her abdomen and threaded through the soft, golden-brown down adorning the juncture of her thighs, then with his lips, sought the delectable rose-scented petals of flesh.

Moving against each other in an oiled ecstasy of delicious friction, they were as sybaritic as any denizens of the ancient Roman empire. Time drifted past them, unnoticed. Rayne was tireless in his invention, leaving no part of her untouched. There was no modesty; they held nothing back. If they retreated, it was for the pleasure of being pursued. If they faltered, it was because flesh and bone could stand only so much.

And then it could stand no more. Rayne, holding her close, opened her thighs and let her feel the firm, hot probe of his maleness. She moved against it, accepting, needing the penetration, feeling desolate and empty without it. Prepared by care and kisses and warm oil, she took him into her tightness, stretching to receive him—took too, the soul-jolting wonder of the joining.

Completion. It was perfect, inescapable. It was hers and nothing could ever take it away. She closed her hands over the rigid muscles of his shoulders and pressed her forehead to him with her eyes squeezed shut. She wanted the moment to last forever.

Then he moved, a slow, experimental searching for greater depth. She caught her breath with the abrupt escalation of rapture. Greatly daring, she eased upon him. He made a soft sound of half-strangled awe. Probing farther, removing carefully, he caught and established a rhythm with the rich and steady tempo of beating hearts.

Soaring, caught in a state of grace, they rode the magic. The warm water surged and splashed, washing around them while its heated perfume rose to invade their senses. Rising, falling, sloshing, plunging, they clung together while euphoria shook their minds and expanded the inner walls of their hearts.

Holding her tight to his chest, Rayne meshed his legs with hers and rolled her over so that she was above him. She thought for an instant that he was sinking under the water while, astride him, she rode him down. But in a moment, the Roman bath was gone. The water became silver-blue fur, the deep, soft pelts of far-North fox. It shimmered with the orange-gold of firelight that was reflected from a roaring blaze on the hearth of the great Gothic fireplace that towered above them as they lay before it. Over the fireplace mantel

was an enormous set of crossed deer antlers. Fiery
mulled drinks sat steaming in tankards beside them.
Outside, a blizzard assaulted the stone walls with snow
and ice.

Resplendent in her nakedness, heated by internal
fires, Mara was lit by the leaping flames as she hovered above Rayne. His eyes glowed with something
that burned even brighter than the fire. Pressing his
hard, strong fingers into her hips to support her, he
began once more to move within her.

This was loving with a barbaric edge, a fragile balance between soul-shifting abandon and fierce desperation. Mara felt the rhythmic internal pulsing of its
splendor. Her skin glowed with it. Her breath came in
hard gasps, and her heart pounded in her ears. Still
they contended.

He was elemental, a force unto himself. She had
thought she had felt his strength, but she had been mistaken. It was bountiful, unceasing, controlled; it was
yet dedicated to this one stupendous service. He was
taking from her as he willed, yes, but he gave ten-fold
in return. Prodigal of his power, he loved with his entire being, as if to stop would be a defeat, or a disaster.

Sweet, sweet disaster, erupting inside with the hot,
liquid fury of a volcano. It roared through her, a piercing consummation so strong she cried out and was still,
stunned into immobility.

He caught her, tumbling her to her back in the deep,
soft pile of furs. With her hair wrapped around him
like a silken shawl, he pressed deep with a final, shuddering paroxysm. It flowed through them, vital and violent, the molten, red-hot rapture of human existence.
Limitless, uncontainable, it had no beginning and no
end.

It was magic of the highest order. But it was not
without cost. They had used the sorcery, and now the
price must be paid.

Their skins cooled. They could breathe again. The leaping fire died to glowing coals. The barbaric scene darkened, slowly fading, became once more only a large low bed in a sleeping chamber of the woodland cottage. Beyond the windows, the sunlight was dying as the earth turned toward the west. They had loved the day away, and now it was nearly done.

Out of the long silence, Mara sighed, reaching to place her palm over Rayne's heart while she lay against his side. Her voice low and as even as she could make it, she said, "I have need of a small boon. Can you possibly grant it?"

"Only ask."

The response was deep-toned and immediate, but she felt the jolt of his heartbeat. He knew what was coming—how could he not?

She moistened lips that were suddenly dry. It was a moment before she could force the words through her throat. "I once thought I could bend in submission to my foe, that it was my duty to abandon all hope of love and to marry for reasons of state. I find I have no taste for that martyrdom, after all."

"Few would even consider it," he said.

She went on, heartened. "I will take that course if I must, but only as a last resort. There is, perhaps, another way."

"Yes, Princess?" he said when she paused.

"A great wizard once suggested that I choose a champion, someone strong and true to fight in ritual combat for my sake, defending me to the confusion of my enemy." She swallowed hard and closed her eyes before she went on. "You are the man I choose. If I ask it most politely, will you extend me this honor?"

Wind rose in the space of a heartbeat, whirling into the room. The cottage and the deep forest were whipped away with the dark expansion of time and distance. They fell into nothingness.

In thunderous transformation, Mara and Rayne were returned to the castle battlements. They stood once again where they had been in the beginning, with the light of the setting sun in their faces. Beyond its walls, the baron advanced, confident upon his charger, displaying the might of his men behind him in order to awe the castle into surrender. The men of the garrison, tired and fearful, eyed each other, while women stood in whispering groups with hungry children clinging to their skirts.

Crowned with a simple gold fillet, dressed in fine linen in rich colors, and with a sumptuous cape of fine red cashmere wool around her, Mara gripped the stone in front of her. Her eyes were dark, and her hair shifted around her stiff shoulders in the spring wind. There was a bloom on her high cheekbones, however, and mystery in her eyes.

Rayne did not wear the brown robe and cowl of the wizard, but stood tall behind her in a knight's tunic and cloak, and with the molded steel of a breastplate armoring his chest.

Beyond these minor changes in dress, the moment was the same as when they had left it such a short time—and yet such an eternity—before. His voice deep and not quite steady, Rayne spoke exactly as he had then.

"Will you surrender?"

Mara considered carefully. It was not easy; there was a disturbing sense of loss inside her, like the failure to retain a wonderful dream on awakening. No matter; the question her wizard had asked of her required a reply. There was only one that she could see.

"Impossible," Mara said. "Impossible, here. Impossible, now."

It was the answer to many things, the final result of everything that had passed between them in an isolated woodland. Slowly, she turned her head to look at him.

He met her gaze for a single instant. In the depths of his eyes was such desolation steeled with resolve that, seeing it, she felt the sudden ache of tears.

His cloak billowed around him as he stepped to her side, coming close, so much closer than he had ever dared in the past. His breastplate caught the fading daylight and glowed with a blue sheen. Then he was kneeling before her, the wind ruffling his dark hair as he inclined his head.

"Command me, my princess," he said.

Chapter Five

The baron swaggered into the audience hall, his every strutting step showing confidence in his victory. Faced with Mara's challenge to settle the outcome of the siege by right of arms, he laughed aloud and slapped his knee at the jest. That was before Rayne stepped forward to present himself as her champion.

The insignia of deer and longbows, quartered, that was etched into the breastplate Rayne wore caught the light of torches and wax tapers. The baron blanched. A big man, well-fleshed, he seemed to shrink while he glared at Rayne's features and tall form.

"Who are you?" the older man said in harsh demand. "What is your rank and title that you dare seek to contest with me?"

Rayne smiled, a movement of the lips that did not affect the chill of his eyes. "I am my father's son."

"A nameless bastard, then."

There was craftiness as well as scorn in the baron's charge. Mara held her breath, for it was the older man's right to refuse to meet a man he considered his inferior.

"My father and my mother took each other in hand-fast marriage," Rayne said evenly.

"Without witnesses, I vow!" scoffed the baron, jutting his chin forward.

"Witnessed by God on high. Who else is required? What wedding at the church door can be more sanctified?" Rayne touched his fingers to the insignia. "Oh, yes, and there was one other present, an old man with some renown as a wizard. He left behind a document, properly sealed, testifying to my right to wear the Ewloe arms."

A handfast marriage—private vows exchanged by a man and a woman in token of their intentions—was more than adequate, Mara realized with some amazement. Such a union was as legally binding as the two people involved wished it to be. The priests might rant about proper blessings, but no such intervention was required; not even a witness was necessary so long as the marriage was undisputed. This meant that Rayne was the true Baron Ewloe, or would have been had his father not renounced his title.

Something like a snarl appeared on the older man's face. "It takes more than a name and arms to be a champion. By what right do you stand for the sister of Prince Stephen?"

"By her faith and trust," came the answer in ringing tones. "Also by my sworn oath to protect her. Will you meet me?"

The baron swore as he set his fists on his hips. "I have no dispute with you."

"The old wizard, my father-of-the-heart, thought otherwise," Rayne returned with cold precision. "He swore it was you who worked upon the man who sired me, telling him he had sinned against God by taking a bride of Christ for his own. It was you who convinced my father that he must set out on a crusade of repentance. Moreover, no man heard him renounce his lands and title before he departed except you, the man who now holds them."

"So you think to take them from me by force with your challenge?" said the baron, rage mottling his features.

"The man who found me in a cave kept me safe

from you for that purpose, aye, even trained me for it,"
Rayne said. "But no. I fight for the freedom of a lady;
that is all. The title you gained by stealth will belong
to the princess if you are killed in the contest."

Mara realized what Rayne said was true. The baron's
lands and his every privilege would be forfeit if he was
defeated. Rayne, though he would meet the man, was
only fighting in her name. She was the one who had
been attacked; therefore the spoils of the battle would
belong to her.

"Then you are twice a fool," his uncle growled, "for
you will die for nothing. I will grind you into the dust
and make mud of your blood. I will carve your carcass
into quarters and feed it to my hounds. And then I will
deal with the woman who would turn my kin loose
against me."

Turning on a booted heel, the baron strode from the
hall. The great door clanged shut behind him like the
clap of doom.

The preparations began. Rayne was a whirlwind of
activity, appearing to be everywhere at once. He organized the details of the coming fight, designating the
moment when the gate would be opened, also which
weapons should be polished and which charger
groomed for his use. He scrounged extra food from
heaven knew where for the children and the injured.
Lending his strength as well as his supervision, he
shored up the castle's defenses against possible surprise attack. In the midnight hours, tirelessly diligent,
he traveled the halls to check that the sentries were
alert, at the same time putting hope and heart into the
defenders.

Some time in the hours before dawn, Rayne visited
the castle chapel. Prayer and fasting were prescribed
before a contest of importance, and he must, of course,
comply.

Mara, lying sleepless in her bed, thought of him

kneeling alone. She pictured him before the altar with his dark head bowed, preparing his soul for whatever the outcome of the meeting might be, and her heart hurt.

Still, something else troubled her mind. There was an important detail that had been overlooked, something forgotten or left undone. It hovered at the edge of her consciousness, but she could not quite grasp it.

It was in the quiet hour just before first light that it came to her. She sat up in bed with a cry, then put her closed fists to her mouth while she stared into the darkness.

Rayne was admitted into her presence less than an hour later. She was dressed and ready, standing in an antechamber where thick candles glowed in tall floor candelabra of wrought iron and a small fire burned on the hearth. She had been gazing into the flames and thinking about the coffee that had been served to her by a man she thought to be a woodland outlaw. All softness was wiped from her face as she turned to receive her champion.

Without a greeting, without a flicker of acknowledgement for his smile or his easy bow, she said, "Where is your weapon you called a rifle? Why did you not bring it?"

Rayne's face took on a stern cast, and he walked slowly to stand before her. "I could not use such a thing for this meeting. It was best left behind."

"Why could you not? Surely the mechanism would work as well in one place as in another?"

"The advantage given to me by its superior destructive force would be too great. To use it to defeat the baron would be as unfair as stooping to sorcery. If I prevail by dishonorable means, then I do not prevail at all."

She stared at him for long moments, a flush rising to her face. With his words, he had openly admitted to being both Rayne Winslow and the wizard. She had been the first to make a slip, of course, by showing she knew he could have provided himself with the rifle if he wished it.

Her voice tight, she said, "You made me think this rifle would be your chosen weapon."

"You assumed it. I never said so." All warmth was gone from his voice.

"You intended I should," she returned instantly. "You wanted me to believe there would be no danger of failure."

Rayne made an abortive movement, as though he would turn from her presence, then was still. A candle flame fluttered on its wick with a popping sound. The gleam of it flickered across the planes of his face, turning it to metallic bronze. His eyes seemed tormented and yet angry, though either expression could well be no more than a trick of the light.

"So," he said finally. "It was never me you required, but the magic of the rifle."

"That isn't true!" She clenched her hands within the folds of her mantel so that her nails cut into her palms. "If you had wanted to be fair, you could have brought two rifles. That would at least have made of it a clean meeting instead of hacking butchery with lance and sword."

"Death isn't any easier for being clean."

She whirled away from him. "That isn't the point. The point is—"

"Yes?" he said harshly as she stopped.

She was terrified for him. Still, to say so in plain words would be to let him know how much she cared. How could she do that when she had no idea what—if anything—he felt for her?

She could command him. He was her wizard, her adviser, her right arm; he had pledged her his loyalty and would risk his life to keep her safe. But none of these things were proof of the kind of love that she required. She yearned for that proof with a painful longing.

When she did not answer, he said, "You lack faith, after all, in my ability to defend you."

"It isn't that," she said, turning quickly. "Only . . . you are far too important for your life to be put at risk unnecessarily."

"Important in what capacity? If you wed the baron, your days of authority will be over; do not be deceived. You will no longer need a wizard. Will you give me a position as your chamberlain, knight of the royal sleeping chamber, then? Will I have the honor of seeing that your bedsheets are clean and sweet, your fire kept burning, and that you have warm water in the morning so that you and your lord may wash away the stains of the night? Oh, yes, and perhaps I can take his place while he is away, soothing your bruises and warming your cold feet—among other things."

She felt heat flare across her cheekbones, but would not look away. "Suppose I said yes, at least to the . . . the other things you mention? Suppose I said that we might become lovers, meeting in secret?"

"No."

The word was like a hammer strike against her heart. She absorbed it, allowed no sign of the agony to appear on her features. With some difficulty, she said, "There would be no . . . obligation to assume that duty, if you did not desire it."

"I refuse not from lack of desire, but from a surfeit of it," he said, his gaze steady upon hers. "Stolen kisses and snatched moments while listening for footsteps is not my idea of loving; I require more. It would be only a matter of time before something said or done made the affair plain. You would be beaten, locked away, even killed. I would be gutted and thrown to the dogs—if I were lucky. Of the two courses open to me, this one carries the greater risk."

He wanted her; he had said so. At the same time, he was telling her that closeness between them was impossible, that her position made it so. She had known how it must be. Yet she had been driven to make the suggestion by a haunting and persistent vision of the intimacy they'd shared.

She could not dwell on these matters. There were decisions to be made.

Drawing a deep breath for control, she gazed beyond his shoulder. "You leave me no choice," she said in strained tones, "except to withdraw my request for you to act as my champion."

"That is your privilege," he returned, his gaze steady on her face even as a white line appeared around his mouth. "I should warn you, however, that there is no purpose in it. Whether I seek the death of the baron on the field of honor or in your chamber, is all one to me. But seek it I must, for I cannot stand by and watch you fall into the hands of such a monster. If I kill him on the jousting field, I will be applauded. If it is in your chamber, I will hang. Either way, my life is in the balance . . . and the weighing has already begun."

She heard the bitterness in his voice, and spoke in response to it. "Perhaps you expect me to hail your courage and your pledge like some woman of ancient Sparta by saying, *'Come back either with your shield or upon it,'*—but I cannot. If that makes me faithless, so be it."

His gaze widened a fraction. He lifted his hand as if to touch her, then went rigorously still. He said in soft amazement, "You fear my death."

A strained laugh escaped her. "What else have I been trying to tell you?"

He watched her for long moments, his eyes darkening with comprehension. Abruptly, his lashes swept down to conceal all expression. When he spoke, his voice was even, and so distant—as if he had already gone from her to the field where he and the baron would meet.

"You have just made it even more necessary for me to defend you. There is nothing more to be said, then, except for you to wish me well."

She swallowed with difficulty against the hard press of unshed tears. "That much, at last, I can do."

He stepped closer and reached to take her hand. Carrying it to his lips, he turned it and pressed a kiss into the palm. Lowering it once more, he stepped back quickly, as if he thought she might detain him, or that he might seek to stay.

His bow was perfection, holding the exact degree of homage that was her due. His knight's cloak flared around him as he turned, swirling at his heels as he crossed the room with swift, steadfast strides. The door closed behind him.

Gone.

He was gone. And she had not given him her favor to wear. She had not kissed him good-bye or felt his arms around her. She had not told him she loved him.

Why? Oh, why? Pride was the reason. Her senseless, unbending pride.

She would have confessed her love if he'd asked, if she had known that he wanted it. She wished that he had forced the issue as he had so many others.

But must she always be constrained to do what was best and right? Could she not forget power and duty and give way to her own needs?

It was too late. She closed her eyes tightly against the press of tears.

No. She would not cry. Not yet. She had that much trust, that much faith.

With a lift of her chin, she moved to summon her maidservant to bring her a cup of hot water steeped with herbs. It might help to warm her body . . . although it could not ease the chill in her soul.

* * *

The match between Rayne and the baron was no
mere tournament, but rather an extension of the greater
battle of the siege. The gathered soldiers formed a pan-
oply of color, with waving flags, trumpeters, and the
flash of heraldic devices, but there was no formal
arena, no wrestling or other games, no feasting, and no
fair.

Mara had not requested a pavilion for her use, for
she did not wish to view the spectacle at close range.
The battlement would serve her as a vantage point.
It gave a clear view of the field, but was not close
enough that she must hear the grunts of pain or see the
spilling of blood. She could discover the final outcome
without being forced to wait until informed of it. Most
of all, none would know her terror. None would see her
grief, or her joy.

The joust began just as the sun had cleared the horizon, lending its golden light. Horns sounded, voices
rose in harsh shouts. The heavy chargers snorted and
pranced, their trappings and the armor of the two
mounted men catching the light with flashes of gold
and silver. Then, with a last salute of trumpets, the
horses were pounding wide-eyed down the field with
their hooves flinging clods of earth as high as their riders' heads. Helmets set and closed, steel-tipped lances
poised, the two combatants thundered toward each
other.

They came together like a hammer on an anvil, in a
mighty ringing of metal on metal. Lances shattered,
and the pieces were thrown with the force of spears.
The combatants heaved backward, rocking in their
saddles. The baron dropped his broken lance as his
charger reared, yet both men kept their stirrups. They
rode past each other and down the field until they
slowed their mounts to a halt.

There was milling and confusion, then new lances

were chosen. Once more the two contestants rode at full tilt toward each other.

Mara snapped her eyes shut this time as the two men met. She heard the cracking wallop of a well-struck blow followed by the rattling thud of a fall. Then came the shouts and yells of the crowd. Only then did she dare look.

The baron had been unhorsed, but was drawing his broadsword as he struggled heavily to his feet. Rayne had lost his helmet; it had been struck from his head by the baron's splintered lance and was rolling across the grass. He was dismounting, half out of the saddle as his squire ran forward to take his horse.

The baron did not wait. With a wild battle yell, he attacked.

Mara stifled a useless cry of warning. With straining eyes, she saw Rayne spring to the ground and draw his sword in a single fluid motion. He met the power of the baron's assault with a determined thrust.

Their great, heavy blades showered orange sparks as they clanged together, scraping edge to edge. There ensued a glittering fury of hacking and slashing. With their swords grasped in both hands, the two men used the strength of their whole bodies and the weight of their armor to put speed and force behind their blows.

The baron was concentrating on Rayne's unprotected head. Rayne parried one blow, sprang back from another. He mounted an offensive in an attempt to get under the older man's guard, but was forced to retreat under a flurry of blows aimed at his scalp. As he danced backward, the red sheen of blood tracked down his face from a slicing wound at the temple.

Sickness rose inside Mara. Her eyes burned and her heart beat with shuddering strokes. She wanted to scream, to demand that the fight stop. The impulse to give up, give in, do whatever was necessary to protect Rayne from further injury, surged inside her.

Two things prevented her. One was the certain knowledge that interference at this point would be a dangerous distraction. The other was the greater certainty that the fight would be over before her messenger could reach the field.

The baron appeared to be in control. Wily, experienced, heavier of frame and well-protected from glancing blows above the shoulders, he bore down on his opponent. Rayne, on the defensive, took the sword strokes that dented his armor at his forearms and thighs. Yet he was more nimble; his swings with his broadsword were cleaner and faster. He could not be overpowered or driven back an inch farther than he intended to go.

As the contest wore on, age and rich living began to tell with the baron. He flagged visibly: his offensive maneuvers lacked control, his swings became wilder. Once, he staggered as he recovered from a hard blow against an opponent who was suddenly not there. His waning strength made him press harder. He struck at Rayne's head as if he meant to cleave it from his shoulders. Teeth bared, he narrowed his vicious gaze to the younger man's hair. Shining in the sun like a flying falcon's wing, it presented a perfect target.

Abruptly, Rayne stopped retreating. Ducking under a whistling roundhouse blow, he swung backhanded into the body of his foe.

The flashing point of his sword struck under the overlapping edges of armor plates, piercing the chain mail there. The baron faltered with a great cry that rang even to where Mara stood. His sword dropped from his hand. He toppled, falling with a clanking of metal; he did not move again. Rayne stood over him, his red-stained sword tip parting the grass.

Rayne had won. Mara had seen it. It was over.

She clung to the stone of the battlement, watching as her men surrounded Rayne. The baron's forces seemed inclined to avenge their leader's death, and for a moment it appeared that there would be a pitched battle between the besiegers and the castle's garrison.

Then Rayne began speaking. Men listened, and slowly the crisis passed. The forces below began to disperse.

Still, Mara did not move. It was over, but where was the gladness, the sense of triumph? She was happy that Rayne was safe and that the siege would be lifted, but surely there should be something more?

It was several minutes before she turned away from the battlement. Her movements stiff, she walked toward the audience hall where she must await the return of her champion from his victory.

Mara had thought he would come to her at once, striding into the hall like a conquering hero. He did not. Instead, the news drifted in that the baron's army was decamping, retreating down the road with their siege engines in tow. A celebration was declared, of course. The retreating army's discarded supplies were raided, and food and drink were prepared with rejoicing. The villagers crowded the hall to eat their fill and drink to their deliverance.

Still there was no sign of Rayne. Inquiries brought no information of value. Everyone had seen him somewhere or other, but none knew where he was at present. No one could say who had tended his sword cut—or, indeed, if it had been tended.

The night wore on. The minstrels played a final drowsy tune. The castle's dogs, those few that had not mysteriously disappeared during the siege, gnawed the last bones under the table. Everyone was half-asleep from wine, full bellies, and relieved nerves.

One moment Mara sat alone at the head table, the next her wizard was standing behind her chair in the silent manifestation favored by his kind. She looked up, saw the brown robe, the cowl. Startled into indiscretion, she sprang up.

"Rayne," she cried, "where have you been?"

The cowl dipped in homage, then tilted. In deliberate tones, the wizard said, "You speak of your champion? He was here, yes, but he has departed. He has a care for Your Highness, and was proud to have been of use—still, he thought it best that he not remain."

He was offering, she saw, a return to their old relationship of princess and adviser. He would be her wizard, always at her side. The passion they had shared need never be mentioned or brought to mind again.

Was that what he wanted—or only what he thought she would prefer? She did not know. Still, it was tempting. He would remain close; she would see him daily. She could explore his mind at will, and extend to him the same privilege. They could grow closer year by year, even if they never, ever, touched each other.

It wasn't enough. She could not bear to be faced constantly with his mask of indifference. That would drive her mad.

"I had thought," she said, "to offer a reward to the man who fought for me. It pains me that he has departed without waiting to see what it might be." She watched him, wondering if he would remember suggesting once that a just reward might be her kisses, even herself.

His voice soft, he said, "He required no reward, but would not willingly have caused you distress."

She tried to see the eyes hiding inside the dimness of the cowl, then looked away. "Yes, well, perhaps it may be as well, after all. I have been thinking that I should gather my resources. I will need a dowry to present to my future husband."

He stirred, coming a step nearer. "It is inevitable that you will marry, but . . . surely it can wait some little time?"

"I fear not," she said pensively. "This affair of the siege has set me thinking that it may be best to go ahead with an alliance; a princess alone is far too tempting a target. In any case, a nobleman of sufficient strength can help influence and control the other barons who might range themselves against my brother. It is plainly my duty to encourage that kind of stability."

"You will be leaving the castle, then," he said quietly.

She pretended surprise. "I suppose I may, depending on the wishes of my new lord. In any case, I will no longer be needing an adviser since my husband will, no doubt, reserve that position for himself. And I fear he may also be jealous enough to forbid me the services of a wizard."

"This noble husband . . . he has been chosen?" There was a strained quality to the words.

"He has," she said simply.

The man behind the cowl was silent a moment, then inclined his head in abrupt acceptance. "There is nothing for me to do, then," he said, "except take leave of you."

She had thought he might fight his dismissal. His quick acceptance filled her with despair, but she had still one more move to make in the battle for the end she desired.

"You will join my brother I expect?" She summoned a determined smile. "I shall miss you, but our parting—like my marriage—has always been inevitable. I would like, however, to extend to you some small boon in token of my gratitude for your understanding and years of fine counsel. You will kneel, if you please."

"I want nothing." That curt phrase, without preamble or title, was an indication of his agitation.

Her smile was bright, though it had a tendency to

quiver at the corners. "I command you this one last time, my wizard."

Still he hesitated. When at last he sank to one knee before her, the movement was graceless, almost unco-ordinated. The stiff set of his shoulders indicated his reluctance and, she thought, revealed how tight was the rein he kept on his emotions. Pressing her lips together to still their trembling, she reached for the small sword she had left ready on the table.

He glanced up at the sound of the blade sliding from its sheath. As she passed it over his head to touch first his right shoulder, then his left, he flinched under the light blows, then drew a sharp breath to speak.

In tones that rang clearly around the hall, she cut across whatever he meant to say. "I hereby confer upon you, Rayne Winslow, wizard to Prince Stephen, son of Reddick, last true Baron Ewloe, the title of your father that has reverted to the crown, along with all the lands, honors, and privileges to which the bearer of the name is entitled. May you wear the rank with the valor you have shown in acquiring it, and live in peace and harmony under its insignia."

Rayne flung back his head to stare up at her. The movement caused his cowl to fall back, exposing his face, but he did not notice. Frowning so that the cut across his brow oozed a fresh trickle of blood, he said, "No, Mara!"

She made a brief gesture indicating that he might rise. "Yes, Rayne, Baron Ewloe. It is done, and noth-ing can change it."

He came slowly to his feet. His tone compressed, he said, "Nothing? Not even if, as a final act of office, I point out to you a danger in your generosity that you may have overlooked?"

"Danger?" She watched him in suspended hope.

"One which may derive from . . . from the honors and privileges of my new title. How far do they extend, would you say? Do I, for instance, have command of the baron's forces?"

"So I would suppose, since they will now be in your levy." Her tone took on an abrupt wariness.

"In that case," he informed her in grim tones, "I could also take up where he left off in his siege. Given my knowledge of the castle's defenses, I believe I could take it in a single day. You would then become my prize."

"You wouldn't," she said as purest gladness rippled along her veins.

"I would. How can you doubt it?"

Her head high, she said, "What of honor, then? I think you once declared it would prevent you from that kind of trespass."

"Oh, I would not take you by force," he said with soft suggestion in his voice, "but I might bend my principles enough to find other means to persuade you to my dominion."

"Such as?"

The words had hardly left her mouth before her mind was flooded with the warmth of sunshine and the scent of bruised bluebells, with the ripple of steaming, rose-scented water against her skin and the silken softness of silver fox fur under her bare back. And more—so much more that she felt feverish with the invasion of it.

"Sorcery?" she whispered.

"Memory, fresh and whole. Returned for a purpose." His smile had a wry twist of remorse. "I was not reared to be entirely noble."

Memory. Yes, she remembered, and it was as if a part of her innermost self, long missing, had returned. On a swift, indrawn breath, she said, "You took that from me. How could you?"

"I had reasons, none of which are important now."

He paused, then said with quiet speculation, "Do you think it will aid my siege?"

"That, I cannot tell," she said with a small shake of her head. "But I see no reason for such an extreme when the castle and all that's in it can be yours by a polite request."

"A request," he repeated, and all expression was suddenly wiped from his face.

"For surrender." She gathered her courage and met his gaze again, waiting with what composure she had left for his answer.

Rayne's eyes widened into black pools of doubt. "I don't believe," he said softly, "that you mentioned the name of your chosen husband."

"Why, the great and noble Baron Ewloe. Who else?"

Beyond where they stood, the music of the minstrels resumed. The candles in the hall wavered and bowed as at the rush of a strong wind, then burned straight and true once more.

Rayne's lips parted with a quick breath. With rasping softness, he whispered, "Witch."

"There is an additional duty that will be required of my future consort," she said, lifting her chin a fraction. "Will you accept it?"

"I don't think—"

"The office was once suggested to me by a wise man and fine wizard. It is the post of my chamberlain."

A slow smile curved the chiseled firmness of his lips, rising to gleam in his eyes. "Knight of the royal sleeping chamber?" he said. With lilting promise in the deep, rich timbre of his voice, he went on. "This is a post I accept with all my heart. The duties attendant upon it will be my honor and my glory. They will be performed with strict industry, to the last of my strength, and with love. The last will be unending, my privilege and my purgatory, my reason for remaining earthbound and my last, best hope of heaven. Forever."

She swallowed on the knot of tears in her throat, the joyous tears springing from the knowledge of a final, overwhelming victory. With difficulty, she said, "You find the terms of surrender acceptable then, my wizard?"

"Yours . . . or mine?" he said, his gaze bright.

"Either. Both. Or only mine. I love you, Rayne."

He closed the distance between them in a single stride and swept her into his arms. Holding her close against his heart, he said thickly, "And I you, princess mine. But as your official adviser, I believe that further negotiation—protracted, diligent, and lasting far into the night—could be of mutual benefit."

"Just as you say," she murmured dutifully, and smiled against the smooth surfaces of his mouth as he took his prize with a kiss.

〽 TOPAZ

Journeys of Passion and Desire

☐ **CROOKED HEARTS by Patricia Gaffney.** Reuben Jones walks on the wrong side of the law—a card shark and a master of deception. Grace Russell has had to learn a few tricks herself in order to hold on to her crumbling California vineyard. In this sexy, rollicking ride through the gambling halls and sinful streets of the 1880s San Francisco, two "crooked hearts" discover that love is the most danger-ous—and delicious—game of all. (404599—$4.99)

☐ **LOVE ME TONIGHT by Nan Ryan.** The war had robbed Helen Burke Courtney of her money and her husband. All she had left was her coastal Alabama farm. Captain Kurt Northway of the Union Army might be the answer to her prayers, or a way to get to hell a little faster. She needed a man's help to plant her crops; she didn't know if she could stand to have a damned handsome Yankee do it. (404831—$4.99)

☐ **FIRES OF HEAVEN by Chelley Kitzmiller.** Independence Taylor had not been raised to survive the rigors of the West, but she was determined to mend her relationship with her father—even if it meant journeying across dangerous frontier to the Arizona Territory. But nothing prepared her for the terrifying moment when her wagon train was attacked, and she was carried away from certain death by the mysterious Apache known only as Shatto. (404548—$4.99)

☐ **WHITE ROSE by Linda Ladd.** Cassandra Delaney is the notorious "White Rose," risking her life and honor for the Confederacy. Australian blockade runner Derek Courtland's job is to abduct this mysterious, sensual woman—only she's fighting him to escape his ship and the powerful feelings pulling them both toward the unknown. (404793—$4.99)

*Prices slightly higher in Canada